SUN OF

"Lares's intricate plot is a wonder, full of surprising connections and revelatory twists. She unfolds the sumptuous world of the book with care and patience, weaving new aspects of magic and startling creatures throughout the story. Her extensive research is brought to visceral life, and I felt she held my uninformed hand just enough. . . . Lares's ideas are magnificent."
—REACTOR

"A fast-paced, smart historical fantasy. . . . Weaving together narrative strands of identity, colonialism, indigenous belief and self-determination with swashbuckling adventure, *Sun of Blood and Ruin* introduces a powerful new voice to the genre."
—*Grimdark Magazine*

"An exhilarating tale of revolution, original magic, and divided loyalties, *Sun of Blood and Ruin* is a triumph. Rich with vivid characters and an immersive landscape, Lares weaves a breathtaking, complex story grounded in Mesoamerican myth that pulls the reader into a fantastical journey of self-discovery, courage, and the meaning of freedom. Don't miss this one!"
—Ehigbor Okosun, author of *Forged by Blood*

"[An] ambitious debut. . . . Ideal for speculative fiction readers longing for a fresh setting, Zorro fans, and those looking for a nuanced historical fantasy treatment reminiscent of Rebecca Roanhorse and R. F. Kuang."
—*Booklist*

SUN OF BLOOD AND RUIN

MARIELY LARES

HARPER Voyager
An Imprint of HarperCollinsPublishers

In loving memory of
Priscy, my best friend
Celia, my grandmother
Gonthrán, my dear uncle,
who always asked, "How's the book going?"

It's going pretty well.

SUN OF BLOOD AND RUIN. Copyright © 2023 by Mariely Lares.
All rights reserved. Printed in the United States of America.
No part of this book may be used or reproduced in any manner whatsoever
without written permission except in the case of brief quotations
embodied in critical articles and reviews. For information, address
HarperCollins Publishers, 195 Broadway, New York, NY 10007.

HarperCollins books may be purchased for educational, business,
or sales promotional use. For information, please email the
Special Markets Department at SPsales@harpercollins.com.

Harper Voyager and design are trademarks of
HarperCollins Publishers LLC.

Originally published in Great Britain in 2023 by Harper Voyager UK.

A hardcover edition of this book was published in 2024
by Harper Voyager, an imprint of HarperCollins Publishers.

FIRST HARPER VOYAGER PAPERBACK EDITION PUBLISHED 2024.

Map design by Nicolette Caven

Library of Congress Cataloging-in-Publication Data
has been applied for.

ISBN 978-0-06-325432-9

24 25 26 27 28 LBC 5 4 3 2 1

THE BASIN
OF MEXICO

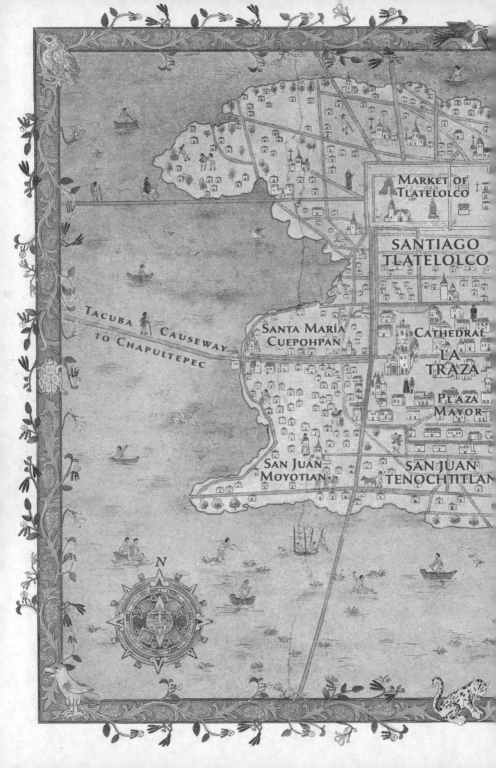

MARKET OF
TLATELOLCO

SANTIAGO
TLATELOLCO

Santa María
Cuepohpan

CATHEDRAL

LA
TRAZA

PLAZA
MAYOR

TACUBA CAUSEWAY
TO CHAPULTEPEC

San Juan
Moyotlan

SAN JUAN
TENOCHTITLAN

N

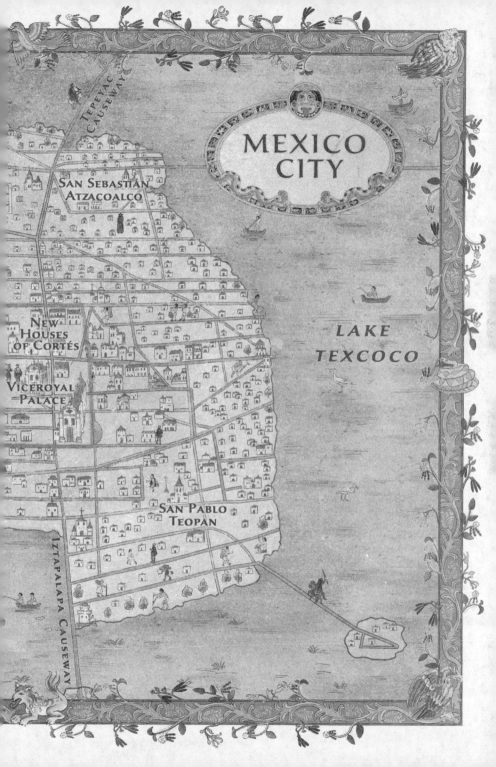

MEXICO CITY

TEPEYAC CAUSEWAY

SAN SEBASTIÁN ATZACOALCO

NEW HOUSES OF CORTÉS

VICEROYAL PALACE

SAN PABLO TEOPAN

IZTAPALAPA CAUSEWAY

LAKE TEXCOCO

A Note on History, Terminology, and Pronunciation

Beginning around 900 A.D., seven tribal groups migrated to Central Mexico from the Seven Caves of Aztlan. In order of arrival, they were the Xochimilca, followed by the Chalca, Tepanec, Acolhua, Tlahuica, and Tlaxcalan. The seventh and final tribe to arrive in the Valley of Mexico were the Mexica, who are referred to as the Aztecs. This term was introduced by modern scholars to refer to the people of the "Aztec Empire" and is not used in this book.

These seven tribes collectively embody the Nahuas or Nahua people, all sharing a common cultural and historical background, including the Nahuatl language. These different groups used names related to their cities or tribes. For example, the Mexica who resided in Mexico-Tenochtitlan called themselves Tenochca or Mexica-Tenochca. The Acolhua people inhabiting Tetzcoco called themselves Tetzcoca, and the Tepaneca of Tlacopan called themselves Tlacopaneca. These three city-states made up the Aztec Empire, describing the Triple Alliance, which Tenochtitlan dominated and later was largely destroyed in 1521 by the Tlaxcaltecah, the main rivals of the Mexica, and their Spanish allies under the command of Hernán Cortés. Much of what we know about the Aztecs was written by conquerors, and the claims that their conquest was an astounding achievement and that the destruction of Tenochtitlan was total has persisted across five centuries.

However, there is plenty of evidence to the contrary. After the conquest, the island where the Aztecs settled and built their capital was still mostly Indigenous; the Spaniards were still outnumbered; Aztec nobility still retained power in colonial Mexico. While this book is fictional and set in an alternate Mexico, it attempts to shatter the myth of Spanish hegemony. Arguing that Tenochtitlan did not, in fact, die is not a new narrative, but it bears repeating, as Mexico City continued to be an Indigenous metropolis well into the seventeenth century.

Despite its offensive nature, I've used the inaccurate term "Indian" or "indio" in Spanish throughout this book to reflect the language and concepts of the time. The error lies with Christopher Columbus who, as the story goes, upon arriving in the New World thought he was in India. "Indigenous," "Indigenous peoples," and "native peoples" are broadly accepted terms, though clumping together a variety of different groups is not ideal, as they each have their own unique histories, languages, and cultures. The best course is to always call people by the name they take for themselves.

Besides Nahuatl, over a hundred languages were spoken in New Spain (present-day Mexico). Many words have variant spellings depending on their English, Spanish, or Nahuatl origin, such as Mexico, México, and Mēxihco, respectively. Variant spellings occur in this book to indicate the language being spoken. For ease of reading, I have chosen not to use macrons (ā, ē, ī, ō) on any Nahuatl word.

Examples of variant spellings:

English	Spanish	Classical Nahuatl
Mexica	Mexíca	Mēxihcah
Tenochtitlan	Tenochtitlán	Tenōchtitlan
Montezuma	Moctezuma	Motēuczōma
Chichimec	Chichimeca	Chīchīmēcah

They tried to bury us.
They didn't know we were seeds.

Mexican proverb

CODEX CHIMALPOPOCA CÓDICE CHIMALPOPOCA

Annals of Cuauhtitlan *Anales de Cuauhtitlán*

The Legend of the Suns

Leyenda de los soles

In the year 13 Reed,
so they say, it first appeared.

En el año 13-Caña,
se dice que vino a existir.

The sun that now exists
was born then.

Nació el sol
que ahora existe.

This is the Fifth Sun,
its date-sign is 4 Movement.

Este sol, su nombre
4-movimiento, este es nuestro sol.

It is called Movement Sun
because on that day it began
to move.

Se llama sol de movimiento
porque se mueve, sigue su
camino.

The old people say,
that in this age earthquakes
will appear.

Como andan diciendo los viejos,
en él habrá movimientos
de tierra.

And there will come starvation
and we shall perish.

Habrá hambre
y así pereceremos.

CHAPTER 1

La Leyenda

The jump between the two buildings is too wide, maybe ten feet. There's only one way I can make it. I gather my vital force, my tonalli, in my legs, and soar from one rooftop to another, my cloak of darkness flying out behind me like a banner.

I rush through the afternoon, fully aware of the lookouts below searching for any sign of trouble. Any trace of me.

I'm all but invisible, and an invisible hunter is a successful one.

Seen from this high up, Santiago Tlatelolco looks grand. The daylight is several shades brighter as it reflects off the limestone buildings, and the streets glisten as if each stone were dipped in precious metal. From up here, I can see the capital and its central square, with Viceroyal Palace to its east surrounded by fountains and lush gardens. The rest of the square is bordered by the cabildo, the cathedral, and the residences of the encomenderos. Beauty fashioned from the remnants of war.

The faintest sounds buzz in my ears. The claws of scurrying rats on tile. Gurgling bellies. Dry lips parting. The vestiges of a conversation from around the corner—"I'm depending on you to make good bargains today, José."

Tuning out the noise of the town, I land on a house made of

1

earthen bricks shaded by avocado trees, with a small plot of crops planted on a raft platform above the water. These floating gardens are abundant along the fresh southern lakes, closer to Xochimilco and Chalco, but chinampas are not unknown in the vicinity of the north. There aren't any inside la traza, the Spanish part of the island, but they can be found here. This is where farmers sow wheat, in accordance with the policies of the viceroy of New Spain, for if the Spaniard is to eat, he must have bread, and if the Mexica are to keep their governments and privileges, they must pay tribute to the vice-royalty and adhere to all Spanish laws.

This particular house, however, raises maize.

It is Nahua belief that once the people ate only roots and meat, until the god of dawn Quetzalcoatl brought forth corn from the Mountain of Sustenance, and from that day forward, they have planted and harvested it.

A soft feathering from the roof's smoke hole curls above the house. Planks of wood form a trapdoor. I tug and it springs open. Inside, the bony Señor Alonso is hunched over a table, frantically unrolling slips of bark paper, reading glyphs and symbols from manuscripts older than him, with ragged edges and stains.

Señor Alonso's curved back proves his life has been one of hardship, like a stalk of corn persevering after a bad growing season. Browned and withered. Not dead but blighted. His tonalli wanes. That's what healers say when the body is not in harmony: tonalli is weak, tonalli is too sluggish, tonalli is flowing too much or too little, tonalli is pooling in the wrong places.

I enter quietly and slow the descent of the trapdoor. One end of my mask escapes my hood, and I tighten the strap back into my bun. My feet touch the floor softly. Señor Alonso knows I'm here, but he doesn't bother to look at me.

"The viceroy's men are coming for you," I say, fighting to keep my voice steady. "We have to get you out of here. Now."

Señor Alonso holds a parchment up to the light from the window as he strains to see better. A fly lands on his cheek, but he's too focused to wave it away. "The Nemontemi days are upon us," he murmurs, in slightly accented Spanish that reveals his native Nahuatl.

The last five days of the year. Unfortunate dead days.

Señor Alonso remembers the tales of his father, and his father before him. Many years ago, no prudent Nahua left their home during the Dead Days, not for food, not for anything. Those who did looked over their shoulders as much as ahead of them. A twig did not crack in the forest or lake water splash without a heart skipping a beat. In the stories Señor Alonso shares, there is sorrow, for he speaks of a world that has all but vanished. He was just a boy then.

"I'm aware," I say, "but you can't stay here, Señor Alonso. They're coming, I tell you."

"Are you aware it's been fifty-two years since the last New Fire ceremony?" Señor Alonso says, gently rolling the scrolls.

I frown beneath my mask. Few still living remember a New Fire ceremony. It only happens once every cycle. The last time the Holy Fire burned, there was great fear of destruction. The Spaniards hadn't arrived, Mexico-Tenochtitlan was the capital city of the Mexica-Tenochca, and Emperor Moctezuma reigned.

If, every fifty-two years, on the last day of the Nemontemi, a blaze isn't ignited atop the Sacred Hill as night descends, the sun will not rise, earthquakes will rattle the ground, and terrible star demons will come from their abyss of twilight to devour the flesh of men. Or so the ancient prophecy goes.

But no one believes in the old ways anymore. Or at least, no one openly admits it. The Spaniards made sure of that.

I jerk my head as the approaching clip-clop of hooves echoes outside. My heart pounds thunderously. "We're out of time. We have to go!"

Señor Alonso looks at me, his gaze soft and steady. "I'm not coming with you."

I press my lips together to stop my cry of outrage. "What?"

3

"I'm not coming with you."

"If the Fifth Sun is in peril," I say, "we can only pray that the gods have not abandoned us and they will allow the world to continue until the Dead Days pass. There's nothing else we can do, Señor Alonso."

I know they're here when a frigid air chills my skin, wrapping around me like a rebozo woven from the snow itself. Their presence feels cold, harsh, and sinister.

A fist pounds on the door. My hand is already on the hilt of my sword.

Señor Alonso seizes my arm. "Don't."

"I won't let them take you," I say, shaking my head. Certainly not without a fight.

"It doesn't matter," he says faintly. "If the Fifth Sun should fall, so, too, will everything else."

The knock comes again, louder this time, more insistent.

"Go," Señor Alonso urges, forcing a smile.

"Please." I shake my head, terrified. "Please don't do this. What about Miguel?"

"My son will make his own choices, and I already know that I will not like them. Tell him . . ." He pauses to steady his voice. His fear for his loved ones doesn't rule him. "Tell him that my last thoughts will be of him."

The sheer cotton cloth behind the two slits in my mask hides my tears. "Señor Alonso."

"You will tell him that." It isn't a question.

I nod. He nods. With a terrible ache in my chest, I push up the trapdoor to the roof just as soldiers kick the wooden door open. They bind Señor Alonso's wrists behind him and shove him out of the house.

I direct tonalli to the center of my palm, flooding it with my life force, my vigor, my essence. I hold up my hand, warm with power. *Do it. End all this.*

Soldiers tie Señor Alonso's ankle to a horse and drag him along the dirt road, his snowy head in the dust. It hurts to look, but it hurts more to ignore. If I look away, I abandon him.

Regathering my tonalli, I take a flying leap and land on the next rooftop with a soft thud. No time to catch my breath. I launch myself back up into a run, tears rolling from beneath my mask.

At the edge of the rooftop that overlooks the town square, I crouch like a vulture. Below me, the tianguis hums with the usual racket of merchants hawking their wares and demanding cacao beans in payment. Every fifth day is market day, just as it was before the Fall, almost thirty years ago. But the once-great market of Tlatelolco is not what it used to be.

The crowd stirs as soldiers enter the square.

Thirteen. Thirteen faces wearing perfectly rehearsed expressions of arrogance. Thirteen rotten pairs of eyes that have seen more death than life. They ride steadily, in an orderly fashion, red capes spread over their horses' rumps, blades hanging beside their dangling boots, one long, one short. Their commander-in-chief rides at the front, the most highly regarded captain general of the viceroyalty of New Spain.

At this distance, he's no bigger than a roach. I hold up my forefinger and thumb to measure him, then I squeeze the tips tight, squashing him.

Shouts of outrage fill the square as the guards push Señor Alonso up the stairs of a raised platform and place his head on a wooden block.

I clench my fists so tightly that if it wasn't for my leather gauntlets, my nails would draw blood.

In spite of the preparations around him, Señor Alonso is calm. His robe is dirty. His face is swollen, bruised, and he's bleeding from his mouth and nose. I can't watch this unfold.

Guards stand in a line at the bottom of the platform as a barricade. They push people back, jabbing with their spears. "Keep your distance!"

With a stony expression, Captain Nabarres dismounts his reddish-brown steed and approaches the guards. Strikingly tall, broad-shouldered, with a bearded mouth perpetually downturned, the man always looks as though he's smelled something foul. He sweeps his red cloak over his shoulder, revealing the glinting breastplate beneath. His hand rests on the hilt of his rapier, waiting for a reason to draw. A valuable sword indeed, finely forged in Toledo. Kings from other parts of the world have wielded arms of Toledan provenance. No blade rivals the superior craftsmanship.

Except for mine.

Don Diego de Mendoza, the governor of Santiago Tlatelolco, moves through the crowd with his Mexica lords. Their bodies are richly clothed in fine mantles, though it's their heads that draw attention. Their headdresses are beauties made of quetzal feathers, ornamented with turquoise and gold.

Captain Nabarres nods. "My lords."

"What is the meaning of this, capitán?" asks Don Diego.

"This brujo," Nabarres replies, gesturing to Señor Alonso, "is accused of healing by incantation and resorting to the use of herbs for witchcraft."

The viceroyalty is highly suspicious of the magical powers of curanderos. Witchcraft, the Spaniards call it, but they don't understand the complex cosmos. What they don't understand, they destroy.

Captain Nabarres's second-in-command, General Valdés, comes forward with a bill of law and reads from it. Witchcraft is punishable by death, with the support of the Holy Church. It's heretical and evil so execution is the correct end.

"Curandería is not witchcraft," Don Diego adds quickly. "We wear the Cross; we are followers of Christ; Señor Alonso's patients are cured through the grace of God. Surely, using medicinal herbs for treatment doesn't merit any type of condemnation."

"This is the work of the Devil, Don Diego." Captain Nabarres holds up Señor Alonso's calendar scrolls as evidence. He raises his jaw and casts his fierce gaze on the crowd. "People of Santiago." His voice cuts easily across the market, trained to carry over a battlefield. "I can't have you all consorting with el diablo, now can I? What sort of chaos would follow?" He says Santiago, of course, because Tlatelolco is too difficult for his European tongue.

"Capitán, let us handle this matter in the cabildo," Don Diego says evenly, although the crowd is in a tumult, and his tone has taken a sharp edge. "We will interrogate the accused and determine his punishment if found guilty."

Captain Nabarres takes a few steps closer to where Señor Alonso is held down by two guards and surrounded by others. "It is well for you that I am a merciful captain general," he says. "Give me the witch, the one who calls herself Pantera, and you will be spared."

Señor Alonso slowly lifts his white head and stares back at him defiantly. "You fool," he says in Nahuatl, "your feeble little mind can't begin to imagine what's coming for you." He spits at the captain general's boots.

Captain Nabarres doesn't speak the Nahua language, but no interpreter is needed.

Yells and curses are drowned out by three long bursts of a horn. I'm being summoned. A dark-haired boy steals through the crowd, leaping out of the way as he races past the guards. There is a wildness to Miguel, like a colt ready to bolt. Jaw clenched, he lurches forward to defend his father. Señor Alonso meets his son's brave gaze before his face hardens and he looks away. Guards close in on Miguel.

I pull the chain underneath my cloak and clench the obsidian medallion in my palm. It's all I have of my father. If he were here now, he'd gather his honorable character and convictions, and justice would somehow prevail today. He was a man of reason, not violence.

But he's not here. I am.

I tuck my medallion back inside my cloak and vault from the roof, my robe rustling like the unfurling of wings. To soften my landing, I push my tonalli downward, sending up a blinding cloud of dust.

When it settles, I come into view. My back is to Miguel to shield him.

All around me, people shout, "Pantera! Pantera!"

"I knew you would come." Miguel holds a rusty blade with a reach half as long as his arm, ready to do his part. "They're too many. What's the plan?"

I look over my shoulder. "The plan is for you to get back."

Miguel protests, but I ignore him as soldiers come at me with arms and anger, one after the other. My fingertips curl as I focus my tonalli into my hand, then I turn to the nearest soldier and release it at his chest. He falls back as if caught by a wind. I strike one in the stomach, another in the face, anyone who stands in the way. A bullet goes right through my robe, shooting down a soldier instead.

Sometimes the gods are kind.

The points of two swords hang in the air, just inches from the nape of my neck. I raise my hands, deluding the men into a false sense of their own power. Then I drop to the ground, spin, and stretch my leg out to sweep the men backward.

"The legendary Pantera," Captain Nabarres says. "Not bad, for a witch." His mouth barely moves as he speaks, as if he's bored by it all.

Sorceress. I scowl, begging my mind to let it go, but it doesn't. *Drive your sword right through him*, it screams at me from the shadows. *Show him how powerful you are.*

I stare into the face of a murderer, but my mind shifts to my most primal self. A wild animal. I circle my foe, all flashing eyes and fury beneath my mask, forcing him to turn constantly to keep me in sight. Captain Nabarres is dangerously close. If I wasn't wearing a disguise, he would recognize me immediately. The thought sends a shudder of fear through me, but I tip my chin up, refusing to cower.

"What's wrong? Cat got your tongue?" His lips twist in a grin under his mustache. "Is that why you're known as the Panther?"

"I do not fight with my tongue, capitán," I say from deeper in my throat to change the pitch of my voice. "It's me you want. Release Señor Alonso."

"You fight with La Justicia?" he asks.

"I fight with all who oppose tyranny." The great Indigenous uprising—I have yet to meet them, but he doesn't know that.

I slowly advance. Nabarres fixes his gaze on my hand, enthralled by the Sword of Integrity, the mysterious composition of the blade glowing with green light. *Damascan steel?* I can almost hear him wondering. *Swedish? French? What?* A Spanish blade will bear the mark and name of the smith who forged it, but Nabarres knows, if he knows anything, he will find no engraving on mine.

I toss my sword, and he catches it.

"The sword doesn't lie," I say as the blade's glowing green fades away. "Integrity eludes you, but you *can* feel its power, can't you? Vamos, capitán. Before the day is over."

I let him come. In a furious flurry of movement, he thrusts the Sword of Integrity with a move that would've decapitated me had I not bent backward. He swings with brute force. I dart from left to right. Enchanted swords have a way of causing problems if placed in the wrong hands. After all, what is sorcery if not a double-edged blade?

When Captain Nabarres raises the Sword of Integrity over his head, it dips behind his back, throwing him slightly off balance. I take the opening and shoot a burst of tonalli. As he staggers to the ground, the sword flies out of his grasp and into mine. In my hand, the Sword of Integrity hums through the air in a blur. Nabarres twists at the last moment. He loses a few hairs from his beard. The sword's tip rakes across his breastplate, which falls to the ground with a clatter, but I don't draw blood.

Captain Nabarres scoffs and rolls to his feet. "The great hero of the people," he says, brushing dirt from his sleeves. "You have so many appearances to keep up, don't you, Pantera? So many masks. You can only hide for so long. You are foolish, girl, and now you prove an unworthy opponent. That is all I need to know to defeat you."

On the outside I remain calm, but my stomach is a seething knot of fury.

"Do it," he orders the executioner.

My head jerks to the side. I'm fast, but not fast enough. The blade falls. I flinch at the sound of it slicing through flesh and bone. The head makes a loud thud as it falls into a basket. Señor Alonso's body twitches and goes limp. A waterfall of blood spurts from his open neck, spilling across the platform.

No, gods, no. My throat burns with a silent scream. I stare at the gruesome sight in shock. If I could move at this instant, I would shift into my nagual. Show Nabarres why they call me Pantera. It would be so much easier to let the Panther settle this, claw him apart. But I can't do anything, not shift, not growl, so I just stand there, wondering if air will ever enter my body again.

Miguel lets out a strangled cry, shoving through the crowd. It seems to come from deep inside him, a chilling wail wrung from a tortured soul, a sound I've never heard a human make. It brings me back to myself.

Captain Nabarres smiles, satisfied with his demonstration. "Hang up the body for all to see what becomes of those who support the witch. As for you, Pantera, I appreciate your appearance. Now I have another criminal to arrest. Get her!"

CHAPTER 2

La Cueva

"Don't let her get away!" General Valdés bellows.

Soldiers quickly mount their horses and give chase. I send tonalli to the soles of my feet, allowing me to jump from the ground and alight on a building.

Why am I running? Predators don't run. They aren't hunted. They *are* the hunters. But no matter how much I yearn to fight, there's more at stake here than my pride.

I blaze across rooftops. My legs fly as if I'm gliding through the air. Riders race below with their firearms drawn. In their crazed flight, they trample the marketplace. Chickens flutter in fright while wooden carts splinter on to the street. A volley of bullets flies after me. A moment later, I become aware of a stabbing pain in my leg, like a nail hammered through. Every step I take intensifies it. Warm liquid runs down my thigh.

I've been hit.

Grimacing, I adjust my mask and push ahead.

I'm on the path leading to the mountains. Without looking back, I find a place in the woods to hide. A cave, which allows me to observe its mouth without being seen. Caves are sacred passageways to the Land of the Dead. Before Christianity, Indigenous priests made

11

appeals to deities here. They visited caves as part of their duties. I don't imagine anyone else ventured inside, especially not during the first of the Dead Days, unless they had a death wish or, as in my case, were on the run. Good judgement be damned.

"Halt!" General Valdés commands. There's a faint mumbling coming from his men. I pick up: "La Malinche . . . fantasmas . . . not going in."

I untie my mask and pull it off. The rear of the cave is pitch black, and if I could shift, I would be able to see in total darkness. However, I don't dare risk draining my tonalli when I'm already injured. What good would that do? I can practically feel my life force leaking out with every drop of blood. I press my hand against my wound, taking in shallow gasps of air, my fingertips touching the nasty scar right below it. A reminder of one of my earliest lessons with Master Toto. It's a long time since I studied under him, but his teachings remain.

I was eight, and I didn't really believe that the stumpy old man could be a sorcerer, much less a real Nagual Master. Compared to him—it turned out—none of the other Naguals could even begin to be called masters. Barely lifting his hand, he delivered a slash across my knee. A cut that could easily have severed my leg had that been his intention.

"You won't always have full use of your body. Learn to fight at a disadvantage."

I blinked away sweat and tears from my eyes. "But, Master . . . I don't know how to fight."

"Good," he said. "Now the learning can begin."

He followed up with a wave of tonalli that sent me flying backward. My stomach clenches at the memory.

I crawl to get a better look at my pursuers. A bellowing shout escapes my lips as my wounded leg brushes a boulder. It echoes loudly around the cave.

A shriek rises from outside. "La Malinche!"

Superstition is a funny thing. If the stories are true, these caves are haunted by the spirit of Hernán Cortés's interpreter, La Malinche. The Nahua girl Malintzin was sold as a slave, given the Christian name Marina, and bore Cortés's children. After winning Mexico for the Crown, he arranged for La Malinche to marry one of his captains. I don't know how she died, but her wails are said to haunt the woods ever since.

"We have to follow Pantera," General Valdés says, "quickly, or she will escape and Nabarres will have our hides. And I'm not ready to die. Ortega, you go first."

"Me?" Ortega squawks. "What about La Malinche?"

I peer over the edge of the cave mouth. Valdés pulls out his long blade and cuts Ortega down. He collapses in a pool of red.

"Jimenez, you're up. Or are you afraid of a ghost too?"

Jimenez rides a few steps ahead. Warily, the general and the rest of the soldiers follow. I cup my hands around my mouth and cry my shrillest, most piercing yowl.

In a panic, horses neigh and rear up, pawing at the air. At least two men are thrown. Others grab fistfuls of mane, trying valiantly to keep their seats. Hooves hit the ground again, and Valdés and his men bolt. Not my finest act of deception, but what can you do, when you can do nothing? Another of Master Toto's sayings. The man always spoke in riddles.

"Ever heard of speaking plainly?" I asked him.

"It's not a lesson if you already know the answer," he replied, balancing a handstand with two fingers.

My eyelids begin to droop. I slide down against a wall, resting my head on the rock behind me. With a whimper, I pull out one of my knives from my belt and cut off part of my robe, then wrap it around my thigh and press the wound firmly to stop the blood from flowing. Although the bullet only grazed me, my leg feels like it's being pulled apart. I think of my master's lessons, remembering what I know about injuries and how to replenish tonalli. I could build a fire, but that would only delay me, and I'm expected elsewhere.

I'm surrounded by darkness, until a ray of daylight finds its way through the mouth of the cave.

That's it.

I need Tonatiuh. I need the sun god.

CHAPTER 3

La Sirvienta

"How can I draw tonalli from the sun?"

I sat with Master Toto on a bamboo raft on one of the many glittering lakes in Tamoanchan. A paradise where buildings grow right out of the ground like glaciers, sparkling like diamonds. Maize never runs out. People don't grow infirm with age. Every day is balmy and filled with the green of the sacred Flowering Tree that stretches endlessly up into the sky, its cleft trunk like the stilts of the gods.

That is what I saw in the ten years I was with my master, not heads being separated from necks. In the few months since coming back to the capital, I've seen nothing but ruin, terror, disease, executions, raids, famine.

"Trees draw tonalli from the sun in the same way they draw water from the soil."

Master Toto always had something to say about trees.

On the eastern side of la traza, hundreds of canoes loaded with goods for the market glide up and down the Acequia Real. It's the largest waterway in and out of the city, and the one supply route over which the Mexica lords maintain some control, though the viceroyalty owns and operates the embarcaderos, the docks in Chalco and

Xochimilco. After the Fall, the Spaniards destroyed the dams and most of the canals to build their churches and residences, which has made fresh water less accessible. The whole island appears as if the gods swooped upon it in vengeance.

I bargain with a boatman for passage on a canoe bound for the southern shores of Lake Texcoco, handing over a small bag filled with three hundred cacao beans. After counting the beans, he raises an eyebrow at me. I could buy the canoe for such a sum. Alas, I'm in no condition to row.

"They're real." My assurance is worthless. Like any currency, cacao beans can be faked. Some thieves remove the outer skin from the bean and fill the husk with sand.

The boatman bites one of the beans in half, then nods.

I curl up between two cisterns filled with the sap of the maguey plant. The canoe bobs unsteadily in the water as the boatman plies the oar. I lie there, feeling the sky and myself one with the sky, feeling the sun and myself one with the sun, abandoning myself to Tonatiuh's warmth. As he rises, so does my tonalli, and as he sets, my tonalli does as well. That is what I know.

I also know that Señor Alonso is dead. Miguel is without a father because of me. Señor Alonso wouldn't have wanted me to dwell on his death, for life is a dream, and only in death does one become truly awake. But then a lone tear traces down my cheek, and almost at once, sobs begin to shake my body.

It was Señor Alonso who, on my return to the city, found me in the main square, dazed and horrified. In ten years, the capital had changed almost beyond recognition, perhaps as much as I had. The palace had undergone substantial renovations. A new, larger church had been erected. The air was thick with an overpowering stench; the ditches coiling through la traza were filled not with water but with sheet-covered corpses.

I stood before one of the ditches and knelt before the dead to offer a few words of prayer.

"I wouldn't get too close if I were you," warned the hunched man who had taken my side.

"What happened to them?" I asked, afraid of the answer.

"Cocoliztli," the man replied.

I stood. "What sort of pestilence?"

"A fever comes first, followed by aches. Then," he explained, "the totomonaliztli—the pustules—start forming. All over, on the chest, head, face, and legs, they appear. People can no longer walk, sit, or even lie on their backs. Eating or speaking causes them to scream in pain, for some have sores on the tongue. The sickness has taken a great many of my people; it's easily caught, so they die alone, with no one to care for them. From morning to sunset, all you see are bodies thrown into the ditches."

"Can it be treated?" I asked, dismayed.

"I apply several remedies to my patients," the man said, wiping his sweating brow, and I wondered if he, too, was succumbing to the plague, "but more die than recover."

Hooves rattled along the cobblestones as a brace of soldiers galloped past us, sending a few passers-by into frightened disarray, including the hunched man. He quickly grasped my wrist, jerking me behind a cart. "If they see you, they'll think you're sick."

"But I'm not sick," I said, puzzled.

The man's expression hardened. "Do you wish to get yourself killed? It doesn't matter if you aren't," he whispered. "Dead or alive. It's all the same to them."

Cautiously, I watched the soldiers. One of the riders halted his horse at a distance from the ditches. "Burn the heathens," he ordered through the cloth pressed against his nose.

I stared at the soldier, my jaw tense. "Who is he?"

"You must be a stranger to the city if you have to ask."

"I've been away for a long time."

"*He* is Captain Nabarres, and you'd best learn to stay out of trouble if you want to survive. Do you have family? Somewhere to go? What is your name?"

I opened my mouth, but the words lodged in my throat. For a moment, I felt compelled to tell him everything: who I was, where I'd been, all of it. But I didn't dare. He wouldn't have believed me, or worse, he would've. Then he'd have asked more questions that I couldn't answer. I knew then I had to lie. To hide not only my own secrets but those of others who'd put their trust in me.

"You can call me Pantera."

The memory leaves me, but the misery doesn't. The pain in my leg is nothing. A mere prick. Whatever it was inside Señor Alonso's core that made him unbreakable, it never diminished—not when he was beaten, not when he drew his last breath.

At the town of Chalco, I hitch a ride on a mule-drawn wagon. The terrain is so painfully pitted, I think my teeth will jar loose. I reel with nausea the entire time, but at least I don't have to walk.

By the time I make it to Puerto Marqués in the bay of Acapulco, one of the main ports of New Spain reserved for the Spanish treasure fleet, Tonatiuh is almost down from the top of the sky. I am drenched in sweat from head to toe, everything hurts, and each step feels like a negotiation rather than an order.

I crouch behind a crate of fishing equipment and peek over the rim. Men are moving barrels of fish along the pier under a cloud of noisy gulls. Guards patrol the dock, idly watching the action. Eleven galleons, large and small, sit at anchor. After wintering in Acapulco, they return to Spain in spring filled to the brim with riches stolen from the New World. But with Spain at war against more than a dozen European powers, attempts to sail back have become dangerous. It's been years since the fleets have brought treasure to the motherland.

At the end of the pier, I see it: *La Capitana*.

If anyone has realized I'm not on board, I'm finished.

I duck my head at the crunch of boots. Two guards stroll by, swords clinking at their sides, laughing at some shared joke. I couldn't fight them if I wanted to. The sun sinks lower, and I'm losing more tonalli with every drop of blood. When my path is clear, I half run, half limp to the pier's edge and dive deep. Frigid water steals heat from my body and salt penetrates my open wound. I choke down a scream. The fog of pain begins to clear, and awareness seeps back. Blood in the ocean draws all kinds of hungry predators. But I can't board the ship disguised as Pantera. I'm not *that* mad. Yet.

The warm, gentle air hums against my skin when I surface. I'm comforted by the turquoise panorama of the Pacific. The salty air. The twilight. Waves raise and lower me, break at the shore, and then return to the sea. I stroke toward the ship and latch on to the underside of the starboard. Drawing from what little tonalli is left inside me, I soar on to the upper deck as though I'm bewinged and cling to one of the porthole ledges. My leg protests. The Sword of Integrity is heavy on my back, but I've always loved the weight of it. The power it possesses.

I wiggle through the round window. My situation would be a lot easier if this was a wider opening, if I wasn't injured and soaking wet, and if my robe didn't keep getting caught on splinters of wood. Knocking over a carafe and a candlestand on my bedside table makes a gods-awful clamor as I tumble inside.

"Leonora?" A frantic voice calls from behind the closed door. "Is that you?"

I slip off my mask, panting. The door swings open.

Inés, my handmaid, stumbles into the cabin and inspects the damage.

"Where have you been?" she demands. Her voice is shrill, stabbing my ears, not her usual sweet tones. "We said before sundown. Didn't we say before sundown? My shadow is almost out of sight. I thought all kinds of things. I was about to send out a search party. Speaking of parties—Leonora!" She hurries over as my legs give out and helps me to the bed, noticing the bloody tear in my outer thigh. "What *happened*?" She sighs and shakes her head, muttering a stream of obscenities in Purépecha during the process.

"Ay, Leonora," she says reprovingly. "You always take too many risks! What if you had been recognized? By Captain Nabarres, worst of all."

"Well, that *is* the point of wearing a disguise—ow!" She pinches my wound together. Blood flows out of the open sore.

"It's bad. You could lose your leg."

"Inés . . . you always say the most delightful things."

"And it's deep," she says, upon further study of my thigh. "The flesh is inflamed. I need to clean the wound." She looks up at me with brown uncertain eyes, throwing me a questioning look.

I nod. "Do what you can."

She stands, tossing her long dark hair over her shoulder. She lifts the front of her huipil and rushes behind a partition for bathing privacy. At first, I think she's fetching me a cool drink, but then she returns with a gourd and empties it over my wound. Freshly passed urine. I clamp my teeth together and desperately suck in air.

Then I lift a brow. "Do you know what you're doing?"

"I know a thing or two about surviving."

When I first met Inés, she was getting by on her wits, picking pockets, robbing shops, conning fools in and around the slums of Mexico City. At the time, I had just returned to the capital after ten years of being thought dead, and I needed a handmaid. An ally, too, with a degree of shrewdness, whom I could trust with my story. And Inés needed not to be hanged for stealing from the viceroyalty. Father's wife would not permit the bastard daughter of her husband and a Mexica woman to have a maid. But Father, believing I needed a friend, allowed me a servant of my choosing, however unusual.

"I'm sorry about Señor Alonso," she says when I tell her what happened, sewing my wound shut. The stitching is rushed and it's going to leave another scar, but at least I'll live. "He's in a better place. He died a warrior's death."

I am angry, so I take no comfort in her words. Why didn't he fight? Why did he surrender himself?

From the bed, I have a perfect view of Tonatiuh dipping behind the ocean. Gliding from east to west, he brings life and light, to this our sun. Unlike the gods before him, he isn't the first, nor the second or third. He is the fifth, and one day, the old people say, he too will meet his death.

My eyes are steady on the horizon; Tonatiuh's last rays reflect on to the water. I watch a flock of gulls fly by, going wherever they want, racing the wind, seeing the world from a different angle, living their lives in freedom. How I envy them.

Inés retrieves something from one of the drawers and offers it to me. "Happy birthday."

I take the small wooden box and shake my head.

"I know. I know. We said no presents. But when have you ever known me to do as I'm told?"

"You're a terrible servant."

She grins. "I know. You just keep me around because I'm pretty."

I open the box to reveal a silver coin. A Spanish dollar that bears the head of Joaquín de las Casas y Lara, with the inscription BY THE GRACE OF GOD. I run my thumb over its surface. I miss seeing his face in person.

When I think of my father, I think of a very sad man. As the first viceroy of New Spain, the king's envoy in the New World, keeping the peace was next to impossible. On his arrival, he found a territory rife with Indigenous and Spanish conflict. Hernán Cortés held the military rank of captain general, but his ambition was to be made viceroy. He had, after all, single-handedly destroyed and razed Mexico-Tenochtitlan, or so he boasted in his letters to King Carlos. But even with the power-drunk Cortés as an enemy, Father solidified society by establishing Indigenous councils and appointing the Mexica royals to govern the barrios in the north and south.

I run my fingers over the obsidian medallion I always keep around my neck, tugging at the long chain, feeling its weight, its glassy surface which is cool to the touch. Sometimes, when I want to see my father again, all I have to do is look closely at the medallion, and there he is in my mind's eye. But there, too, is misery and rage. I remember my cause, the reason I donned a disguise. Father's efforts to counter the harm wrought by his own people made him powerful enemies in court, influenced by Cortés. He opposed them, but in his final sickly days, the tyrannical Spaniards became bolder in their abuses. And so my work began.

We used to play hide-and-seek, my father and I. I wasn't a skillful hider; I would flatten myself under beds or slip behind thin curtains with my feet poking out. But I was a good seeker. I never told him, but I could somehow hear his heartbeat from another room, smell the heady scent of the cempasúchil blossom used to rinse his shirts. He would walk around, opening and closing doors with a dramatic swish, tossing aside pillows, peering inside my toy chest. "Leonora," he sang. I can still remember the rush of exhilaration as he searched for me. I would come out laughing from wherever I was, and he would wrap his arms around me. In those memories, my father is strong and true, like this coin, not the way he looked when the plague took his life. Little did either of us know I would continue to play hide-and-seek, long after my childhood days were over. Even after all those years, I'm still hiding in plain sight. Only now, it's not a game, and I'm never found.

I squeeze the coin. "Where did you get this?"

"Wouldn't you like to know?"

"I don't want you stealing, Inés. The risk is too great."

"And how exactly is what you do so safe and morally acceptable? I don't see why it's fine for you to go around killing people if I can't swindle them once in a while."

"I don't kill people," I say, even though my hands aren't clean. "You don't need to steal. I can get you anything you want."

"Are you an advocate for the law now, Leonora? This is an unlikely turn for you."

"I'm an advocate for preserving the integrity of your neck."

Inés finishes nursing and dressing my wound, then moves to my head. She jabs a hairpin into my scalp, fastening my new headdress. I would never let anyone else touch my hair, rich as it is in tonalli. Although I can't see what she's doing, I feel her weaving loops and thin braids with hairpins. I didn't say I wanted an intricately braided coiffure, but the style shows wealth, grandeur, and importance.

Tonight, I will see the man I am to marry for the first time. On my return to the capital, my father's wife wasted no time. She saw opportunity in the recently widowed Prince Felipe, the king's son—a chance to be rid of me and increase her own standing. She arranged our betrothal, forging an advantageous alliance. I can almost hear her telling me that if I am to be the future queen of Spain, I can't look like the king's scullery maid. Dull as a rusted spoon.

"What do you think he looks like?" Inés asks.

"Who?"

"The prince."

"He must be repulsive." The taste in my mouth is as bitter as my answer. "Why else would he have declined to send his portrait?"

"At least we know he's not a wrinkly old man." She is quiet for a moment, then she somberly says, "If you leave to join him as his wife in Spain, who will defend the people here?"

"La Justicia."

"When have the rebels come down from the mountains? They fight for their own survival and nobody else's. Pantera is needed in the capital."

"If I don't wed His Hideous Highness, there won't be a capital to defend." I push my headdress back. The thing is chafing my forehead. "This is duty, not desire. I can't kill my way out of this one. There is nothing Pantera can do."

"There is something Leonora can do. Pray. It can't hurt. And it might bring you the peace you seek."

"Where are the teteoh, Inés? Look around. Do you see Quetzalcoatl here? Tezcatlipoca? Are they in the statues? In the temples?"

She sighs. "Why do you hate your gods so much, Leonora?"

I don't hate the gods. The teteoh form, shape, and are all things. I just won't be ruled by them.

"I think the better question is, why don't you hate *yours*? What has Kurikaweri ever done for you? Did Xaratenga give you power? Immortality? Did they save your mother from death? Did they prevent your brother from falling to the dreadful pox?" I shake my head. "The Spaniards have taken everything from you, and you still wish to appease your gods who let them?"

Inés closes her eyes against my tirade. "My gods, like yours, have their limits . . . my lady." She words it delicately, trying to avoid provoking me further. But she means, *don't mock the gods. Or you'll unleash their wrath.*

When Inés has finished making me presentable, I'm in a crimson silk gown embroidered with flowers. Red. The color of Spain, Andalusian dancing, Rioja wine, the spilled blood of toros. I'm dripping with precious gems. My hair cascades down either side of my face and falls just short of my waist like molten obsidian.

Inés brings me my lace gloves. "Ready?"

I slip them on, pulling until they cover the blue patterns inked on the backs of my hands.

To the Spaniards, today is a day of celebration, of triumph and high hope for the future, heralding the beginning of what could be a union of two worlds, the Old and New Spain.

A beginning approaches, too, for the Nahua, for believers like Señor Alonso, for at the close of the Dead Days, the sacred tonalpohualli and solar xiuhpohualli calendars will commence on the same day. Every fifty-two years, this cycle starts again. It's either the beginning of a new cycle, or the beginning of the end.

Here I stand at the threshold of a new year, and all I can think of is the past. I think of home. I think of family. The people who took me in and raised me. How I wish I could return to Master Toto, to my friends, to that place where beautiful life-giving flowers bloom. Memories come and go, and they're all I have, memories of the place that shaped me.

"How do I look?" I ask.

"Like a Spaniard," Inés replies.

That's who I must be now. The other half of me. The enemy.

I knew, when I decided to don the mask of Pantera, that this wasn't going to be easy. To pretend to have an interest in this life, in these Christians and their god, in the dull chat of courtiers who don't know the world outside their walls. The games they play. For position. For power. For influence.

Certainly, it would be a difficult and tiresome game to play, to smile and act the demure maiden. But over the past few months, I've perfected the art of keeping up appearances and protecting my identity.

I nod to Inés to throw open the door, then lift my head like a queen at her coronation and walk out with dignity.

My charade is tragically good.

CHAPTER 4

El Príncipe

Vicereine Carlota decides I shall have the most glorious birthday the New World has ever seen. This woman, my father's wife, has never liked me—not when Father brought home another woman's babe, not when I returned to the capital, no longer a child. At best, she is distant, at worse she is cruel. She is no family of mine.

At the stern of the ship, a lively band plays music for Spanish courtiers, dons and doñas and their kin. Dancers twirl to the rhythm of guitars, clutching the folds of their long skirts. There's enough food to feed a battalion. Wine is flowing like water. Such extravagance, but it's not for me. Not really. What a show Vicereine Carlota has put on. She'll go to great lengths to present an opulent picture so that no one, especially my betrothed, might doubt our wealth and power.

A few days ago, a letter with the Spanish royal seal arrived on behalf of His Royal Highness, Prince Felipe, saying a storm had washed him on to the shores of Acapulco Bay and his ship required repairs. The vicereine was radiant. Thrilled.

Rather than inviting the castaway Prince Felipe to the palace to meet in person privately, she insisted we go to him and welcome the prince to the New World aboard a ship of the Crown.

The meeting couldn't wait, for the surest way for a Spanish prince to get lost is to allow him to travel freely over strange ground. The alliance is of great importance, and hallelujah, God our Savior has sent us a blessing, and when God gives us favor, we must answer immediately to His goodness. Or so she said.

The pain in my leg makes me quiver, but I right myself, moving slowly across the main deck. Half-hearted birthday wishes and murmured compliments follow in my wake. Everyone from the palace is here, dressed in their finest to honor Prince Felipe.

Captain Nabarres stands by the dance floor, stern as he watches the dancers. He smiles when he sees me. To sense another's tonalli, I need proximity, and as I approach him, it settles on me like a blanket of cold that turns dew to frost. "My lady," he says, lowering his head. "Feliz cumpleaños. May fortune and health be with you."

I nod courteously. But I don't forget who murdered Señor Alonso. I can still smell his blood clotting under my nose, and the image of Miguel crouched over his father's corpse enters my mind.

"Is your leg bothering you, señorita?" he asks. "I noticed your ladyship limping."

"I bumped my knee, is all."

"You're shaking, señorita. Should I send for the doctor?"

It's possible Captain Nabarres isn't aware that Pantera was struck with a bullet. But if he finds out.

I paste on a smile. "Nonsense, capitán. It's nothing." I give a twirl, my skirt swishing about my legs. "See?" I don't flinch, but I bite down on my back teeth to keep from grimacing. If Master Toto can remain straight-faced when kicked in the groin, I can hold my smile.

"Leonora, there you are," Vicereine Carlota says. I thank the Thirteen Heavens for small mercies as Nabarres focuses on her. She looks resplendent in her golden gown. The top half of her hair is knotted in a high bun, while the bottom half hangs in curls. Most strikingly, her hair is as dark as possible. Her handmaids have been dabbling it in tea seeds. Any gossamer hint of white, and she'll have them whipped like disobedient children. Everyone has reason to please her.

She folds her hands, rosary beads interwoven through jeweled fingers, at her waist. "Must His Highness grow old waiting to meet you? A lady is never tardy."

"A lady is never too eager," I say with a haughty toss of my head.

The clarion notes of a trumpet sound, and a herald appears in the thick of the crowd. I grit my teeth involuntarily at the blast. Guests crane their necks to see. "Her Excellency Vicereine Carlota de Sepúlveda y Olivares and Lady Leonora de las Casas Tlazohtzin."

Guests lower their heads until Vicereine Carlota has settled in her chair on a dais with the viceroy, who says nothing but hears everything. Even though Viceroy Jerónimo is the sovereign leader in New Spain, ruling in the name of King Carlos, and wields absolute power, my half brother is only fourteen. Vicereine Carlota acts as regent. Everything, large and small, is decided by the vicereine, along with her numero dos, Captain Nabarres.

A path is opened by men at arms coming down the stairway from the upper deck.

Once again, the herald sounds a ringing call on his trumpet. Resting his instrument on his hip, he shouts, "His Highness Prince Felipe of Asturias and Girona, Duke of Milan, son of His Royal Majesty King Carlos and Queen Isabela of Portugal, God rest her soul."

I sit on a stool next to the viceroy and watch as all eyes turn to the young royal approaching us, with half a dozen guards trailing behind him. His face is nothing special, but what he lacks in defining features he more than makes up for in continental charm. Of all the aspects of his appearance, only his attire is truly arresting. His velvet stockings match his black doublet, edged in gold cording. A black cape hangs in broad folds from his shoulders, and the feathers in his bonnet flutter among gold pins in the sea breeze. Sensing his tonalli confirms my impression. Under all that glitter, his tonalli feels ordinary, not too warm, not too cold.

This is the man who is to be king of Spain. With the death of his first wife, he has to remarry to secure the succession, an infanta from Spain or a princesse from France, and I am neither, but this is no impediment to Vicereine Carlota, who is unstoppable in her plotting. She claims his arrival was a generous gift from God. It seems that by some miraculous power, Prince Felipe survived a storm at sea and washed ashore stripped of all but his life. Miracles are for Christians. I don't believe in them. So how exactly is he here?

Prince Felipe stops before the dais and gives a small greeting in Latin. I don't speak the language. From the vicereine's smile and my brother's polite nod, I can only assume the prince is expressing his delight at arriving in the New World.

Pleasantries out of the way, he turns to me and speaks in Spanish, a romantic language more appropriate for courting.

"Lady Leonora, an unfortunate storm has brought me to you, but it gives me great joy to congratulate you in person on such a felicitous day." He takes my hand in his and kisses it. His pale skin stands out against the dull cream of my gloves, as if he's never seen the sun.

"Your Highness is most kind," I say loudly enough for everyone to hear my greeting. My appearance is gracious and entirely ladylike. I'm like a painting from the palace gallery. I fix my social smile in place and welcome His Highness to New Spain. "Bienvenido a la Nueva España, alteza."

He grins, looking at me from beneath his pale lashes. His blue eyes glow under the torches shining above his head. "Forgive my candor in admitting that I thought your portrait a deception, Lady Leonora. I did not think it possible for a person to have one brown eye and one green—surely, a fanciful painter's most daring leap of imagination. But now, it is plain to see you are the masterpiece. Your beauty is quite enough to embolden a man."

Masterpiece? He's barely arrived, and his words are already sticky sweet, like agave nectar. Well, I suppose that's why he came.

His voice is overly loud and precise, as if he's reciting a sonnet. He entertains magnificently. If he wants a show, I'll give it.

I smile coquettishly. "Goodness, alteza, you flatter me." If only I had a fan to flutter over my face, the theatrics would be complete. "It saddened me to hear His Highness declined to send his own portrait. I feared, perhaps, my appearance was not pleasing."

"My lady, you please me immensely. It is a delight for me to look at you. My portraits don't quite emulate my likeness. But now that I am here, I shall have my portrait painted by the first skillful artist who arises in my domains. But it could never compare to so miraculous a beauty." He inclines his head gracefully.

"The night is a celebration," he continues, "but also a beginning. As you know, the king's health has worsened, and he is considering abdicating the throne. In the interest of ensuring a smooth transition of power when the Lord calls my father to resign Spain, my first order of business is to settle the succession of the Crown. As I am his heir apparent, the king has given me his consent to wed Lady Leonora."

"Praise Him." Vicereine Carlota beams. "The three most important moments in a woman's life are the moment of proposal, the moment of marriage, and the moment when she provides her husband a son."

What a tedious life.

The prince shifts his eyes to my brother. "Excelencia, do I have your blessing to marry Lady Leonora?"

Viceroy Jerónimo's mouth opens and closes, as if at war with himself over what to say. "If my sister does not wish to marry you, then I see it unbecoming to give my blessing."

For a moment, I see Jerónimo for the child he is, under the carapace of the viceroy that he has to be. My dear brother. It's not his wish that I leave for Spain, not after believing me dead for so long. This boy's first word was "no," despite everything else they taught him to say. He couldn't have been coached into a response now either.

I have to bite the inside of my cheek to hide a smile.

Vicereine Carlota does not smile. She pins Jerónimo to his chair with a venomous look. Then she banks down her seething emotions, squares her shoulders, and turns to the prince. "Alteza, I apologize that my son dares behave as a common child, forgetting he is the viceroy of New Spain."

Prince Felipe gives a polite smile. "That's quite all right. It is the way of children."

I may be two years shy of twenty, but he's not much older than I am. I let boldness overtake me. "Wasn't His Highness merely thirteen when he became Duke of Milan?"

"Ah, yes," Prince Felipe says, "but age is just a number. I've always been aware of the world around me. How seeing must become observing, because the smallest details give way to new discoveries . . . leading to a new world."

"What an ambitious agenda," I say offhandedly.

The silence is broken almost immediately by the vicereine's laugh. She does that a lot. "My Leonora has humor and a tongue, alteza."

"No os preocupéis, mi señora. I've always said: never has the world made a queen of a girl who does what she is told and says nothing of her own. I like Lady Leonora. She is strong-willed, for all her beauty."

Strong-willed? What exactly does His Highness think he knows about me?

Prince Felipe shifts his gaze to me, and his grin broadens. It's not the eager smile of a man to his wife-to-be or the secret smile of a lover. No, his increased heartbeat tells me it's something else. But what?

Courtesies over, Prince Felipe motions an attendant forward. He hands the vicereine what I assume is the obligatory betrothal letter presenting the bride price. As Vicereine Carlota reads the letter, I glimpse its contents. Clothing. Money. Exotic meats. Jewelry. Various fine silks. I manage to avoid rolling my eyes. Just barely.

"Why, alteza," she says, the joy in her voice unmistakable, "you honor us."

"If it pleases Her Excellency, I am willing to take your daughter without a dowry. I have met Lady Leonora and that is enough."

No dowry? Preposterous. Even poor families manage some kind of dowry for a daughter. Does Prince Felipe think our house so low that I would marry undowered? Does he wish to marry me out of pity?

"You shall have my Leonora, alteza," the vicereine swiftly declares.

I hold my tongue, but it's not easy. Vicereine Carlota controls the coffers. It's too sweet an offer for her to refuse.

The look of relief crossing Prince Felipe's face confirms my suspicion. There is *definitely* something off about my betrothed.

Soft music begins in the background, and Prince Felipe asks for a dance. I'm waging an internal battle. Every movement, every shift of weight nearly steals my breath, and with this dressing wrapped around my leg, there is no way. "I'm a terrible dancer . . . alteza."

"A pity. I'm an excellent dancer." He holds out his hand.

"I have every confidence that you are."

I'm almost grateful to be saved when Vicereine Carlota distracts Prince Felipe with more introductions. But when his attention turns elsewhere, she pulls me to my feet and grips my arm, her nail guards digging painfully into my skin like talons. "Debéis comportaros," she says, her voice menacing.

"Define *behave*."

"Stop acting wild. This is no time for your temper. A prince is never refused. It's past time you were wed, Leonora. You ought to give thanks to God that by some miracle He has chosen *you* to be a king's wife."

"Which god?"

"That is pagan talk!" she fumes. "I will not listen to it. How many times do I have to tell you? There is only one God."

"He is not my husband of choice." I didn't mean to sound so vulnerable, but I couldn't stop myself from saying the words.

"Choice?" she says, almost offended by the word. "Leonora, did your Indian mother not teach you how the world works? Your blood is tainted. You have no choice. You do what you're told."

I bristle. My mother, if she were alive, would never force me to marry. Father spoke of her lovingly, the Mexica woman named Tlazohtzin. She passed before I could form any memories of her; the rigors of childbirth weakened her, and she went to Tonatiuh. When women die giving birth, they die the most honorable death, just as warriors who fight and die in the battlefield. They become divine women, and their teyolia, their spirit, becomes a companion of the sun. My mother's warrior teyolia lives in me.

"Until I am queen of Spain," I retort. "Then *you* will dance to whatever tune I sing."

I don't wait for her angry retort. Instead, I turn and tell Prince Felipe it would be my honor to dance with him. With an immaculate bow, he holds out his arm and escorts me to the dance floor. His arm daringly circles my waist, then he lifts my right hand and positions it on his shoulder. He is so close I feel his tonalli brush against mine. It feels sticky, fuzzy, as if struggling with itself.

You can do this, Leonora.

The prince takes control as we flow in graceful arcs, performing wide, sweeping turns and pirouettes around each other. Elegance at its finest. Pain at its truest. With every step, my leg throbs beneath my silken dress. It gets harder and harder to ignore as the prince raises and twirls me. I can't help it. I let out a yelp.

"I'm sorry about that. You're lighter than I expected. It's not too uncomfortable, is it?"

"Not at all." It's torture trying to bend my knee at the appropriate angle and dance on a swaying deck without wobbling or veering sideways. I feel my dressing start to slip. I spot Inés among the servants, and she shoots a concerned look my way.

"I believe you will find my company most enjoyable, Lady Leonora," Prince Felipe says. "I am a man of honor and stand strong in my faith, my family, and my service to my country."

"It seems unnecessary to ingratiate yourself with me, alteza. I'm already marrying you." Without a dowry, no less.

"I am merely speaking the truth, my lady," he says graciously. "I'd like to get to know you. I've no intention of being trapped in a loveless marriage. Again."

"I was very sorry to hear of your wife's passing."

"There was respect and mutual understanding with Manuela. Not love."

"Love is for commoners. You cannot lead with your heart if you're to accomplish a single thing of significance. Very few can."

"Thank you for your good counsel, my lady, but you are being unfair."

"Now, that doesn't sound like me," I say, lifting my chin to meet his eyes. "What do you have to gain from this alliance?" It evidently isn't wealth. Certainly not position.

"A wife. A family."

The rise in his pulse is subtle. He is a fantastic liar.

"There are many princesses for you to wed in Europe who might give you that. Future kings do not simply marry for their own pleasure, alteza." He's a foreigner. Perhaps his intent is to endear himself to his subjects. Still, why would he attempt to gain my affection?

He smiles. "I know, it's hard to believe. I will admit I can be . . . passionate. I recognize just how much King Carlos and Queen Isabela have influenced my life. My parents . . . they had the greatest love for each other until my mother's death parted them. It inspired me, you see."

"The people from here . . ." I say, "they have this . . . belief. They call it the Nemontemi, the Dead Days. The last five days of their solar calendar. During this time, the gods rest after a long year. Demons and wicked forces are able to roam the world. Disease, death, and chaos spill out from the Land of the Dead. No activities are planned, lest something dangerous occur.

"They don't call the Nemontemi period 'the Dead Days' for nothing.

A person unlucky enough to be born during the Nemontemi is expected to have a difficult and unhappy life. Do you know what day it is today, alteza?"

"The day of your birth?" he replies uncertainly.

"Yes, and the first day of the Nemontemi. A wife like me could bring you misfortune . . . ruin, not the love you seek. You see, I'm cursed. I'll ask again: What do you have to gain from this alliance?"

Prince Felipe seems hardly perturbed. His expression remains casual. "I am a man of God. I don't believe in pagan superstition. If you don't expect fortune to look your way, that doesn't mean it won't. When my father abdicates the throne, all Old and New Spain will bow down to you as my queen. It shall be so."

Whether I like it or not, I can't escape the vicereine's promise that I will wed Prince Felipe. I will bed him, bear his children, and live with him for the rest of my life. I might learn to enjoy the prince's company. But leaving Mexico will give me no pleasure at all. I've never been to Spain. I was born here. The mountains, the lake, the forest, the valley—they are in my blood. This is my home.

Then, too, there is something about Prince Felipe. Mouths sometimes speak falsehood, but tonalli never lies. Scent. Sound. Those are things I trust. Most often, a lie will be accompanied by fear. Fear of being caught. Fear of the truth. But what can a prince have to fear?

The melody finishes, and the prince looks down at my neck. "Your necklace is quite unusual."

My gloved hand rises protectively to my medallion. "It was a gift from my father."

"Ah, a family heirloom. That would make it very special." He clears his throat and forces a grin that dimples his cheek. "You wear it well. Another dance, my lady?"

A lady approaches us then and curtsies. "Príncipe Felipe." I make a little face of disdain at her disregard. "Please forgive my forwardness, alteza. We have not been introduced. I am Amalia Catalina de Íñiguez y Mendoza, Countess of Niebla," she says, pulling her shoulders back, accentuating her breasts beneath her dress.

"Lady Amalia." Prince Felipe lowers his head stiffly. "A pleasure."

It's hard not to notice the spots on the left side of her face, though they are largely hidden by a dusting of powder. The Lady of Niebla contracted the pox upon her arrival to the New World, which left her marked. Often this will mean the ruin of a young lady looking to marry, but it does not deter her; Amalia "La Viuda" has been married thrice.

Her long hair falls in wavy tresses, like a golden waterfall. She is draped in the extravagant ebony duchesse favored by the House of Habsburg, her gown heavily embroidered with gold thread and adorned with pearls symbolizing purity. She does not, for one moment, look as if she's grieving her third husband's death.

"You dress in black, Lady Amalia?" I ask, lifting an eyebrow.

She smiles, but it's cynical. "I am no longer in mourning."

"Widows are expected to wear full mourning for a year."

"Are we now?" She presses a heavily ringed hand to her heart, feigning concern, a mock pout shaping her lips.

"Seeing as you've been married three times," I sneer, "I'd say you are somewhat of an expert in the matter."

Lady Amalia narrows her eyes, her cheeks reddening. "I do believe Viceroy Jerónimo is looking for you, Lady Leonora. He wishes for you to join him."

"Looking for me, why? I am not hiding."

"It sounded important."

Lady Amalia is not a woman of impulse but of calculation. She won't hesitate to exploit an opening if she finds one to her advantage. She is a nuisance but also my means of escape. I suppress a retort and drop into a brief bow.

The moment I'm out of sight, I breathe a sigh of relief. The cut on my leg burns, as though my blood has become poison, intent on destroying me from the inside out. I hobble down the stairs below deck and make my way lower inside the ship, clenching my jaw as I go. As soon as I let down my guard, all the recklessness catches up to me, giving me a painful reminder of my fragility. I'm so concentrated on taking gentle steps that at first I don't think anything of the sudden warmth pressing into me. The night is stuffy and heavy as usual, nothing more, but then I feel myself heat up, as hot as if I am on fire.

Impossible.

No mortal I know exudes tonalli like *that*.

CHAPTER 5

El Pirata

I probe the unknown tonalli, letting its heat wash over me. Male. Powerful. Commanding. I quickly follow it to the cabin where Inés nursed and dressed me. There, I press my ear to the door.

There is movement inside.

Trinkets clank together as the intruder rummages through the drawers, not worried about stealth. He doesn't care if he's caught, or he thinks he can't be. I don't like either theory. My leg might be giving up the pretense of holding me upright, but I still have my spirit. I brace myself and step inside.

The intruder is a contradiction. He wears military ceremonial dressing—breeches, padded doublet, and a scarlet buff coat with hanging sleeves. This charlatan fits the basic formula for a viceroyal guard: solemn appearance, flawless jacket and shoes, tall. He makes a virile impression.

But he doesn't stand at attention. He doesn't even look up from his search. I've never met a guard who didn't acknowledge me.

He's a pirate, and a cocky one at that.

His long hair is tied in a bundle, brown like his skin. I'll admit, he's easy on the eyes, and his tonalli is exquisite, but I loathe pirates with a fierce intensity. Horrid scoundrels, rascals, and bottom-feeders who plunder and pillage for their own gain. Not unlike the Spaniards.

"Who are you?" I ask, polite. For now. As an entirely reputable lady, I can't terrorize him into giving me answers. Not right away.

In the thin glow of the candles, his youthful skin doesn't match his weary expression, as if he's worn out by incessant toil—and yet his tonalli blazes, betraying his vigor and potency.

I lift an eyebrow. What in the Nine Hells is he doing here?

Puerto Marqués, the small harbor named for Cortés after he inherited the title, is a favorite spot for pirates; they attack and rob vessels laden with treasure. This pirate sneaked aboard a Spanish treasure galleon with a cargo of silver and jewels, a pirate's Holy Grail. Yet he's in my cabin, turning drawers and cupboards inside out.

My eyes snap to the loose floorboard next to the bed. I breathe a sigh of relief at seeing it hasn't been pried open. Otherwise, he would've found my mask and the Sword of Integrity.

The pirate has the audacity to carry on his looting as if I'm invisible. He doesn't bother to threaten me. I hate him for it. I am worth threatening.

"I asked you a question. I will have an answer."

Finally, he turns around and gives me a bored look. But then his eyes catch on something and his expression changes into a grin. He swiftly crosses the cabin toward me. The full force of his tonalli hits me, making my limbs feel boneless. Before I can gather my wits, he's standing right in front of me, his attention on my chest. Then he yanks away my medallion before quickly wrapping it in a cloth. I pause a moment, blinking under the influence of his tonalli, but then a memory bubbles up like an effervescent geyser.

My father is lying on his deathbed. "Promise me, Leonora," he says. "Promise to never take it off. Always wear it close to your heart."

"Lo prometo, papá. It'll never come off."

I take a step forward, my teeth lengthening into deadly points. I stop the shift before my mouth elongates into a snout. My heart pounds, and my body reminds me I have a bullet wound on my leg. I fight back the rush of anger.

"I'll be on my way, señorita. Buenas noches," the pirate says with a pleased nod.

Master springs up in my mind like an apparition.

Ignore the principles of Nagualism, and you will have left the Nagual Path.

I cannot kill this man, much as I want him dead. I try to think of what a poised society lady would do in such a predicament. With great theatrical pomp, if not star quality, I lunge for the door in an effort to block the exit. "Stand back, thief! You're not going anywhere. Guards!" I cry out imperiously, but no one comes.

"Por favor, get out of my way, señorita." There is a proud strength to the set of his shoulders, a brashness in the tilt of his head.

"Guards!" I shout again. Pantera is always surrounded by guards, but now that I actually need one, they're nowhere to be found.

"I've been rude." He puts a hand on his chest. "I admit I didn't know you'd be wearing the mirror. You didn't look directly into it, did you?"

Mirror? I close the distance between us in a few rushed strides. "I demand you give it back this instant."

He flashes his teeth in the widest smile I've ever seen. It's all teeth. Nice teeth. "You have my permission to search me for it, but you're going to have to be very thorough . . . señorita."

I don't flush easily, but my cheeks burn. I pick up a candelabra and hold the brass weapon in the air.

"All right. I can be reasonable," he says, grinning at my ire. "Which pocket is it in?"

"Hand it over, thief. I'm not going to ask again."

"Ah, see, theft implies ownership. How can I possibly be stealing something that isn't yours to begin with?"

"My father gave it to me!"

"I know." From the inside of his jacket, he retrieves the cloth with my medallion inside it and holds it up for me to see. "You have no idea what this is, do you? I understand you're upset, señorita. Don Joaquín was a good man. He was wise and just. But he did not understand the specific dangers of wearing a g—"

The pirate's next words are cut off by a blast that rocks the ship. I lose my balance and fall, but scramble back to my feet and grab the door handle to stand up.

Another blast.

This time, the pirate and I are thrown across the cabin, and I give a cry of horror when my medallion flies out the window. We land in a heap . . . his back crushing my bad leg. Gods, the pain is worse than being shot again.

"Get off me!" I shout, but I can't hear my own voice. The cabin spins. My vision fades in and out as my feet leave the floor. Strong arms lift me. I tip my head back and see stars spinning white across a solid black canvas. I catch a brief flash of light. A shooting star slides across the sky. *Star demons will come down from the heavens to devour the flesh of men.*

How can something so beautiful be so feared?

CHAPTER 6

La Maldición

There's so much noise.

"Leonora."

My eyelids are heavy, but Inés's voice pulls me awake.

"Where am I?" My voice is a croak. Like I've forgotten how to speak. I clutch fistfuls of the silky bedsheets, looking around. Blurry shapes start to look familiar. Sunlight pours through wispy curtains that billow in the warm breeze.

"You're safe. Rest."

I squint to see Inés by my bed, silhouetted against brightness. Her big brown eyes, pert nose, slightly bulbous at the tip, a brightly colored wrap swathing her dark hair.

"Someone found you lying on the beach in Acapulco," she says. "You were brought back to the palace."

"Someone?"

She pours a cup of a red beverage from the bedside table.

"Drink. It tastes like strawberry." She holds the glass to my mouth, tipping it slightly. I take a sip and immediately spit out the bitter remedy.

I bite back a groan and grab my throat. "Are you trying to poison me?"

"It's herbal vinegar. Mixed with myrrh, worm-grass, black-seed oil, and some frog venom. It helps reduce pain. You must drink it."

I do so, begrudgingly, glaring at her all the while.

With a roll of her eyes, she shakes her head. "I'm glad you're awake. You snore unbearably. How are you feeling?"

I don't answer until the glass is empty. My eyes tear from the effort of forcing it down. I sit up, coughing at the vile aftertaste. My pounding headache, racing heartbeat, ringing ears, and throbbing leg only make the dizziness worse.

"Like I'm being poisoned."

"Yes, well, the expectation isn't for you to enjoy it, but it *is* good for you."

"How long have I been in bed?"

"A couple of days."

I tense. "How *many* days?"

"About a week."

"A week or a couple of days? Which one is it?"

"Why does it matter?"

The Nemontemi is over. It's a new year. No earthquakes. No star demons. The Fifth Sun didn't end. "You're right. It doesn't." *It's just a prophecy.*

She puts the back of her hand to my temple. "You're burning up again." She leans over me and presses a damp cloth to my forehead. It smells lemony, like yarrow leaves. "Viceroy Jerónimo sent the doctor to examine you. I dismissed him before he was able to look at your leg. Don't worry. The leeches are doing a fine job now."

Leeches? I look down. Bloodsuckers cover my thigh, so many that it's nearly black. Groaning from the effort, I sit up and start flinging leeches. The plump ones explode against the walls and floor in a splash of blood. I shudder, watching those still attached twist and squirm on my leg. One particularly greedy one, an especially fat little predator, has moved on from my wound and is now feeding on my inner thigh. I pull the bulging worm away, but it's latched on tight. How I don't choke and faint is beyond me.

Inés huffs. "You're not supposed to remove leeches by force."

"Get them off!" I say, resisting the urge to move my leg. Inés reapplies a giant leech to the site of my wound, and I swat her hand. "I said get them off!"

She locks her hands on her hips. "Do you want to lose your leg, Leonora? If you don't let them feed, you won't last more than a day. Now shut up and lie back."

Reluctantly, I obey. I stare at the ceiling, clenching my fists as I struggle to do as she says. "I can't believe the legendary Pantera is scared of leeches. Didn't you grow up in the jungle?"

The most dreaded demons are known to assume the shapes of insects. "I didn't grow up in the jungle," I say. "I grew up in a city nestled in the jungle. I don't like bugs. Leave me alone."

"Worms."

"What?"

"Leeches are worms," Inés says matter-of-factly.

"Fine," I huff. "I don't like things that wriggle."

She lets out a deep sigh. "Leonora . . . Leonora . . ." As Inés tucks a pillow under my head, the fight leaves my body. She flops down on the bed next to me. "After the shipwreck, I didn't see you, and I thought the worst . . ." She clears her throat.

"I don't know what to tell you, Inés. You're stuck with me," I say in a jesting tone. "Now, someone attacked *La Capitana*. I'd very much like to know who."

"We don't know it was planned."

I lift an eyebrow. "There was an explosion on a galleon filled with treasure and we don't know it was planned?"

"It was an accident," she says, tugging on her earlobe. "A sail caught fire."

"If you're going to lie, Inés, do it convincingly."

"I'm not lying."

There's always much more information in what she's *not* saying.

"What are you not telling me?"

"Gods, Leonora. You almost . . . you nearly died. It's too much for you. You must focus on regaining your health."

"I can do this all day, Inés. What are you hiding from me? What happened while I was sleeping?" I sit up with effort. "If you're not going to tell me, then I'll find out for myself."

"All right, enough!" she says. "Captain Nabarres believes La Justicia was behind the blast."

And there it is.

I frown. "La Justicia?"

She exhales, as if resigned to her next words. "I don't think it was them. I think Captain Nabarres needed La Justicia to strike first—or appear to. It's not above him to lie to fuel the war. He's burned down pueblos to the north since the explosion."

La Justicia territory.

After the Fall, when the Spaniards conquered Mexico-Tenochtitlan, those who survived were allowed to continue their daily lives but forced to embrace Spanish rule and Christianity. Mexica nobility took on the governance of the Indigenous barrios surrounding the city, and the Spaniards did their best to completely erase any reminder of the past in the capital. Indigenous temples were destroyed, libraries with sacred books ransacked, holy ceremonies and festivals prohibited, and people who still believed in the old gods were punished. Pagans, they called them. Heathens.

So, some forgot about the ancient ways, either because they really believed in the new faith, especially after Our Lady of Guadalupe appeared to the Indigenous Christian Juan Diego on Tepeyac Hill, or because they did what they had to do to continue living.

But not all surrendered. Rebellious tribes formed La Justicia and took refuge far away in Snake Mountain, where they learned to resist. To shout *enough*—enough abuse, enough oppression, enough of the Nailed Christ.

Unfortunately for Captain Nabarres, Father didn't grant him the authority to wage a war, since the rebels didn't pose a threat to political stability. The truth? The war was too costly to pursue. Then, too, the Crown passed the New Laws to protect Indigenous peoples, outlawing slavery in New Spain and imposing severe restrictions on encomenderos—men who were conquistadors, sons of the first conquerors, some women and Indigenous elite, and anyone sufficiently well connected—forbidding these landowners from passing down their encomiendas to their families, as well as requiring them to pay for Indigenous labor. But that didn't stop the encomenderos. Despite King Carlos's best intentions, the encomenderos resented such limitations on their power and immediately set out to protest these laws. Even though Father pushed for their enforcement, they went ignored.

When La Justicia rose up in arms, hardly anyone was surprised.

I've stood in the shadows and heard enough council meetings descend into slander to recognize deceit when I hear it. If Captain Nabarres thinks he can orchestrate an elaborate plot and point at the nearest rebel to wear down the resistance, he can think again.

"Where do you plan on going in your robe?" Inés calls after me as I make for the door. "Leonora, you have to rest. Get back in bed. You're not well."

"I'm fine."

"You're not."

I rip another leech from my leg.

"Stop that!"

I turn around. "Señor Alonso is dead. Pueblos are up in flames. I can't just sit in bed. I have to do something, Inés."

"This is beyond madness. Look at you! You're standing there on one leg with the other bleeding. All I'd have to do is blow and you'd fall over. You can hardly walk. You'll have to use a stick."

"No, I won't." Just to prove her wrong, I put my foot down. It sends a jolt of pain up my leg.

"And what is it you plan on doing without your sword?"

My eyelids flutter. The Sword of Integrity.

"Leonora de las Casas Tlazohtzin, there's no way I'm letting you leave this room. I should add that there are two guards standing outside just in case you get any ideas." She scoffs, shaking her head. "If your father could see you now, he wouldn't believe it."

"Cállate."

"Did I strike a nerve? At least you had a father. Your mother wasn't butchered. And your brother didn't catch the dreadful plague. Do you know what happens to little girls with no family?"

Cállate, I want to say again. My father fell to the sickness, and she knows it. But she's right. Inés has suffered through unimaginable pain. Defeated and angry, I take my bruised pride and limp toward the bed.

"Otro día, Leonora. Live to fight another day."

I wake that night gasping. I'm lying in a pool of sweat. The air feels like the blast of a furnace. I close my mouth, feeling fangs slip back into my gums. My skin squirms as if ants are gnawing at my flesh, and I scratch my arms, trying to ease the sensation, until I realize I've drawn blood. Lifting my hands, I see long, sharp claws. I recognize the symptoms. Nasty side effects of not shifting often enough.

Shifting is a lot like hunger. My mind and body won't find rest until the need has been satisfied. I resist the shift every time. I have no control of myself without control of my own body. I can put off dealing with it, but sooner or later, my body will take over and force the shift. Nature always wins. The nagual always wins.

There are some complications.

Nagual Apprentices aren't permitted to shift without the supervision of a mentor. I haven't shifted since I returned to the capital. Without guidance, the result is unpredictable. I've heard the stories. Tales of Naguals who, after remaining in their nagual form for too long, have gone feral, forgotten their humanity, or worse, become trapped in their nagual permanently. If something were to go wrong during the shift, Nagual Masters, and some more advanced sorcerers, have the ability to take another person's nagual altogether.

There's also my injury. It hasn't fully healed. The shift would be more taxing, and very painful. I could fail. Not survive the process. Bleed out. If a nagual dies, so does the person to whom the nagual belongs. Master Toto said the Nagualist arts help awaken us to our true nature, and that by shifting, I can become more myself. But I fear losing control. The first time my body forced the shift, Master Toto was fast enough to stop me.

When I began my apprenticeship, Master Toto taught me how to shift into my nagual, and this practice lasted for all my ten years with him. A decade of learning to master one nagual. Sorcerers must have patience and perseverance to walk the Nagual Path, which can take a lifetime, depending on your nagual—or naguals. There have always been whispers of those who can shift into more than one animal, but such a sorcerer is likely divine, for what is time to an eternal being? Tezcatlipoca, the god of sorcery himself, is a fowl, an owl, and a weasel, though his strongest connection is to the jaguar.

I pull my father's tarnishing coin from under the pillow and flip it between my fingers. Señor Alonso is dead, my medallion, mask, and the Sword of Integrity lost to the sea.

I turn over and pull a pillow over my head, hoping to muffle the Panther's roar in my head. It's too late for this foolishness, and I need sleep, but my body only cares about the release. I need to run.

Instead, I bury myself under the covers. It's going to be a long night.

Every day my tonalli gets stronger, but standing up makes my hip ache terribly, leaning forward is a nightmare, and walking is torture if I don't tread slowly. Ridiculous.

By the end of the week, I've memorized every crack on the wall, the pattern of the rug, the exact folds of the gauzy curtains on the canopy bed, the candles on the chandelier, and the intricately carved moldings of the cornices. I can't take it anymore. I need my sword.

Vicereine Carlota and I sit in one of the palace's inner courtyards drinking tea. It's a rare occurrence. For my birthday, she presents me with a piece of jewelry: a gold-and-green brooch in the shape of a rose, outlined all in pearls.

"A belated gift, I know, but . . . well . . . the circumstances were beyond my control," she says. "Exquisite, isn't it?"

"It is splendid, but I cannot accept it."

"Why not?"

"I don't have need for it."

"Nonsense," she says. "You are the future wife of the next king of Spain."

I sigh, pinning the brooch to my dress. "You're in good spirits today."

"It is the day the Lord has made, and so is a day of rejoicing," she says into the steam rising from her cup. "The Bible tells us, 'an eye for an eye.' I will see the rebellion dealt with rightly, La Justicia crushed, peace restored. I swear before God Almighty, our Lord Jesus Christ and la Virgen María, our enemies will pay for the atrocities they've committed."

I've never been to La Justicia's stronghold in Snake Mountain. I've never made the pilgrimage deep into the forest, where a great ahue-huetl tree is said to envelop the pyramid-temple at the top of the hill. I haven't met with Sin Rostro, the faceless face, the leader of La Justicia. But I have heard La Justicia's beliefs spread through the island, passed along second- and thirdhand.

"La Justicia calls for justice, and calls for it peacefully."

"Peacefully?" She balks. "Then why do they have weapons?"

"To protect themselves, I suppose." *Obviously.*

"It's only a matter of time before they're gone. And Pantera. I intend to see her punished too."

I look down at my hands. I despise the gloves. They're itchy and the lace makes me feel like I'm touching the world through a piece of tablecloth. They're a reminder of how much I hide. But more importantly, they're a reminder of *why* I hide.

"Please, let's not talk about the witch," I say. "All I hear are tales of bloodshed. Is it not possible to talk of more joyful things?"

I regret the words almost the moment they leave my mouth, as she falls into a frenzy about my wedding dress. "Blue," she says. "It has to be blue." I look at her, and her face is radiant. "No, black. It is much favored at the Habsburg court."

"What of the curse?"

Vicereine Carlota goes still. "What of it?" she asks quietly, holding my eyes as if daring me to answer.

I draw a terse breath. "Death in battle. That's what the seer—"

"You will hold your tongue," she says, "or I will hold it for you. You are *not* cursed. That is pagan nonsense. I'll have no part of it." She says it with such conviction that I almost believe her, then I remember this is Vicereine Carlota we're talking about. She is a woman of many facets, of contradictions. Christian, yet deeply superstitious. She consulted Indigenous lore and became interested in ancient magic out of desperation to escape her shameful childlessness. There are stories she drank mule's urine, supposed to increase fecundity, as well as rabbit's blood. Eventually, she did conceive. But whether her pregnancy with Jerónimo was aided by a Christian miracle or pagan remedies, or neither, is anyone's guess.

"If it's such nonsense," I go on, "why are your palms sweating? Why does your voice tremble? Could it be that you are afraid? Could it be that you believe I will never be queen?"

"¡Callaos, niña! No sabéis lo que decís . . ."

There was a native man at my baptism. As the priest said his prayers and poured water on my head, this man came forward and predicted my destiny. Those who were present heard him say my birth date was too unfortunate, and that only one out of ten babies born during the

Dead Days can find happiness. He warned I would die young in battle. Father didn't concern himself with this curse all those years ago. There was simply no time to lend it credence, not with the encomenderos for enemies and rebels gathering to rise in the mountains. And Vicereine Carlota hardly bothered to listen to the ramblings of a native man. But who's to say she hasn't come to believe in the curse? And now that she needs me to honor the alliance with Prince Felipe, perhaps she fears it.

In the middle of the night, when the air cools and the crickets sing, I'm just a girl afraid of death, wanting to grow up and see more of the world, taste more of life. But I am a child of the Nemontemi; my death has been foretold, and I'm not long for this world.

CHAPTER 7

El Temblor

Speaking requires tonalli.

It's the first thing I learned as an apprentice to my master. To cultivate tonalli, one must first take a vow of silence. Or as Master Toto would say, "swallow a lot of saliva."

After not saying a word for days, my questions came rapid-fire.

"What is tonalli?" I asked.

"It is your life force."

"I know, but what is it? Is it divine energy?"

"Yes. No."

"Can you see it?"

"Yes. No."

"Can you touch it?"

"Yes. No."

"Does everything have tonalli?"

"Yes. No."

Master Toto always contradicted himself.

The memory fades away. I'm kneeling in a pew inside the cathedral, not that I've come to pray. This is one of the few quiet buildings in the plaza where I can calm my mind.

I'm in one of the chapels, listening to my own breathing. The exchange of air. The silence is supposed to recenter me. I inhale and exhale, trying to guide tonalli to the injury in my leg. But despite my best efforts practicing tonalli manipulation for years on end, Master Toto said I have a "monkey mind," always jumping from thought to thought. Sitting still and thinking about nothing felt like wasting time when I could've been learning how to fight.

My mind flutters over images of Señor Alonso's head falling into a basket. Why couldn't he have died in battle? The glory of a warrior's death. I grieve for the unfairness. I tell myself his death was honorable, but trying to convince myself is as futile as the Our Fathers and Hail Marys that Fray Anonasi makes me recite for penance after confession.

Despite my meditating for hours, nothing changes, including my peace about the situation.

The vaults above the high altar are decorated with praying sculptures, frescos, and a marble Christ. The church has been years in the building, ever since Cortés and his entourage of invaders ripped down Tenochtitlan to pave Mexico City over its ruins. As with all the new palaces and buildings, the cathedral was built to impress, to intimidate and defend against the natives, to serve as a reminder of power and who holds it. Everywhere I look, I see wealth. It cruelly belies the existence of the people who were living here before the conquistadors arrived. I can't take the briefest walk without being reminded of the slaughter that took place here.

As a little girl, I didn't understand why I wasn't allowed to leave the palace. For eight years, I did not see the outside world. Father said it was dangerous. I did not understand the violence and horror around me.

I was too young to recognize the smell of death emanating from the blood-seeped stones used to rebuild the city.

But I was old enough to remember.

I still remember those lonely years. I still remember the thrill of doing the forbidden, sneaking out like a thief, getting lost in the woods, and the fear of not being able to find my way back home.

I was gone for ten years.

Now, my true home is somewhere else.

The balding, sunken-eyed Fray Anonasi greets me with a most woebegone expression, mumbling in Latin. I don't know if he prays for me not to go to Hell, or if he thinks I'm the spawn of Satan. He never fails to make a rushed sign of the Cross when he sees me.

"Are my horns showing today, padre?"

His face blanches as he clings to his rosary beads. "Señorita Leonora, this is the house of God," he says sharply. "You would do well to allow the Lord's grace and mercy to transform your soul in His holiness."

"Sí, padre," I say demurely.

He walks away in a huff.

The church is utterly still, utterly silent, so that each noise is intensified. I can hear the crunch of gravel under someone's shoes, whispered conversations, a distant snore. Or I can block them out, as I often do with background noises.

Inés makes her way up the several flights of stairs to reach the chapel. Her feet barely touch the ground. No one else walks like that, like morning mist rolling in from the sea.

She takes a seat on the bench in the row behind me. "Prince Felipe wishes to speak to you."

I pull myself up to sit. "I know," I say. "I heard you talking. You didn't have to come all this way."

"How far away exactly can you hear?"

"I don't know. Sometimes I can hear a whisper from across the palace, sometimes not at all."

How is it that you can hear silence, yet you never listen? Master argued.

"How is your leg today?" Inés asks.

"I can't run or shift or fight if that was your intended question." She breathes a sigh of relief, but then I say, "I swear to the gods, I'm completely harmless," and that provokes a little chuckle.

"You are many things, Leonora. But not harmless."

"I'm fine. As long as I don't walk too far in one stretch. I have a strange gait. People might notice."

As we head out of the chapel and disappear down the stairs, I make out a soft, almost hushed rumble of thunder. I go still and listen to what I think at first is my own blood pulsing through my head.

"Inés, do you hear that?"

"Hear what?"

It now sounds like the teteoh are fighting among themselves with lightning bolts.

Except, it's not coming from the sky.

It's coming from the ground.

As I reach the staircase landing, a rolling boom gives fair warning of what's to come.

No time to think. Safety.

"Come," I tell Inés, holding out my hand.

"What?"

"Now!"

Startled, Inés lifts her skirt and clasps her hand with mine as she steps down on to the landing. At that moment, the ground begins to shake, releasing tension in a violent jerk. We curl up in balls and grab on to the railing.

"It's over already." As I speak, the temblor dies away. "Are you all right?" I pull her up to stand.

She nods. "How did you . . . did you hear it coming?"

Earthquakes will rattle the ground, and terrible star demons will come from their abyss of twilight to devour the flesh of men . . .

It's just a prophecy. Then why is my heart pounding?

"It can't be . . ."

55

Inés blinks. "What can't be?"

"You believe in coincidences, don't you?" I ask, but I already know she doesn't. She believes in her Purépecha gods—and fears them.

She shakes her head. "What are you talking about?"

"When was the last time an earthquake struck?"

She frowns in confusion. "What does it matter? It was a little tremor. Such shaking happens here all the time."

"This one was different," I say. "It was loud. It came from nowhere."

"They're earthquakes, Leonora," Inés says. "They're sudden and unexpected. We don't know when they will occur, nor how large they will be."

"I don't hear the birds," I murmur.

"What are you *talking* about?"

"The chachalacas." I lean against the wall to take a breath and lessen the pain in my leg. "Never mind. Forget about it. You're right. It's probably nothing. We should return to the palace."

I don't speak to anyone as I make the long walk from the cathedral to the palace. A flurry of motion pounds in my ears. Screaming voices, clashing objects, thumping footsteps, all of it crashes into me from above and below, every direction. As the noise thickens, I focus and force it into the background. Finally, I lock in on Viceroy Jerónimo's voice and hobble in its direction.

Viceroyal Palace is a gigantic quadrangle of interior courtyards, winding alleys, and galleries. In many ways, the structure is more defiant than graceful, with its high walls, crenellations, and buttresses designed to keep out enemies. Every so often someone will lose their way in its rambling interiors. I come up the stairwell and round the gallery on the second floor, hurrying to the viceroy's office.

"Lady Leonora," Prince Felipe says, hurriedly approaching me. "Did you feel the earthquake? Are you hurt?"

Realizing I have an audience, I don my usual guise of damsel in distress, throwing myself into the prince's arms and breaking into hysterics. Palace guards and attendants bustle toward me. The prince gestures at them to take a few steps back.

"You have nothing to fear, my lady. As I join my life to yours, I promise to protect you from any harm that might come your way."

Does he have to be so nauseatingly amorous all the time? I pull away and give him a dazed smile. "Gracias, alteza. I am unharmed."

"Praise God."

"Indeed. My handmaid said you wanted to see me."

"I did, yes. I'm sorry to have interrupted your prayers."

"The shaking would've interrupted them anyway." His heartbeat roars in my ears, and I grit my teeth to stop myself from showing discomfort. "They happen quite often," I go on. "Most of them you don't even notice." I again offer a smile, but it's forced.

"Let us not dwell on such unpleasant matters. Perhaps some diversion would do us some good."

"Diversion?"

"If this is to be a love match, we really ought to get to know each other a little better. Do you not agree, Lady Leonora?"

I stifle a groan. "Wholeheartedly."

His blue eyes gleam with triumph. "Would you enjoy a horse ride with me? We could travel the short distance to Chapultepec. I have not seen much of the valley yet. I'm told the trees are very old, and that Hernán Cortés himself sat weeping at the base of one of them after being defeated in battle. Can you imagine? What stories they might tell."

My chest tightens. The last time I ventured into the woods I didn't return for ten years. *Doesn't he know?*

"Recibid mis sinceras disculpas. I should not have spoken as I did, dear lady." *He knows.*

"No, no. Some fresh air would be pleasant," I say, trying to control the tremor in my voice. "I do so love to ride. Chapultepec is quite a landscape. The trees are magnificent."

"Moteuczoma's daughter Doña Isabel says they were his favorite," he says.

I lift an eyebrow.

"What?"

"You said Moteuczoma, alteza."

"Is that wrong?"

"No, alteza. It is the emperor's name in Nahuatl," I say. "You won't hear any Spaniards pronounce it like that."

"Yes, well, that is what Doña Isabel calls her father."

Prince Felipe is charming and has an exquisite taste in clothes. But there was a twitch in his left eyelid when I noted the pronunciation. The only surviving heir of Emperor Moctezuma, Tecuichpoch, christened Doña Isabel after the Fall, lives in Spain. Since her removal she has become a devout Christian. She was only a little girl when her father fell. It's been almost thirty years. Who's to say she still speaks of him? Or speaks Nahuatl at all?

"Of course," I say. "I thought His Highness might return to Spain after the attack on *La Capitana*."

"I assure you it takes more than a disorganized act of war to ruin my plans, my lady."

"I admire your spirit, alteza," I say, "but a ship was purposely sunk. People died. How can we be certain there won't be another attack?"

I soften my expression and remind myself it's not a lady's place to speak her mind, let alone put forth any kind of ideas, even though I keep wondering who could've blown a Spanish treasure galleon.

I, of course, have my suspicions.

La Capitana was the largest galleon in the New World. It carried the most treasure of all the ships in the fleet. There are rumors circulating about La Justicia possibly trying to overthrow the viceroyalty. Yes, La Justicia had the motive, opportunity, and nerve. Perhaps even the means.

But one thing doesn't make sense.

The attack happened on the first day of the Nemontemi. The Nahuas who still believe in the old gods fear the Dead Days.

Then again, La Justicia is made up of different tribes, not only Nahuas, so the attack could've been carried out by someone else.

None of it will matter if the prophecy is fulfilled.

Prince Felipe falls silent. Or maybe I stop listening. A familiar rush of heat blows past me, scorching my skin like the blast from a furnace. I know right away whose tonalli it is. There's no mistaking it. No other tonalli threatens to blister me as if I'm on fire.

"Is something wrong, my lady?" Prince Felipe says. "You look flushed."

I unfurl my fan and wave it in front of my face. I discreetly scan the corridor. He's here. Somewhere. "I'm afraid I'm not feeling well."

"Is there something I can do?"

"Your Highness is most gracious, but if it be your will, may I take my leave?"

"Do rest. I look forward to our ride." Lowering his head, he turns and walks down the hall.

Below me, Captain Nabarres and a small force of his men pound up the stairs. They pause at the landing as Nabarres shouts for his page to fetch him his rapier. Every soldier seems to have the same height and build. In fact, every soldier looks precisely like the one next to him.

Except for one. His tonalli hangs thick and heavy in the air, as if he can't contain the power inside him.

The pirate.

CHAPTER 8

El Teniente

He must've felt my stare because he looks up and sees me, standing above him at the top of the stairway. His brown eyes hold mine, and I can't help the gooseflesh that rises on my arms any more than I can help the stab of anger in the pit of my stomach.

There's that smile again—that knowing, damnable smile. I hate his smugness. I hate that he's standing so perfectly composed. That one corner of his mouth curves like he's invincible and knows more than me.

As the men come up the stairs, I clasp my gloved hands together in front of me, hoping they don't notice they're not quite steady.

"Lady Leonora, I'm glad to see you're in good health," Captain Nabarres says.

"Why wouldn't I be? The quake wasn't so bad, and it passed quickly."

"I was told you were bedridden. Your handmaid was emphatic about it. She feels it will require a month, perhaps longer, before you're fully recovered from the attack on the ship."

As he speaks, I feel the weight of the pirate's gaze pressing on the side of my face, watching, studying my demeanor, my movements. I catch it for a moment with as much composure as I can bring to my aid, then before I can be drawn in, I let my eyes wander. *I don't know what game you're playing, but I can play it too.*

"The Lord himself couldn't keep me in my bed for a month, capitán," I say.

"Introduce me to the señorita, will you, capitán?" says the pirate.

According to custom, he must first be introduced before speaking to me. And I must be faultlessly graceful and charming in all situations.

"Lady Leonora, this is Lieutenant Ayeta, a new officer in the service of His Excellency," Nabarres says, indicating the pirate. "An outstanding interpreter in the Indian language."

I almost scoff. The pirate is dressed like a don. The white of his doublet bounces off his brown skin, and a silver chain with a cross pendant dangles from his neck. An almost convincing Christian façade. Does this man truly think to pretend? What a pitiful amateur.

The pirate steps forward with an audacity to rival Quetzalcoatl himself. Like he owns the sky, the wind, the cosmos. The arrogance. No—he is more like Tezcatlipoca. The trickster god is notorious for sowing discord and deceit, concocting the most dastardly of plots for his own gain.

I don't offer my hand, but the pirate lifts it anyway. I didn't realize that I had formed a fist, and he uncurls my fingers to lay a kiss on my knuckles, as though taking away my anger. The warmth of his lips cuts through my lace gloves. A sparkle in his eyes tells me that he can see how it disturbs me.

"Your servant, señorita," he says, all politeness and charm.

His tonalli envelops everything around him: an invisible, fiery force luring me with its warmth. He feels like the sun, like lying on the beach under the shade of a palm tree and still absorbing the heat. I've never met Tonatiuh, but I imagine his tonalli is something similar. I'm inadvertently caught in a dreamy, otherworldly haze when I begin to feel myself burning. A thread of panic unwinds in me, and my immediate reaction is to put as much distance between us as possible.

"While I am from Cuernavaca," he continues, bringing me back to myself, "I have been baptized and confirmed in the Lord's Church.

My life is Spain's and always ready to be exchanged for that of my country's enemies." He says the corrupted word the Spaniards use for Cuauhnahuac, the land stolen from the Tlahuica people.

"Speaking of which, what is this I hear about a masked defender who calls herself Pantera? They're saying that she's the finest swordswoman in all New Spain and that she is a bruja, among other things. I saw posters in town offering a sizable reward for her."

"Ah, yes, I've heard some disturbing talk about the Panther myself," I say, my voice calm, my expression tender. "Too dramatic an alias, if you ask me. They say she was in Santiago Tlatelolco the other day and started a commotion. I positively do not believe any of us are safe with that bandida on the loose." I turn to Captain Nabarres with my best look of concern and dismay. "Why was the witch there? What did she want? And why was she not captured?"

"The actions of a criminal are not an ideal subject for discussion with a genteel lady such as yourself, señorita," Nabarres says.

"I do try to refrain from such vulgarities myself, but this Pantera will surely strike again. I wonder . . ." I pause. "If she *is* a witch, would this not make her difficult for ordinary men to capture? Say, someone like yourself . . . capitán?"

Oh, how I enjoy pricking the man's pride. His lips twitch in a wince, but I can hear his teeth grinding as he fights to keep his temper. "If she *is* a witch, then she will burn like the rest of them."

I struggle to keep my composure.

"It's only a matter of time before she's unmasked," Ayeta says.

"Fine spirits, lieutenant," I say. "You sound sure of yourself." Maybe he knows more than he's saying. My stomach muscles tighten. Nerves? Ridiculous. A quick chill prickles my skin. Fear? Absurd.

"As sure as God as He looks down on us, señorita."

"Yes, well, let us pray you find this Pantera," I say with a wry smile, "and that no harm befalls you when you do."

*

The skirt of my heavy dress swirls around my ankles, hissing against the polished floors. Once I'm out of sight, I press against a wall and clutch my leg, pain creeping through it, then I separate General Valdés's voice from the surrounding noise. He's joined Captain Nabarres, the pirate, and the other guards.

"What news of Pantera?" Nabarres asks.

I lean my forearms on the railing overlooking the inner courtyard, pretending to muse.

"None, capitán," says Valdés.

"None?"

"We have put up wanted posters offering a reward of fifty reales and combed the valley," says Valdés. "There's no trace of her. She hasn't been seen for weeks. The bounty on her head makes her fair game for anyone who wants to make a hefty fortune."

"The pescadores at the bay," Valdés says, "they found something. A sword, they say, with the arms of its guard shaped like two serpents."

A smile tugs at my lips. Finally, some good news.

"Bring it to me," says Nabarres.

"Capitán," Valdés says, "we don't have enough men to win the war against La Justicia, respond to natural disasters, secure the palace, chase after a witch, and retrieve a sword."

"If you'll allow it, capitán," Ayeta says, "I'd like to offer my advice."

"Go ahead, teniente."

"We have vowed to serve our Holy Faith, the Crown, and the viceroy of New Spain. We may not have enough soldiers, but I'll share with you a truth you won't hear in Spain. Cortés didn't lay siege to the Mexica with just his men. He had allies, capitán. Native allies to fight on his side. Here, my people know, it was the Tlaxcaltecah who brought Tenochtitlan to ruins, not Cortés."

After a long pause, Nabarres says, "You speak as though you have a plan. What do you propose, teniente?"

"I propose we make some new friends."

"Valdés," Nabarres says, "ready the men and the horses."

"Ready them for what?"

"To move."

"Yes, capitán."

I stop listening and slip down the long winding corridor. I'm smiling, filled with joy at the thought of being reunited with my sword, though I must act quickly, before Nabarres gets his hands on it.

The next moment, my smile disappears as I catch sight of the pirate. He still carries himself with confidence, his boot heels clicking loudly against the pavement, drawing women to him as peccaries draw jaguars. Freshly powdered ladies duck behind fans to hide their smiles as he walks past them. I could suggest hobbies, perhaps helping to avert the end of the world, but such talk would have me swatted with one too many fans by one too many ladies.

"Hello again," the pirate says, stopping a few paces before me. "Señorita, you look troubled. Have I done something to upset you? If I did, I must make amends for my faults."

Very well, I think, *if he wants to put on an act, I can play that game.* "There is no trouble at all, lieutenant. But as scripture says, 'Consider it all joy when you encounter various trials.' The Lord uses hard times to help us grow in our faith. He delights in those who put their hope in His unfailing love."

"Are you always this pious, señorita? I remember you having more vigor the last time I saw you."

Ignoring is an art that helps you practice patience. Master's words. *This world will get a rise out of you. It is wise to remain unfazed and take things with as much levity as you can.*

I never was a good student.

I can't stab the man, so I straighten up and throw my head back, flipping my long hair over my bare shoulders. "Are you always this dull or are you exerting yourself today?"

His face brightens. A glance into his eyes—the heat, the contempt, the lies gathered like a perfect storm—has me gritting my teeth like I'm biting down on a strap of leather.

"I'm soon to be wed, lieutenant. It is not proper for an engaged lady to be seen associating with a complete stranger. Now, if you'll forgive me, I have more pressing matters with which to concern myself. Perhaps someone else can entertain you, like those ladies who keep staring."

His gaze slides to the sophisticated damsels in question, who are still tittering behind their hand-painted, lace-trimmed fans. He clears his throat and offers them a cordial nod, then his eyes land back on me. "Not interested."

"Not pretty enough?"

"Not enough bite."

I can't believe he has the gall to show his face here. "Who are you?"

"You may call me Andrés. That's my Christian name. You're welcome, by the way. For bringing you home safe and unharmed."

The urge to take a step forward and blacken his eye is almost overpowering. I have to remain calm. I have to push down these thoughts, hard as it is.

"You're a funny pirate, aren't you?"

"I'm not a pirate, señorita."

My face flushes, because I already know he isn't. He is something much more.

"Where is it?" I whisper harshly.

"Where's what?"

"My medallion."

"Bottom of the ocean, I reckon. Trust me, it's for the best."

"Give up your play, thief," I say, shooting him a stare of death. "You might fool Nabarres, but you don't fool me. Why are you here? Whose jewelry are you after this time? Should I put away my brooch?" I finger the green gem pinned to my dress. "It's an emerald, though I'm sure you knew that."

He focuses on my chest briefly, then meets my eyes again. "You ask a lot of questions, señorita."

He would do well to answer them. Unless he wishes to be strangled in his sleep.

He doesn't seem worried. At all. He wears his imperiousness as if it's merely another piece of clothing.

"I would prefer not to quarrel on our first official acquaintance, Leonora."

My smile turns frosty, the fragile mask of polite interest melting away. "I have no desire to be amicable with you. And I don't remember giving you leave to address me so familiarly. I am Lady Leonora, or miss, until such time as I say otherwise."

"My apologies, señorita. I'll try not to be any further trouble to you. I'll leave you to your *pressing* matters." He bows dramatically low and walks away.

Andrés de Ayeta is a problem.

CHAPTER 9

El Virreinato

My heeled slippers strike the wooden floor of the corridor like hooves. Every step sends a burning ache through my leg, but I have no time to waste.

Even before I reach the council chamber, I can hear my brother speaking.

". . . Don Diego de San Francisco, the governor of San Juan Tenochtitlan, is requesting we aid efforts in the south and send supplies to the affected barrios of San Juan Moyotlan and San Pablo Teopan," he is saying to Vicereine Carlota and five of his councilors, including Captain Nabarres. As president of the Audiencia de la Nueva España, the highest governing council in New Spain, Viceroy Jerónimo oversees the administration of the court. "I want every soldier, every guard, every hound to dig the wounded out of the wreckage and direct the homeless to shelter. Organize laborers to clear the rubble from the streets. The viceroyalty will pay for it."

My blood chills. The earthquake must have struck harder in the barrios. The end is closer than I thought. I hasten my pace, biting my tongue against the pain.

Vicereine Carlota scoffs. "We might as well become beggars."

"If we leave people outside, they will fall victim to the pox,"

Jerónimo says. "I'd rather be poor than spread the plague further on top of everything else."

"Let me remind His Excellency that we are at war," the vicereine says. "We cannot win a war if we don't defend our home. We cannot defend our home if we don't feed our soldiers. We cannot feed our soldiers if we don't have sufficient coin to carry the viceroyalty through to the next year."

"Don Diego is a respected nobleman in the barrios," Jerónimo says, "and he belongs to one of the wealthiest Indian families. King Carlos has recognized his service in the war in Nueva Galicia. We, too, must show a gesture of good will."

I halt before the guard posted outside the council chamber.

"The Audiencia is in session, señorita," he informs me.

"I have a matter of great importance to discuss with the viceroy," I state brusquely.

He nods. "Por favor. Wait here."

"I am Leonora de las Casas Tlazohtzin. I do not need to be announced."

Before the guard has a chance to speak further, I shoulder past him and let myself inside.

Cino Mondragon, Minister of Intelligence, chortles as I step through the doors. "My lady, are you lost?"

"I know where I'm standing, Don Cino." I notice a small spot of ink between my glove and my sleeve, and I snatch my hand back, quickly pulling the glove back into place. "If I may be so bold—"

"Accumulating knowledge is my duty . . . but I do not know why you are here, lady." He lifts an eyebrow.

I'm reminded that I am not at the top of society. I am not a peninsular, gachupín, blue blood, mainlander, a Spain-born Spaniard. I am Spanish on my father's side, but my tonalli carries the blood of my Indigenous mother. I am a mestiza caught in the nepantla, the space between two worlds. At baptism, you are assigned a caste for life. You cannot better your caste, nor improve your lot.

The viceroy raises a hand. "Let her speak," he says, drawing every eye in the room to him. It makes me grin to hear his commanding tone.

"Gracias, excelencia," I say. "You must stop all construction in the capital at once."

Don Bartolo de Molina shakes his head despairingly. "We cannot halt work right in the middle of it, my lady. It is prohibited." During his time as Minister of Development, he has overseen the entire rebuilding of the capital. "Some of Spain's wealthiest families are under the assumption that we will soon have housing for them. I have an obligation to get the job done as quickly and efficiently as possible."

"As you all know," I say, "the city was built on an island. The ground shakes . . . violently. We're like a bowl of jelly. I certainly wouldn't want us to be in violation, but we must show some flexibility, before we lose everything."

"Lose everything? We will recover from the earthquake," Viceroy Jerónimo says.

I glance at Captain Nabarres sitting at the opposite end of the table. "Go on," he says. "Tell us your thoughts." The challenge in his voice is unmistakable. It digs under my skin as Vicereine Carlota gives me an icy glare, raising prickles until I feel my temper beginning to stir.

The life of Narcizo Nabarres revolves around the vicereine. As her closest confidant, Nabarres serves as both Minister of Defense and Captain General of the Spanish military, making him one of the most powerful men in court. One might say he is entirely devoted to his duty, especially as he commands the army and Spanish guard to observe everything that could be of possible interest to Vicereine Carlota—who attends church, who avoids or talks with whom, who may be plotting against whom, who goes where.

I stand up straighter and roll my shoulders back. "Your duty is to defend this land and its people. You have an obligation to protect lives. We must lessen the impact of disaster before it occurs. We will not withstand the next quake."

"If I understand what you are saying, you want me to stop progress on construction because of an earthquake that might not happen?" Don Bartolo asks.

"The earthquake *will* happen," I say. "It could happen tomorrow. It could happen right after we walk out of this chamber. It could happen three days from now."

Fray Anonasi eyes me shrewdly. "Are you Minister of Earthquakes, Lady Leonora? Or do you believe yourself to be above God? Only the Lord knows what the future holds."

"No, padre, but the prophecy—" I blurt before I can stop myself.

"What prophecy?" Viceroy Jerónimo says.

I hesitate for a moment. "The Nahua people . . . they believe in a prophecy. It's said that this world is not the first. There were four that came before and were destroyed. The fifth world, ours, will come to an end through earthquakes. All will go dark and star demons will come down from the sky to devour us all."

A ripple of laughter passes around the table. Vicereine Carlota watches this with detached interest, as an artist might watch paint dry.

The viceroy lifts an eyebrow. "Star demons?"

"Yes. Tzitzimime," I say, nodding. "Creatures that dwell in the darkness of the heavens. When earthquakes rip the ground apart, these demons will swarm upon the survivors, all will perish, and the prophecy will be complete."

The look of weariness on my brother's face makes him appear ancient. "Gracias, Lady Leonora. That will be all."

"No, that is *not* all," I say, more sharply than I intended. "If there is another earthquake, if these creatures come here, then *that* will be all."

"Enough," Vicereine Carlota says with strained patience. "Enough of this pagan folly."

I meet the viceroy's gaze evenly. "This has been prophesied since the beginning of time by the people of Anahuac, the true owners of these lands. If there is anything to be done to avert that fate, it behooves us to consider it fully."

"¡Basta ya!" Pushing her chair back, the vicereine staggers to her feet. "Clear the room," she says, entwining her jeweled hands in front of her stomach. There is a flurry of boots as the men stomp out. "You too, Jerónimo." She raises her eyebrows, waiting for any sign of argument from my brother. Of course, there is none. The door closes behind him.

She moves to pour herself a drink, then relaxes in her chair. Her silence is dangerous, like the silence of a snake deciding whether to strike. For a brief moment, her eyes are set upon her goblet in idle thought. Then she takes a sip of wine and draws her gaze back to me. Her voice comes softly, but it's still commanding. "Heresy is an offense to God. Fray Anonasi will see you at confession."

Impulsively I reach for my medallion, seeking my father's comfort, but my neck is bare. "Father would not sit idly and do nothing," I say spitefully.

Vicereine Carlota holds her head a little higher, her eyes sharper. "That fool?" She scoffs. "No, he certainly would not be idle. He'd be busy with his Indian whores."

Ever since I was a child, she's held this over me, this condemnation. She hunts for ways to remind me that I am inferior—lest I forget for one moment—for my heretical beliefs, for my mala sangre, for being my father's bastard.

"You always hated him because he loved my mother," I snap.

"Yes, he loved her," Vicereine Carlota says flatly, "but I didn't hate him. He gave his life to help the Indians, and look at them. They're still as oblivious as ever. What is a head without a brain? Useless. I intend to keep mine."

"And what good is a brain without a heart? You never loved Father. You love power above everything else," I say bitingly.

Father was the sun, always bringing the people hope.

Vicereine Carlota is the night, the darkness they fear.

CHAPTER 10

La Playa

The sea breeze wafts between the rocks, providing occasional relief from the muggy air typical of Acapulco Bay. I go eastward of Punta Bruja, which despite its fittingly bewitching name, is clear of danger. Dressed in black, I blend into the shadows. I've devised a mask from a rebozo, but it keeps slipping. I take a deep breath, fill my lungs with the scent of the sea, and adjust it.

Gulls and pelicans squabble over the little fishing village of Puerto Marqués. It's an eyesore straggling along the shoreline. *La Capitana*—what's left of it—sits dead in the water. Some of the other galleons have now drifted ashore. Viceroy Jerónimo dispatched a salvage team to remove the wreckage from the port, but the beach is still strewn with tattered sails and planks of wood.

A colony of sea lions lounge on the rocky shore, settled in for the night, oblivious to my intrusion. I creep along the dock, careful not to turn my back on the animals.

Captain Nabarres's strong voice echoes inside the fish house, a large shack on the side of the pier. He gives orders to the fishermen as though they are his own crew. I crouch behind barrels of tuna, seeking a glimpse of the captain general. Several of his soldiers, including General Valdés, gather around him as he sits at a table talking to the harbormaster.

Wind gusts against my face, bringing the stink of seaweed, smoke from the other side of the beach, patches of guano, and a million other odors. It's so overwhelming that I cough. Loudly. A soldier turns toward me. Fortunately, night hides me and the sea lions start barking. Much as I like a good fight, I'd rather not attract an unnecessary one, with a failing leg and a feeble mask.

"We wish we could help you . . ." the harbormaster is saying in Nahuatl, "but we've told you all we know. Someone came looking for the sword and stole it. I don't know who he was. It was dark, I didn't see his face."

He?

Lieutenant Ayeta interprets the harbormaster's words. "We're too late, capitán. Pantera was already here."

I lift an eyebrow at Ayeta's wrong translation. That lying, two-faced thief! At his words, Nabarres stomps his feet and bangs his fists on the table. "Pantera!" he hisses. "How did she *know*?"

I tighten my mask and step out from behind the barrels.

A mousy soldier with shaggy hair is the first of Nabarres's men to come around the fish house and see me standing in his path. "You're . . . you're . . ."

"¿Qué pasa, amigo?" I say. "Is there something wrong with your throat? How about some water?"

I feint toward him, and my eyes crinkle in a smile at his reaction. He recoils in fear, stumbling backward, and plunges underwater. I'm annoyed that he scared so easily.

Sea lions bark their disapproval, push each other around, and jump onto the dock, lurching and bellowing, full of aggression. Betrayed by sea lions. Any other time I would laugh.

Nabarres and half a dozen soldiers burst out of the fish house in a flurry of drawn swords and forbidding glares. Any other time I would fight.

"Pantera," Nabarres snarls.

I spread my arms wide and bow slightly.

"She's surrounded, capitán," General Valdés says, his blade leveled. "This time, she's not getting away."

Nabarres smiles into his beard. "What is your plan, witch? Are you going to fight with your devil's magic?"

"This is quite unnecessary, capitán," I say. "I've not come to fight. I've been absent the past few weeks and heard you were looking for me. You know how gossip gets around town. I didn't want you to think I was dead, so here I am. How are things for you, capitán? Still harassing honest workingmen, I see."

"What are you waiting for?" Nabarres draws his sword and swirls the tip. "Fight."

I step back. The floorboard groans under my boot. Nabarres will pay for his crimes. But not today.

"Forgive me, capitán. It seems I have interrupted a private meeting, and your men must be tired from the journey. Why don't you rest, muchachos?"

A sharp kick on the loose board beneath me sends the guards into the water in a magnificent sweep. An entertaining view by any standard.

Seething, Nabarres attacks furiously, hoping to drive me off my feet and make an end of it. But he strikes the air. I whirl and push a barrel to tip it over. Its contents slosh out across the floorboards.

Barrilete.

Momentarily taken aback, the remaining men shift their gazes to a family of bellowing sea lions charging straight at their dinner, yellow teeth bared. I jump on the overturned barrel, launch myself into the air, and dive into the water. Swimming toward the beach is a battle— fully clothed, with a bad leg, through choppy water—but I'd rather ache than be dead. I will not perish here, not like this, lost like another grain of sand in a great expanse of sea.

"I want her alive!"

Well, that's something Nabarres and I can agree on.

It's so dark they can't see a horse's length away. I'm gone, and no one can tell in which direction I went.

When I reach shore, I stagger on to the sand. I crawl, then collapse, shivering from the cold. I lie there, among ship debris and splashing waves, trying to catch my breath, and begin undoing my mask.

"Tsk, tsk, tsk. I wouldn't do that if I were you, Pantera," a familiar voice says in Nahuatl.

No one sneaks up on me. No one. I do the sneaking. Until now.

I should've picked up his scent, heard his footsteps. In the darkness, his tonalli is not at its zenith, but I still recognize its owner.

Groaning under my breath, I struggle to my feet and turn around. Some ten paces away, Andrés de Ayeta leans nonchalantly against a palm tree. The moonlight creates shadows on his face, accentuating the hard lines of his jaw, the fullness of his lips which are pursed in amusement. He's clearly enjoying my attempt to escape.

How in the Nine Hells did he know where to find me? My stomach clenches like a fist. If I can sense his tonalli, can he sense mine?

"What *would* you do if you were me?"

He smiles, amused by my Nahuatl or the question—I don't know.

"I'd walk away." He places a hand on his cazoleta, one of the swords attached to his belt. "You will find only death upon this beach. I take no pleasure in killing, though I should tell you I do it quite well."

A snort escapes me. If he thinks he can intimidate me, he's wrong. "You? You're going to kill me?" I would love nothing more than to see him try.

"I would rather not," he says, "but I suppose that's up to you."

"What is your name?" I ask to maintain my façade. Leonora knows his name. Pantera doesn't.

"They call me Ayeta."

"I take it you've heard of me, Ayeta?"

"I have."

"Then you'll know that I, like you, have also killed a number of people, though I, also like you, take no pride in that. But I, unlike you, did not do it with this much talk. No, no. I duel, sword against sword, woman to man, woman to woman . . . at about the distance we are now."

He smiles then tips his head, as if contemplating what to do with me. "They say you're a witch. Is it true?"

I open my arms. "I am as you see me. I heard what the harbormaster said. My sword, Ayeta. I know you have it, and I want it back. Now."

"No."

"Listen here, you . . . whoever you are. I was raised in the jungle. I've faced flowers scarier than you. You'd be wise to hand over what is mine."

"No."

I take a step forward, defiant, and pain jags up my leg. I'm more vulnerable than him. Most often in a fight, the one who tires first dies.

My right elbow shoots forward as I fling one of my knives, merely to provoke a reaction. It passes his neck with less than an inch to spare and hits the palm tree behind him.

He doesn't even flinch. "You missed."

"I meant to."

The second knife is meant to gauge his speed and skill. I aim it directly at his chest. Before it can strike him, he unsheathes his cazoleta at impossible speed and swats it out of the air.

My eyes narrow to slits. *Interesting.*

"Those will do you no good here." He draws a shorter blade from his belt and tosses it to me. "Show me, Pantera," he says as if he has nothing better to do.

He was right before. I should walk away. I know better than to attack him in my current condition. I shouldn't let him goad me, and the chances of me getting badly hurt are high, but I can't help myself when I have a weapon in my hand.

We circle each other, making small feints to see how the other will react. I'm not going to kill him, but he doesn't need to know that.

Our weapons meet. I already know he's quicker than he looks. Lighter, too. His sword moves faster than my eye can follow. You can tell a lot about a man by the way he wields a blade. It is a dance of death, and Ayeta whirls out of my reach, his feet shuffling across the beach, then lunging in to draw blood. Effortless. We chase each other, but my bad leg slows me, and I can't hope to keep dodging his strikes for long. I hate fighting on sand.

I retreat to where the ground is wetter and firmer and swing my sword in tandem with a burst of tonalli. Given my present condition, the result is a meager trick, nothing compared to an actual destructive attack by a Nagual Master, but it'll have some effect. Yet, before my weak blast hits him, he holds up his blade and splits it right down the middle.

"Who are you?" I pant.

His face is calm and blank, but I hear his ragged breathing. "I'm Andrés de Ayeta."

"I don't know many people who can deflect a tonalli attack."

He makes a sound almost like a laugh.

"Unless . . . you're a wizard."

That strange half laugh again. "I'm not a wizard." He puts his sword back into its sheath. "I've seen what I needed to see. Keep it," he says, looking at the blade he gave me. "Perhaps it will help you against Captain Nabarres."

He starts walking away, and I feel my face flame crimson. I will have my sword and his blood.

"Look at me," I say. Then, louder, "I said look at me! What kind of coward walks away from a fight?"

Fury taking over, I slash my sword to send a flurry of sand at his face. Sputtering and coughing, Ayeta lurches backward, and I move to close the distance between us, then thrust my blade in a horizontal blow that cuts his cheek wide open. It's a deep gash. Ayeta remains still, his eyes on me, his chest heaving as he catches his breath. His gaze is unreadable as it moves across my mask, but his heart is pounding. He doesn't have to scream for me to know he is in pain. As if he can hear my thoughts, he smiles, and I notice the red around the wound slowly begins to disappear as his skin knits itself back together.

What in the Fifth Sun?

"There she is!" General Valdés yells from a distance.

"Until we meet again, Pantera," Ayeta says.

The following morning, I ache terribly. Even though I escaped, I don't have my sword and it feels like I'm still running, looking over my shoulder, watching my back. Fear looms like a dark cloud at the back of my mind, the prophecy constantly reminding me that it can descend upon us at any moment.

As the days pass, I begin to wonder if the earthquake was just a coincidence, but that little bit of doubt lingers. And try as I might to forget, my own fate is ever-present. I've been doomed to die since I was placed in the womb of my mother. We are all appointed to die, but it's a strange feeling when you know your life will end early. It's all about the waiting. If the waiting doesn't kill you first.

Meanwhile, Inés battles contrary emotions—she is both pleased and displeased with me, for I sneaked away in the night without her awareness, but I did manage to procure a blade, the toledo given to me by Ayeta. It's the length of my forearm. A very nice letter opener. Inés doesn't understand why not possessing the Sword of Integrity is a problem. Where others see a mystical weapon and obsess over the Sword of Integrity's origins, Inés sees a piece of cold metal. "The weapon does not make the warrior, Leonora," she says. "Remember that."

I've never been separated from my sword. Without it, I'm not myself. I'm a blacksmith without a hammer, a scribe without a pen.

Evening comes, and with it, the same feeling of powerlessness. At least I'm still walking. At least I'm still breathing.

At least.

When did I become this person?

Is this what I do now, excuse myself?

I keep waiting for an epiphany, for Master to show up and tell me what I must do, for that moment when all of this will turn around.

"Is Her Ladyship's appetite lacking tonight?" Prince Felipe asks at dinner, after I skip the platter of meat. The dish is served garnished with the tails of bulls that fought against matadors in glittery suits in the latest Fiesta Brava. Oh, what brave men repeatedly stabbing, spearing, and taunting a bull to death for spectacle. Vicious brutes. I should like to see them gored by the bulls instead.

Viceroy Jerónimo, Vicereine Carlota, and a few of the wealthiest courtiers in the colony are loudly dressed and loudly behaving, talking over each other. I feel the heat of the vicereine's searing glare from the head of the table. I can take bullets and swords, but I cannot escape her wrath. "Serve Lady Leonora some rabo de toro," she says, beckoning to one of the servants.

Never mind the diners eating with their mouths open, how dare I disregard the main course? The height of rudeness.

I fight back the queasiness roiling in my stomach. I'm not only given a mountain of bull tail, blood blackened, swimming in sauce, nudging a pile of potatoes, but a knife as well; it lies atop my folded napkin. Slowly, I pick it up, feeling it rest comfortably in my hand. I have more in common with this dinner knife than I do with these people. Sharp. Ready to cut.

"Is the food not to your liking, my lady?" Prince Felipe looks down at my untouched meal, then back at me.

"I confess I've never liked the taste of bull, alteza." The stink of the meat threatens to push me over the edge.

"But," the prince says, "it is the custom after a corrida."

"A most vicious and barbaric custom."

Vicereine Carlota speaks. "Alteza, it is clear Lady Leonora is not herself. She is recuperating from a bout of ill health. Green sickness, I'm afraid."

My hand tightens around the knife I'm holding.

Of course, she would save face, but green sickness? Despicable. Eating is a symbol of wealth and power, two things Vicereine Carlota worships. Special bulking diets are tried to ensure that those of marrying age will be attractive. Doctors warn women of the consequences of not marrying as soon as their cycle starts. If a range of symptoms then appears—pale skin, faintness, odd eating habits—the only diagnosis possible is the disease of virgins, otherwise known as green sickness. The cure? A dose of a man's seed.

This woman will never be appeased. If I speak, it is too much. If I am silent, I am reproached. If I am friendly, I am too forward. If I do not put on a bright face, I am too proud. If I do not eat, I am green sick.

Prince Felipe clears his throat as Vicereine Carlota has just made it known that if I don't soon marry and fulfill my function as a woman, my womb will wander, my health will falter, and I will run mad, because virginity is for nuns, and even they are wedded to God. Behold the curative powers of intercourse. I am screaming inside.

But she is right about one thing.

I'm not myself.

This is my epiphany.

The strange thing about leading a double life is that you may suddenly find the double life leading you. One side is always hidden from the other, and often contradicts the other.

Lady. Warrior.

Human. Nagual.

Spanish. Mexica.

Who?

This absurdity weakens me. All the lying and pretending is poisoning my tonalli.

"Sorcery has nothing to do with magic," Master Toto once said to me. "It is not simply wielding great heaps of tonalli and playing out our fantasies. You must become yourself. Your true self."

"Who is that exactly?" I asked. "This fabled self that I'm supposed to be?"

"There is no true self," he replied.

I never understood the riddle.

Which is the real face? Leonora or Pantera?

CHAPTER 11

El Paseo

Days after the earthquake, there is great concern over the latest outbreak of the plague sweeping the island. The conquistadors, Cortés and his band of treasure-seeking men, brought it with them: with a touch, a sigh, a sneeze, a prayer, they gave it away like a gift. The pox spreads its terrors in the shacks of the poor and the palaces of the rich. The number of dead is becoming fearfully large. No one is safe from the blistering pestilence—my father certainly wasn't—except those who have already survived the sickness. It won't visit you twice.

Due to the palace being fumigated to clear the contagion, I'm awake at a wretched hour. Inés makes sure that the washing tub is ready, filling the carafe with hot water, and placing the towels and sponges near at hand. She then selects a suitable dress, airs it properly, and lays it on the back of my chair, ready for me.

"I'm sorry to hear you've come down with green sickness, my lady," she mocks, rinsing away the soap. "Perhaps I should mix you a tonic?"

"Ah, you have jokes today."

"So pale, so wan, and looking like a ghost. The sign of love's frustration. We must take urgent steps to combat the disease," she says. I hear the smile in her voice.

When I have been combed and dressed according to the demands of the day, I limp into the kitchen. The servers and chefs stand to attention as I creak open the door, then relax when they see it's only me.

I sniff the air. "Epazote?" I say, reaching for an apple from a basket.

"You have a good nose, señorita," one of the head cooks says as he prepares breakfast. "A sprig of epazote leaves gives beans a delicious flavor."

"It also makes them less gassy," Inés says, walking in behind me. "Leonora." She moves closer to me and looks around, making sure no one hears us. "What good are you to the people if you collapse from starvation in the middle of battle?"

I take a bite of my apple.

"You might not be green sick, but you cannot fortify yourself with one piece of fruit. You need a proper meal. Respect your body."

"I am not starving myself. I am focusing on myself."

Fasting helps me replenish tonalli. The Panther's hunger has reached near-violent proportions, but that same hunger makes my humanity stark and raw. It's about getting my body in proper balance. Once I achieve that, tonalli will begin to flow. Nagualism draws from the philosophy of tending to yourself first. Bring order to the chaos.

Inés sighs. "Your power doesn't lie in your magic, Leonora," she says. "It lies in your ability to remember who you are when they try to make you forget."

"You are just full of understanding today."

"I am clearly wise beyond my years."

I shuffle out into the plaza, carrying a bundle of apples. The warm air isn't nearly as oppressive as it can be. I hear the heat is quite dry in Spain, especially in the south, and some of the newer Spanish settlers struggle with the sticky temperatures accompanied by swarming flies, gnats, and mosquitoes. The plaza buzzes with activity: Spaniards, mixed castes, and Indigenous men and women coming and going, riding in horse-drawn coaches, strolling through nearby shops, promenading in a line for confession, propelling canoes with long paddles up and down the main canal along the south side of the palace.

The promise of rain is in the air, and for a moment, I'm full of high hope, until I feel myself in the presence of something powerful. It's overbearing, and I hate it. I look around, clinging to that hatred, then I see a rider on a white Andalusian making his way across the plaza toward the palace.

The horseman comes to a halt in front of me, then he springs down with ease and removes his helmet. "Buenos días, señorita."

I greet Ayeta with the same excitement I felt for my bull-tail stew last night. At the beach, he spoke Nahuatl to Pantera, the language of his people. Hearing him speak Spanish now reminds me of his deceit, and it makes my face burn.

He gives me a concerned look. "I heard you were sick. How are you feeling, señorita?"

By now everyone in court must know that Lady Leonora has come down with a sudden case of being untouched. The fact that *he* knows this is even more infuriating. If he makes one single joke about it, I am going to claw his eyes out.

"I am as you see me, lieutenant." I meet his eyes with an icy glare.

He gives me a wry smile. Then he takes a deep breath, as if inhaling a pleasant scent. "It's a fine day," he says. "I expect to become wealthy quite soon."

"Is that so?" I say dryly.

"The reward for the Panther's capture is now a hundred reales." Not enough, in my opinion. "Perhaps I will buy a purebred like Bonita here." The mare bobs her head and nudges Ayeta's shoulder slightly. "Tell me something, amiga," he drapes one arm over her neck, "horse to man . . . do you think the bruja will surrender?"

Never.

Bonita snorts, as if in response.

"You are closer to finding the witch, then?" I say casually.

"I'm not at liberty to say, señorita," he says, "but . . . between us, I think she'll find me."

"Really? And why is that?"

"Well, you see, I have something that belongs to her."

It's clear to me that Ayeta took the Sword of Integrity from the fishermen in Puerto Marqués before Nabarres could lay his hands on it. The question is, why? To use it as bait and lure me, or to satisfy some ulterior motive? It doesn't matter. I will have my sword soon enough.

"You know," he says, "I can find no one who speaks against her. I also cannot find anyone who can give me much of a clue as to who the girl might be." He holds my gaze. "I don't suppose you know who she is under that mask of hers?"

I slowly inch myself closer to him until his breath warms my face. Being near him is dangerous, like standing next to a furnace. I feel the strong pull in my midriff. He remains still as I offer an apple to Bonita.

"*If* I did know who Pantera was, I would collect the reward myself," I say. "I should like to see the witch in action, though. I hear so much about her skill with a sword. It seems no one can talk of anything else these days."

"Captain Nabarres seems to think it highly likely that this Pantera is a native warrior. A rebel skilled with a sword."

I stroke Bonita's muzzle, letting her eat the apple. Her tongue tickles my palm. "And what do you think?"

"I think," he says, "she is something else entirely."

A flare of panic grips me. He doesn't know anything. He couldn't possibly. I smile in gentle amusement, wondering what kind of magical tricks he has up his sleeve. Andrés Ayeta is a wizard. He has to be. But is he a good one?

"*Trouble* is what she is, lieutenant," I say. "The sooner this bandida is brought to justice, the better. Much as I'd love to continue our conversation, His Highness and I are going for a ride. I suggest you be gone by the time I get back."

"Or?" He crosses his arms. "See, that kind of threat is usually followed by an 'or.' 'Or else I will feed you to the hounds.' 'Or it will end very unfortunately for you.' Something like that."

It's too early. Too early to fight with him. "It's feeding time at the sty. There's a sounder of swine you'd fit right in with. I don't care where you go as long as it's away from me."

He shakes his head, chuckling. "You bewilder me, señorita. You could fillet a fish with that tongue. You remind me of the ocean. Never still. Never at rest. Always heaving and tossing your salty bitterness. But when a storm comes along, you are untamable."

"Are you suggesting that you're the storm in this metaphor?"

"Why? Are you feeling a tempest raging?" He lifts a suggestive eyebrow.

"More like you're ruining an otherwise nice day."

I turn and walk away, feeling his eyes on me until I round the corner and disappear from his view. My fury grows, the cracks in my mask widening.

Whoever angers you controls you. When you let someone make you angry, you're giving them absolute power over you.

Master's words are like mosquitoes buzzing round my head. Andrés de Ayeta is a far more effective pest. I kick a bale of hay inside the stables to quell my frustration. But that achieves nothing except to send a searing pain up my bad leg.

I hear a throat being cleared.

Prince Felipe takes a couple of steps forward, and his soft blue eyes catch the morning light. Apparently, he spoke and I didn't hear.

I blink. "What?"

"I said, do you feel all right, my lady?"

"Yes, I feel fine," I say, then remember he thinks I'm afflicted with love fever.

"Are you sure?"

"Sí, sí. I insist."

"Muy bien." He glances down at the bundle of apples I'm carrying.

"Is that what you're bringing with you?" I nod and he beckons to one of his attendants. "Put this with my things."

I choose a horse from the stalls, deciding upon a gelding that seems suitable in temperament and height, considering one of my legs is splinted and thickly bandaged. He's a beauty, with a solid tan body and a black tail and mane. The horse looks at me. Something trustworthy about his gaze makes me step forward and hold out my hand. As his head comes down, he sniffs at my gloves then gently licks my palm.

"I don't have sugar cubes," I say, "but I do have apples. If you look out for me, I'll look out for you. Deal?"

The horse tosses his head with vigor, his tail swishing. I've always had a fondness for wild things. Scrambling onto the back of the horse, my feet find the stirrups and my body remembers the feeling of a horse between my knees. I take a loose grip on the reins and shift a little forward in my seat.

Prince Felipe grabs the horn of his horse's saddle and attempts to put his foot in the right stirrup. The horse rears, and the prince finds himself on the ground.

My horse nickers, his teeth bared, his head turned, as if the sight amuses him.

"Now there's something you don't see every day, eh?" I say with a laugh, patting the stallion's neck. "You have to mount from the horse's left side."

"Right," he says, pulling himself to his feet and dusting off his clothes. "Right you are."

We cross a fine, paved road, divided by a great, solid aqueduct which conveys fresh water to the city. The Mexica were ingenious in devising a series of canals to bring water to the city, for mitigating thirst and for bathing. A dozen guards ride behind us in silence, their bodies almost unmoving in their saddles, trying to ward off the sticky humidity. Their discomfort at wearing stockings, mail, sallet, and plate protection, is clear. These are too hot in the daytime, even with the sun out of sight and the trees veiled in mist. The foot soldiers, bearing heavy halberds and banners for the patrol, are none too pleased either. The viceroy was generous, offering a party of his men to accompany us. No one forgets that New Spain is at war.

Chapultepec is a short distance west of the palace. We ride beneath giant ahuehuetes, trees that were already old when Emperor Moctezuma was a boy, and still stand tall and vigorous today. Here were his gardens, his aviary, his fishponds, his zoo, his bathhouse at the base of the hill.

Unease crawls up my spine, like a spider leaving a trail of silk. Sitting on my horse in the muggy breeze of the hot morning, I begin to shiver. Memories haunt me. That combined scent of vegetation and moisture seeps into my skin. It's just like when I was a child afraid of the deadly insects, plants, creatures, or whatever else the woods offered up. I'm eight all over again.

"Are you cold?" Prince Felipe asks, snapping me back to the present. "You're shaking."

"I was for a moment."

"Is that why you're wearing gloves?"

It's because the ink on my hands is the surest way to give away my identity. "Ladies never ride ungloved, alteza." I notice there is a mosquito buzzing about him. "And unlike your hands," I say, "mine won't be getting bitten."

"Ah, mosquitoes don't bother me."

"New settlers find them unbearable, alteza," I say. "If I didn't know any better, I'd say you were previously . . . settled."

"What can I say? I'm not especially delicious."

I offer a soft chuckle and let the prince feel good about himself.

"You know," he says, "they don't pierce the skin right away. They take a while before deciding where to dig in. I've noticed white is effective in repelling mosquitoes. You, on the other hand, in that red dress, remind me of a matador taunting a bull with his cape."

"For a Spanish prince recently arrived from the Mother Country, you certainly know a lot about the wildlife."

He shrugs off the observation. "My governess taught me more than manners and etiquette."

I seize the opportunity to question him. "I understand you were considering the daughter of the king of France for betrothal."

"Elizabeth, yes, but she's quite unfit for marriage."

"How so?"

"She's five."

"I see," I say. "Were other brides suggested for you?"

"Mary Tudor, the heir to the English throne."

"What happened?"

"She's a spinster. Hardly suitable for childbearing."

"Who else?"

"The Archduchess of Austria. She is my niece. I don't understand what this has to do with us," he says. "It seems like you're interrogating me."

It takes some effort, but I manage to conjure an innocent smile. "Just making conversation. The truth is, I am ashamed, alteza. I have been so wrapped up in our marriage plans, I didn't think to inquire if there was someone with whom you had intended to spend your life. I do not wish to interfere if—"

"You're not interfering," he says, in a tone that suggests the subject should be closed. "My companions until now have only been . . . for the night, so to speak. There is nothing to come between us. What about you?"

I shift uncomfortably in my saddle. "I was gone for ten years, alteza. There is no one."

"Please forgive me. It's not my intention to cause you discomfort."

"You're not making me uncomfortable."

"I can't imagine what that had to be like for you," he says. "May I ask how you became lost in the woods?"

I snap to attention, pulling the reins of my horse.

"Is something wrong, my lady?"

A brief sound. I barely register it. I signal the patrol. "At ease!"

The raising of weapons. The clenching of fists. Rattling quivers. All this I hear in the space of three heartbeats.

CHAPTER 12

La Emboscada

A bowstring tightens.

From the forest to my left, an arrow whizzes just inches over my head. Its feathers ruffle my hair. Had my frightened horse not moved like lightning, I would have lost my scalp. He almost unseated me. Lucky for me, but not for the foot soldier behind me. The shaft buries itself in the man's throat, and he collapses to the ground, gasping his last breath in a bloody froth.

"Get down!" someone yells. "Take cover!"

An ambush converges on the sandy trail of Royal Road.

It extends along all routes of escape, so even if we run away, we're still going to die.

Archers fire from the forest on either side of the road. There must be a dozen of them.

If I stay where I am, I'll be killed.

The best thing I can possibly do is move, move, move.

Though reacting to an ambush is a little trickier when you're mounted, hitting the ground is a valid, fear-driven instinct.

Another murderous arrow whistles out of the fog, and I dive toward Prince Felipe. He yells something incoherent as we fall, then we scramble for cover. Our horses flee. The prince clumsily draws his sword, crouching behind a tree to survey the situation. Except, if he stays put, an arrow will find him.

The patrol mills around in a panic, searching the forest for the enemy. If the fog wasn't so thick, they'd be able to open fire. A guard's voice thunders, but he falls dead a moment after he scrambles to his feet to tend to his fallen comrade. An arrow hits a horse, then passes through the animal's crownpiece, head, and neck to enter the rider's heavy breastplate, a thing which seems both incredible and impossible. Foot soldiers shout back and forth at each other, not knowing whether to pull back or advance on the company of unseen archers firing with discipline and deadly accuracy.

Prince Felipe and I drop flat on our bellies. I study an arrow that embedded itself in a soldier's sallet. Long and thin, tipped with some kind of volcanic rock that makes for excellent penetrative qualities, even against Toledan steel.

Rebels.

For a moment, my head feels as hazy as the fog around me. Maybe the fog is somehow inside me, as I am inside it. Leonora should run, not look back. At the same time, Pantera begs me to fight. But I don't have my guise. I don't even have my sword. The gods must be laughing.

The prince staggers to his feet. "What are you standing for?" I whisper-yell. "Stay down!"

"They're hiding in the trees! Shoot up!"

"Get on the ground!" I somehow shout under my breath and pounce on his back. He grunts as we stumble face-first into the dirt.

"What are you *doing*?" he grumbles.

I press my hand against his mouth. "I'm trying to save your life. Look around, alteza. How are we to survive with you shouting away our location? Now, are you going to be quiet?"

He nods, and I uncover his mouth.

"Listen, they'll see you coming long before you can stop them.

You'll have to run after I lead them away. They won't notice you while their attention is on me. Do you understand?"

"That's it, then. The problem is solved. I will simply go on my way and leave you here." He scoffs. "What kind of man do you think I am?"

"A dead one if you don't do as I say."

I can't think straight, and if things go on this way, we'll both be dead before I figure out how to get us out of this mess while our hearts are still beating. The most important thing is to keep my wits. To start with, Prince Felipe needs to shut up.

"I'm sorry, alteza." I choke him out in about fifteen seconds and wait until he convulses and snores. Time for his siesta.

As I get up and brush myself off, I look upward; the fog rolls low over my head. The prince was right. The archers must be hiding in the trees. They can see us, but we can't see them.

A large figure lunges at me from the fog. I throw my hands up.

"I surrender!" I repeat it in Spanish, Nahuatl, and in broken Purépecha, but my attacker rages toward me, hair whipping around. I sprawl backward, then his red-painted face is up in mine. He's taller than I am, and a good hundred pounds heavier. And he isn't wearing any covering.

"Stop!" I say, struggling in his grasp. I don't want to hurt this man. "Listen to me! Please, no more blood!" He acknowledges my words but although he seems to understand, he still sees me as an enemy.

The warrior slaps me hard across the face with the flat of his palm. My cheek blazes hot, and the pain in my leg rebounds intensely. His hands wrap around my neck, squeezing my flesh. Stars sparkle across my vision. No one's coming to save me. I'm on my own.

"Please, stop!" I try to shout, but I'm at the mercy of a man whose people have been shown none.

Inés's words ring in my ears. *Your power lies in your ability to remember who you are when they try to make you forget.*

Each second is an eternity as fear engulfs me, debilitating my mind and body.

Remember who you are when they try to make you forget.

My ribs heave up and down, but no air comes. Dizziness.

Remember who you are.

Trapped. No way out.

Remember.

I'm a sorceress. I say it over and over in my head. I look up, but Tonatiuh is shadowed by the low clouds, so I desperately try to draw tonalli from the earth, the trees, the wind, the leaves, anything and everything. Absorbing just enough, I flatten my palms against his chest and blast him against a tree.

"Leave," I say, my breath rushing out, "before I decide my face is the last thing you'll ever see in this world."

The warrior comes at me in a rage. I can bring this fight to the ground. I can put him on his back but choking him is out of the question; he has a neck like a tree trunk. Even if I'm more agile, more skilled, he's bulky enough to crush my bones beneath his weight.

I remember His Sleeping Highness is hidden under a pile of leaves. My fingers search for his weapon, find the hilt, and manage to plunge it into the soft flesh of my attacker's lower abdomen. He barely groans at the impact of the Spanish fashion accessory, protected by layer on layer of flesh, but I can weaken him and cause pain. In a desperate effort, I go for his groin. Stab, stab, stab. Blood sprays as the dagger wrenches free, splashing down the front of my dress. He's too shocked to struggle, to even know what's happening. Finally, I drag the dagger across my attacker's throat.

A hand goes to my cheek, swiping away tears. "Go to Tonatiuh, warrior," I say.

I let the bloody dagger fall to the ground, trembling, making sense of it all. *He's gone. I killed him.*

For a moment, it grows eerily quiet. Standing just within the margins of the forest, I look up to see our remaining guards beginning to emerge with caution. I feel myself shaking, knowing how this is going to end. They'll be dead within thirty seconds. Then the archers will come after the prince and me.

I might not have the mask of Pantera, but I have the next best thing.

On this foggy morning, with the mist of battle dripping off me, and the stench of fresh blood in my nostrils, I have to shift. I *want* to.

I strip behind a tree and hide my clothes. I move my body into position—on all fours, head down, feet and hands flexed, back arched. I chant a prayer to honor the god of sorcery Tezcatlipoca, asking to be able to shift on demand as I am . . . out of practice. I've become so accustomed to my human form. Then, a second prayer, not to let me fail, hoping I am a true Nagual. It's been so long since I've prayed to the teteoh I don't know if they will even answer, but I am desperate. *Help me.*

Shift, Leonora. Focus. You can do this.

Shifting will use up nearly all my tonalli, and I'm uncertain if I will have any left to fight with, much less shift back, but I can't show the rebels my face. Not my human one.

Come on, come on, come on.

I ignore the echo of Master Toto's voice in my head, telling me not to do this, for I cannot do this alone. I lack control already, but when I lose control completely, I am dangerous.

But Master Toto is not here. If he were here, he'd understand. He'd know I have no other option. This is not a game. This is my life. I will live by choice, not chance. His voice roars louder, but I drown it out. He raised me. He trained me. He dismissed me. Now I curse him for interfering.

Moments pass but nothing happens. Sweating, I try harder to focus. Nothing. I feel a tickle in my throat, and I grunt, but then nothing.

Please, Tezcatlipoca. Let me not fail.
If I fail, I'm dead.

If I fail, Prince Felipe, the king's son, is dead.

The consequences would not only be detrimental to the interests of Spain, upsetting the balance of power. There's no telling what King Carlos, already mourning the loss of his beloved Isabela, would do if he came to learn his only surviving son, inheritor of his crown, has been murdered by rebels.

As I pray, my skin starts itching intensely. I take a deep breath and give in to the shift.

A panther's heart is smaller than a human's. For the heart to shrink, it first has to stop beating. All the panther's other organs are smaller too, so while my human heart is dying, my liver and kidney are also failing. My throat, gullet, and vocal cords are tearing and reforming. The damage alone can kill you. But the animal drags you through the Nine Hells and keeps you alive and conscious, enduring every second.

My skin stretches. It feels like someone is inflating my entire body, and it itches like the pox everywhere. The sensation deepens, and I try to block the pain. I'm being flayed alive. My muscles twist and snap. Knee and ankle joints reverse. Fingernails lengthen into claws. I can take the pain now because anger has consumed me.

You cannot run away from who you are, Leonora, Master promised. *Your nature will betray you.*

Master was predictably sage. Nature always wins. The Panther is my animal companion. We share the same soul, and I cannot fight who I am.

I feel every second of the shift. By the time the fur starts to grow, everything hurts, everything is swollen, and I'm feral enough to murder a village.

It's over. The Panther is alive.

I don't need to see my reflection in water to know what I look like. Black coat. Different-colored eyes, one brown, one green. A sleek body some seven feet long. Once I told Inés that there's no such animal as a black panther because any panther found in the New

World is simply a black jaguar. We have spots, like tawny jaguars, but they are harder to see because of the dark fur.

I blink. The colors of the forest have changed to shades of gray. I lift my nose and swivel my ears to the back of my head, instantly alert. After shifting, my already keen senses sharpen.

I see better, smell better, and hear better.

I have plenty of strength in my shoulders, so I'm able to take Prince Felipe by his jacket and drag him far enough away to hide him from the archers. I have to be careful because I have extremely sharp teeth, which could easily pierce through his skin. The arrows have stopped firing, but I'm not in the clear yet. I scan the woods, looking this way and that, catching glimpses of expertly crafted arrows, hatchets, and armor.

The archers come down from the trees and out of the fog. A few dozen cluster around; men with nude, red-painted bodies.

I'm the only one who can end this. With a growl, I leap from the bushes, claws extended, landing on all fours and exposing myself fully to their view, sides heaving, catching my breath. Before, I saw them as dangerous foes. Now I see people—people who can kill, yes, but who can also be killed.

Their leader is young, his face rigid with fury, a man I would hesitate to lock eyes with, let alone cross. When he speaks, I don't understand. There are over a hundred Indigenous tongues and even more dialects.

A trained Nagual can suppress most of their instincts when in animal form. I can listen to the other archers spout angry words at each other without pouncing. But I've been human for too long. I'm not strong enough to resist. The Panther is at the front of my mind.

If they run, I *will* chase.

If I chase, I *will* kill.

Usually, when you come across a jaguar, it is already too late. The ambush emerges from nowhere, and the cat is already on you. Some of the archers, confused about seeing a jaguar in the forest, slowly start to retreat. I hiss. *Don't do it. Don't do it.* The leader holds up a hand, instructing his men to stay put.

But all it takes is for one person to make a sudden movement. By then it's too late, and no one wants to be the last one left behind. The archers make a run for it.

It happens in an instant. I claw my way to freedom, ripping innards from squirming bodies as screams fill the air. The leader manages to escape. For a moment, a dismal silence prevails. Then the sounds of the forest slowly resume, indifferent to the blood that has been shed.

I pick up speed, darting around trees. Leaves crunch under my paws. Wind ruffles my fur, chilling, invigorating. I'm not as fast as I should be—my bad leg holds me back—but the more I run, the lighter I am, the less pain I feel. Straining every muscle, I keep running, too fast to think, to even realize I'm barely touching the ground, and I trip and roll over my own hind legs. I tumble to a halt and shake myself off, then throw open my jaw to roar. There is no greater feeling in the world than to be as one is. This is what true Naguals must come to realize within themselves. They are none other than themselves, and the Nagual Path leads to the nature of one's self, the real self. This was the essence of my training.

When the high runs its course, I start worrying if Prince Felipe was savaged in my absence. My shift back to human form is torturous. I yank on my clothes and, to my astonishment, my horse returns to me. He has an arrow lodged in his rump, but he seems impervious to it. Such a beast! As I withdraw the arrow, I say a prayer to the god of animals. "There, there, amigo. That's what a good prayer to Tezcatlipoca gets you." I press my forehead to his. "From now on, you will be Valiente. You are a warrior, a brave one."

When I find him, His Royal Highness is breathing slowly, and in odd bursts. I wake him.

Prince Felipe groans. "Where . . . am I?"

"They're gone," I say dismally. "We're safe." For the time being.

Raising himself on his elbows, he pushes sweat-dampened strands of hair back from his forehead. "You're hurt," he says, looking at my bloodied dress.

I shake my head. "It's not my blood."

As he stands, he brushes dirt and leaves from his sleeves and notices his jacket, torn by my fangs. "What—?" he mumbles, trying to make sense of it all.

They're gone because I killed them. I'm a murderer.

As Nahualli, I made a vow to follow the Nagual Path, swore my life to it, promised to walk in the nepantla—the middle—for the earth is slippery, and there is the always-present risk of falling from the path. There can be no life in a world without balance.

This day, I lost control. I betrayed my oath.

CHAPTER 13

La Culpa

Jerónimo's eyes are wide with horror when he finds me and Prince Felipe in the stables. He calls for the guards to fetch the doctor, aid the prince to his bed, and be discreet about it.

"What do you mean *dead*?" he asks in alarm. "You can't possibly mean—"

"I mean dead," I tell him. "Your men are all dead."

"You must be wrong. Are you sure?"

"It seems that way," I respond tiredly. "We were able to flee before they could do us any harm."

"They? Who are *they*, Leonora?" Jerónimo presses, his tone tense and hard. "What did they look like? I demand answers. I need to know. I consider this an act of war."

"I didn't see them."

He needs someone to blame, someone to hold responsible and so shroud his own culpability. He can blame his god, or he can blame himself.

Jerónimo peppers me with more questions. I've had very little sleep, or food. I've fought twenty men, my flesh is bruised in half a dozen places, my leg wound is almost tearing open, and my head feels like a tangled ball of wool. So I shrug off the questions and retreat to my bedchamber.

I'm sitting alone in my bloody dress when Inés barges through the doors. "My lady!" Her voice comes out in a breath. Her scent immediately brings comfort. Rosemary, sage, mostly lavender.

"It's just me," I say, dismissing the formality.

She lifts a burning candle from the nightstand and holds it to my face. "What happened? How bad is it? Where are you injured?"

"I'm unharmed," I tell her. She lets out a sigh of relief. "We came under heavy attack in the woods. They used their archers to hunt us down. It turned into a massacre."

She presses a trembling hand to her mouth. "La Justicia?"

"I don't know."

"Why were the rebels so close to the capital?"

"I don't know."

"What do you think they're planning?"

"I don't know."

"How is the prince?"

"Sleeping. He'll live."

"What about you?"

I shrug.

"You're here, and you're safe," she says. "That's all that matters."

"Sit with me," I say.

"I'll draw a bath."

"Sit, Inés," I say. "Pull up a chair."

"A chair?" she asks, her eyebrows in surprised bows. "But . . . it is not proper."

As with everything else in the palace, the rules are ever more obnoxious. Resting is considered a privilege. Further folly dictates the type of seating one is entitled to. The rank goes from an armchair, to an armless chair, a sofa, a high stool, a low stool, or no seating at all in the case of the help.

"I don't care," I say. "You're my friend. My only friend."

In the soft light of the candle, her cheeks tinge with color. She glances down at her hands. She gives a crooked smile, then she composes herself and sits next to me on a chair with no arms.

Silence falls as we gaze out the arched window facing the plaza. A burial detail carries fallen soldiers while palace guards keep a sharp lookout for another attack, their forms shadowy under the moonlight.

"I would very much like to know about you, Inés."

"You know me, Leonora. You know everything about me."

"I don't know what makes you who you are. Tell me about growing up and what you wanted to be and how you see yourself now and what you live for."

She raises her eyebrows. "All that?"

"Your dreams when you were a little girl."

"It's hard to dream when you're deep in a nightmare." She sighs. "I wanted to be as brave as my mother. I still do." Her mother. She fiddles with the black cord draped around her neck, wrapping her fingers protectively around it. "This is the only thing I have of hers. I took it from her after she . . ." Her voice trails off.

"When the soldiers came to my village in the middle of the night, they were targeting children. There was no warning. Children were shot, stabbed, burned alive. Mother dragged my brother and me out of bed. We were so afraid, but not my mother. She ran up to a Spanish soldier upon his horse, making herself a target so we could escape."

I know how the story ends, but this is more than Inés has ever shared.

She takes a breath to steady her hands. "She put up a fight. She was so brave. Captain Nabarres seized my mother by the hair, cut off her head. And before he burned her body, he took her head and paraded it on a pike."

I can almost see . . . Inés, a frightened child, wondering why her mother was so savagely torn away from her.

"We ran," she says, "carrying what we could on our backs. I still remember the smell of burning flesh as my brother and I left everything behind. I cannot rid myself of the smell. It must have seeped into my soul."

She lets out a shuddering sigh.

"This world has sharpened you into a blade, Inés." I reach out and squeeze her hand. "You are the bravest person I know. Your mother would be proud."

She squeezes my hand back and then lets go, sitting straighter. "My gods didn't bring me all this way to leave me. They kept me alive for a purpose. They will not deny me my vengeance."

"And your father?" I prod.

Suddenly uncomfortable, she pushes to her feet. "A white man. A coward."

"He lives?"

"Alive or dead, he is nothing to me," she says coldly. "Enough. Let me take a look."

She removes my bloody clothes, and I grimace as she slings her arm around my waist, puts my arm around her shoulder, and helps me climb into bed. When she sees my leg, she curses under her breath. The shift tore the stitches open, and I am bleeding. Worse yet, the cut has lengthened. She sews me back together again. Twenty-two stitches. That must be a record for me. She's meticulous at keeping the sutures small and close together this time, not wanting me to have a large scar.

"Inés," I say as she slips on my nightgown. "Do you think *I'm* a coward?"

"I think . . ." she says, "you were put in a very difficult position. You said they were going to kill you. You had no choice. You were only defending yourself."

"Was I?"

"You were brave enough to save Prince Felipe."

"Brave," I say, the word feeling unfamiliar on my tongue.

"Yes, you behaved with courage."

"No, I behaved like a child. I wanted to be safe, but I wasn't going to show His Royal Highness what I am. I put him to sleep. I thought, What if he dies? I wouldn't have to marry him. I wouldn't have to go to Spain. It would make my life so much easier. I wasn't brave or courageous or helped by my gods. I didn't save the prince because it was the right thing to do. I saved him because his death would have made things worse. The king's son, murdered by rebels. The war would never end. There would never be peace. The only reason the prince is alive is because I'm selfish. The only reason *I'm* alive is because I'm an animal."

Would I have let Prince Felipe die were it not for his status? Is doing the right thing because it serves a greater purpose good enough? Or is that just another form of selfishness? Am I just too proud? Do I know for sure what's right?

These questions haunt me.

"Anyway," I say, "it doesn't matter. If the end of the Fifth Sun is near, I should make my peace with my gods."

"Don't talk like that," she says angrily. "The world isn't ending."

Inés is Purépecha, but she knows of the Nahua prophecy. Violent earthquakes and flying sky monsters.

"How do you know?" I go on. "How do any of us know?"

"The Dead Days are—"

"Over. It's a new year. Yes, yes. I know that. But what if Señor Alonso misinterpreted the days? What if," I fight past the knot in my throat, "he was wrong about the year?"

The Fifth Sun can only be destroyed during the Nemontemi. Or so the codices say. Even then, there aren't many who can read and interpret the calendar.

"Go to sleep, Leonora." She pulls the sheets over me. "We'll talk about this tomorrow."

"I'm not a good person, you know? I've . . . I've done bad things. Some horrible things. I've killed people. I've offended my gods. If

104

I'm going to die," I say, thinking about my foretold death in battle, "I don't want to take it all to my grave." I want to live. But destiny always runs its course.

"You're not going to die. It's all in your head."

I chuckle softly.

"What?"

"Ollin used to tell me that," I say, smiling.

"Who?"

"My friend. We trained together in Tamoanchan." We grew up together. Ours was not an ordinary friendship. We were inseparable, until Master Toto dismissed me, and then we weren't, and I went. And that was the last I saw of the Nagual Warrior Ollin. How I miss my friend.

"When we were little," I say, "I had trouble sleeping. I would see this terrifying beast, and I'd wake up and hide under as many blankets as I could, because so long as I did, nothing could harm me. Ollin would try to make me feel better and say it was all in my head. He was right. The beast—it was in my head. Eventually, I learned what it was."

Inés scrunches her forehead. "What?"

"Me," I reply. "The Panther. She visited me in my dreams. It's how your nagual reveals itself to you."

Go to sleep. The first Nagual Truth. To discover one's nagual, one must first go to sleep.

I drift off to the drumming of her heart, but in my dreams, they come for me. The archers from the woods. Their screams of horror as they resisted demand to be heard. I see their faces. I cannot escape them. I don't deserve to. Now is when I'm least proud of what I am, for I killed and failed to uphold my oath to follow the Nagual Path. I jolt awake and sit in the dead calm of the night. Forcing myself to go back to sleep seems pointless.

I tie on my mask and disappear into the darkness.

CHAPTER 14

El Sanador

I scurry out the servants' passageway, heading along the narrow, badly lit corridor. Viceroyal Palace keeps its help as invisible as possible. And plenty of lovers find the back corridors convenient when slipping out of one bedroom and into another. I walk quietly on the cobbles, careful not to attract attention.

The entrance to the cuartel is at the foot of the watchtower. Below the barracks are the dungeons and torture chambers. Dangerous territory.

With my head down, I proceed across a walkway that keeps me out of sight of the night watch, scanning my surroundings for potential threats with my other senses. Inside, I scurry through a labyrinth of corridors going in different directions. I hold on to the wall, resting my leg. When the pain lessens, I can walk. When it returns, I can only wait until it passes. Perhaps I should curl up here in the dark and damp and let myself be taken away to the next life, but I'm too stubborn.

The cuartel is the main military residential area where the soldiers responsible for defending the viceroyalty live. Ayeta must be here. The midnight air carries a trace of his tonalli, guiding me with perfect precision. Torches line the outer walls at the end of the pathway where two guards sit playing cards on a foldup table. If I remove them, it won't take long before the alarm is sounded. Too risky.

Taking off my mask, I swaddle a bundle of fabric from my robe and cradle it against my chest. I rumple my hair and pinch my cheeks to redden them. I go forward, bracing myself for what I'm about to do. If it saves me from death, I'll do it.

I keep to the light against the wall—surely they can see me.

"You," one of the guards says.

"What is your business here?" the other asks as he stands.

Aside from Nabarres's closest men, most soldiers have never actually set foot inside the palace, much less know what I look like. I clear my throat. "I would like to go to my husband."

The first guard sneers. "Who is your husband?"

"Lieutenant Ayeta."

The two guards look at each other.

"Andrés? We didn't know he was married," the second guard says.

"There, there." I bounce my bundle of fabric up and down in my arms as if shushing it. "My little one has been fussing all night."

I turn to leave just as the standing guard says, "One moment."

I face him. His hands are on his belt, which holster an array of weapons. "Tell your husband to transfer to the larger houses for soldiers with families."

"I'll do that. Buenas noches."

When I'm out of sight, I slip my mask back on, my pulse pounding at my temples.

I reach the door of his room. *Please be unlocked.* When I turn the knob, the door creaks open. Just stepping inside makes my breathing rapid and shallow. Ayeta is sleeping under the covers with a girl whose arm is draped across his bare chest. I move over to the bed on the balls of my feet and straddle him, knife poised.

With a dagger to his throat, he finally stirs awake. The woman sits up in a flurry and gasps, clutching a pillow against her breasts.

"I need you to be nice and quiet," I say to her, "or else your sweetheart here loses his head. Can you do that for me?" She gives a quick nod. "Good. Now get out. And don't even *think* about raising the alarm if you know what's good for you."

"He's—he's not my sweetheart," she says in a panic, slipping on a robe. "He's not my anything. I swear. We just met."

Andrés clicks his tongue, feigning insult, as if he hasn't fully registered that he has a knife at his throat. "I thought we had a nice time."

The woman nervously looks at him, then at me, and back at Andrés. "It was . . . pleasant enough."

"What part of *get out* wasn't clear to you?" I bluster.

She rushes out the door.

"It's nice to see you again, Pantera," Andrés says, reclined under me. "How did you get in here?"

"I'd be more concerned about the blade pressed against your neck if I were you."

He sighs, as if I'm already too much to bear. "Why are you on top of me?"

"You stole something of mine. I want it back."

"You do know I heal, right?"

"Don't test me." I push the dagger further into his skin.

"I didn't steal your sword. I took it for safekeeping."

"Lie. Steal. Is that all you do?"

He gives another cluck of exasperation. "You insist that I tell you the truth and then you don't believe me when I do. You're impulsive and you let your emotions get the better of you. These are not good qualities for someone who hides behind a mask. How much longer do you suppose you'll be on top of me? I'm warning you . . ." I don't realize how tightly I'm squeezing his hips with my legs until he gives me that stupid smirk of his.

Straight away, I lean back, and Andrés props himself up on his elbows.

"Don't even think about it," I say, leveling my blade at him. "I don't want to have to hurt you."

"That's the difference between us, Pantera. I would hurt you without a thought if you stopped me getting what I wanted."

That's when I jab my blade into his palm. It cuts through the skin. A rivulet of blood runs down his wrist.

Andrés curses under his breath. "I promise you I am the least of your problems."

I can't determine if I'm furious or confused.

"Tell you what," he says, "why don't you move the blade out of my palm and maybe I can stop bleeding?"

As soon as the blade is withdrawn from his palm, he grabs my wrist and flips me so now I'm flat on my back and he's on top of me.

He pins my arms above my head. "Let. Go."

I do as he says. As much as I want to slash his throat, I want my sword more. "For someone who can heal, you sure are scared of a blade."

He releases his hold. "I can feel pain, if that's what you want to know."

He's hovering between my legs and supporting his weight with his arms held out on either side of my body, his fists clenched. I thank the Thirteen Heavens that the sheets are still tangled around his waist.

And then he stands up, letting the sheets fall as he walks toward his wardrobe. I gape like he just sprouted an extra head. It's a good thing my mask hides my burning cheeks. My eyes flicker over the elaborate maze of ink on his body, wondering about the story behind the symbols. I push myself up from the bed and turn my head, listening to the rustling of clothes.

"Why do you avert your gaze? Do you find me so repulsive you can't even stomach the thought of looking at me? Is that it?"

I *wish* I found him repulsive. It would make things so much easier. If I keep my anger burning, I can ignore the rush of desire pulsing inside me. Until this very moment, I had not the faintest idea lust could be so consuming.

"Come on, Pantera. My nakedness can't be what you find so shocking. Don't tell me you've never seen a naked man before?"

My mouth is annoyingly dry. "I've seen plenty," I snap. Young Naguals who aren't clothed after shifting back from their nagual. Many warriors fight stripped bare. But Ayeta's nudity is different. Unsettling. I keep trying to look at the ceiling, at the window, or at the door. Anything and everything but the obvious.

"So, what's the problem? It's just a body. I have one. You have one." I hear him pull on pants. "You know, you really have a flair for the dramatic, Pantera. Couldn't you have found a better time than the middle of the night to come looking for your sword? Or are you here for something *else*?" The provocative drawl raises gooseflesh on my arms.

I refuse to let him go further with his assumption.

"Don't think too hard, lieutenant. You might hurt yourself." I get up off the bed. "Where's my sword?"

"In its sheath."

He thinks he's so funny. "Where've you put it?"

"In a safe place. I'll give it back. Come by another day."

I narrow my gaze, trying to read him, but he gives me nothing. "What is your price?"

"My price?"

"You want something in return."

"I don't."

"Everyone wants something in return." He wouldn't have taken my sword otherwise.

"Not me."

I hesitate, wary now.

"If you're going to start trusting me, Pantera, I should tell you that I can heal you."

"What?"

"You're bleeding."

My heart quickens, and I look behind me at the bed. Its white sheets are stained with a second patch of red. One for his hand. One for my leg.

"What happened?"

"None of your business. It's just a cut." The pain I can tolerate, but why must I lose blood? I selfishly wish the sun would rise in the middle of the night so I could replenish my tonalli. But there's no arguing with Tonatiuh.

"Pantera, much as I enjoy bantering with you, I'd rather we not be enemies," he says. "Healing can be very exhausting . . . dangerous even. In your case, I can mend your leg since the wound is still open. That is, if the legendary Pantera isn't too proud to accept my help."

My lips pressed tightly together, I collapse on a chair by the window, fighting to keep control of my reeling senses. Andrés crouches in front of me, and for a long, long moment, he looks at me.

"Is that a yes?" he asks.

I take a shuddery little breath, slumping further down in my chair. I lift my robe, exposing the tearing where the stitches have come undone. Again. It looks worse than at the start. The bruising has turned a mottled black.

Saying yes means exposing myself to his touch. And not just his touch but his tonalli. I'm losing more of my own tonalli by the minute, and the less tonalli someone possesses, the colder it becomes—but that's not the only reason I begin to tremble. I'm not treading carefully enough. But if I say no, he will have won. He will know that I'm afraid, that I feel far more at risk than I did when I was in the woods. He's still looking at me, enticing me with his gaze. It occurs to me that he might want me to feel his power, to frighten me, show me what he can do, or he might truly want to help me—which seems the least likely. No one is that altruistic. Regardless, it won't do to give in to my fears. For the second time in a day I ignore Master Toto's disapproving voice in my head.

"Yes," I finally say.

"Pantera."

"What?"

"You need to relax."

I don't realize I'm gripping the chair tightly. "What difference does it make if I'm relaxed or not?" I ask in an irritable voice.

"Because I need to concentrate, and I can't do that with your heartbeat pounding in my ears."

"Why are you helping me?"

"I'm a healer. It's what I do," he says, "and I don't see a line forming behind me. Try to be still."

I say nothing, but underneath my mask, I squeeze my eyes shut and bring my lips together. Then his hand presses on my wound, and I stifle a scream. I nearly push myself to my feet and bolt but latch on to the chair instead.

"I know it hurts," he says. "I have to find the damaged places and repair as much as I can."

"It doesn't hurt," I say through clenched teeth.

"Your wound I can heal; your pride I cannot."

The heat of his hand against my chilled skin sears worse than a branding iron. It's taking all my willpower to sit still and not cry out. I will not cry out. Tears threaten to leak from my eyes as tendons straighten and surfaces smooth, then the pain starts to lessen, and as it does, it is replaced with a.feeling I can only imagine is similar to being in Omeyocan, the thirteenth and highest heaven, dwelling place of Ometeotl, creator of gods and humanity and all that exists. Andrés's tonalli bores into me like a tree burrowing in its roots, violently ripping away at the earth. I'm in a trance. But then Andrés groans, and I open my eyes to see him pull back his hand. He tilts to one side and flops down wearily against the bed.

"That was," he says, "more than a cut."

I test my leg. There is no sign of injury. Not even a mark. Extraordinary. As soon as I rise, my blade returns to his throat.

He regards me a moment in silence. "You know, most people would say thank you."

"What in the Nine Hells was that?"

"I'm not sure. It's never happened before."

I grind my teeth. "What kind of wizard are you?" I also want to know why he stole my medallion, but I can't reveal my true identity.

"I told you. I'm not a wizard."

"Then what?"

"A man."

"Don't," I say, "don't insult me. Your tonalli is not that of a mere man. I have not sensed another like yours. What *are* you?"

He shrugs. "I don't know. No one else has ever asked me that."

"Never?" It seems impossible.

"Never."

Andrés de Ayeta is a professional liar, slipperier than a wet fish, but I believe him. Perhaps that is the worst torment and the reason I'm angry. I believe him because his tonalli whirled through me and took root, twitching with a living power all of its own. I believe him because I *felt* him.

CHAPTER 15

El Sol

Early the next morning, my eyes open wide. I take one great leap from the bed and wake Inés.

She springs up frantically. "What is it? What's happening?"

I toss her a sparring sword, and she looks confused, her eyes half-closed and hair disarrayed. She makes a little face, gives me an incredulous glance, then shifts her gaze to my leg. Her eyebrows go up, and she blinks. If she didn't know any better, she never would have guessed I was near death last night.

"How?" she gasps.

With a smile, I nod for her to follow me to the lake, not far from the palace. Tonatiuh barely whispers his light, but already the air is steam, blowing on us.

We spar. Inés twists her wrist hard and high. The point of her practice sword hits me right in the chest. I'd be dead if it was the real thing. After the explosion on *La Capitana*, I hadn't been able to train with her, but she's naturally quick and light on her feet and becoming better at predicting my moves. Her swings are sharper, more precise.

"Don't do that," she says, dropping her defense.

"Do what?" I brush a few strands of hair out of my face. My forehead is damp with sweat.

"Let me win. I don't want you to let me win. Let's go again," she says. "And this time, at least *try* to dodge my attacks?"

"Very well," I say. With a quick motion of each hand, I wrap the ends of my sleeves around my fists, then I bring my right foot and sword forward, angling it up.

She matches my stance and comes at me, bringing her sword down in a clean, straight slice. I pivot out of the way and flick my own weapon in a move that would've cut her belly open.

"Don't study my moves, Inés. Pay attention to my blade. Contain your chest and pluck up your back, loosen your waist and liven your wrist. Your only opponent is up here." I tap a finger against the side of my head. "If you can remain calm while someone is trying to stab you, then you can face just about any adversity life throws at you with ease."

She blows out a breath and straightens, glancing skyward at the call of an eagle.

I adopt Master's sword style, pointing my blade toward Inés from the top of my head while my left fingers are posed and readied. Then I attack.

"I wasn't ready!" she shouts.

"Do you think Captain Nabarres is going to wait for you to be ready? He's not going to let you draw your sword. And he's not going to stand idly while you are distracted by a bird."

I leap into the air, my feet lashing out swiftly and with force. A release of tonalli sends Inés backward, along with a grove of trees that bend as if blown by the wind.

"That's cheating!" she grumbles as she pulls herself off the ground.

"No, that's winning."

"How do you do that?" she asks, red-cheeked and soaked in perspiration.

Once, Master Toto said to me that if we try to define tonalli, we do not understand it. Its very nature is unpredictable, ebbing and flowing, always changing.

Sorcery has nothing to do with magic. It is not simply wielding great bursts of tonalli and playing out our fantasies. You must become yourself. Your true self.

"There are three souls in the body," I say, and bring up my sword to where her liver is. "Ihiyotl, the source of our emotions." Then her heart. "Teyolia, knowledge and wisdom." Finally, her head. "Tonalli, life force. Everyone and everything has tonalli. Controlling it is the hard part."

I explain that tonalli is derived primarily from the sun. It can be gained or lost, and travels when you sleep, sneeze, yawn, or are startled, entering and leaving the body as when a window is opened to freshen the stale air. For the most part, the kind of tonalli a person has depends on when they were born, but through intense and focused cultivation of the mind or body, it can grow more powerful. I've heard tales that after the Fall, Emperor Moctezuma's tonalli was so strong that upon his death his relatives consumed his ashes so as to be filled with his royal tonalli and impart it to their future heirs.

"Tonalli manipulation is a technique developed by the Old Ones in the Fourth Sun," I continue. "The greatest sorcerers can lift a person in the air, crumple a chair into a ball, vanish into nothing . . . take flight."

I can draw tonalli from Tonatiuh, people, animals, rocks. Objects usually have a lot less tonalli than living beings. For the most part, I can manipulate my tonalli, guide the flow of it within, and gather it from my surroundings to increase my power. I can even release my nagual soul from my body, free to travel without shifting. But it's one thing to manipulate one's own tonalli and quite another to manipulate that of someone else. This relies heavily on tonalli control.

"Control is the only route to mastering tonalli," Master Toto said.

"How do I control tonalli?" I asked then.

"You don't."

The lesson was absurd. Trying to control tonalli is like trying to control whether or not the sun shines. It's an exercise in futility. No matter how much I trained, tonalli did what tonalli does.

Inés is rapt. "Show me."

"I can't."

"Because you didn't complete your training?"

"I know the spells, I just can't do them," I say. "My father said my entrance to this world was at night." I chuckle at the misfortune.

"So?"

"So my tonalli is weak, depletes easily." In the absence of the sun, it is common for Nahua babies to rest near the family hearth in order to absorb tonalli from the fire, but such a rite is completely pagan, and I don't know if my mother believed in the old faith. "Some people simply don't have enough tonalli, and then there are some who have a lot and don't know it. Though I've never met someone with tonalli like . . . never mind."

"Predictable," she says like the word sickens her.

"What?"

"You've taken a liking to him."

"Andrés? Don't be absurd. He healed my leg, is all."

"If it's so absurd, how did you know I was referring to him? Do you even trust him to return the Sword of Integrity?"

"Enough talk, Inés." I point my practice sword at her. "Let's go."

"No." She wipes sweat off her forehead with the back of her hand. "I'm done."

"Done? This is war, Inés. You fight to the last breath."

"We've been at it for hours," she says tiredly. "I'm thirsty."

"Is this how you will avenge your mother? Asleep on your feet?"

"Don't you dare."

"Your mother was murdered, Inés. *Murdered*," I repeat.

"Será mejor que te calles."

"You're too tired. It's too hot. Is this how you will punish Captain Nabarres?"

"¡Cállate!"

117

"Show me how you will honor your mother!"

She pushes forward and takes control. As if someone else has stepped inside her body, she comes at me, quick and deadly, forcing me to stay on the defensive, around and backward nearly to the edge of the hill. Her eyes are a knife in my ribs, a burning stare that will last as long as it takes her to cut me down.

Now it is a real fight.

She spins in the air and grazes the side of my head, a hair's breadth away from my face. I'm so surprised by the move that I drop my guard, and Inés tears the blade from my sweaty hands. The wood breaks with a sharp, flat snap. In that instant, she strikes me in the knees. She goes for my weakness. Pain explodes in my legs, and I stumble to the ground, gasping for breath.

"Leonora!" she pants, rushing to my aid. "Are you hurt? I didn't mean—"

I glance up. It's not reprobation in my gaze. It's thrill. "Very good."

She offers her hand and pulls me up to stand as a horn bellows in the distance, followed by another and another. That's three times. Pantera's call.

My legs burn as I run, my black garb flapping behind me. Tonatiuh in the sky is brighter now, almost blinding, lengthening my shadow. I'm not running at the speed of a panther, but there's a new lightness in my step, and I don't have to stop to catch my breath. My sword hinders me. I find it strange that it isn't as heavy as the Sword of Integrity, yet I feel it a burden on my back.

I run farther, faster. I follow the smell of burning reed and loam, the screams of the desperate, and the cursing of soldiers. Distant at first, then nearer. The horn leads me to the outskirts of Mexico City's traza, the Spanish area of the city, surrounded by Indigenous barrios on all sides. At the edge of la traza lies Mexicapan. The smallest barrio. I dodge people and animals running the other way, past a slaughter-house, a convent, and a church, for no community in New Spain can be complete without a place of worship dedicated to the Christian faith. Many Nahuas live here, and other peoples too, who have been made to recant their beliefs. Spaniards generally avoid Mexicapan, the bad barrio, which smells like blood and carcasses all the time.

It is engulfed in chaos, overrun by soldiers, fires, and corpses strewn on the ground. I race around a burning hut and see a soldier dragging a woman out of her home, her hair gathered in his fist, and her little daughter crying out as he forces her mother down. "¡Mamá! ¡Mamá!"

"Release her," I shout at the coward.

He looks up, trying to work out where the sound came from. "She's mine," he says. "I can do what I want with her. I bought her."

"I'd be very cooperative right now, if I were you."

"Or what? I've heard of you, witch," he sneers. "You never actually kill anybody."

The child comes to me and clings to my leg, and all I can think of is Inés, the way her mother was beheaded before her eyes and her brother fell to the pox, and she was left destitute.

"I do now." I pluck my throwing knife from my belt and hurl it at his face. No sound comes out of his mouth as he goes down.

"Go now," I say to the woman and her daughter. "Don't look back."

Fresh blood calls to the Panther. Smoke whirls all around me, and I emerge with my sword ready, looking for more men to kill. I kick a Spaniard into the smoldering remains of a house.

Captain Nabarres is shouting for his men to burn everything, but *someone* has loosened the saddle straps on their horses, and when they trot forward, the mounted soldiers fly off their seats. I smile underneath my mask.

Down the row of prisoners, men and women scream for help. The old and the ill fight where they stand or are cut down. The children are left with the dead for company.

I kneel in front of a prisoner. "What happened here?"

The man looks at me with horror. "The viceroyalty has imposed a tax on my family, and I cannot pay. They're taking me to the mines. Taking all of us!"

"Hold still. I'm going to free you." I grit my teeth at the injustice, pulling at the bonds locked around his hands.

A soldier comes at me from the side, and I push to my feet and slice my sword through his stomach. Ayeta. My chest heaves with deep, ragged breaths. He stands still, his sword red to the hilt, his wound starting to heal.

When he tosses something at me I catch it then open my hands. Keys. If Ayeta could see my face, he would notice my bewilderment. Why is he helping me? What is he planning? What is he getting out of this?

Before I can dash the thoughts from my head, Ayeta wheels to hack down a red-bearded Spaniard. He disappears into the smoke, and I hurry back to the prisoners to unlock their shackles. As a pair fall away, iron clamps heavily around my own wrists, so tight the metal edges nearly cut through my gloves. I look up at my captor, one of the prisoners I released. He is apologetic, crying and shouting, "He has my family!"

"The Panther, trapped at last," I hear my enemy gloat. Behind me, Captain Nabarres saunters over with casual arrogance, as if giving a toast. He knew I would come and free the prisoners. Did Ayeta know? Was this *his* trap?

Standing next to him, his most loyal right-hand man General Valdés nods to the men. "Remove her mask."

They approach cautiously, and my bones start to crack. My thumbs, then my fingers, retract into my hands and become paws with claws. I'm able to break through my chains, gloves tearing apart in the process. My hands quickly shift back before anyone sees. Once I'm free, the soldiers, five or six of them, look at each other not knowing what to do.

Nabarres can hardly contain his fury. "What are you waiting for, idiotas? Seize the Panther!"

The men surge forward, and I swing my sword at their skulls.

"How is this going to go, Pantera?" Nabarres says. "Are you going to run from me like you always do? Run, run, run!"

I'm angry. Corrosively, self-destructively angry. I whirl in the air, my sword slashing round my head, and a wave of tonalli rushes through the ground. The shock of it sends Nabarres and his men soaring backward. The debris settles, and I look up to see the sun. The smoke is gone. So is the fire. There are fallen trees, broken branches, and leaves. A long silence spreads, so thick and full of confusion I stand there wondering what caused this. It's as if the teteoh stirred up a tempest. Except, of course, it wasn't the gods. There is only one person I know who uses tonalli with the force of a storm. Master Toto. I look around, expecting to find him, but instead I see Ayeta on his back, propping himself up on his elbows and waving the dust from his face.

We lock stares, and he beams at me, as if he just witnessed the second coming of Quetzalcoatl to reclaim his kingdom.

It takes me a moment to realize.

This power came from me.

CHAPTER 16

La Condesa

Days later, I sit in Sunday Mass. Fray Anonasi tells us to confess our truth and everyone takes a moment of silence to contemplate the sins they've committed.

There's a brief silence, and I close my eyes trying to feel something like God in the room. Fray Anonasi says I must give Him time to change my pagan heart. After all, a man died on a cross for my sins, rose from the dead, and put his life inside me. But I don't believe in sins, or commandments, or stories of men who revived the dead or turned bathwater into ale. Christians and their myriad of saints. There is only light and dark, motion and stillness, order and chaos. Duality. Like the double god Ometeotl, who is both female and male. They fathered and mothered themselves, as well as the universe.

As I shake the fog out of my head, my gaze roams to where Captain Nabarres stands at the back of the church, and I remember him flying through the air and landing face down in mud. That blast was like nothing I've done before, not even close. I don't have the tonalli for it. An attack like that should've drained me entirely, but I had power, more than I've ever felt. I thought Nabarres might not have survived, but then he resurfaced and rode off on his horse.

*

The memory lingers after Mass. I walk through the palace corridors until odd looks and whispers swirl around me. Gossip is the favorite pastime in court, and I cannot escape it.

This is a palace for socializing, where you meet others by accident in the courtyards or the entertainment rooms frequented by lords and ladies who play parlor games and billiards, enjoy comedies, operas, and spectacular parties. I go the long way around to my chamber to avoid the burning stares, and Inés is waiting for me there, her face grave.

"Leonora." Her voice is low and calm, as if she thinks I'm already overreacting. That only makes me angry. "I just heard . . ." she says, and I glare at her, daring her to finish that sentence. "There are rumors."

Every muscle in my body tenses. "What rumors?"

"Lady Amalia is with child. Her handmaid says she hasn't bled."

"La Viuda? What do I care what Lady Amalia does?"

"She was seen leaving Prince Felipe's chamber through the servants' passageway a few weeks ago."

"*What?* Why?"

"Well, Lady Amalia is young and fertile . . ."

"If Lady Amalia's reputation is any clue, then, by the gods, she planned this romantic encounter. She would not have put herself in a vulnerable position if she was not certain of the outcome." I pace the length of my room, my mind reeling. "It's only been a few weeks. Isn't it too soon? How can they already be speculating about pregnancy?"

"When you're a widowed countess trying to win a crown, sooner is better . . . my lady."

My heart shrivels in defeat. She's right. I hate that she's right. I sweep out of the room and thunder through the palace. I'm grateful for the long walk, the chance to order my thoughts. Lady Amalia is not only young and fertile. She's also ambitious and politically astute, always ensuring her future.

I reach the building where Prince Felipe resides, one of the new houses built for Hernán Cortés, secluded from the common gaze. The high walls and archways are covered with tapestries, and its rooms are scattered with gold dust, collars, fans, and other wondrous golden ornaments. It is a glittering sight.

The very layout of Viceroyal Palace is designed to reflect the hierarchy of court. The farther one ventures, the fewer people are admitted through the guarded doors.

"I wish to see Principe Felipe."

"Your pardon, my lady," the footman says, "but su alteza real is asleep. Perhaps it would be better if you came back at another time."

"Asleep? The sky is alight. I demand a word with him."

The guard footman seems uncertain for a moment, then ushers me into the room.

I go through the antechamber and Prince Felipe is lounging on a velvety chaise, his head resting against the armrest, his eyes half-lidded. He's wearing an open-necked tunic without a belt and no trousers. I clear my throat. "Alteza."

He stands and his loose garment flutters dangerously. "My lady. What can I do for you?"

"I missed you in Mass. I've come to see how you are faring."

"Do you mean after we were attacked by a horde of rebels? I wasn't feeling well, but I am on the mend. Thank you, my lady, for your concern."

"Viceroy Jerónimo wishes to host a dinner in your honor."

"Tonight?" His voice has an edge of unease.

"Unless His Highness has a prior engagement." The bitterness drips.

"No, no, of course not. It's only that my shoulder aches and I'm confined to bed rest."

I give him an incredulous glance. "I don't appreciate being made a fool of, alteza."

"My lady?"

I walk to the wardrobe and open the double doors. As I suspected, from the strong masculine scent, warm tonalli, and the vein pulsing in his throat, a man steps out. A native man.

"I can explain," Prince Felipe says, sounding defeated. "Leave us," he tells the man, who avoids his gaze and exits through the servants' passageway. "It was the last time. I promise. From now on, no one sleeps with me until you join me, and after that, only you will share my bed."

I take a breath and clasp my hands in front of my waist. "You didn't mention your nightly companions were men, alteza."

"They haven't all been men. There have been some women too."

"Like Lady Amalia?" I say furiously. "Is it His Highness's wish to make me the laughingstock of this court? First, you take me without a dowry as if I am the town whore. Cows have more use than a bride without a dowry. Now, you bed La Viuda. I've scarcely gone anywhere today without someone giggling or whispering behind my back."

The prince must feel the stab of my anger. His own face colors. He reaches for my hands, his blue eyes pleading. "I'm deeply sorry, my lady. I should have considered your feelings before. We are betrothed. I should not be indulging my pleasures with others."

I wrench my hands from his. "My feelings? Do you think this is about my feelings?"

For all I care, Prince Felipe can wed and bed Lady Amalia and ride off into the sunset with her. No prince, no wedding. That would take care of my problem. But . . . I will *not* become queen to cope with my husband's conniving mistress, with no part in anything except the production of heirs. I will not be played by some upstart countess who's hardly finished burying her husband and is already plotting her next move.

The prince frowns. "I don't think you're jealous, my lady, but you're clearly making yourself ill over this. Please, don't be upset."

I chuckle, livid. "Upset is what happens when you need to relieve yourself and your chamber pot hasn't been emptied. This is about power!" I shout because it's obvious, or at least, it should be obvious.

It's all that matters. "I don't care if you bed a man or a woman or a creature with horns. Ours is a marriage of convenience." Or rather, inconvenience. "Nothing else."

"*Don't*," he says sharply. "Don't say that. It's not enough. We must commit ourselves fully. How can I swear undying loyalty and devotion to you if I do not mean in body as well as in mind? I will be your husband in truth, not just in name. I will share my body and my heart with you and you alone from this moment on. This is the vow I am making to you and to the Lord."

"You would hardly be the first prince to indulge in male companionship."

"That is neither here nor there!" he snaps. "I have many obligations to my father and to court!"

"So?"

"So, until I father a son, I will not be directing my attentions elsewhere. A king must sire a son before he can rule without challenge. It is my destiny and rightful inheritance."

I nod to the wardrobe. "Who is he?"

"No one."

"That's not what it looked like. He seemed important to you."

"He is no one." His tone hardens. He scrubs a hand down his face. "I'm . . . I'm sorry. I made a mistake. It will not happen again. Lady Amalia means nothing to me. It was merely one night."

I laugh bitterly.

"You are not the first man to fall prey to Lady Amalia's allure. Rest easy, you will not be the last. She seduced her late husband Don Gascon de Parada into a wedding in much the same manner."

"The circumstances are *nothing* like each other."

"Perhaps, but considering the child growing inside Lady Amalia's womb, I'd say she's succeeded." I shake my head. "Sort out your priorities, and quickly. This isn't the time to lose your head over a girl, alteza."

"Yes, my lady, I was wrong," he says, getting down on his knees.

"I beg your forgiveness, humbly and penitently, for this insult to you. It will not happen again."

"Get up."

"I beg it."

"That is not necessary. I will see you at dinner."

On my way out, I refrain from slamming the door behind me. I don't know who I'm angrier at—Prince Felipe, Lady Amalia, or myself. Maybe I'll just divide my ire equally among us. I turn a corner in the hallway in a swish of heavy brocade and step out into one of the little gardens, under the arch of its balcony.

"You appear to be in a good mood today, señorita. Unless I'm mistaken."

Andrés is standing to my side, a few steps behind me. "You *are* mistaken," I reply crisply.

"Ah. How are the wedding plans coming along?" he says as he leans on the railing. "All set for the big day?"

"Tell me something, lieutenant. How is it that men are the stronger vessels if the wiles of a girl reduce them to unthinking fools?"

He tips his head, looking at me with pensive eyes. "You don't strike me as the sentimental type, señorita."

"My apologies, lieutenant. Excuse my ill manners."

"It seems foolish to worry about trivial things when there is so much else to worry about."

"Yes, well, sometimes you need the little worries to put the big worries into proper perspective. What is that?" I ask, sniffing as he moves closer to me. "You smell terrible. Like lemon or something."

He sniffs his armpit. "It's called soap."

"I don't care what you call it. You smell like su alteza when he's courting. It's an assault on my nose. I much prefer your natural scent." I clear my throat. "Don't you have things to do, lieutenant? Like search for the Panther?"

He yawns. "I'm sorry, señorita. I've not had much sleep. It seems I've taken up a wife and child recently."

"She must be a nuisance like you."

"Oh, quite so," he says. "Three times, now, she's tried to kill me."

"She sounds lovely."

I knew Lady Amalia was my enemy the moment she introduced herself. "I am Amalia Catalina de Íñiguez y Mendoza, Countess of Niebla," she said to me, giving equal weight to both her title and names, pronouncing them without a pause in between. That was months ago, when I returned to the palace, and I remember thinking she looked like an angel. Well, the priests say that the Devil was once one too. She knew more about the world than I did and seemed more sophisticated, and I felt ashamed of being a mestiza, for I ranked below the Iberian-born countess and therefore did not have the same power or influence or social status.

Gossip around the palace tells me more and more people believe she's carrying Prince Felipe's child. There's already talk of whether or not the prince will make her mistress of the court when he becomes king. With me on the way to becoming queen, Amalia "La Viuda" has turned the position of royal mistress into the nearest thing. She presents herself as a faithful subject to the Crown but has no loyalty to anyone except herself. Married and widowed three times before she was my age, the servants joke that she has conquered more men than Cortés has conquered lands. Her third husband, Gascon de Parada, a wealthy Basque don, well regarded as one of the discoverers of the mines in Zacatecas, was apparently not as good a businessman as he was an explorer. He died in poverty and the marriage was childless. But even that was not a loss for La Viuda. Lady Amalia requested financial assistance from the Crown in recognition of her husband's contributions.

Dealing with the power-hungry countess is the last thing I want to do, but I must.

I lash my wits together, striding through the corridors toward Lady Amalia's bedchamber. I find her settled in a chair by an unlit fireplace, a chessboard on a marquetry table before her. Though she's in her nightgown, a scarlet robe over her shoulders, and her long golden hair brushed loose, she's like a stained glass window, bedecked in colorful jewels.

I take a few steps inside, noting that most of the walls are covered in bookshelves.

"Lady Leonora. What an unexpected visit," she says softly, as if she is too nobly bred to raise her voice. She has the lispy accent of peninsular Spanish.

"I've come to play chess, of course." I sit across from her, and she lifts an eyebrow. I can play a decent game. Her face, which is usually powdered to perfection, is bare. I don't think I've ever seen her naked skin. It's scarred from the pox, but she's a beautiful woman, even in court where beautiful women abound.

"White moves first," she says.

I study the board, then slide my pawn forward one square.

She lifts her small hand, moving her own pawn opposite mine. "I enjoy chess because you must think several moves ahead."

"Is that what you're doing now?" I maneuver my knight's pawn. "Thinking ahead with Prince Felipe?"

"What holds for the game, holds for life. You cannot win if you don't make a move." She caresses her flat stomach. "I am pregnant with possibility. I give thanks that the Lord has blessed me with a child so soon. I have hopes that it may be a boy."

I strain my ears for any signs of life in her belly. There is just gurgling.

"Do you plot against me, countess?"

"Not so much against you as for myself, Lady Leonora." How else can a poor widow make her way in the world? "You'll find life is a lot like chess: the best prepared with the cleverest strategy will always win. Oh, don't look so dreadfully stricken, my lady. I'm far too young to be a widow forever. Men use their swords—I'm sure you know which kind I mean. We women use our wits. In the end, it's the same game."

I look down at the board, frowning. She has a clear line to my king. When did she get her queen over there? How did I miss that?

"Do you know which is the most powerful piece?" she asks.

I blink, simultaneously thinking of my move and an answer. "Protect your king. It's the first rule of chess."

"Kings are lazy bastards," she says. "Queens do all the work. They are in the thick of battle while kings watch from a safe distance. The king is certainly important, but he is not the most powerful. Some may argue the queen has formidable power because she can move in any direction. But see, pawns are such fascinating pieces. Often overlooked as insignificant, yet they can be promoted to queens and depose kings. Don't you find that interesting?"

I sigh. My king can't go anywhere. It will be checkmate in four moves. She's played *me*, not the pieces.

"My mother has a saying: 'No matter what a woman does, she must have the heart of a lady, but the spirit of a man . . . anything less would be unacceptable.'" She leans back in her chair, chin lifted, as if thoroughly pleased with herself. "Jaque mate," she says, and gives me a blinding smile. "Another game?"

CHAPTER 17

La Cena

I emerge from my chamber at sunset, dreading a troublesome dinner.

In the dining hall, the Spanish elite are seated according to rank.

Lady Amalia enters as if she is a queen crowned, with her mother Doña Cayetana walking next to her, and a hush spreads through the room.

She glides toward me like some kind of ethereal apparition. I wonder if her feet are touching the floor; they are hidden under a black-colored farthingale that exemplifies Spanish taste and sobriety.

"My, I *love* your brooch, Lady Leonora. Is that an emerald?" She leans forward to examine it, fastened on the front of my dress. Instinctively, my hand rises to touch the gem. "Where in the wide world did you get such a treasured jewel? A fake, surely. All emeralds are heirlooms of the Crown. Everyone knows Queen Isabela possessed a spectacular collection."

Something about her words makes an odd sort of sense and that enrages me more than anything else she's said so far.

"It was a gift," I say stiffly, ignoring the insult.

"From whom?"

"Why, my betrothed, of course," I lie merely to provoke her, and I'm not disappointed. Her lips pinch together, her jaw sets, and her eyes flicker with brief annoyance. A crack in her armor. I happily take the win.

But then Amalia lifts her chin and says, "Prince Felipe has given me a gift, too. The gift of life within me." She stares down at her belly, cradling it. "Praise Him."

I clench my fists behind my back. I won't give her the satisfaction of seeing she's angered me. I won't be her pawn. I offer a smile and move to my seat. I'm sure then that La Viuda will continue to make trouble, and I'd better be prepared to deal with it.

Dinner is served. Each course has nearly twenty dishes. Fine dishes that taste of nothing, I'm so fatigued. I am seated among the greatest Spaniards in the New World, and I long only for my bed. All I want to do is sleep. Although, when I go to bed, I dare not shut my eyes because that is when the archers from Chapultepec come for me.

I've seen crows feast on their own kind. They tear at the flesh, pecking and pecking. That's how the archers take a little bit of me at a time. I'm like a frightened child, fragile and damaged, hiding under whatever cover I can, hoping the crows don't find me too.

At one point, around the tenth course, I think I will fall off my chair. But I must hold my head high as if I am not weary, and smile and smile, and absolutely under no circumstances state an opinion. God forbid I exude confidence and enjoy the talk of men. So far, I manage to sit back and stay quiet. That is, until the discussion reaches a point where I have to either speak or burst.

"Are you saying that *you*, capitán, will be the one who discovers Pantera's identity?" I say loud enough for my voice to command the conversation.

Nabarres leans forward, eyes flashing, and says, "Why yes, Lady Leonora. I can and *will* defeat the legendary Pantera and unmask her. Who better than me? For one thing, of all the people seated at this table, only I have actually seen La Pantera. For another, there is none better with a sword in Spanish America." Immediately, several others around the table agree with this statement.

132

"If you're the only one who has seen the Panther, are you certain you're not chasing after your own imaginings, capitán?" I conceal a smirk in my wine as I take a sip.

His irritation grows. For all his talk, for all his evidently earnest obsession with unmasking Pantera, there it is, plain on his face. Shame.

"The witch is real," Nabarres says. "She's real as you or me, my lady."

Lady Amalia studies her fingernails. "All this fuss over a girl in a mask. I'll never understand it." She helps herself to a pastry. "The confections, by the way, are superior."

"What is your opinion in this matter, excelencia?" Doña Cayetana asks Jerónimo.

Jerónimo's lips compress into a bitter line. "Pantera this. Pantera that. Must I always hear that name? Already my head aches, and the day, it has been insufferably hot. Can we not dine in peace?"

"There can be no peace as long as the witch is free," Nabarres says.

Vicereine Carlota sighs dramatically. "What can we expect of someone without the saving grace of Jesus Christ?"

I make the sign of the Cross. "God help us."

"This Pantera is a woman of action, though her interests run counter to mine." All eyes turn to Prince Felipe as he continues. "Whoever Pantera is, she seems to be, at least in the minds of the people, a hero. Simply saying her name in town inspires them to rebel. I admire what she has done, but I wonder how it must feel to fight for something and never be acknowledged for it . . . her family . . . her friends . . . they might never know the girl behind the mask."

"Sentimental weakness on your part, if you'll allow me to say so, alteza," Nabarres remarks.

"I can't help being sorry for her, whatever she's done," the prince says. "The girl is hunted, and each minute her pursuers are closing round her."

"Serves her right, alteza. She richly deserves it," Nabarres says. "It is the result of her own bad behavior."

"It makes you wonder, doesn't it?" the prince replies confidently. "Where would we be if only we received exactly what we deserve?"

The dining hall quiets, except for a muffled snicker from one of the servants.

The prince then raises his goblet of wine, nodding. "To Capitán Nabarres, our bravest and best."

Vicereine Carlota smiles, but her eyes don't. "Excelencia, it is time."

My brother folds his napkin on his plate. Pushing back his chair, he stands and clears his throat. "Alteza, dons, doñas, distinguished guests. I thank you for being here tonight. It is an honor for my mother, the viceregent, and myself to extend su alteza real a warm welcome to México. I am very pleased that I have the opportunity to show our guests not only our beautiful capital, but also New Spain."

The dining hall breaks into a round of applause. The viceroy raises his hand. When it is quiet enough, he continues.

"Looking around us, it is easy to despair. Earthquakes, the pox, attacks from La Justicia, and the masked witch. We must not only celebrate our friendship with the Crown but find solutions to these grave issues. Unity is more important than ever. In pursuit of a better tomorrow, our interests are very closely connected. It falls to me, and it brings me great joy, to give Príncipe Felipe my blessing to wed my sister Leonora."

He pauses and an excited murmur sweeps the dining hall. He waits for silence again.

"The viceroyalty extends its best wishes for you both. I very much look forward to seeing what new cooperative ventures may come out of this pairing. May it symbolize the harmonious union of Old and New Spain. To the bride and groom! ¡Salud!"

I lift my goblet. This is not love. This is business.

"What of su alteza's child?" Lady Amalia asks, cheeks scarlet, her temper getting the better of her. She catches my gaze and holds it. I don't look away.

"Your . . . condition," the prince glances pointedly at her flat belly, "has no relevance to my marriage. I abide by the will of God."

Lady Amalia's glare could burn holes through the tapestries. She rises and slaps her hands on the table, rattling a few dishes and cups, and curses the bitch of a mother who bore him.

Vicereine Carlota slips a spoonful of pudding into her mouth, Jerónimo bites into a pastry, Prince Felipe holds up his goblet for the cupbearer to fill. No one seems to react as Lady Amalia hisses and stomps out of the dining hall, which proves what I already know to be true. Although widowed, unchaste, and presumably carrying a bastard child, Lady Amalia Catalina de Íñiguez y Mendoza, Countess of Niebla, is a blue blood.

Doña Cayetana gets up from her chair. "All praise be to God for the miracle that is growing inside my Amalia's womb." She brings her goblet to her lips, drinks, then looks at Prince Felipe. "I am certain that God has called on my daughter to give birth to the next king of Spain. She is destined to bear su alteza's son, who will have the blood of a *true*," she looks at me, "Spaniard flowing in his veins. This is the divine promise of the Habsburg line."

How is she certain of what her god wants? How does she know what Lady Amalia's destiny is?

Doña Cayetana comes from the royal House of Jimenez, who trace their ancestry back to the greatest Castilian nobleman and war hero, El Cid. The family connection is so far away, Lady Amalia and Doña Cayetana are more closely related to Adam and Eve than to El Cid. This minimal relation shouldn't mean anything at all four hundred years later, but alas, it does.

It's known that the Crown struggles to preserve marriages between peninsulares, Spain-born Spaniards, but it also has an interest in allowing Spanish men to marry women of lower castes, which they hope might encourage the rebels to stop fighting and come down from the mountains to establish ties with Spanish families. As I'm thinking of purity and Doña Cayetana continues making her case, I turn my head slightly, distracted by the sound of scurrying footsteps beyond the palace walls.

I hear their army before I see them: boasting, clattering weapons, a bristling sea of men and women.

Rebels.

But at that moment, Doña Cayetana goes limp, her jaw falling open as her goblet of wine slips through her fingers and falls to the ground. As if seized by a spasm of pain, she puts a hand to her throat and stumbles to the floor.

"Poison!" someone yells.

Blood trickles from Doña Cayetana's nose and ears, streaming down to her neck. Red, I note. Not blue.

Dons and doñas at the table shriek, all dropping their cups. Guards close in on Prince Felipe, the viceroy, and vicereine, and they are yanked from the room as shock and fear takes over the dining hall.

I take this as my cue to leave in search of three things: Inés, a weapon, and a disguise.

In that order.

CHAPTER 18

La Justicia

I manage three out of three.

"Bar the doors," I tell Inés, pulling my black guise over my head. "Don't open them for anyone but me. Inés, did you hear me?"

She emerges from a corner of my bedchamber, hooded in black herself. "You're out of your mind if you think I'm staying here to die."

"I won't let anything happen to you. I promise."

"Leonora, no one is going to look at me and think, 'Ah, yes, one of us, just some innocent servant who's suffering.' I have a white father. I am like you. They're going to take one look at me and it'll be over. Quickly if I'm lucky."

"Don't you have a weapon?" When I ask, she looks at me blankly. "Rebels are near, Inés. If you come, I expect you to protect yourself." I hand her one of my swords. "Stay behind me."

She nods and we slip out of my chamber, robes rustling, keeping to the shadows of the corridors. The deep toll of the palace's bell echoes around the walls. Normally this would signal Sunday service, but it is nighttime and the clanging that pounds in my ears is chaotic rather than melodic. A warning. They've breached the gates. My hands sweat inside my leather gauntlets. Ahead, in the dim light of the candelabras, two rebels stand in our way. This is the great fear of the viceroyalty—an invasion from La Justicia, an army of ruthless and highly skilled rebels sweeping down from the mountains, coming at us in numbers beyond counting.

"All alone, are we?" says the bigger of the two in Nahuatl.

"Please, let us pass," Inés says calmly in her native Purépecha.

The second warrior moves toward me. "Lower your hood."

If I don't give them a look at my face, I'm dead. If I give them a look at my face, I'm dead.

"Lower. It."

"Please," Inés says, "we are on the same side. We don't want any trouble."

The first warrior laughs. "Hear that? She wants peace and love. There is only war and blood, little girl. You sleep in this palace?"

Inés gives a sullen shrug. "Yes, but—"

"You eat in this palace?"

"Yes, but I—"

"You shit in this palace?"

This time, she stays quiet.

"We are not on the same side," he says. "You're a *traitor*." He spits out the last word.

"Don't call her that," I say.

The warrior grumbles between clenched teeth. "Little girl? Or traitor?" He walks up to Inés, getting very close.

"Leave her alone."

"Or *what*? What are you going to do?"

"What I am going to do is not important," I say in their language. "But it's important that you leave her alone, or else you're going to find your answer very quickly, and I don't think you're going to like it very much."

The rebels trade angry glances, spitting out a dozen words in Nahuatl.

There is intent in their eyes, a killing intent.

Now. The time is now.

Flexing my fingers, I will two balls of tonalli into the center of my palms and blast the men upward. They thud against the ceiling before dropping to the floor.

"You didn't have to kill them!" Inés wails.

"They'll live," I say. "But we won't if we don't get out of here. Now."

I jerk my head around, as does Inés, at the sound of an approaching horde. The floor shakes with pounding feet. I snarl and run, kindling enough force to meet them halfway. They are not easily turned away. They come at me, again and again, roaring their battle cries as though their victory is only a scream away. A shrill cry resounds. I startle and turn to see Inés cutting a woman's chest open. The rebel falls, and Inés drops to the floor beside her to close her eyes, says a quick prayer, then vomits when she sees the attacker is still alive, wheezing in terror.

"I'm sorry!" she cries, over and over. "I'm so sorry!"

The woman's blood pours over Inés's hands. There is nothing to be done but send this warrior to Tonatiuh. I plunge my sword into her throat. Inés closes her eyes at last with trembling fingers.

"I can't do this!" Inés sobs.

"Listen to me," I say. "This is battle, and you will be killed where you stand. Either they die, or you do. It's not going to be you. Do you understand?"

She nods, panic clear in her eyes. "What do we do?"

"We have to hide."

We run around a corner, only to be confronted by more rebels.

"Leonora," Inés breathes.

"I know. Get back."

I don't want to fight them; I certainly don't want to kill them, but again, I have little choice in the matter. And at the moment, I'm only thinking of Inés's safety. I come up against ten, twenty warriors advancing on all sides. I take my share of blood, and my share of wounds. Shifting my eyes to Inés, I hear a rebel say to her, "I'm going to kill you, you traitor bitch." I cut him down so she doesn't have to.

The fighting rages all night. The Spanish soldiers endure, for a while. They have no chance to surrender. They are bested by rebels hacking them down with great skill. The ground is strewn with bodies, some dead, some only wounded.

Another warrior is upon me. I trip and land on the floor, and he stands over me to thrust his spear into my gut. As it's coming down, he drops suddenly, pierced through the back.

Inés nods at me, breathless, her face flushed, her sword wet. She reaches for my hand to lift me up. I nod back at her, then turn and leap into a knot of warriors.

My tonalli begins to wane. Blood trickles down my face; I can hardly see, and the skin on my knuckles is shredded, but still the rebels keep coming. I am so fixed upon every weapon coming at me I don't notice Inés's absence right away. I stop breathing. My head twists around. Where is she? Where did she go? Glancing over my shoulder, I see the bodies of the slain. I almost envy them; the dead don't have to suffer the weight of doom.

With a burst of speed, I run to my bedchamber, the dining hall, the library, the kitchens, the courtyard. I sniff the air and catch a hint of her scent, somewhere in the outer buildings of the palace, and I move in its direction. She's inside one of Cortés's houses. I can't get there fast enough.

"Inés?" I say, creeping quietly through the door. An owl screeches. I tug my hood over my face, as far as it will go, and continue walking. Paralyzing fear buzzes through my body, triggering my defenses. I am not alone.

Some fifty rebels shuffle out of the darkness. One of them has Inés about the neck, a knife pressed to her throat.

Prince Felipe.

He must have seen us fighting together. I've never felt so many resentful emotions at once.

I think back to the day we met on *La Capitana*. He looked every inch the regal prince. But beneath the black-and-gold sparkle of opulence, he was hiding something. Now, I know what.

Himself.

It's why he never sent his portrait. Why he fabricated an elaborate story about a storm pushing his ship to Acapulco Bay. Why he didn't want the fuss of a dowry—a negotiation over lands and riches that would have surely exposed him. Why his tonalli felt strangely ordinary. It's because he's not the king's son. He's no more than a clever imitation of the real Prince Felipe, a spy for the rebellion. A charlatan who was able to fool the entire court, including me. An imposter. A very good one.

"You will not take another step, or you will be sorry, Pantera," the imposter says.

"Or *I* will be sorry?" I still, barely keeping my composure.

"Put the blade down," he says. "Don't make me slash her throat."

I think to show him the end of my sword but loosen my grip. "If you try, your life is forfeit. Consider that before you bring harm to yourself."

"I don't see how you are in a position to give me orders. You're surrounded."

"Did he do that to you?" I ask through gritted teeth, pointing at Inés's face, which is streaked with red. Her cheek is slashed open. I promised Inés I wouldn't let anything happen to her. I promised.

"Kill him, Pantera!" Inés says, struggling against the imposter's hold. "I don't care if I live or die! Do it!"

Rage fills me. I lower my blade, letting the tip touch the floor, then drop it. "You've seen what I can do with a sword," I say. "Do you *really* want to see what I can do with sorcery?" No one moves. No one says a word. No one does anything. "Bring me your leader. I wish to speak to him."

"So speak," a stiff voice says. A man in a wooden helmet shaped like a jaguar shoulders his way to the front of the group. The more elaborate the helmet, the more renowned the warrior. I've never seen a Jaguar Knight. After the Fall, I didn't think there were any left. He motions to the others to leave, and the room empties, leaving only the leader, the false prince, and another woman, whose face is covered in red-and-blue war paint.

The imposter releases Inés from his grip, and she stumbles to my side.

"You speak the common tongue?" I ask.

The leader nods. "I'm afraid we weren't introduced the first time we met."

The first time?

He removes his helmet. I examine him. Beneath the grime and blood, he looks somewhat older than me, but his eyes are ancient.

I never forget a face. Not even one I first saw inside a wardrobe. I remember him from Prince Felipe—the imposter's—bedchamber.

"I am Nezahualpilli."

"Are you Sin Rostro?" The faceless leader of La Justicia.

"We are *all* Sin Rostro. We are one face, one voice. For years we've lived in the forest, building an army and preparing to fight a war we did not seek, but a war we are determined to win nonetheless."

"La Justicia," I say.

He nods.

"Was it you?" I ask, barely above a whisper. "*La Capitana*. Were you behind it?"

"I was on that ship. Why would I risk my life in such a way?" the imposter says.

"Who's to say what another man thinks."

"Here's what I think," he says. "Neither of us are who we say we are . . . Leonora."

A flutter goes through my belly.

"Leonora . . ." The imposter tilts his head to the side, his gaze full of certainty, like he's testing my resolve, daring me to deny it. "You talk like Pantera—you act like Pantera—you fight like Pantera—you *are* Pantera."

I lower my guise. There's no point now in lying about who I am.

"You might know the face behind the mask," I say, "but you don't know the first thing about me."

"Yes, I do," the imposter says. "I know first things, second things, third things. To start, you choked me to sleep."

"I was trying to save your life!" I snap.

"You were trying to hide your identity!" he shouts back. "When I first met you, I was impressed with your candor. Then I remembered someone who was exactly the same way, a woman willing to stand up for what she believed. What better way to fight injustice than to assume a disguise of some sort—to make people believe that you are something you are not, Pantera?"

I am quiet, withdrawing into myself. Bracing.

"Enemy of my enemy," Nezahualpilli says, "do not worry. We have no intention of revealing this to anyone. Your secret is safe with us."

"You invaded the palace," I say, barely managing to keep it together. "You murdered innocents. You wounded Inés. One of your own tried to kill me in Chapultepec. You slaughtered a dozen soldiers with deadly arrows and took our horses. Is this how you seek justice?"

"Were they unclothed?" Nezahualpilli asks.

"What?"

"The men who attacked you."

"What does it matter?"

"It matters," Nezahualpilli says, "because the bow is not our principal weapon. We have been accused of many things, and we are guilty of some of those. But we did not sink *La Capitana*. Nor did we ambush you in the woods."

"Children of the Wind," the woman with the red-and-blue war paint says. "They're the best archers in the world. So brazen they run into battle with no covering at all. It has a startling effect on the Spaniards."

"This is Eréndira," Nezahualpilli says. "She sees all."

Inés steps forward. "Uanancha . . . Eréndira?" *Princess.* Inés has taught me a little of her language. She says something else that I don't understand, then something I do. "My . . . my mother told me stories about you when I was little. I thought you were dead."

The woman—Eréndira—gives a sly smirk. "I am old, but I am difficult to conquer." She does not seem old. To me, she has youth, strength, and a beauty that sharpens that proud smile.

"You were attacked by the Chichimeca and their prince, Xico," Eréndira says, her dark eyes set on me. "The Chichimeca fiercely dislike intrusion into their territory, which happens to contain mines your people are exploiting for silver. They assault mining camps and ranches, especially caravans traveling Royal Road."

I am reminded of the Spaniards' twofold mission: to exploit the region's mineral wealth and convert its native population to Christianity.

"The Chichimeca are angry," Nezahualpilli adds. "They are fierce and formidable, and they have learned to ride horses. I must say I am impressed. You survived their attack."

"Your imposter is alive because of me. Now leave," I say, my attention on Nezahualpilli, "take your men and women with you, and you will be spared death."

The usurper scoffs. "I told you, Neza. She's as stubborn as a mule," he says to him, then turns his head toward me. "I was foolish to think that you of all people would understand."

"Me of all people?"

"You fight, just as we do," the imposter says.

"Listen, Nezahualpilli—"

"Call me Neza," he says.

"Neza, there's one understanding we need to reach," I say, then look at my betrothed. "He *is* going to marry me."

The imposter quirks an eyebrow. "But . . . I am not a prince."

"Exactly." The vicereine doesn't know that. And what she doesn't know *can* and *will* be used in my favor. "The plan has changed. You want justice. I want freedom. You might not be an imposter, but my betrothal to the true Prince Felipe remains very real. I can do nothing for La Justicia if I am to leave for Spain to marry the king's son. So, I will marry you instead."

"If you were queen," says the imposter, "you'd be in a position of power to help."

I chuckle. "I'd have a fancy crown all to myself, but a queen consort has no power. That has always been vested in kings."

Neza and the imposter exchange glances.

"If I say no?" the imposter asks.

"Your choices are incredibly limited . . . alteza," I say. "You might have ended lives tonight, but you will not save your rebellion like this. You and I will wed, so long as no one discovers who you really are. After the wedding, you will tell the truth. I have been deceived, but regrettably, we are already married. In this way, I will not become queen. I will stay here, making clear my desire for the building and enforcement of Indigenous laws, and for achieving justice. I ask no man to die, or even to bleed."

"We are past peace," says Neza. "This is war. We are here for Pantera, not Leonora."

The imposter blows out a breath. "The plan was to gain access to the palace, find out its weaknesses, and acquire information about everything that goes on in court. It was never supposed to come to this, Leonora. We cannot marry. My hair and skin are fair, and my eyes are blue. Do you think that is a coincidence?"

"Probably not."

"My father made powerful enemies in court. Enemies that would see me dead should they know I was still breathing. Does the name El Mestizo mean anything to you?"

"Should it?"

"I am Martín," he says. "Martín Cortés."

Cortés. That is a name that carries its weight in the New World.

I scoff. "That's a nice story, but I happen to know Don Martín lives in Cuernavaca. You are not the heir of Hernán Cortés."

"There are *two* sons of the conqueror—both named Martín," Eréndira says.

"You're right. I'm not a don." The imposter shakes his head. "My father also named my younger brother Martín. They call me El Mestizo because I'm the bastard son of Hernán Cortés and Malintzin. You may know her as La Malinche."

"Whoa," Inés breathes. "You're Doña Marina's son?"

La Malinche has many names. She was a Nahua princess, slave, interpreter, negotiator, known for her role as Hernán Cortés's translator. Regarded as a traitor to her own people, as she served the conquistadors, she is not revered by many. Translator or traitor? I don't know. But the son of Cortés and La Malinche has both European and Indigenous blood. He is a mestizo, like me.

I frown. "That's . . . not possible."

"And, yet, here I am, the firstborn. Don Martín Cortés y Zuñiga is my younger brother. I'm Martín Cortés El Mestizo. Martín after the Roman god of war. Martín in memory of the soldier-saint, Martín de Tours. Martín in honor of my grandfather in Spain. My father liked the name."

"Well, congratulations, Martín, bastard of Cortés," I say. "Your father was a greedy murderer."

"I am *not* him," he says angrily. "I might look like him, but I am not Hernán Cortés."

"Then why are you telling me this?"

"It seems fair, as we know so much about you, Pantera," he says.

"You need more than a mask and a sword to fight off what is coming," Neza says. "You need an army."

A knot tightens in my stomach.

"I'm building an alliance," Neza says. "We will take back our rightful place in this world. We owe it to those who died fighting, to our brothers and sisters, our fathers and mothers. We owe it to them to see the day when we can say three things: we did not consent, we did not give up, we did not surrender.

"Pantera's efforts against the white invaders have not gone unnoticed. We have heard of your reputation and good work. Join us. We need warriors and . . . whatever else you are."

"Don't you understand?" I protest. "That's what they want you to do. You are seen as a danger to New Spain. If you fight, then they win. The viceroy listens to opinions which differ from his own. Let me reason with him. If it doesn't work—"

"When," Neza interrupts.

"*If* it doesn't work," I say, "then we do it your way. Do we have a deal?" I hold out my arm.

For a moment, Neza considers my proposition, then he tucks his hand into the crook of my elbow.

CHAPTER 19

La Regente

The first thing I do the next day is go to Vicereine Carlota. She is in her chamber, vigorously fanning herself while a guitarist plays a melody. Her relaxed behavior betrays her arrogance; how little she cares for the lives of those she sees as beneath her, those who fell in last night's battle.

"It was you, wasn't it?"

The guitarist winces at my raised voice and slides his finger along the wrong string with tragic force. With a roll of her eyes, the vicereine makes a small motion of the hand, and he slips out the nearest door.

"You're going to have to be more specific, cariño."

"You sank *La Capitana*." I slam my brooch on the small table in front of her. "Some birthday gift you claimed from the salvage. Don't even try to deny it. Lady Amalia has it on good authority that all emeralds are reserved for the Crown. This brooch could only have come from one place. A treasure ship bound for Spain."

"Yes," she says indifferently, as if I asked whether she wants her bath drawn. "My plan worked, or at least as much as I allowed it to."

Murderer! I want to shout, but the screams of those who died by my hand stop me. Instead, I curse in Nahuatl.

Snapping her fan shut, Carlota gets up from her seat and slaps me. How dare I speak the language of the Indians?

I absorb the blow, so horrified I can barely speak. "Why did you do this?"

She walks to the window and flutters her fan. "See for yourself."

I go to her side. In the grand courtyard below, guards put prisoners to work, cleaning up the aftermath of La Justicia's attack. At least ten mangled corpses hang like cuts of meat from trees for everyone to see. I glance away, my stomach heaving.

"We cannot sustain this war," she says. "The cost is too great. We don't have enough soldiers, weapons, or horses because every day they are stolen by the savages. I have written letters to the Crown about the events of the war and how dire the situation is, with the heathens attacking us in such great numbers. You must marry soon, Leonora. It is your duty. I give them a queen. They give me an army."

"Sinking a ship overloaded with stolen riches from the New World to replenish the viceroyal purse makes you no better than a common thief," I grit out. "In fact, it makes you worse."

"The whole is greater than the sum of its parts. If you're ever to rule, you must learn to forsake such things in the face of more important needs."

"I almost died!"

She dismisses the claim with a lazy wave. "Do you believe I would put the king's son and his future bride in danger? You were safe, until you decided to wander off. Didn't I tell you to dance with the prince? Perhaps my methods were a bit extreme, but every war has its casualties."

Her words are a kick to my gut. I gasp for air and lean on the sill to keep standing. "Casualties like Doña Cayetana?"

She sighs as if I am tiresomely stupid.

"You poisoned her. That much is abundantly apparent. The wine—you had it waiting for her. I know it was you."

"You are either an ally or an enemy," she says. "Doña Cayetana was an enemy."

"Because she spread the news about Lady Amalia's pregnancy to the entire palace?"

"Because she was not an ally."

I know something the vicereine doesn't. Lady Amalia is no longer a real enemy because Martín is not a real prince. He is the son of a conquistador. He will never be king. Whether Lady Amalia is with child or not, she will never be his mistress. Once I wed Martín and secure my stay in the capital, we'll tell everyone the truth. Then Lady Amalia will be nothing more than a distant memory.

"Have you no shame?"

"Shame? I am doing God's work," she says flatly, her face like stone, as if I am no more than a dramatic child. "God did not simply create the world, populate it with people, and then leave them to muddle through on their own with no oversight from Him. Rather, God is in control of His creation. If it was God's will that Doña Cayetana die, why should I feel guilty? I've done nothing terrible."

God's will? What kind of hypocrite orders Doña Cayetana's murder and then enforces laws that condemn the killing of innocents? With every word a new wave of anger flares up inside of me.

"Did my brother agree to this?"

As if my words summoned him, the door bursts open and Jerónimo walks in.

"I agreed to no such thing," he says, his voice soft, but full of impending thunder.

Silence descends for a moment, then the vicereine says, "This is a private conversation."

He takes a quick step forward. "Do not speak to me like I am a cupbearer. I've heard it all."

"You forget who addresses you," the vicereine says, her head held high with scorn.

"You forget who addresses *you*. Soy el virrey. You are my proxy. You rule on my behalf, not on your own. You bow to me!"

"I bow to the king," she says bitterly.

"I was appointed by the Crown to rule this territory. I am sovereign. Bend the knee, Lady Mother." She doesn't. "Bend the knee and swear fealty to me."

Vicereine Carlota kneels before him. It is a moment of victory, but I do not revel in it.

"I have heard your confession, Lady Mother. You have committed murder and treason. You are to travel to Cuernavaca. Cortés built his hacienda there, which he left to his son Don Martín, the Marquess of the Valley of Oaxaca." The imposter Martín's younger brother, the worthy son of his father. "It has become a gathering place for our Spanish lords, who love to wander about its gardens. Don Martín is the heir of Cortés and could prove himself an enemy of the viceroyalty when he becomes of age. You are to position yourself inconspicuously and watch him. You will meet with no one else and do nothing except send me letters on his capacities and intentions. You will be served by my people; your own servants will be turned away. Do I make myself clear?"

Vicereine Carlota pushes herself off the floor. "House arrest? Don't be silly."

"You may stay down on your knees."

"For the love of God, I am not the criminal here. The real enemy is out there! I am your mother! I am the vicereine! You can't just banish me from court."

"Spare me the protests. It's simple," he says, with a casualness that almost puts me at ease. "I will name someone to fill the position, seeing as you can no longer serve."

"You don't have the authority to decide such a matter."

"No, I do not, which is why *you* will, unless you prefer execution for poisoning Doña Cayetana or prosecution by the Crown for sinking one of their galleons and robbing its treasure. God knows what other atrocities you've committed."

I give the tiniest smile. In that moment, I forget he is my little brother, a fourteen-year-old boy. He is the viceroy of New Spain.

"But who will be viceregent?" Vicereine Carlota doesn't hesitate to nominate Captain Nabarres. "Narcizo has the greatest prestige in the Audiencia."

Captain Nabarres? Not in this world.

"I think you misunderstand. I have someone in mind. It is not easy to rule on the king's behalf," the viceroy says, his voice business-like. "I need an intelligent counselor who cares about this colony and its people as much as I do. I also need a counselor capable of under-standing my mind and heart. This person would be able to share—and occasionally lift—the burden of my power." As he says this, his eyes shift to me. Me? He wants *me* to be viceregent?

"Jerónimo," Vicereine Carlota says calmly, trying her best to hide her irritation, "you can't possibly think—"

"You may not speak my name."

She assumes her humblest expression. "Excelencia. Leonora is not a suitable candidate. She is a mixed-blood. She lived a pagan child-hood. It's entirely against protocol. Council will never agree to such a demand."

"Then you had better try your hardest to convince them otherwise, Mother," Jerónimo says. "There is no one else I trust to hold power for me. You will do this. We must ensure that the viceroyalty stands strong before Spain. King Carlos was impressed by Father's achieve-ments, and that is the only reason I have filled this office, but this administration cannot survive on his memory forever—and neither can we."

As viceregent, I suppose I could wield some power. Not to mention it would allow me to fulfill my side of the bargain with La Justicia.

I've been baptized twice in the Christian church, neither time by my own consent. Once as a babe, and again as an adult when I returned to the palace, to make sure I wouldn't burn in Hell for my heathen upbringing. Peninsulares hold the best administrative and religious posts, having both prestige and social status. The Crown doesn't allow mixed-bloods political power, for we were weaned on the milk of Indigenous mothers and nurses and have breathed only pagan air. They think there is no solution to this condition, that it makes us weak. They are wrong.

Vicereine Carlota sighs and shakes her head, needing all her will to restrain her temper. "New Spain needs a firm hand on the tiller. You are making a grave mistake."

"I have made my decision," Jerónimo says.

"May God help us if this colony is to be run by children."

Quietly regal in my long-trained purple brocade, I stand before the viceroy's most trusted advisors, watching as Vicereine Carlota joins the other ministers seated around a refectory table beneath an enormous painting of a young King Carlos. The portrait serves as his proxy.

"It is my wish," Vicereine Carlota says in a firm voice, leaving no room for anyone to doubt her authority, "that Lady Leonora be appointed regent in my stead while I recover my health and strength."

There are raised eyebrows and widened eyes. As expected, the proposition stirs controversy. All members seem fully aware of the implications of my appointment. Vicereine Carlota intervenes, instructing council she wants me to take over despite my lower caste and speaking in favor of an immediate announcement. Jerónimo supports a quick decision. Vicereine Carlota nods to me that I can take a seat. The meeting lasts well into the afternoon and the servants bring refreshments. Apparently, this is common because everyone keeps working as they eat, deciding on demands from every courtier for a hearing, for a place, for a slice of land or a favor, or a post.

I find myself rubbing my gloved hands against my skirt underneath the table. My dress and hairpiece itch. My whole body burns. I scratch at the trim of my corset, then hide my hands underneath the table again. I try to take a deep breath, but the bodice is too tight.

Maintaining control of the colony is a full-time job and requires a sure hand. Someone untrained can easily lose control. Someone like me. I'm sure this is why the vicereine suggested I attend the meeting, to make me realize how little I know about how the colony is run. What I do know, what I have known since my infancy, is that I'm a child of the Nemontemi. I can't escape my curse. I should've been sacrificed the moment I left my mother's womb, for what kind of life could I live, born under an unlucky day sign? Fated for misery and misfortune. What good would I do? What *can* I do? If I'm destined to die young, to fall in battle, am I making things worse by delaying the inevitable?

Eventually, Vicereine Carlota and the men retire, leaving me alone in the room with Jerónimo. He remains seated at the table, his pen scribbling quickly across a page.

"I'm outlining an entry for my history. We accomplished quite a lot today." He adds his page of notes to the stack beside him, looking up with a smile. "I like us working together."

"I must be honest with you," I say. "I don't think I should be regent. I will serve as your counsel in any matter of court, but I'm not suitable for the regency."

He sits back in his chair. "Because of your lower caste? Leonora, I'm the viceroy. Do you think anyone thought that would happen? Father certainly didn't. He never taught me anything. The job is mine nonetheless. We all do as we must. Is it Captain Nabarres? I know you don't like him. This was a rather unusual meeting. They don't always run long."

"I'm afraid it's more complicated than that."

"What is it, then?"

"I am cursed, brother."

"What?" He scoffs. "You are *not* cursed."

"The seer at my baptism, he predicted this. He foretold I would die young in battle in the Fifth Sun. Your Excellency, this *is* the age of the Fifth Sun."

He stares at me tiredly. His pudgy cheeks are blotchy. "This man predicted your death?"

"He did."

"What a terrible burden to place on someone."

"Perhaps, but it has always been mine to bear."

"Leonora, you are a child of God," he says pleasantly. "Be assured He loves you. Let Him carry your worries. Through His goodness and grace, I know you'll fulfill your duties as regent with the utmost loyalty and dedication."

I may have been gone ten years, but Jerónimo is my blood, my brother. First there was just me, then he came, and as his older sister, I swore to protect him, to be by his side no matter what, teach him all I knew. I watched him grow. In my best memories, my brother is there. But I'm looking at him now, and I no longer see the two-year-old running from the artist tasked with painting his portrait, climbing into my arms to take comfort. He is the viceroy of New Spain, and to become his trusted counsel, to ask his cooperation with La Justicia, I must gain the viceroy's trust, not the boy's.

"I've never told anyone how I got lost in the woods that day," I say, my throat tightening, the memory alive as though it happened yesterday. "I was not allowed to leave the palace. I wanted to see something of the world that lay beyond these walls. The glimpses I'd had of the outside merely had the effect of increasing my disquiet. I pleaded with Father. I was always met with the same answer—the times were dangerous, rebels could be lying in wait for me, I would be assaulted, perhaps beaten to death. Someday I might be able to come and go as I wished. I didn't understand then, but I do now. He was afraid . . . of the curse, though he never admitted it."

Looking back, death would've been preferable. But I was given no choice, and Father was practical. Isolation was the better alternative. Mourning the loss of a child while a rebellion was stirring would only have weakened the viceroyalty.

I take a deep breath and exhale. "I was always a restless child, with a restless mind. When I did finally leave, the occasion was not a joyous one. I wandered too far into the woods. I couldn't find my way back. Then . . . I saw people. Natives. They took me in, fed me, and cared for me."

"Where did you go?" His voice turns sad. "Why didn't you come back? Why didn't you tell us you were alive?" he asks, searching my eyes for answers.

I look down, and in the silence that stretches between us, I hear all the reasons that I can't voice. I can't tell my brother about the place in the misty sky where beautiful, life-giving flowers bloom. I can't tell him that there I vowed allegiance to Totoquilhuaztli, better known as Toto. Chief of Sorcerers, Creator of the Book of Destinies, Nagual Headmaster . . .

My master.

"I wanted to," is all I say.

"Ten years, Leonora," he says, "and everyone thought you were dead. We grieved for you."

"You were a boy of four then."

"You are my family. You are my sister. Father never stopped looking for you. When everyone else had given up, he didn't. He couldn't."

"I know I am different," I say, "I'm not what I was. Death stalks me and this colony. The threat is—"

Jerónimo holds up a hand to silence me. "What happened is past. You are not cursed. El diablo is the enemy, prowling around like a roaring lion looking for someone to devour."

"You don't understand," I say sadly.

"You are just like my mother, thinking me stupid."

"What? No, Jerónimo, that's not what I—"

"I have heard your curse, but do not expect me to open my mind to the influence of the Devil. Scripture condemns those who practice astrology, divination, and sorcery. Nothing is done outside of God's control. He either causes or allows everything in keeping with His divine plan. We will drink to your new position. That is all."

156

"Drink?" It seems outrageous.

"Yes. And I will pray for you."

"What about Prince Felipe?"

"What about him?"

"Have you forgotten he is to be my husband?"

"He is welcome to stay in the palace until you are wed and leave for Spain. Then I will either find a more suitable viceregent, wait until I am old enough to rule, or find myself a wife. Whichever happens first."

"That will take time, Jerónimo," I say, "time you do not have." *Nor I.* "How long before King Carlos sends another viceroy to replace you?"

"We will hasten the wedding."

"That is not your decision to make," I argue. "It's the king's."

He groans in frustration. "Why are you opposing me?" He turns his attention to his pages and waves a hand at me. "Leave."

"But I—"

He levels me a harsh glare. "I said leave."

It's hard to bite my tongue, but if Jerónimo is to start trusting me and doing as I advise, I'm going to have to prove we're on the same side.

"I wish to speak to our heavenly Father," I say. "Will you pray with me?"

His mouth forms a hesitant smile. He can't refuse. "Yes, of course."

We kneel beside each other on the floor and hold hands. Jerónimo makes the sign of the Cross. "In nomine Patris, et Filii, et Spiritus Sancti."

I clasp my hands together. "Beloved Father, I ask you to grant me the wisdom I need to guide Jerónimo on Your chosen path. To do it with integrity and diligence. Please, dear Lord, keep my brother safe in Your care."

I don't feel His presence. I don't know Him, and I don't care to. But I do care that Jerónimo cares for Him.

"Amen," he echoes. "It's nice to hear you praying."

I smile demurely and look at my hands. "I fear I'm not doing it correctly. Will you show me?"

He beams, as if the sweetest words poured into his willing ears. He puts his hand on mine. "Nothing would make me happier."

Progress.

CHAPTER 20

La Espada

Inés is released from the infirmary, where she spent the past week. A deep, diagonal cut takes up most of the right side of her face. I try not to react when I see it and condemn everyone who was involved. It isn't easy. My anger is visceral. As she steps inside my chamber, I lock her arm with mine and we move toward the window bench, causing a cluster of pigeons to burst into flight.

"Come and sit. I have your favorites today," I say, indicating the small table where a dish of thick, sweet chocolate, and a plate of churros sit along with a teapot.

"Are these my welcome-back presents?"

When we're both seated, I pour the tea. "I just want to talk." I drop a lump of sugar into her cup.

"Talk?" Inés raises an eyebrow. "Oh, I understand. No one's tried to kill you since last week. The boredom must be overwhelming."

I sigh. "That didn't seem so bad. Go ahead. Do your worst."

"Do you think about the people you've killed?"

I nod. "All the time. I also think about the people who I haven't. Believe it or not, there was a time when I didn't dare kill a spider."

"The first time you killed, you told me that you were scared."

"That's why I did it." I frown. "Because I was scared, not because

159

I was afraid of doing it. Fear can make you do things you never thought you would."

Inés carries the weight of war. Taking lives is not easy. The person whose life is taken is dead in a few seconds if they're lucky. But the one taking the life dies a little more each day. Because of the Spanish, Inés grew up alone on the streets, sleeping anywhere and doing what she could for food—stealing, breaking into houses, fending for herself. She has a gentle heart.

"I'm sorry you had to kill. You had no choice," I assure her, hoping to ease her conscience. "It wasn't your fault."

She narrows her gaze, and I notice her furrowed eyebrows. For a moment, they're all I can look at. I focus on them instead of the bright red scar on her cheek.

"I'm not angry with you," she says. "That night . . . it just brought back memories. Memories I wish I could forget."

"Your mother?"

There is so much in her silence, so much she still won't say. A torment in her mind. Some scars are invisible. I know Inés carries her share.

She reaches for a churro, dips it in chocolate, and begins to nibble. "Is there something you want to ask me?"

"Does it hurt?" I say softly, my gaze lingering on her scar.

She gives me a smile, which *does* hurt. "It pulses," she says, fingering the mark gingerly. "Sometimes it throbs."

"Oh." The word comes out like a lament.

"Don't look so morose, Leonora. It's only a scar. I think it adds character. So, did you miss me?"

I chuckle.

"What? I like to hear sweet nothings every now and then. Come on, how much did you miss me? Very badly, rather badly, or only a little?"

"I suppose it *was* rather dull without you," I say, but in truth, it felt like the longest week of my life. If something happened to her . . . I kiss the top of her head, hugging her tightly. This isn't me, this tender, affectionate being, and yet it's who I am right now. She draws it out of me.

"The woman," I say, "the one you called princess."

"Eréndira," Inés replies.

I nod. "You said your mother told you about her."

"Yes." Inés smiles as if remembering a sweet moment. "When Cortés was done with Tenochtitlan, he turned to Michoacan, the home of my people. The king had a daughter, Eréndira, seventeen years of age. She didn't submit to the Spaniards. My mother told me she learned how to ride a horse, a white stallion, and soon they became inseparable."

"If she was seventeen then," I say, "that would make her old. She seemed youthful to me, full of warm tonalli."

Inés looks at me over the brim of her cup as she takes a sip of her tea. "There are many stories about the princess. In one of them, her father the king was tortured and killed, and Eréndira fled on her horse to lead a resistance against the Spaniards."

"Then what happened?"

"You will have to ask her," Inés says with a shrug. "She was never seen again."

The jaguar is an elusive cat. It sleeps during the day and hunts at night.

Wearing my guise, I sit quietly in Andrés's room, hidden by shadows. He enters, shrugs off his jacket, and tosses it carelessly toward a chair. It hits, then slithers to the floor. He doesn't bother to pick it up.

"Someone's in a sour mood," I say.

He slumps on to the bed and rolls up his sleeves, exposing thick forearms, then bends over to pull off his boots.

"What do you want, Pantera?"

"You know what I want. Where have you been?"

"Supplying Captain Nabarres with more of the sage advice that led him to station his men all around the perimeter of the palace, armed and ready to take action against an attack."

An attack?

I shoot up from my seat. "You *knew*. You knew of La Justicia's plot to attack the palace and you warned Captain Nabarres. You are a spy and a traitor."

He sighs. "I have ears in every crack and crevice of these lands. That does not make me a spy. I roll in the mud with an animal like Nabarres and exaggerate to gain his confidence. That does not make me a traitor."

"It makes you exactly that!" I snap. But then I think about my own theatrics to earn the viceroy's trust, and I fall silent.

"Ask yourself how they would have been able to enter the island undetected."

I scoff. "Unbelievable. No, no, actually quite believable. Predictable in fact. It makes complete sense. You're a liar, Andrés. A liar, a thief, and a pretender. Is there nothing you won't stoop to?"

"I'm confused as to what you're upset about. Is it because I didn't tell you La Justicia would invade the palace?"

I don't know where his allegiances lie. I can't ask. I refuse. We're not partners. We're not friends. We aren't on the same side. He doesn't work for me or owe me anything. We aren't committed to each other. I remind myself of that.

"All those slaughtered . . . blood was spilled. And for what? The future? There'll be no future if the prophecy—" I bite my lip to keep from saying more.

"Prophecy?" he asks, brows knitted.

I breathe deeply, taking a moment to compose myself. "A better man would've stopped the attack from happening at all."

Fortunately, I rouse his temper more than his curiosity. "Pantera . . ." he says with strained patience, "if you think I planned this, or that scratching Nabarres's back is how I wish to spend my days, you are gravely mistaken. I have my own agenda."

"Oh, *really*? And what would that be? Capturing Pantera for Captain Nabarres? Are you personally going to deliver me to him? Is that why you were in Mexicapan?"

He crosses his arms. "Tell me to go."

"What?"

"If I'm such a nuisance to you, tell me to go and I'll go."

"You're offering to walk away?"

"Say the word, and you'll never see me again."

I waver.

"You may not like me, Pantera. You may not agree with what I do or how I do it, but you know as well as I that I am privy to information about nearly everyone and everything in the colony. I'm also a notorious fiend and unfailingly prone to deceit, but I have answers to questions you don't even realize exist yet. Consider it in your best interests to ask me to stay."

My laugh is short, strangled. "You are mad."

"Right, then. Good luck finding your sword," he says, then walks to the door.

Nine Hells. "Stay," I blurt out, more loudly than I intended.

He turns around. "Say it again."

"Do you want me to sing it to you?"

"Say it again."

My sigh is almost a groan. "Stay."

"You have to understand something, Pantera. Without words, there is no peace. Captain Nabarres is a great orator; he can charm birds out of trees. He speaks Spanish and Latin and has won positions of power thanks to his eloquent speeches, but he does not speak Nahuatl. It's important to seal alliances with my people, negotiate, win them over, and all this can only be done with a tongue Nabarres lacks. He would give half his life if he could master the language.

"Though I am instructed in Christianity and took the name Andrés de Ayeta after the Spanish priest who baptized me, I am Tlahuica. Nabarres doesn't know how faithful I am to his words or how capable

I am of betrayal. He has another interpreter, a shipwrecked Spaniard who lived among the Tlaxcaltecah for years and learned the language. Nabarres feared I would double-cross him and had that man nearby just in case. But after sharing intelligence with Nabarres about La Justicia, I have his trust and there's no further need for the other interpreter. Now I am Nabarres's voice. The *only* voice."

That makes Andrés equally powerful. But is he equally wicked?

"I know you don't trust me," he continues. "We are strangers still, in spite of our previous, shall we say, close encounters." He stands. From a hiding place in the wall, he retrieves a scabbard and brings it to me.

My heart beats rapidly. I grip the sheath and pull out the sword, *my* sword. My anger instantly disappears as I take hold of the hilt and lift it, craving the comfort of its power, the coolness of the metal. You have not held a sword until you have handled the Sword of Integrity.

"It's heavier than I remember." I turn the blade in the moonlight, as alive with exhilaration as the first time the blade chose me. We are bonded. A spark of hope ignites within me, the anticipation of good things to come. I haven't had hope in so long that it's as foreign as it is welcome.

And as quickly as it comes, it disappears.

"No, no, no," I mutter to myself, waiting for the sword to recognize me. "This can't be happening."

"What can't be happening?"

"It doesn't glow green at my touch!"

"What kind of sword does that?"

As I hand it to him and he closes his fist around the handle, a quiet gasp escapes my lips, as if I am again relinquishing my soul, my life, my power.

"Only one who has integrity can light the sword. The Sword of Integrity fights true—for me alone," I say bleakly, facing away. "At least it used to. I'm no longer worthy."

"Pantera?"

I turn around to see a green glow in his hand. *His*, not mine.

Impossible, and yet it is happening.

I sigh and speak in a low, broken voice. "The Sword of Integrity is a powerful weapon, and in the wrong hands it could be disastrous. Sometimes you choose the sword. Sometimes the sword chooses you. It seems to have chosen to serve you next," I say sadly. It has forgotten my hand, and now knows his.

Andrés looks at me, searching my mask for what—I don't know. "You said you grew up in the jungle. Who taught you how to fight?"

"You wouldn't believe me if I told you. No one would."

"Oh, I don't know. I've heard a thing or two in my day."

"If we're getting to know each other," I say, "then I want to know who you really are."

He opens his arms wide. "Look at me. I'm not the one wearing a mask."

"We all wear masks, Ayeta. Mine is just more obvious than yours."

He draws a sharp breath. "I would say that you owe me considerably more than I owe you. Where did you learn how to fight, Pantera?"

"Tamoanchan," I croak. The oldest Nahua tales speak of the place in the misty sky, the abode of the gods, but the lore has been lost since the First Sun, and its true location is shrouded in legend.

He gives a snort of almost laughter.

"See? I knew you wouldn't believe me. What I told you is the truth. Either you believe me or you don't. I don't care."

"Assuming such a place exists outside your head, why did you leave paradise?"

"I didn't," I reply stiffly. "Not voluntarily. My master dismissed me. Something about me being erratic, wild, and untethered. I wasn't a good student. I didn't want to practice the way he wanted me to." I would say more, but my throat closes, and I have to tilt my head up to stop the tears that threaten to spill. No one ever asked me if

165

I wanted to be a sorceress. Master just said it was my destiny, and when I failed to live up to his teachings, he abandoned me.

Even watching me through my mask, Andrés must see that I am about to fall apart, right here, right now, because he does exactly what I need him to . . . nothing at all. I didn't want him to do anything, not try to understand me, nor fix my anger or sadness, offer me advice, a word of comfort, a solution. I just wanted him to listen.

"A sword that doesn't glow green is still a sword," he says, "and that's a fine thing to have when enemies are all around."

He flips the Sword of Integrity and offers me its handle. I take it before climbing out the window.

CHAPTER 21

El Plan

Tonatiuh is the color of blood as his rays stream through the windows of the council chamber, yet my mind is clouded with gray.

"La Justicia is building an army," Captain Nabarres says, sweeping his gaze around the table, meeting the eyes of each member of the Audiencia in turn. "They plot against this viceroyalty. If we don't fight back now, it might as well be theirs."

"How strong are your convictions, capitán?" Bartolo de Molina asks. "Are you prepared to die for them?"

"What do you know of war, Don Bartolo? Tell us," Nabarres says in a bored voice.

"I know nothing of war," Don Bartolo says, "but I know La Justicia is a snake with many heads. We cut one head off, two more grow in its place. We've no chance of withstanding another attack. We need all able soldiers here. These lands—they are not ours to do with as we will. They never have been. The sooner we accept that, the sooner we can begin to understand what role exists for us. And if that role is to live as guests, then so be it. It has to be better than being dead. I, for one, am sick of a war that has been raging for so long."

"Excelencia." Nabarres levels his gaze at the viceroy. "Now is the time to bring the fight to the enemy. In the name of Spain. For our king. For our god."

Fray Anonasi crosses himself. "We have tried to civilize them with religion. My apostles have established schools and churches. They will not be civilized. They refuse. They worship pagan gods who take on many forms, and they will not recant their faith. Nothing remains for us to do but deliver all that God's justice demands."

"Leonora?"

I turn to look at the viceroy, lost in a haze.

"You're my counsel," he says.

"Of course." I straighten in my chair, my spine crackling with tension. "You are fighting an old war, excelencia. Thousands of men have been sent to their graves. Not to mention, if there is another quake, there will be more fatalities. Peace is the only reasonable solution that allows us to continue our existence."

Don Cino is overcome with fury. "Peace? Those animals murdered my wife! They delivered her head to me!"

"Why?" I ask.

"*Why?*" He guffaws. "Since when have the savages needed a reason to kill?"

I exhale harshly. "We don't call them savages, Don Cino."

"Did I call them savages? Is that what I said?"

"You did."

"Her Ladyship will forgive my insolence," he says, his words coated with derision. "Should I have said barbarians? Brutes? Monsters?"

I bite my tongue to keep the wave of angry remarks from spilling out of my mouth.

"Cino, *por favor*," Don Bartolo says in a sharp whisper.

"My deepest sympathy for the loss of your wife, Don Cino." My words sound hollow, but I mean them. "No one else needs to die. We can end this war."

"Absolute nonsense." He harrumphs in disgust. "You think if we stay here, with our arms crossed, the indios will magically leave us alone?"

"No, not magically," I say. "With reforms and the enforcement of laws. Speaking of which, the Crown passed the New Laws to abolish the encomienda system and ensure the just and moral treatment of Indigenous peoples. Why have they been ignored?"

"Diplomacy!" Don Cino, himself an encomendero, spits out the word. "They sent me her damn head! We might as well sit here and braid each other's beards until our enemies are beating down our walls. *Again!* The rebels are allying themselves with any and all forces to revolt. My men tell me the bruja Pantera was recruited by La Justicia, and when the full treachery of their plot against us was revealed to her, she did not reject it."

"Your men?" I say, trying to keep my voice level. He doesn't know that. He can't.

"I am Minister of Intelligence, my lady."

"And what was Pantera's response? Did your men tell you that? What was it? Tell me, Don Cino, tell me her words exactly."

Captain Nabarres leaps from his chair, suddenly furious. "Am I surrounded by children? What do you need to see? The rebels here with swords drawn at our throats? All of us in this room are targets! They know where we are. What's stopping them from attacking again?"

"Change or return to Spain," I say. "Those are your options."

"Careful, señorita," Nabarres says.

"Have I offended you?"

"You overreach."

"Enough, capitán," the viceroy says.

"Excelencia," Nabarres says, "I've grown weary of doubters. This is fearmongering of the worst kind, and I will not stand for it. We are not deserters. We are conquerors."

Viceroy Jerónimo leans forward on his chair. "What is it you're proposing, exactly?"

"The indios believe they are agents of their pagan gods, chosen people with a divine mission to rule and take responsibility for the passage of the sun across the sky, which requires human hearts and blood. You see, this is not a war being fought over territory, to seize land, or for plunder. It is a war of ideas, of beliefs as to how many gods there are and whose god is the true God. That's what we're fighting here. This is our enemy. Not La Justicia. But an *idea*. How do we fight paganism?"

Nabarres flattens a map across the table. "Through my allies, I have gained an understanding of their religious beliefs and learned of the symbolic importance of the ahuehuete. This tree can be found growing within Coatepec, here," he says, pointing to an area on the map. "The indios think it is their connection to their false gods. We strike at the heart of their movement and sever the artery through which their faith is supplied, and then we shall see how the heathens survive in a world without their gods."

My grip tightens on the arms of my chair. Coatepec. Snake Mountain. La Justicia's home.

I feel like kicking something, shoving my fist through the wall, flying across the table at Captain Nabarres, punching him until I make a hole in his head.

Instead, I eye him defiantly and say, "La Justicia outnumber us. They are composed of different clans and have settlements spread across the forest. Much of the mountain is under their control. To attack even a quarter of their known communities, you would have to divide your army into nothing more than raiding parties that would make La Justicia laugh."

"Which is even more reason to attack *now*," Nabarres says. "I don't plan to fail."

Jerónimo holds up a hand. "I've heard enough. I must seek guidance from above."

Captain Nabarres takes a deep breath as he places his palms on the table and leans over them. "Perhaps, excelencia, we should discuss matters of war when hair grows between your legs."

Jerónimo jumps from his chair, dead white. "I am not a child!" The scream echoes around the room. "I will do whatever I think is necessary, whatever is required of me to protect this colony! No one, not *you* or anyone else, will tell me any differently!" His voice is shrill and uncontrolled. "Understood?"

"Yes, excelencia."

"Then rest, capitán. Gather your men. Make love to your wives. Tell stories to your children. Eat hearty. We shall raise lions to the sky within a fortnight."

He means war.

Nabarres smiles, fondling his beard with bejeweled fingers. "That is a sound plan, excelencia."

I bridle at the amusement in Nabarres's eyes and at Jerónimo's command to strike Snake Mountain.

"Everyone seems to forget one important fact," I say. "While Vicereine Carlota recuperates, *I* am viceregent. Not to put too fine a point on it, but for the time being, my word is law. And my word on this matter is that there will be no attack. War cannot be the answer. It hasn't been. It is not now. It never will be."

"Out. All of you." The viceroy's voice cracks through the council chamber like a whip, and the men shuffle out of the room. When I turn to leave, he stops me. "Not you, Leonora."

When the door shuts behind the last member, I say, "Don't you see what is happening here? You've allowed Nabarres to bait you, Jerónimo."

He looks disappointed to the point of exhaustion. "I thought I could trust you, sister. And I am deeply saddened to find I was mistaken."

"Brother, you can. You *can* trust me. You came to me. You sought my counsel, and I have given it. I wish you well, as I must. I know you want to do right, but is this how you intend to make your mark on history? By setting in motion the destruction of these lands?"

"I'm afraid your . . . association with the Indians has clouded your judgement."

"It is not I who has clouded judgement," I retort.

"You are much too rash, Leonora, and your tongue is an unruly demon. How will God speak to you if you are never quiet?"

"If Father were here, he would not do this. It isn't right."

"But he's not here, is he?"

His words sicken me.

"What happened to you?" I say, shaking my head. "You used to believe in Father's vision, Jerónimo. To bring together the Old World and the New. Our father helped the people, protected them. Do you know who you are anymore?"

He sits back in his chair and caresses the arms of it, as if he's remembered why he's sitting in it at all. "Soy Jerónimo de las Casas y Sepúlveda, virrey de la Nueva España. God has made up His mind. He put me in power, now I must do His will."

I am silenced by this. That his God, the White Christ, would wish war and bloodshed on His creation is a frightening thought. Who is this God in His heaven with all the angels, and what is His will? Surely not death and destruction.

"Hernán Cortés," I say. "One of the greatest conquistadors of the New World. And yet, he spent years seeking recognition for his achievements and support from the Crown. He died a forgotten and embittered man. Is that what you want, Jerónimo? For your life to end in failure?"

"It is your loyalties that concern me," he replies, his tone harsh. "I appreciate your efforts, Leonora. I always want to hear what you have to say, but I cannot have you opposing me at every turn. I act as I think best, and I don't need your permission to defend the colony. I am not a child who can be frightened. I am not my mother's puppet. I am not a man who shrinks from what must be done. I am devoted to protecting Nueva España, and I view this responsibility with the utmost solemnity." His voice contains a petulance that I've not heard before. "You may go."

I stiffen as if I've been slapped. Viceroy Jerónimo didn't appoint me regent because I was the best person available for the position. It had nothing to do with my capacity as advisor, and it definitely had nothing to do with the fact that we're brother and sister. It was never about working alongside each other for the greater good of the colony. It was about getting rid of an inconvenient, more powerful adversary: Vicereine Carlota. I stand but a hair's width from crossing the dangerous threshold of challenging the viceroy's authority. Maintaining my cloak of service to my leader requires long deep breaths and the self-control of a Nagual Master.

"You may judge me as rash, brother," I say, "but I alone dare to assert the truth. Our gathering has tired me, and since a demon seems to have built a mansion in my mouth, I am going to bed." In case the mockery is missed, my next words make it explicit. "May the Holy Spirit control my tongue!"

Part of me understands Jerónimo and the pressure he feels. Unlike my father, who was selected by King Carlos for the prestigious position of viceroy on merit, my brother needs to prove himself worthy and gain the king's support and respect. For Father, greater weight was given to ability than birth. Father didn't bear a noble title, but he was a military man, and that was of central importance for a colony that was in turmoil, and so he was catapulted into a political position as viceroy of New Spain.

I walk up and down my chamber, wondering if I'm mistaken in trusting my brother. If Neza was right and we are past peace. If anything else can be done. Perhaps, I'm the one who doesn't know Jerónimo anymore.

"Pantera would fight," Inés says when I tell her Nabarres will attack Snake Mountain. She trails a sea sponge over my shoulders in small circles, careful not to touch the cuts and bruises scattered around my body. I'm slumped in a washing tub, knees against my chest, staring morosely ahead.

My mind swirls, like the water around me. I rest my braided head back on the edge of the basin. "Yes, she would fight. Then she would screw up and ruin everything."

"Do you remember why you began to wear the mask?"

"To give them something to fear."

She dips the sponge into the water, then runs it along my arms. "You wanted to inspire hope. Right now, there's no hope and nothing to fear but destruction."

"All they see when they look at me is Spain, Inés," I say grimly. "One glance and they think of me as the enemy. That's the only way they *can* view me. That's the real reason I wear a mask. Why I wear gloves wherever I go. To fool people. To pretend I am something I am not. If they knew who I was underneath the mask, they would not cheer. They would not call out to me."

She sighs, bracing her hands on her thighs and pushing herself to her feet. I hear her moving around, lighting candles, preparing the bed, choosing a nightgown from the wardrobe, finding my slippers.

I lift myself from the tub. "Please, don't be upset."

"I didn't say anything."

"It is the tone of your silence."

"How can silence have a tone?"

"What you think is silence, because you don't know how to hear, is full of sound. I can hear five different sounds in your silence without counting your labored breaths."

"And what do you hear?"

"Disappointment," I say sadly. "Inés, I . . ." My voice trails off into thought. "I'm too Spanish for the natives and too native for the Spaniards. Don't you see? I don't belong anywhere. I have no place. So where do I go?" This has always been my struggle. Neither side accepts me fully. I'm tired of the separation between my two halves, the border that divides both worlds, assimilating one side while going back to the other, speaking the language of the invader and the language of the invaded, back and forth until I become lost somewhere in between. This is the nepantla, neither here nor there, neither this nor that.

Inés comes to me, drapes a robe over my shoulders. "I know your discomfort. You must make peace with the story you were born into, Leonora. You didn't create this. It's not your fault. You can't change it. But you have power, and a responsibility to use it. You are grown from a white man's flesh and a brown woman's womb. Own it. You help no one by disempowering yourself." The conviction in her voice is unwavering. "The people need you. They need Pantera."

"Do they?" I ask, feeling the robe cling to my wet body as I pull it shut and tie it at the waist. "There's no happy ending, Inés. I will marry Martín to stay in the capital and attempt diplomacy. It's what my father would have wanted me to do."

"To the Nine Hells with diplomacy!" she snaps. "You are a warrior! Warriors need war!"

"I'm tired of fighting!" I thunder back.

"I don't even know who I'm talking to right now. This isn't you. The Leonora I know loves to fight."

"I don't know," I reply morosely. "I used to be so sure of myself, of what I wanted, and what I was doing. Ever since Ayeta showed his face and I lost my medallion, I feel like I've been missing something . . . a part of me."

"Your medallion? What does that have to do with anything?"

"I don't know!" I say again. "I don't want to fight, Inés." I pause, afraid I'll start crying if I continue, but I do. "When I look at you, it all comes back. I did *that* to you." I point at her scar. "I'm the reason you were hurt."

"We've been over this. I'm not angry at you."

"Well, you should be!"

"Do not feel sorry for me," she says firmly. "I survived a wound nobody expected me to. I shall be honored. Not disgraced. My gods have something great in store for me." Her words cut me like a cold winter wind.

I look away, gathering my galloping thoughts as if I'm taming a wild horse.

"You're just going to throw it all away?"

I look at her. "Throw *what* away?"

"Your power! The mask. Your spirit."

My legs give out. I shouldn't be this tired. I plop down on a chair with a sigh, staring down at my bare feet.

"I've been working on something for you. Something better." I look up to see a grin appear on her face. I follow her to a chest hidden in the gloom beneath the bed. She sinks to her knees and opens it. I hold my breath as she rises and takes a couple of steps toward me, holding a black mask.

Pantera has donned many guises. This one is far more practical than most: the full-sleeved blouse is loose and more breathable, cinched around the waist; the bottom fitted to my legs, useful for running. It's all black, with some discreet golden circles on the cloak resembling the Panther's rosettes. It must've taken her hours to assemble and sew all the markings.

"Do you like it?" she asks.

"It is majestic."

"Why don't you try it on?"

"I'm sorry," I whisper. "I can't."

"Why not?" she asks, searching my eyes for a clue, but I lower my head. "Answer me!"

"I am not worthy!" I shout back at her.

She groans. "Oh, the sword. The damn sword! Who cares? You are a sorceress! For the gods' sake, you are a panther! You don't need a weapon. You should understand this once and for all. You *are* the weapon!"

"*You* don't understand," I say, shaking my head. "Inés, my actions have angered the gods."

"You mean *your* gods."

"Yours or mine—is not all great evil sent from their hands? I must pray. Is this not what you recommended to me? What happened to all your talk about praying?"

"Oh, I prayed, Leonora. And Captain Nabarres was put in my path. I will not allow him to take Snake Mountain."

"Inés," I say as she makes for the servants' passageway. "Where are you going? Nine Hells, Inés! They've hurt you already! You want to give them your life too?"

She halts but doesn't look at me.

"What if something happens to you?" My voice shakes slightly. I couldn't bear it.

She gives me a glance. "I know you're afraid. I'd be afraid too if I was fated to die in battle. Fear isn't a bad thing. It's how we find out what we're made of. But, Leonora, don't you see? You'll never know if you let fear stop you."

Master Toto once told me a warrior accepts their destiny, whatever it may be. He said a warrior fights to change things, and nothing can deter them from that purpose. He also said that the only way we can change is to accept ourselves as we are. I can't stop the curse, the prophecy, the shivers, the fear, or the pounding of my heart, but if this is my destiny, if I was born to fight and die, so be it.

I sigh. "We'll need Valiente."

Inés frows. "What?"

"After we make ourselves ready, decide what we need to take, what we can carry, gather our supplies, and pack them tonight, we'll need Valiente. We leave at first light. Meet me at the stables."

She gives a little smile in the soft candlelight. "Where are we going?"

"Snake Mountain."

In the morning, Valiente snorts loudly as I mount him, as if he knows we have work to do.

"All right." I laugh as he paws excitedly at the ground. "We're going."

I've been too afraid. But I cannot live in fear. I realize now that to die in battle would be the greatest bliss. Tonatiuh honors his fallen warriors in the House of the Sun, the Third Heaven, where you can sip the sweetness of flowers and enjoy splendor without end. There is no higher joy than accompanying the sun god in his travels from the east to his home in the west. Better to die with my sword in hand than in my bed.

I give Valiente a good scratch on the neck. I wait for Inés, as we agreed, but when time passes and there is no sign of her, I trot out of the stables and into the plaza to find her.

Instead, I find Captain Nabarres alongside his men. He is staring at me with blazing eyes.

"Viceregent, are you headed somewhere?"

Guards rush in and surround me, forming a circle with me at the center. I lock eyes with Andrés, my stare an act of violence. How foolish I was to think I could trust him, to think his intentions were good. However formidable I find his tonalli and however much he's helped me, I cannot trust him.

"Snake," I say under my breath. He looks away. I dismount and tether Valiente to a tree by the cathedral.

The commotion catches the attention of Viceroy Jerónimo as he's leaving church. "Capitán, what is the meaning of this?"

"Lady Leonora, you are under arrest for crimes committed against the viceroyalty of New Spain."

CHAPTER 22

La Pantera

"On what charges?" Jerónimo demands furiously.

"Treason, sedition, conspiracy, thievery, murder, assault with deadly weapons, rebellion, attacking Spanish troops, heresy, witchcraft," Nabarres says. "I do not have enough fingers to continue counting, excelencia. Lady Leonora is in fact the masked bruja Pantera."

"Leonora . . . Pantera . . . ? Surely, this is a joke."

"Oh, I am quite serious. The bedmaids found this in her room," Nabarres says, holding out one of my knives. Traces of blood line the edge. My heart leaps into my throat. "She is a traitor to this colony and to *you*, excelencia."

Jerónimo lifts an eyebrow. "A knife?"

"A knife made of flint, excelencia," Nabarres says. "This is no Spanish knife. It belongs to the Panther. It belongs to *her*."

"Capitán," I say evenly, "are you so desperate to capture the bruja that you would accuse *me*? I found the knife the night of La Justicia's attack. My handmaid was wounded. I was alone. I feared for my life."

Nabarres laughs. "Excelencia, your sister is fooling you. Can you not see the evidence that is right before your very eyes? The masked bruja appeared around the time Lady Leonora returned to the palace. She lived with the indios. She is one of them. She fights with them."

"It's no secret she's defended the people," Jerónimo says with a dismissive wave. "My sister fights injustice with her words, not a knife, capitán. I cannot believe that you would stoop so low. All you have provided me with is conjecture . . . nothing of substance. My own sister would not lie to me about who she really is. Right, Leonora?"

My stomach twists at the hint of doubt in his voice.

Some legends are best left as that and nothing more. Master Toto never said hiding would be easy. He said it would be necessary.

"I am not capable of such deceit, brother," I say, my throat tight. "There is no possible way I could be Pantera. I am the least likely person to be her."

"Your disguise is brilliant," Nabarres says. "Your acting skills do you credit, Lady Leonora. You are one of the best performers among us . . . however, I am not fooled any longer. Excellency, I would not make such claims if I did not believe I was correct. The facts will bear themselves out. Only one woman can be Pantera. She has been here all along, right under our noses. Pantera and Lady Leonora have never been seen together." Nabarres casts a proud glance at me. "That is because they are physically the same."

"You are trying my patience, capitán," Jerónimo says. "Where is Pantera's legendary sword, her mask, eyewitnesses to support your accusation? You have no evidence to prove that my sister is Pantera."

"Excelencia—"

"No, capitán! You've risked your reputation, your very position without proof to support your claims. A man of your stature and experience should not have rushed judgement to convict an innocent woman. I expected much more of you."

"This is *your* doing," Nabarres snarls at me.

"Your obsession with the bruja has put you in this position, capitán," I say. "I fear you are not well."

"Enough of your tricks. You are Pantera . . . I know that you are! If you aren't, then why hasn't the bruja shown up to rescue you? Don't bother to answer that. You cannot be in two places at the same time."

"There is nothing that I can say or do to convince you that I am not Pantera," I say. "It would be a waste of time. But I will say this. Had you become the leader you should have been when you arrived from Spain, defended the colony and its people justly, there would be no need for Pantera . . . whoever she is."

Nabarres waits a moment, as if savoring his next words. "Your gloves." He looks down at my clasped hands. "I'm certain I've never seen you without them, my lady. Why is that?"

My heartbeat thrums in my ears. "My hands get cold."

"In this heat? You know, Pantera wears gloves too. I thought, quite possibly, she wore them to protect herself. Or," he says, voice menacing, "to hide what lies underneath. Like the mask she dons."

"Hide what?" Jerónimo asks.

"Oh, I don't know. A marking on the skin, perhaps? A humming-bird on the side of her right hand."

He saw it . . . In Mexicapan, I shifted my hands to slip from my chains. It was either that or let Nabarres's men remove my mask. I can't breathe. I can't think.

"Preposterous," Jerónimo fumes. "Leonora, show him your hands."

"What?"

"The sooner you do, the sooner we can all return to our duties."

I briefly meet Andrés's eyes. Something like sympathy fills them. Whatever fear I felt a second ago is replaced by rage. I am a sorceress. I don't need his pity.

I hold his gaze as I start taking off my gloves, tugging first at one finger then another. But then there is a whistle followed by, "*Pssst . . . Capitán Nabarres!*"

We crane our necks up toward the roof of Viceroyal Palace. I squint, looking directly up into the sun. As quickly as it blinds me, a cloud passes, shielding my gaze from the light. My vision clears, and a black-masked figure clothed in darkness peers down at the scene below, commanding respect, ready to do her part. She looks dangerous. Deadly. Completely feral. Someone very far removed from her real self.

The Panther, in the flesh.

"Capitán, Pantera is here!" a guard shrieks.

Nabarres scowls. "Gracias, Morales. Your powers of deduction are truly remarkable."

Please, don't let it be her, I pray to any god who might be listening. *Please, don't let it be her. Let it be anyone but her.* I try to convince myself, but it is futile. I already know it's her. *How did she get up there?* I panic and take a step forward, but Andrés holds me back.

"Easy, señorita," he says. "You don't want to do something you'll regret."

The only thing I regret is not wetting my sword with his blood. I fight the urge to spit in his face, knee him where it hurts the most, let loose my anger and hatred.

I look to the roof as the masked girl says, "I hear you've been looking for me, capitán. Miss me?"

Nabarres looks perplexed as his head turns toward Pantera, then toward me, then toward Pantera again. He then takes a couple of steps forward, hands on his hips. "Have you come to surrender yourself, bruja?"

"Oh, no, no, no. I most certainly have not come to surrender," she says. "I am here on business."

That voice, sweet but venomous, like a cake sprinkled with poison.

"What business could a criminal have?" Nabarres asks.

"Seven years ago, you murdered a woman simply because it pleased you. You took her head and paraded it on a pike before you burned her body. She was my mother."

"You've come to punish me?"

"I've come to settle my affairs once and for all," she says, unsheathing her blade. It shines green in the sunlight. Green.

They'll have her head. Even if I confess, they will still have her head. I have to stop this.

I whistle for Valiente to come to me. He looks up and about, and starts my way, but he is hitched to a tree. I whistle again, and he breaks loose with a colossal burst of strength, yanking the tree from the earth, roots and all, like a stopper from a bottle. He tears along at a gallop, dragging the tree behind him and casting men in all directions. Those who remain standing leap back to dodge his thundering hooves, and the rest scramble to get to their feet. His muscles ripple under his groomed pelt and his powerful legs.

"¡Es la bruja!" one of the soldiers says. "She's doing this!"

"Is there not a man among you?" Captain Nabarres rails, regarding his men in disgust. He unsheathes his sword and drives it into Valiente's side as he passes.

"No!" I bellow.

I rush to him as he neighs in pain and collapses to the ground. What I feel is not human, it is twisted and distorted. It burns like fire lacing my veins, and all that consumes me is the desire to kill.

Inés dashes away. Nabarres leaps on his horse and rides at breakneck speed around the palace, chasing after her.

I kiss Valiente, dry my tears, and stand. When no one is looking, I soar and land in a crouch on the lower, flatter roof of Viceroyal Palace. Wind smacks my face like a cold fist. As I skip across buildings, I scan the streets below and look over my shoulder to see if any guards are following me. But they are too focused on the fleeing Pantera to notice me.

Run, Leonora. Run. Faster. My heart beats wildly. But not from the running. It's the fear. Fear so thick that I can smell it. Taste it. Feel it coating my skin.

I catch a flash of Pantera's hooded robe unfurling as Inés stops near the edge of the roof, and without any hesitation, sends herself flying into the air. She lands on ropes that are strung in an alleyway, bearing laundry. She goes down with them, accumulating pieces of clothing as she falls. I curse and leap after her, sending tonalli to my feet to slow my descent.

Inés lands on her back, groaning and wincing.

"Are you all right?" I pant.

"I've been better," she croaks.

"Nine Hells, Inés. That was—"

"Impressive?" She's wearing my mask, but I can tell she's amused from her voice.

"Reckless."

"Admit it. You're impressed."

"You think this is funny?"

She yanks a pair of breeches from around her waist. "It's a little funny."

I offer my hand to pull her up, and she takes it. "Come on, let's get out of here."

"Did we lose Nabarres?"

I listen for the clopping of hooves, for voices. "I think so." Then again, I'm breathing harshly, and my heart is pounding fiercely. "I don't know."

I give her costume a look.

"What?"

"Nothing. You wear it well. It suits you."

"I'm sorry about your horse," she says, removing the mask. "I know you had a special bond with Valiente."

I nod and look away, willing tears not to spill. My rage threatens to burst free at any moment.

Inés slips off Pantera's robe, uncovering her blouse and skirt, then we scurry discreetly down the alleyway and into the shadows.

"What now?" Inés asks, walking next to me. "How do we get to Snake Mountain?"

"I'm not sure." I grip the strap of the Sword of Integrity's scabbard around my shoulder. "Nabarres knows who I am. I have to be careful."

"What he knows is that he saw someone *else* wearing the mask of Pantera today," she says smugly.

"He's not a fool, Inés. He'll come after me. And if Jerónimo finds out Nabarres was speaking the truth . . . I don't know what he'll do."

"So we'll trick him too."

I stop walking. "You shouldn't have done what you did."

"What do you mean?" Her dark eyebrows twitch. "Nabarres was going to find out—"

"I know *why* you did it," I snap, "but it was a mistake. I would have found a way out. I always do. You didn't need to put yourself in that position."

She crosses her arms tightly. "So now you're angry with me?"

"Have you forgotten what they did to Señor Alonso? I haven't. They'll have your head too, don't you understand? You're my friend. You're the closest person to me now."

"Perhaps. But now we have a little more time to make sure that doesn't happen, haven't we?"

I shake my head in frustration and continue walking.

"Leonora."

I turn around to face her. "Do you really think it'll be that simple? Nothing Nabarres does is simple. You of all people should know that."

Inés sighs and briefly closes her eyes. "I can take care of myself."

"That's not the point!"

"Then what is the point?"

"They're all dead."

"Who?"

"My mother. My father. Señor Alonso. Valiente. Everyone who comes close to me gets hurt."

I nearly lose my footing as a sudden pain forms behind my eyes. Inés grips my arm. "What's wrong?"

Enormous tension is building up inside me, weighing down my senses and making my head pound. I wince as the pressure tightens around my temples. The sound moves through the earth as waves move through the water, though it's not water that's rolling, it's air, being pushed as if through a giant blowhorn. Inés can't hear it, but I can.

"We must get to the palace," I say in a smothering panic. "Now."

Her face creases with utter horror. "What? Why?"

The rumbling in my head becomes clearer and louder. "There's going to be another earthquake. A bad one."

CHAPTER 23

El Terremoto

Before Inés and I even reach the plaza, the alarm-bell starts clanging. We stop at the entrance of the Old Palace, the building where the servants' quarters are located, and look up, seeing the bell swing so violently I think it'll rip itself from its scaffold.

"I don't know how long we have to move everyone outside." My voice is controlled as I battle the fear that threatens to consume me.

"Take this entrance." Inés nods toward the main doors. "I'll cover the side exits. I'll try to get out as many people as I can."

I'd prefer she stay here, but Inés has never been one to shy away from danger when she can help. She *won't*. "Just . . . be careful."

She jerks her head in agreement, giving me her most reassuring grin. "Don't be afraid, Pantera."

I run inside, colliding with frightened and confused people scrambling for safety. Panicked voices fill the air as I race across the halls and up the stairs, banging on doors and shouting, "Everyone out! Get out!"

I don't dare wonder about families with children, the sick, the aged, those who will not evacuate in time, Jerónimo, wherever he is. No amount of worry can do a thing against a threat like this. For the ones in the barrios, for the ones farther away, I can do nothing.

But that can't matter. Not now, when all seems hopeless, and I have to focus on those who I *can* help. I direct everyone I find toward the nearest exit, then round a corner and slam into Ayeta's chest. "Lieutenant, an earthquake—!"

"I know!" he yells back over the din. "What are you doing? You're going the wrong way."

He knows about the earthquake? "There're still people inside. We can't leave them."

Ayeta blocks my path. "There's no time. We have to go."

"You can either help me or get out of my way."

"Any moment now the ground will shake beneath your feet and you're arguing with me?" He groans. "You're exhausting, señorita."

"Leonora!" a familiar voice wails.

I turn around. Inés is surrounded by a press of people fleeing, some of them through windows, others determined to open a path to safety. She shouts herself hoarse inside the crowd, trying to push forward toward me. Ignoring their protests, I elbow someone out of the way to get closer, extending my hand. Our fingers almost touch. Almost. She's shoved back by the crush of bodies.

"Inés!" I bellow.

Ayeta seizes my hand. "We won't make it out. We have to take cover now."

A deep rumble announces the earthquake's arrival. Ayeta and I are separated as the floor tears open between us. At the same time, a chunk of plaster collapses from the ceiling and fills the hallway with choking dust. I hit the floor coughing, my vision obscured, and I crawl toward the wall, curling up as small as I can to shield myself from the cascade of debris.

"Inés . . ." I rasp, still coughing. "Inés . . . where are you?"

I hear her voice in snatches, but the deafening noise envelops me and forces me to press my hands to my ears. I can hardly hear myself wheeze as the building crumbles with each tremor roaring through the ground.

Everything falls. Stars. Angels. The Mexica. The Old Palace is falling apart.

We all fall, in the end.

Immense terror grips my heart. There is no mercy in the shaking, no grace, only the wrath of the gods. I cry, shaken to my core as a blazing beam plows into the floor beside me, on fire from a collapsed candelabra. I survey my surroundings with wild eyes. I'm going to die. Andrés is probably dead. All I'm doing is delaying the inevitable.

It gets hot. Unbearably hot. Fast-moving flames singe my cloak. The Sword of Integrity's weight has always been a comfort, but now it feels oppressive on my back. As the Old Palace rocks, and I expect every instant to be burned or buried alive, I look up to see a roaring jaguar with golden-brown fur leap from the fire. It tears through the flames, and no sooner do I stop shouting than I see it walking on two legs toward me, dressed in the attire of a guard.

"Andrés?" The word is a gasp.

Hauling a tapestry from the wall, he throws it over me to douse the smoke and crouches at my feet. My head involuntarily drops into his chest. The fire engulfs us, and I distantly feel his arms wrapping around me. I sag against him as if he's all I have left. A sickly stench of ash and burning flesh permeates the air.

When the shaking finally stops, Andrés hoists me up with a firm arm and points to the stairway. It's in terrible condition, but this place is going to burn with us inside it. I nod dizzily, grabbing on to him. I'm burdening him, but he gives no indication of struggling with my weight, says nothing to make me let go. With the tapestry draped over us, we struggle through the debris, weaving through the fire and keeping our eyes focused on the stairs. Together we make our way down. The second we stagger outside into the courtyard, we roll in the dewy grass and gasp for breath. Every inhale feels like shards of glass imbedding into my lungs.

I sit up and choke on my next breath. Flames are ripping through the Old Palace. Tendrils of smoke reach into the night sky, escaping the inferno. Nothing will be left. Nothing but charred earth.

Inés. My eyes fill with tears.

I beg Andrés with a shake of my head not to say what I know he's thinking, pleading with him to allow me a fragment of hope.

"Please," I whisper, my throat dry. "Please."

His brown eyes soften with something like pity. "Maybe she made it out."

He wraps an arm around my waist and pulls me to stand. The Old Palace collapses, the top floor falling on to the next one and the next. Dust spreads like fog.

My ears ring with the wails of those seeking friends and relatives, the cries and groans of the injured and dying, calling for help. Andrés rushes to a pile of rubble where a small hand is moving. Scurrying behind him, I begin to scrape away the ruins, and he stops me. "Don't touch it. There are still embers." He throws a beam of wood to the side and lifts out a girl who was trapped. Battered, covered in white dust, she straightens her clothes and brushes her thighs, screaming in pain when she realizes her skirt has burnt into her skin. Andrés says something to her in a language I don't understand.

He gently sits her down and heals her. Then it occurs to me . . . Andrés is unscathed.

A jaguar sprang through the fire.

He sounded the alarm.

Andrés is no wizard. He's a sorcerer.

He heard the earthquake, like me.

He's a Nagual, like me.

Questions are on the tip of my tongue. "Andrés."

"Are you hurt?"

I shake my head.

We turn around as more shrieks pierce the darkness.

"Go," I say. "See to the others."

After hours of looking for Inés, I find a bloodied Prince Felipe, or rather Martín Cortés, just outside Viceroyal Palace. His legs are caught under a fallen beam. I try to lift the beam, but it shifts, falling on his legs again. He's in so much pain he doesn't notice when I let out a small burst of tonalli from my hands, pushing the beam off him.

"Can you walk?"

He nods, but with a wince. "Neza . . ." he mutters hoarsely. "Do you think he's safe?"

"I've no doubt he's alive. Come on." I put an arm around his waist and help him to his feet.

He coughs through the settling dust. "I have to be sure. I have to see for myself."

"There's been an earthquake. You can't just charge off toward Snake Mountain, Martín."

A guard springs forward to aid his prince. "¡Su alteza!"

Martín waves him off. "Ya, ya. Estoy bien."

"His legs are hurt," I tell the guard. "He needs a doctor."

Martín leaves with the guard. Behind me, Jerónimo is issuing orders while frantic servants attempt to straighten up the mess around him. I stop the nearest servant by clasping her shoulder. "Leave that," I say. "We need a headcount, including all the servants." Especially all the servants.

She hurries away, appearing glad to have something useful to do.

"Leonora." My brother's voice is loud.

"We need to know who's missing."

"Yes, I agree. Are you injured?" He squeezes my shoulder.

I shake my head. "The gods—*God* kept me safe."

"Praise Him." He clutches the Cross at his neck. "I've sent men to determine the full extent of the damage and do a room-by-room search for survivors."

I brush bloody curls from his forehead. "You're hurt." He shuts his eyes for a moment, as if my touch soothes him, but then he pushes my arm away as Minister of Development Bartolo de Molina approaches us with quick steps.

"Excelencia, the Old Palace is wrecked," says Don Bartolo. "The Old Courtyard is blocked here. It looks like a good portion of the trees came down. We haven't heard of any other collapses yet, but we will have lost dozens of buildings. There are bound to have been deaths, with a tremor this severe."

A burning animosity takes me over. "People have died needlessly," I say. "Had you heeded my counsel, we would not be suffering the impact of disaster. You had the means, but you did nothing and now people have lost their lives. Do not expect sympathy from me."

It's been a day since the tremors stopped, and I still haven't found Inés. She could be trapped. The not knowing is killing me.

The walk to my chamber does nothing to settle my frayed nerves. In the sitting room, some dozen servants hop to their feet and curtsy as I step inside.

I wave a hand. "Sit down, girls."

After the collapse of the Old Palace, the viceroy issued an edict that any courtiers employing personal servants in the palace have to house them in their own rooms for the time being. None of these girls are mine, of course, but many Spaniards left their help out in the halls.

"You're very generous, señorita," one of them says.

I couldn't just leave them out there. Some of these girls left their families to come and work at the palace. They have nowhere else to go.

"We should be able to use the offices in the administrative wing of the palace," I say. "With any luck, we can have everyone settled somewhere by the end of tomorrow."

"We hope your selfless example will inspire others to make room for displaced servants, señorita."

"No news of Inés?" I ask, my voice tremulous.

They shake their heads.

I frown. *Where are you, Inés?*

*

Jerónimo and I spend the next few days traveling to San Juan Tenochtitlan and Santiago Tlatelolco to deliver food and supplies. Dozens of houses crumpled, and there were casualties, but it is not as bad as we feared. I'm relieved that many escaped death because the alarm-bell drew them outside. Andrés's warning saved lives.

Some five blocks east of Viceroyal Palace lies Atzacoalco, or San Sebastián as the Spaniards decided to call one of the four original quadrants of Mexico-Tenochtitlan, after yet another saint, of course. Although the poorest and smallest barrio, hundreds of people, young and old, ailing and able, neighbors and strangers, all hurry to the streets to lend a helping hand. Some of them don't have much, but their spirit is powerful and tells me we can push back, even against the will of the gods. No tremor can topple their resilience. They give me hope that we can work together to create a better Mexico for all.

Children's laughter and scattered applause draw my attention to a young girl wielding a wooden sword with a ragged black cloth for a mask. She play-fights two child "soldiers." A few passers-by cheer and clap and call out to her.

Jerónimo sighs, as if feeling the start of a headache. "Even the children want to be Pantera." He looks around the streets. "Salcedo," he says to the commander of his patrol, "send word back to the palace that every tapestry is to be stripped from the walls and used for tenting. Have all the damaged furniture and any timbers recovered from the Old Palace broken up and distributed as firewood."

Salcedo nods, then issues orders to two guards, who salute briskly and trot away.

A woman with a tear-streaked face approaches and desperately clutches my hand.

"Is the world ending?" she cries. "I cannot find my children! I would rather the world end than go on without them!"

I press her hand in both of mine. "What barrio are you from?"

"Cuepohpan," she says, as would someone before the Fall, then she realizes her error and corrects herself. "Santa María, señorita."

I squeeze her hand and speak to her in Nahuatl. "Tla xiyauh tiyanquiztli Moyotlan. People from Cuepohpan are leaving word for their loved ones there."

The woman looks up at me hopefully and hurries away, still weeping.

"What did you tell her?" Jerónimo asks.

"We need to direct people from Cuepohpan to the southern plaza in Moyotlan." I thrust my chin toward the departing woman's back. "Many workers go into la traza for their own and for their employers' errands, and Spaniards conduct business and pleasure in the barrios all the time, so people may want to look for loved ones in more than one place."

Jerónimo nods. "Good idea."

On our return to the palace, I'm exhausted but hopeful. We will recover.

When I come inside, Andrés is standing by the entrance, hair disheveled, face haggard, eyes shadowed by dark circles.

"Leonora . . ." He clears his throat, frowning slightly, as if he's just remembered his station. "Señorita."

"What is it?" I fear the worst.

He is already at the door, beckoning me to follow.

I'm filled with an inescapable dread as Andrés and I walk between the rows of tents pitched near what's left of the Old Palace. The groans of the wounded rise from different parts of the camp, weakening as we pass each tent, and then they seem to cease altogether. Andrés pulls aside one of the tent openings.

I pause in the entry. Twenty or thirty bodies, covered in sheets, are lying side by side on the ground. Andrés crouches next to one. He lowers the sheet to reveal her face, her sweet face, bloodied and bruised. I forget how to move. I forget how to breathe.

"She will be buried at the Christian cemetery," Andrés says quietly.

My lips quiver. "Leave us."

He nods and walks away. The moment he steps out of the tent, something breaks loose inside me, and I fall to my knees. Inés is dead.

I rest my head on her chest, weeping. I don't know how long I stay there, slumped over her, holding her, sobs wracking my chest. I can no longer sense her tonalli. Upon death, tonalli remains near the body for four days to retrieve scattered pieces of itself left behind. Her teyolia is gone. But where did it go? What god does Inés now serve?

It's the way we die, not the way we live, that determines where we go in the Nahua afterlife. The Thirteen Heavens are reserved for those whose deaths come early or tragically. To the First Heaven travel the souls of those who die from drowning or certain diseases, or have particularly violent deaths. There live the moon goddess, the god of wind, and the god of rain. The Third Heaven, the realm of Tonatiuh, is the destination for fallen warriors and women who die in childbirth. But Omeyocan, the home of the god of duality, Ometeotl, is the highest of the Thirteen Heavens. The god-goddess is joined by the souls of children in this golden paradise, where they are protected from ever having to visit the cold and dark land of the dead, Mictlan. For, once there, in the underworld, a person cannot leave. It's not a place of demons and punishment for sinners, like the Christian Hell; rather, it's a journey, though with trials. I've always thought of it as a way for people who die of old age or natural causes to let go of their mortal life, as the longer one lives, the more time one needs to leave the flesh behind.

Inés didn't die an unremarkable death, so her soul won't go to Mictlan. Her end did not come in battle, but she died fighting. She will go to Tonatiuh.

This is my belief, but the pain is still unbearable.

I press my lips to her forehead and wish my dearest friend safe travels.

CHAPTER 24

La Boda

The days pass, but my grief doesn't. I'm kneeling at the altar in my best brocade, but it is not to pray to the Christian God. Beside me, Prince Felipe—Martín—is a vision in gold, his blond locks crowned with a bridegroom's wreath resplendent with precious stones. He looks like a gilded god. I take his hand before Fray Anonasi, His Excellency the Archbishop Montúfar, and clergymen, ready to swear to be a wife, bear children as if I am nothing more than livestock and devote my life entirely to my king. It is my wedding day, but it is not the flame of love that burns in my heart. Misery curdles my gut, boiling like volcanic sludge.

"You are a fortunate man, alteza," Archbishop Montúfar says, pulling me out of my stupor. "The Lord has chosen a virtuous woman to be your wife. Go forth, then, with this knowledge and confidence in your heart."

"From your mouth to God's ears, excelentísimo," Martín says. "Lady Leonora is a woman of multiple colors. She has shades of gray and orange and red and yellow and green and brown, much like Mexico City itself. Now that I think about it, she reminds me of my mother. She has the same spirit, the same fire; a woman misunderstood by many."

His real mother. La Malinche.

Martín leans in and whispers, "It's easy when you tell the truth."

Archbishop Montúfar solemnly calls upon anyone who knows a reason why the prince and I should not be married to declare it. If Inés were here, she'd speak now; she wouldn't hold her peace.

"Nabarres is going to attack Snake Mountain," I say under my breath as Archbishop Montúfar turns around for a moment.

I could've done things differently. I could've told Martín sooner. I should've. Though Inés's death and the impact of the earthquake were at the front of my mind. I suppose some part of me foolishly believed Nabarres would abandon his ambition to do battle, what with more pressing matters demanding attention. But Nabarres saw an opportunity. If La Justicia was vulnerable, it would be the perfect time to attack.

Martín blanches. "When?"

"He marches at first light," I say quietly.

"Are you sure?"

"I am."

"Neza . . . we must warn him. How do we get out of here?"

I give him a look, as if to say, *You know how.* "It's easy when you tell the truth." I nod, encouraging him.

Before, Martín was reluctant to make his lies known, but now, it's as if a certain desperation emboldens him. When Archbishop Montúfar faces us again, Martín loudly declares, "I know a reason, Archbishop Montúfar."

The cathedral erupts in noise.

Appalled, Archbishop Montúfar asks, "You're objecting to the union, alteza?"

"I cannot bind myself forever in holy wedlock to Lady Leonora. I confess I do not belong here," Martín says brazenly, turning around to face the wedding guests. "I have been hiding my identity. My name is not Felipe, nor am I the king's son. I am an imposter. The real crown prince is in Spain, and he has no knowledge of my falseness.

I have lied to you all. I am not a prince. I am not a don. I am not even a real Spaniard."

His words are drowned out by the rising din of shock from the scandalized wedding guests. Jerónimo stares bewildered, and I put on my best pretense of surprise and indignation.

Wandering through dungeons in the dead of night is not my preference for entertainment. Criminals, rapists, murderers, thieves, drunks, deviants, and all manner of shady characters can be found in El Hoyo Negro, the black hole of Mexico City. But there I am, cursing under my breath as I crawl through a small recess in the wall used for emptying chamber pots. I carry the Sword of Integrity, and I'm wearing the disguise Inés made for me. She wore it last, and it makes my heart ache.

I emerge from the tunnel to land softly on a pile of hay, then tiptoe down the dark corridor. No guards in sight. That doesn't seem right, but who am I to complain?

The prisoners are sleeping. Also good. The last thing I need is angry criminals raising a ruckus, attracting attention from the guards. Martín is sleeping too. After his outrageous admission, he was promptly arrested and away he went.

His stone cell has one entrance and no windows. Given enough time, a person can forget their own name in a place like this. Total isolation. No sound, no light, no furniture of any kind, only moldy hay, the stink of festering sewage, and the icy grip of death. I pick up a pebble and toss it through the bars. It strikes Martín's back.

He peers over his shoulder with one sleepy eye. "Leonora?" He quickly pushes himself up and takes a step closer to the bars. "It's about time you showed up. It's not exactly a picnic in here. I'm sleeping with cucarachas, rats are running wild, and I have to relieve myself in a bucket."

"Oh, my apologies, alteza. Can I get you some wine? Maybe some cheese?"

"You can get me *out* of here!"

"Why don't you say that a little louder? I don't think the other prisoners heard you."

He glares at me, seething with exasperation. "Don't be cheeky, Leonora. I've had a perfectly glum day while you were out gallivanting. I don't appreciate your sarcasm, and I don't appreciate the position you've put me in." He crosses his arms in a huff.

"Well, at least no one knows you're the son of Cortés. You're going to have to dig your way out."

He scoffs. "What?"

"I don't have the key and all the guards are posted outside the building. I brought a shovel."

"A shovel?" He gives me a brief look of annoyance. "Have you gone mad?" He chortles, then stamps his boot on the ground. "Hear that, my lady? That's *rock*."

"It did not escape my notice."

"Do I look like the kind of person who can dig a hole in rock, crawl through pipes full of waste, climb over high walls, then walk out the front door to freedom?"

I take in the details of his appearance, noting his lithe and slender form, his soft features, his clothes of silk and ribbons. "No. You look like the kind of person who is especially meticulous about his grooming. Nevertheless, a shovel is your only way out." I hand it to him through the bars. "Now dig . . . alteza."

He groans.

"You know, I'm trying to get you out of here, Martín, so why don't you save your eye rolls for when they count?"

"Why don't you save your eye rolls . . ." he mocks in a shrill imitation of my voice.

"Do you want me to leave you here?" I demand.

"That's not what I said."

"Well, then cease your racket and dig. We haven't got much time. Nabarres and his men are already on their way to Snake Mountain."

Despite his grumblings, he drives the shovel into the gravely earth with a clang that sets my teeth on edge. His efforts don't even make a dent. "Care to help? Maybe use your magic to open the lock, witch?"

"Sorceress."

He wipes the sweat away with the back of his hand. "Isn't that the same thing?"

"Yes, because now is *exactly* the time to be discussing how witches differ from sorceresses. Let me go and find a chair to make myself comfortable while we're down here risking our heads."

"Are you finished being saucy?"

"No. Is that what you think I can do? Magically open locks?"

"I have no idea what you can do," Martín says. "I've heard stories."

I could do it. In theory. If I had tonalli control.

Martín takes a deep breath, the sole of his foot poised. When he exhales, he plunges the shovel into the ground, pressing his boot more fiercely against the blade this time. It sinks in deeper. But he doesn't dig up much, for all the effort that went into the push. "Why do I get the feeling you're enjoying this?"

I grip the iron bars, looking up to see where they are joined. I pull on them, but they don't budge. "I promise you I take no pleasure in waiting."

He begins to retort, but I hear something else and lift my forefinger to my mouth to quiet him. "Someone's coming."

I spin quickly around and slip back into the darkness, and as stealthily as I disappeared, I reappear and come up behind the guard on duty. I pounce on him, wrapping my right arm tightly around his neck and pressing my left against the back of his head. As I feel his body go limp, I release my hold and lay him gently on the ground. I search hurriedly through his clothes and find the key in his shirt pocket, then unlock Martín's cell.

"Is that how you put me to sleep in the woods?" he says as I wrench the door open.

"Take off your clothes."

"*What?*"

"I doubt very much you have anything I haven't seen," I say, quickly pulling the guard's shirt and pants off.

Martín glares at me, snatching the garments out of my hands. "You know," he says as he removes the rigid and highly decorated fashion of the Spanish court, managing to convey his displeasure, "if you wanted to see me in my underpants, you didn't need to resort to a jailbreak."

"If I wanted to see you in your underpants, Martín, I would have undressed you myself."

"Now what?"

"Now," I say as I drag the guard into the cell and stuff a stocking into his mouth, "you put your acting skills to good use."

"What about you?"

"Don't worry about me," I say. "Do you remember where the Chichimeca attacked us in the woods?"

He nods.

"Meet me there. I have two horses waiting for us."

Nodding again, he turns around.

"Martín?" I say to his back.

He looks at me.

"Hurry."

CHAPTER 25

El Bosque

We urge our horses on for all they're worth and ride without stopping toward Coatepec, Snake Mountain. I nearly fall out of the saddle several times as I succumb to weariness, but my horse carries me faithfully. Until he stops suddenly, almost throwing me over his head.

I straighten in the saddle. "Why didn't you wake me?" I mutter to Martín. He's on foot, leading his horse to a nearby stream. "Didn't I tell you to force me to stay awake?"

"I thought it was a rare opportunity to see you at peace, and I took it." He takes off his horse's bridle, then pats and strokes it. "It turns out, you snore. Even when you rest, you're at war. Did you know you also talk in your sleep?"

A terrible habit for someone with secrets to keep. Inés took every chance to joke about it.

"What did I say?"

"I don't know. I didn't understand the language. But you did murmur a name. Andrés . . . *Andrés*. Don't tell me the legendary Pantera is in love?"

I don't know if I'm just too tired to argue. As I climb down from the horse's back, my knees buckle. I grab for the reins, steadying myself, wincing as my torn muscles protest.

202

"You don't have your feet fully under you yet," he says.

With only the glow of a full moon, darkness presses in. A breeze stirs the air, then disappears, like the breath of a ghost. Frogs croak and crickets chirp. Ahead, a waterfall tumbles down the rocks. "Where are we?"

Martín mops his forehead with the collar of his shirt. "No man's land." His voice is a whisper, as if he's afraid of who might overhear. "That's all you need to know."

"What, you don't trust me?"

"It's for your own good, Leonora."

"Mine," I say, "or yours?"

He sighs. "There's a path leading to Snake Mountain just beyond the waterfall. It's the shortest route, but horses never manage the trail. Best to go on foot from here. We follow the snake doctors."

"Snake doctors?"

He points to a cloud of damselflies flying about, glittering in the moonlight like blue-winged jewels. "Caballitos del diablo. It is said they tend to injured snakes. There are a lot of those on Snake Mountain."

We unsaddle our horses, turn them loose, and continue our march.

"My father was not a good man," Martín says, ducking under a branch. "He had eleven children, maybe more. Three Catalinas, two Marías, two Leonors, two Luises, two Martíns. He didn't have much imagination. I'm his firstborn, but my brother Martín was his favorite. He's a mirror of my father. Educated, refined, with all the honors and wealth. I am the broken mirror.

"I was born here, but I sailed for Spain with my father when I was six. But I heard the stories of what he did here. Cortés would never have conquered without La Malinche, my mother. When she was no longer of any use to him, he had her murdered. Is there any justice, I ask myself, in all this?"

I step over a gnarled root. A pair of lizards scamper from the brush and disappear. "Is that why you joined La Justicia?"

He walks up to a tree and places his hand on it, closing his eyes for a moment. "They say her spirit haunts these woods. She wails for Cortés every night."

"Do you believe that?"

"It doesn't matter what I believe. That is what everyone believes," he says miserably. "I didn't know La Malinche. If I ever met my mother, I don't remember."

"I understand," I say. "I know very little of my own mother. She died giving birth to me."

"And your father?" Martín asks. "What do you know about him?"

I frown. "What do you mean?"

"Well, I mean . . ." he says, "you must know . . ."

"Know what?"

"Nothing . . . never mind." He looks away. "We're almost there."

"You can't start saying something and stop, Martín."

The bushes rustle behind me. Something like giggling, faint voices and laughter, echo through the forest, and I spin around. "Did you hear that?"

"The children don't like seeing people around these parts," Martín says.

"The children?"

"Well, they also don't like to be called children. Chaneques," he says. "Small creatures with pointed ears and the face of an old child. They guard the forest. If there's one thing chaneques are, it's territorial, and they very much resent intruders. Stay close, and they'll leave you alone."

"I know what a chaneque is." I just never thought them to be real. I've heard that chaneques attack without warning, and they attempt to startle their victims to steal their tonalli because they don't have tonalli of their own.

An owl screeches and Martín stares up into the trees.

"It's just an owl," I say, but as the bird takes flight from its perch on a high limb of a tree, uttering its eerie shriek, I notice it is much too big. In all the years I have walked the woodlands, I have never encountered a lechuza. An evil omen. Screech owls are denizens of the underworld. Messengers of the Lord and Lady of Mictlan.

"Trust me," Martín says, "that is no ordinary owl."

I believe him. The lechuza swoops above me. I duck out of the way, but I lose my balance and stumble backward. I feel awkward and clumsy and most out of place here. I need the Panther.

"Turn around," I say to Martín.

"Why?"

"Because I'm going to undress now."

"I doubt very much you have anything I haven't seen," he teases.

"Do you want to see what I can do or not?"

He obliges, and as he does, I fall on my knees and surrender my body to the Panther. My bones start to crack, and my nose elongates into a muzzle.

When the shift is complete, I grunt, and Martín whirls to face me.

He looks at me for a long moment, taking me in. If I could speak, I'd ask him to say something. Finally, he smiles. "Pantera. Of course." He comes to me and reaches for my clothes. "I'll take care of those for you." I hiss and he flinches. "You've made your point, Leonora."

As a human in the forest, I'm food. As a panther, I'm at the top of the food chain. I'm home. I rake the forest floor with one paw. Home. I rub against a tree, feeling the bark scratch the skin beneath my fur. Home. I dip my tail into a stream to lure fish, teeth bared, claws bared, eyes focused, and I dive and seize my catch in my mouth. Home.

I swivel my ears. My senses, trained and tautened by long years of danger, recognize the soft shuffling of feet, right legs moving in unison and then left legs, matched by the beat of hearts. I know the threat now, and I'd be reckless to stay a panther. I'll be depleted of my tonalli. Martín leaves my clothes behind a dense thicket, and I shift back there, more hurriedly than my shift to a panther. I slip on my disguise and come out. Martín is unmoving. He already knows we're not alone.

"Get on the ground," he tells me and sinks to his knees. "Acting the wrong way, saying the wrong words, or even thinking the wrong thought can get you ripped to shreds in a matter of seconds. Don't resist."

I oblige.

There are howling cries, then we're surrounded by at least ten rebels bearing arms and torches. At the sight of Martín, they relax slightly, but when they see a black-clad figure in a mask, they quickly go to their weapons in readiness.

"Stand down!" Martín yells in broken Nahuatl. "She's with me!"

One of them swiftly turns toward me, his spear aimed at my chest. It's edged with jagged bits of obsidian, designed to pierce Spanish armor with ease.

"Chipahua, don't!"

I glance up at my attacker. Both sides of his head are shaven, leaving one long braid in the center. I've only seen a Shorn One depicted in books. In Tamoanchan, I learned that none are more skilled than the elite warrior order of the Shorn Ones.

"Chipahua," I say his name with a nod, but he steps forward, preparing to attack.

"Stop, Chipahua!" Martín comes between us. "Pantera has Neza's protection! Lower your weapon!"

It doesn't matter who I am. Not to Chipahua. All he knows is I'm intruding on La Justicia territory, so I throw my hands up and say, "I surrender."

Chipahua doesn't look like the kind of man who smiles, but there's something there—curiosity maybe.

"I surrender," I say again. "You cannot kill me. There is no honor in that. I can't imagine you'd go against your oath as a Shorn One. So what are we doing? I'm generally much more useful when I know what I'm doing."

I take a deep breath to keep my body from trembling with fear.

Chipahua's eyes are cold, hard. He doesn't need a reason to kill me, and if he really wanted to, his spear would already be embedded in my throat.

With a show of reluctance, Chipahua nods to one of his men who kicks my back so that I fall on my stomach, then binds my hands with some kind of rope that smells like coconut and burns my wrists.

Martín and I are led deeper into the forest. Chipahua and the others easily negotiate the terrain, thorny vines, tendrilled branches, and thick mud—more like sludge, really.

"How long before we get to Snake Mountain?" I ask.

Chipahua pushes me forward.

"Chipahua . . . I like your name." I look over at him, eyeing the red ink climbing up his arm. "What does your tattoo say? Is it your oath? To never take a step back in battle?"

He ignores me, all business.

"Is it true you have to perform twenty brave deeds to become a Shorn One?"

He shoves me again. This time, my knees hit the mud. One of them strikes a rock, sending a wave of pain through me.

"Oh, come on!" Martín says. "What's the point of hurting her?"

As we trudge through foliage, the forest becomes alive with different sounds: exciting, mysterious, joyful, frightening. But I do not fear the forest. You're only afraid of what you don't know. Despite its snakes coiled in the trees, insidious spiders lurking underfoot, ants with their stings, the forest has been kinder to me than men have. I'm more closely related to jaguars, eagles, and rabbits than to humans.

I am part of the wilderness, and the wilderness is a part of me.

CHAPTER 26

La Montaña

Ahead, the sacred hill of Coatepec looms.

At the top of Snake Mountain, a temple emerges from the lush forest. I don't allow Chipahua to assist me in climbing the steep staircase of the pyramid. Skulls are stacked on wooden poles, like an abacus. As we enter the teocalli, the temple, we leave this world behind and step into another. Limbs of the majestic and imposing ahuehuetl tree grow from the walls. The trunk soars skyward, and its roots curl through and around the stone pillars like gigantic serpents, as if holding the temple in place.

It is believed they reach down into the ninth and lowest level of Mictlan, the underworld. The trunk represents life in the Fifth Sun, and its highest branches touch the heavens, where they attract the attention of the teteoh. No other plant grows as tall, is as beautiful, provides as much shade, or receives as many offerings from its people, of flowers, honey and coins, even animals. To harm such a tree, a symbol of the universe, a connection between all three worlds— Mictlan, the Fifth Sun, and the Thirteen Heavens—would invite the gods' wrath.

Martín rushes to the front of a crowd assembled before the temple's dais. Neza sits in a chair with a high back in front of a wall of snakes carved into the stone. I believed Neza to be Sin Rostro, the leader of La Justicia, but with his mantle the color of the sky, ear flares, sandals sprinkled with precious gems, and a panache of royal green plumes on his head, it's apparent he is the tlahtoani of Snake Mountain. At his side is a young woman, presumably a queen, the Lady of Coatepec.

"Neza!" Martín says urgently, halfway up the dais steps. "I need you to hear what I have to say." With a nod of Neza's head, Martín goes on. "You have less than a couple of hours to get the people to safety. The Spaniards are coming."

A murmur resounds through the temple.

Neza stands and goes to Martín. "Are you hurt?"

"Did you hear what I just said? As I speak, an army of Spaniards about ten or twenty thousand strong is heading this way." Martín grabs Neza's face between his hands so he will look into his eyes. "Please, you cannot stay here."

I stare, bewildered, from behind my mask. Martín has acted impulsively. To touch the tlahtoani is sacrilege and invites instant death. Only family have that privilege. Chipahua and several others are quick to reach for their spears.

Neza does not flinch at Martín's contact. With no loss of composure, he pulls away from Martín and motions for his men to stand down. Then, he makes his way down the dais steps toward me.

"My lord," I say, realizing Neza is a king. Immediately, I go down on one knee, then press a finger first to the ground, then to my lips, the traditional greeting to those of high rank. "Martín speaks the truth. The Spaniards know your location. They know everything. You have to leave or you're going to die."

"You were brave to come here, Pantera," Neza says placidly. "We kill or capture anyone who might venture too close to our stronghold. The danger we know all too well. We've gathered our warriors." He waves a hand, indicating the men and women congregated in the temple. Different peoples. Different clans. La Justicia.

They've been warned. *How*, I want to ask, but my answer comes instantly as I turn to follow Neza's line of sight.

One of the tribes clears a path for a figure who makes his way to the front, betraying not the slightest emotion. My mind is sent reeling, unable to comprehend what my eyes are seeing.

"Andrés." My cheeks flush, and I am grateful for the mask that hides them. "You're La Justicia?"

His only acknowledgment is to raise his chin.

He is splendidly dressed in an embroidered red-and-white tilmahtli knotted around his neck. It's a distinctive cloak, brilliantly woven with snakes in whirlpools. The more elaborate the tilmahtli, the more advanced the warrior's rank. What's more, it's knotted at the front, over a breastplate. He is a lord. He is the leader of his people.

On their armor and shields is a symbol: a tree with three branches. I'm not familiar with the emblem, but then I remember Andrés once told me he was from Cuernavaca, the land Cortés seized from the Tlahuica. Cuernavaca is what the Spaniards call Cuauhnahuac, since they can't pronounce it. In Nahuatl, it means, "among the trees."

To his sides stand four other men, all chieftains from what I can tell by their garments and beaded sandals. I don't recognize all the symbols, but some of them seem to be Nahuas.

I shift my gaze back to Neza. "You're going to fight, my lord?" I ask, as if the idea is preposterous, but in truth, I'm not surprised. They are La Justicia.

"Snake Mountain is where we all found a home after the Fall," he says. "Here we will stand and fight. We shall be accompanied by the spirits of our ancestors, our murdered fathers and mothers, our brothers and sisters. If we cannot bring salvation to our people, then here we will fight and die."

"Then I will fight with you," I say, "for the ones who have already perished and crossed into the afterlife. On my sword I swear it." Inhaling, I shut my eyes and summon every ounce of tonalli I have left. I concentrate on my nagual, long enough to feel my soul leaving my body in the form of a luminous, silvery-black panther. Screams fill the temple, and some stumble back as the glowing shape of my nagual approaches with a roar. "You don't need to be afraid." I speak the Nahua tongue. I command the Panther, and she relaxes on her side. "I am as you see me."

I shift my gaze to find a staff being thrust toward me.

"This witch is a murderer!"

I reel from a blow across my face, my back smacking into the ground. I shake my head, forcing myself to ignore the piercing pain in my cheek, and adjust my mask. My vision is black at the edges, but I recognize my attacker from the woods. The man Neza called Prince Xico.

"The witch did not look human when she was slaughtering my men, but it *is* her. She is the Panther. She killed my cousin!"

"She murdered our husbands!" a woman behind Prince Xico cries out. "We should take her head right here!"

"No! She has the nagual of the Black God!" someone from Andrés's clan yells. "This would anger Tezcatlipoca!"

"Kill her! Kill her!" the women chant. "Kill the witch!"

My face is wet. I taste blood. "You may choose!" I say over the angry shouting. "You may choose to send me to my death for what I've done, but the Spaniards will be here before Tonatiuh rises. They have cannon, firearms, trained horses, swords made of Toledan steel, and they are led by Spain's most celebrated warlord, a man whose passion for glory is matched only by his determination to enslave or murder as many of your people as he can."

"Are you saying the battle is already lost?" Neza asks.

"I'm saying I'm ready to do it your way, my lord."

Many within the tribes quiet down, curious to hear more of what I have to say.

I spread my arms wide. "If you wish to cut me down, go ahead. Do it now. Here I stand at your mercy."

Prince Xico charges at me again, swinging his staff like a sword.

This time, Andrés yanks on his braid and pulls him down. "No, my lord," he says, wrapping an arm around his neck in a stranglehold. "The girl cannot slash a white throat if she's dead."

"I am not your enemy!" I say more forcibly. "I am not seeking to destroy you. I am not without flaws or fault, but the Spaniards are coming, and I'm standing here eager to fight." I extend my hand. "If you'll let me."

Prince Xico looks at my hand, then back up at my mask. He wrenches himself out of Andrés's grasp with a growl, pushing at his chest. "I have not finished with you yet, witch," he says, before storming off.

From the crowd, a young man steps forward. "Pantera is an ally," he says. At first, I don't recognize him. He looks older than the last time I saw him, haggard and more seasoned. Señor Alonso's son Miguel. I smile at him, though he only sees my mask. Miguel tells his story, the death of his father, and all listen. "My lord, let her fight under your command."

"It is not my command," Neza says. He looks up as the screech of an owl fills the sky. "It's *hers*."

A lechuza circles above, the same one Martín and I saw earlier. As quickly as a shadow vanishes in the sun, a young woman shifts into the bird's place. Two long braids hang from each side of her face, streaming over her brown mantle. It's not until she's coming toward me that I know who I'm looking at. The last time I saw her was the night La Justicia attacked, and she was covered in red-and-blue war paint. Inés told me all about the indomitable Princess Eréndira of the Purépecha people who taught herself how to ride horses and fight against the invaders. But Inés did not tell me the princess could also take the form of an owl.

If I wasn't wearing my guise, they would see my raised eyebrows. Nahualli are not the only ones who assume the form of an animal. Eréndira is a chichtli mocuepa; her magic is chichyotl, the sorcery of witches who can shift into owls. The stories of owl witches seem to vary from person to person. For some, they are vengeful spirits. For others, they are women of darkness who made a pact with the lord of Mictlan. In all the stories, however, they are able to transform into screech owls with enormous wings.

It seems Eréndira is respected, and the people wait to hear what she has to say.

"Beneath the mask of our own struggles, we are *all* La Justicia. And while in the past we may have fought against each other, against a foe like Spain we will unite." She looks at me. "We will unite against the white invaders, and we will triumph."

Eréndira speaks with boldness, confidence, and compassion. She speaks like a woman who knows what she's doing.

She reaches for my forearm and grips it firmly. She's seen my face before. She knows who I am underneath the mask. "Thank you for standing with us, Pantera."

"My brothers and sisters," Neza says, "you set foot on those hills, and you make them not a meadow but a battlefield. This is *our* land! May our gods give us victory!"

CHAPTER 27

La Verdad

Martín's calli is a four-sided hut with a smoke hole in the center of the thatched roof and a reed partition that shuts off a small corner where I lie stretched out on a woven mat. It's a single story, as only high-ranking noblemen are allowed to build higher.

Someone throws open the drape covering the doorway.

Andrés enters carrying a platter. His movement is quiet, but I don't startle. I half expected him to come. I wanted him to.

My stomach growls, unladylike, at the smell of food. I sit up on my mat, suddenly conscious of how hungry I am.

"I thought you might want to eat," he says, setting the platter on the table next to me.

I survey the dish. There are tamales wrapped in maize husks stacked on a plate. Peeled halves of avocados. Beans and a bowl of maize porridge. The sweet baked leaves of the maguey plant, and my favorite, chirimoyas. A jug of cold pulque and frothy chocolate to wash it down.

If he thinks I'm going to eat all that, he has never been more right.

"Aren't you hungry?" he says, seeing me hesitate.

Starving.

"Are you so afraid of letting me see you, Pantera?"

I would need to remove my mask. I would need to disclose my secret, bare myself to him. I push myself up from the floor and pace the hut, my mind racing. If he knew the real me and all I've done, would he reject me? Would he think I'm a murderer? A fraud? Why do I even care what he thinks?

"Eat," he says. "You're going to need your strength." He straightens to depart.

"Andrés," I say as he is leaving. He turns around. "Lord. I don't know what to call you."

"Tezca. Tezcacoatzin is my Tlahuica name."

"Tezca."

I walk up to him, intensely aware of his tonalli, already imprinted and remembered so well. We stand there for a moment, neither of us uttering a word, and the intense stillness is broken when he lifts his hand toward my face.

On instinct, I grab his wrist.

His brown eyes bear down on me with unnerving intensity. There's a discomfort in my chest, not quite painful, but like my heart is swelling up and pushing against my lungs, grating my ribs. Slowly, I begin uncurling my fingers one by one, loosening my hold. I'm trembling and the little hairs on my arms are standing up, even though I'm not the least bit cold. I hear him breathing and he can hear me breathing and my knees feel near to buckling. He moves his thumb under my chin, tilting my head up. And then he undoes me. He removes my mask.

His face shows no surprise. He looks into my eyes as if he sees something there, like he really knows me.

I feel positively undressed. This is me. I'm not wearing a dress or jewelry. I must look ready to fall over in a faint, covered in sweat, mud, and blood, my hair wet from a combination of all three, as well as the forest dew. Animals are cleaner than this.

Tezca goes to sit on the table and grabs a cloth, wetting it in a basin. I sit beside him and tuck a loose strand of hair behind my ear.

I wait for him to say something, but he seems more inclined to press the cool cloth to my cheeks.

"There you are, señorita," he says when he's finished wiping away the grime. He smiles, and I smile, which is perhaps the first time something of the sort has happened between us.

"How long have you known?" I ask quietly.

"I suppose I always knew but wasn't sure," he says, "not until you said something to me. *I am as you see me*. Do you remember that? I'd heard the same words before. Pantera said them to me the first time we encountered each other on the beach." He meets my gaze. "I see you as you are, Leonora."

I sigh. "You could've told me."

"I wanted it to come from you," he says, "when you were ready."

My stomach rumbles, reminding me there's food on the table. I eat like a starved beast. I slurp the chocolate in great gulps, shove down the tamales, chew the avocados. I make no attempt to justify my poor etiquette.

The first sip of octli goes down smoothly. It is sweet, a little yeasty. Pulque, as it is known to the Spaniards, was once considered the milk of the gods, its consumption restricted to emperors and their priests, but the Spaniards have transformed it into a cheap party drink and the viceroyalty a significant moneymaker from tax collection.

I sink my teeth into a perfectly ripe chirimoya and let out a small, involuntary moan as the sweet taste washes down my throat.

"If I knew you'd be so pleased about food, I'd have fed you earlier."

I wipe my mouth with the back of my hand. "Are you a Nagual, too?" I know the answer, but perhaps he'll care to talk about it.

Everyone is a Nagual. It is Nagualist belief: every person is a Nagual and everyone has a nagual, an animal that shares its soul with you. But only sorcerers have the ability to shift into their animal form or to command their nagual to do their bidding. It requires an exchange of tonalli. If you're hungry, it gets hungry, and if someone kills it, you die.

"Tezca."

"I don't know," he says. "I don't know how it happens. It's just something I do."

"Something you do? That's . . ." I say, "not possible. One is not simply born a sorcerer. You must've had training, years of practice to possess the tonalli you do. Whenever I'm around you, I'm more powerful. Haven't you noticed? That kind of tonalli can only belong to—" I stop myself. My lips tremble. "You're not human, are you?"

He looks at me for a long moment, as if weighing something. "There was a woman. She came to my mother when I was born, and she visited me several times during my youth. She spoke to me of my father, said I inherited my nagual from him."

"Your father? And who would that be?"

"Tezcatlipoca."

I shake my head because I didn't hear right. I can't have. "Your father is the Black God?"

"Quemah."

This revelation makes me feel faint. The first god, Ometeotl, both male and female, gave birth to four sons. Over the north presides the Black God, Tezcatlipoca, the First Sun, lord of sorcery, the night and darkness, patron of war and discord. He, together with his brothers Quetzalcoatl, Xipe Totec, and Huitzilopochtli created the lesser gods and the world.

"So, what, you're a . . . teotl?" As I'm asking the question, I realize that, as the Black God's son, he must have god tonalli, far superior. No—he *is* this divine force. Tonalli comes from the dual god Ometeotl, reaching humans in the womb. God tonalli, however, is teotl, which makes up everything that exists, including itself. This force doesn't come from anywhere. It has no beginning, no end. It simply is.

"I'm not a god," Tezca answers. "I was born of mortal parents. I rely on food, water, and sunlight for nourishment. The tetcoh rely only on power drawn from worshippers. Prayer, sacrifice."

I blink, dazed.

A silence falls, and I concentrate on drinking my pulque, as if the answers to the questions plaguing me lie at the bottom of the cup.

"Go ahead. Ask," he says.

"What?"

"I know you want to ask."

"Are you immortal?"

"Ahmo," he says, "but that's not the question you truly wanted to ask."

"Why did you take my medallion?"

"You really don't know, do you?"

I take another sip of my pulque.

"The Dark Mirror is a dangerous weapon," he says. "It belongs to my father. Tezcatlipoca uses his mirror to spy upon his subjects, read minds, sees into anyone's darkest fears. It corrupts everyone who wears it. It is said that few can endure the Black God's gaze." He tilts his head, regarding me with curiosity. "*You* did. Now how is that possible?"

I, too, wonder this, but the pulque has created a soft fire inside me, and I snort, already fuzzy and warm. I feel the ground rocking beneath me, and my head is swimming.

"Get some rest," he says as he stands. "It's going to be a long day tomorrow."

I gulp the last of my pulque. "Tezca." I get up from my seat, closing the distance between us. "If I die tomorrow, will you burn me and send my teyolia to Tonatiuh?"

"You're not going to die," he replies firmly.

"Don't you know? My death has been foretold." I hiccup. "I'm cursed, so . . . if I am to fall in battle, I suppose I'm permitted to make a fool of myself." Our lips are but a whisper apart.

He takes a step back. "Leonora."

I frown. "Don't . . . don't you want this?"

Tezca sighs, as if those four words nearly undid the last of his restraint. "You're drunk."

"So?"

"So I don't go around bedding any woman who shows me the least bit of attention."

"You don't?"

That seems to make his expression turn cold. "What makes you think I'm not particular about my bed partners?" he says, distinctly annoyed.

"Well, what else can I think from what I've seen? Am I supposed to believe you are a man of discriminating taste?"

"Leonora," he says sternly. "If you want to say goodbye, write a letter. If you want *this*, have a little respect for me."

"Or maybe you're afraid," I say to his back as he walks away. I tell myself it's the pulque talking, not really me. But alcohol can't talk.

He faces me and crosses his arms. "Afraid of what?"

"Of us."

"Why would that scare me?"

"I just told you. Because I am cursed," I say confidently as if I didn't just slur my words. "I am fated to die in battle. So, yes, I think you're scared, just plain scared, of being with me, if only once, on what could very well be my last night beneath the Fifth Sun."

Silence hangs in the air, then Tezca tilts his head, his eyes cutting through me. "Not used to getting turned down, are you?"

"Your tonalli is certainly powerful, but it is depressed."

He scoffs. "Depressed?"

"What did you think happened when you healed my leg? I felt you, your blood, your aches, your life, all of it in me. You have a lot of anger inside you. You don't open up to people, nor do you trust them. You carry a great burden, and you dwell on what you could have done differently. It weighs you down. I don't know how many people you've lost, but I know it can't be easy going through that pain. And I think that's really terrifying for you."

His gaze is intense, serious, and I can hear his heart racing. "It can't be that I'm not interested, it has to be that I'm afraid of being with you. Is that right?"

"You know what I do when I'm terrified? I act tough, even when I'm not. I see you as you are, Tezcacoatzin."

I go to sleep, drunk and alone.

I wake to the blowing of a conch horn. I am on my feet before my eyes are even open. In my sleepiness, I think the distress call is a summon for Pantera, but it only blows once not thrice.

Martín is a blur in the dark. "They're here."

I reach for the Sword of Integrity beside my sleeping mat. I fight with the straps of my sandals and slip on my padded vest. "Will you fasten it for me?"

"Aren't you going to wear your guise?"

My eyes flit to my cloak, hanging on the back of a chair by the hearth.

"It's not dry," I lie. Every time I put it on, I think of Inés wearing it.

Martín pulls at the strings of my vest.

"Tighter."

"It will slow you down."

"I can't outrun a bullet." I slide my scabbard over my head. "Where's your armor? You need protection too, Martín."

"Oh, I'm not going anywhere. Someone has to hold down the fort, you know." He laughs nervously. "We can't have this place falling to pieces with everyone away, can we?"

I am quiet, looking at him.

"Don't worry about me, Leonora," he says with a smile. "I'll be all right. Now go."

I lean in and give him a tight hug.

"What was that for?"

"You're a good man, Martín El Mestizo," I say, then slip out into the night.

I say my prayers to the god of war, Huitzilopochtli, looking at the hummingbird inked on my right hand.

Warrior, come to our aid. There is war, there is burning. Guide my sword arm. Let her sing in battle.

CHAPTER 28

La Batalla

Tonatiuh still hides below the horizon, but the pre-dawn light illuminates a banner along the summit of a high ridge. With no wind to blow it, the flag of the Crown hangs like a dead thing on its pole.

"Hold steady, warriors." Eréndira's voice comes from the front of the line. "We attack on my command, not before." She tips her chin at me, and I nod in agreement. If we're to battle, the Spaniards will have to come down the hill. It's necessary to maintain formation. We the ranks stand shield to shield, weapons in hand, one mind and body united in a single purpose, all waiting for the signal to strike.

Neza's tribe is beating drums and blowing conch-shell trumpets and bone flutes. Jaguar and Eagle Warriors dressed like their namesake animals stand in all their feathered and colorful glory, perfectly suited to the forest. A few Shorn Ones, who have the honor of being first in battle, are at the front. Chipahua is among them, probably burning with impatience to shed blood.

We form a square several ranks deep, and I'm in the corner of the shield wall, which means there is no one to protect me on my right. I have an old shield with a loose handle. My armor has holes. I'm wearing a helmet shaped like a bird, for neither am I nobility nor do I have rank high enough to wear a decorated helmet, but it at least covers my face. I am the weak link in an otherwise impenetrable shield wall. The Spaniards will try to overrun my flank. I'd be lying if I said I wasn't terrified. But I must win my place. I must prove my worth.

"Shields!" Eréndira commands, and all at the same time, those in the wall kneel, placing their shields upright in front of them.

Someone tugs my arm. I look to my left and she is only a girl, a girl too young and innocent to understand war. She looks no older than twelve, with her face and bald head painted in red patterns. Her name is Zyanya, which she explains means "forever," so Zyanya is forever. "You must kneel," she says in Nahuatl. I drop to one knee just as the second rank raises their shields, interlocking them with those of us in the front so our attackers face a double wall. So long as we keep our shields firm, we will be safe enough.

"What did you do?" I ask Zyanya.

"Do?"

"You're in the shield wall." Clearly, someone wants her dead.

She looks at me, says nothing. Her eyes are kind. They remind me of Inés.

"Spears out!" Eréndira shouts the next order. Spears immediately thrust out of the shield wall from the line of warriors behind me, with such ferocity I flinch. Zyanya doesn't.

I would guess there are more than ten thousand of us: seven clans, mostly Nahuas, banded together to form La Justicia—Tlahuica, Mixtec, Raramuri, Purépecha, Tlaxcalan, Chichimeca, and Mexica.

Across the field, the Spaniards hold the hill. It seems neither side is willing to make the first move. I remain crouched behind the barrier formed by our shields, with the Sword of Integrity in my right hand. The day is getting warmer, and I am getting thirsty. Still, the two armies don't move.

A low rumbling begins, as if the ground is clearing its throat, and then there are shouts from the enemy ranks. Wiping the sweat from my eyes, I look forward through a small slit in the shield wall. I glimpse four legs in the distance, then eight, and twelve, and in a second more than forty. The foot soldiers' chests are armored in mail like the horses' and their masters'.

The Spaniards have hounds—wolfhounds, greyhounds, and mastiffs the size of ponies, trained to fight and kill with the utmost ferocity, and they relish human flesh.

"It is a good day to die," Eréndira says. I can hear the thrill in her voice. "Tighten it up. Stay in formation."

I still can't see very well, but I can hear the snarling packs and the oncoming charge of cavalrymen. "The line won't hold!" I say in a panic.

Eréndira remains calm. "It will."

I push myself up from the ground and take a couple of steps toward her. "Listen to me," I say. "You may all be fierce warriors, but when the hounds overrun us, and they *will*, you're going to witness what a massacre really looks like, and this battle will be over before it even begins."

"Protect the flank, Pantera," she says. "That is an order."

I curse under my breath and fall into step, teeth clenched.

"Brave or stupid, which one are you?" Zyanya taunts.

The very nature of our formation demands strict obedience. The wall is disciplined, bodies tensed, feet braced, waiting for the shock of impact. I am filled with fear. I debate the plan. Seconds pass like minutes.

"Gods above me!" The men around me take up the rhythm. "Gods above me!"

All along the ranks, warriors join the chant.

The Sword of Integrity quivers for a second in my hand. *Huitzilopochtli, come to our aid. Help us bring down our enemies. If I've been fully armed and ready for war from the very moment of my birth, help me bring down my enemies.*

"Let them fly!" The order rings out from Nucano, the Mixtec chieftain.

With a snap of bowstrings, a cloud of arrows whistle through the air, then hit their targets. I do not know how many hounds fall dead in that instant, but a second flight hails down to bury their shafts into the flesh of men and animals alike. That slows the Spaniards down briefly. Prince Xico and his Chichimeca archers are in the trees, firing from the forest canopy. A mixture of excitement, fear, and elation all makes my legs jittery.

"Signal the advance," Eréndira says to the man beside her, the Raramuri chieftain Rahui.

"Throw!" he bellows.

At the command, a barrage of spears and javelins are released from his line, one after another, pinning about a third of the Spanish horsemen to the ground before they come within fifty paces of us. Rahui surges ahead, stamping his bare feet against the earth. I watch him dive into the midst of the Spanish cavalry at a full sprint, moving farther and faster than any man should be able to in the rough terrain without shoes. The sight is so incomprehensible, I frown. He runs like a predator intent on his prey, and the warhorses flee as if possessed, which disrupts their formation.

"Come, my enemy! We will battle!" Eréndira yells triumphantly. "Ready yourselves, warriors. Try to stay out of trouble," she says, before throwing herself into the field as though her life is nothing.

I look above the rim of my shield. It is a scene of carnage, Toledan steel against obsidian-edged wood. A terrible sight. It is then I first see Chipahua fight, and marvel at him. He cuts down men as if harvesting wheat, leaving behind a gruesome trail of blood. Then he emerges from the brush and hurls a snake at the first unfortunate soldier who crosses his path.

"Welcome to Snake Mountain!" he shouts proudly. *Mad bastard.*

In the middle of this chaos, a Spanish cavalryman forces his horse through a cluster of adversaries. One of them plucks him from his saddle as if he's a leaf lifted by the wind and flings the soldier to the ground. The horseman rises and when his helmet comes off, revealing honeyed curls, a tubby face, and a bloody nose, my heart stops.

Jerónimo.

I let loose a cry. "No!"

My brother has his sword and his spirit, but he's never been more in danger than now. I glance nervously to my right, searching for the threat of a flanking movement. To my left, Zyanya is breathing in short spurts, either because she's squatting behind her heavy shield, or because she's scared, or both. Hold the line. Stay in rank. Shield to shield. That is the plan. But the greatest wisdom of Nagualism is to lay no plans. Maybe Zyanya will be all right because her shield is bigger than she is. My hands tremble. *Do it, Leonora, just do it.* I follow my own instincts. I tell Zyanya I'm sorry and adjust my helmet.

"Gods above me!" I roar a panther's call and pick up a speed born of desperation. Jerónimo is fighting warriors left and right. I'm there in three bounds. The Sword of Integrity cuts through the air as it slices into one of the attackers.

I turn back to my brother. "Go now, quickly!"

Jerónimo looks overcome. "Why are you helping me?"

A second warrior charges at me, swinging his club for my head. I shove him back with a burst of tonalli.

"Who are you?" Jerónimo says.

"Get out of here!"

Hauling himself up into the horse's saddle, he takes off the way he came. Captain Nabarres, mounted on his steed alongside General Valdés, watches the scene from his vantage point on the hill.

A scrawny soldier aims his sword at my chest. I leap out of the way, but it gashes my arm. I look down at the blood seeping out, then back up as a second Spaniard rushes over, and I lift my blade to cut them both down, but to my surprise the second soldier drops to the ground and swipes at my opponent's shins. He'll never walk again. But he won't have to. The soldier plunges his blade into the man's neck.

My unexpected friend removes his helmet and nods to me before hurling himself at the enemy, shouting war cries. He wears Spanish armor, but he's not a Spaniard. I look around and realize Nabarres is aided by hundreds, maybe thousands of Indigenous men.

There is simply no way Nabarres made allies on his own. He lacks the language, the awareness, even the understanding necessary to determine which tribe to ally with. Only the people from here have this knowledge. I whip my head and Tezca is shouting at the false Spaniards to give the white demons something to remember us by, and they do, hacking mercilessly. I smile, witnessing the result of his plotting, the reason for him aiding Nabarres. He infiltrated the Spanish army. The belly of the beast.

A scream from behind makes me turn back. A Spaniard falls from his horse with so many arrows sticking out of his armored chest he looks like a prickly pear. I am in the thick of battle and death is on every side. I run straight and catch a Spaniard's ankles with my sword as I pass him, leaving him for someone else to finish. It is not him I want. I jump over corpses piled high, my eyes on the red cloak Nabarres is wearing over his armor.

"Narcizo!"

I start up the hill, chopping, whirling, soaring, and lunging. The Sword of Integrity is wet with Spanish blood.

"Narcizo!"

I close in, dodging and countering every blow and slash thrown at me. It's not easy, but I think of those who are no longer with me: Inés, Señor Alonso, my father and mother, Valiente, and I'm suddenly invincible, though I broke our shield wall and that will not be without consequences. When I reach the top of the hill, General Valdés shouts for mercy but receives none. I plunge my sword into his chest, then dig my foot into his bloody flesh to drag the Sword of Integrity free.

Captain Nabarres, like a good general, calmly dismounts his horse. I remove my helmet and drag my sword in the dirt as I move toward him, my breath coming in ragged heaves.

"So it *is* you," he says amusedly. "Where is your mask, Pantera?"

"I want you to see my face before you die, Narcizo."

"It's bad form to choose a sword that has already defeated you."

"I'll take my chances."

I swing the Sword of Integrity, all savagery and anger, and let her edge do the work. It's a good stroke, but Nabarres unsheathes his blade, meeting mine with a loud clang. My arm has grown weak, and the blow rips the Sword of Integrity from my grasp.

"Some legend," he says with a mirthless chuckle. "You think you're some kind of hero, girl? You're a criminal, a murderer, and a traitor. Tell me, Pantera, how does it feel? How does it feel to betray your own people?"

"You are not my people," I say bitterly.

Below, the Spanish are retreating from the fury of La Justicia, their army running, escaping on horseback. The wounded and dead lie thickly on the ground, baking under the unrelenting sun.

"Se acabó, Narcizo," I say, breathing hard. "There's no chance of getting out of this alive. Surrender and I promise I will kill you quickly."

Nabarres kicks my sword further out of my reach and points his own at me. "Just what is it you think you've accomplished today? You killed a couple of soldiers, maybe a dozen. But you know as well as I that it is far from over. The war will continue. Do you know what your problem is, Pantera?"

"I'm looking at it."

"You can't win against me," he says. "Yes, you are younger, faster, and you are a good fighter, yet you fail every time. Do you know why? Because your pursuits are misguided. You don't know what you're doing. I do."

In a blur of motion, he is upon me, slashing the air with his blade. I dodge his swings, twist out of the way, looking for the quickest way to end the fight. Tearing off my armor, I somersault over him and strike him a passing blow, with a kick to the back.

Nabarres wavers forward, squares up, and faces me. "Nice trick," he says. "Is that what your forest friends taught you?"

"No. This is." I don't have my sword in hand, but I do have a paw with four sharp knives. I whirl, feeling my nails lengthening into claws, and I rake them across his face, drawing blood. Nabarres stumbles back, his eyes widening as he presses his gloved hand against his cheek.

"That's going to leave a scar," I say. "Don't worry. It won't matter once you're dead."

Screaming, he lifts his sword and charges in my direction, but in his haste, he steps on the spilled guts of General Valdés and slips. Before he can steady his footing, I pick up the Sword of Integrity and slide it horizontally, and he knows then: he knows he is going to die. And I know the day will feel like victory.

There is a hiss of air and an arrow hits the end of my sword, knocking it from my hand. I glance over my shoulder. Instinctively, I lean back, dodging another arrow by a scant inch. The next arrow I manage to catch in mid-air. With blurring speed, Prince Xico leaps from the trees, his long dark hair floating loose from its braid as he barrels into me. We tumble down the hill in a tangled heap of arms and legs, branches and vines tearing at my skin. I land with a loud thump on a mossy rock in a nearby stream and lie breathless from the impact. Aching from head to toe, I pick myself up from the onrushing water, sopping wet.

"I told you I was not finished with you, witch," Prince Xico says, his dark eyes holding a challenge.

My tongue darts out to lick a cut on my lip. I look up the hill and see Nabarres fleeing on his horse.

I react. Badly. My shift is rushed, torturous. The fury gives me strength. I don't feel the pain because the anger completely takes over. I run and leap into the air, and before touching ground, my toes become paws, my tail sprouts from behind me. I roar my loudest, most terrifying growl, a deep, chesty sound, and charge at him.

Prince Xico comes at me. He is fast, snake fast. He wants to carve a hole in my chest, and he will not rest until he has done so. I know this because I killed his cousin and men in the woods and because he's carrying a tecpatl, an obsidian sacrificial knife, meant to rip out hearts. I pounce on him, and he flies backward. I feel his weapon nick the side of my neck and slash across my shoulder. My fur is thick. It's only an irritating scratch. My teeth clamp around his shoulder, but his knife stabs again, this time into my underbelly. I let out an agonized hiss. He thrusts it deeper. I feel it rasp against bone as it scrapes my ribs.

The roar of a wildcat rumbles and Prince Xico is torn away from me. I lift my gaze to see a jaguar shifting, then Tezca is standing over me, in full battle regalia. It's the second time I've seen Tezca's nagual, and I think about how he can shift his clothes along with his body. That technique is more complex. It requires the utmost skill and discipline, two things that are beyond my capabilities, as Master Toto often reminded me.

Prince Xico pushes himself up from the ground, cracks his neck left and right. "This is not over, Tezcacoatzin." If anger were visible, the air would be crimson. He disappears into the thicket without another word.

My heart thuds dully. I pull back, feeling my bones snap, muscles shrinking, fangs retracting.

I am naked, of course. Completely nude for Tezca to see. Master Toto says vanity is an odd human concept. Nothing natural should need to be hidden.

I touch my side. My fingers come away covered in blood.

Tezca approaches me. Sitting back on his ankles, he sighs a sigh edged with a groan and raises a hand to my wound.

"No," I say weakly. "Don't."

"You will die."

"I am ready."

"I am not."

"There is nothing we can do to stop the inevitable."

"Yes, there is. I can close the wound."

"This . . ." My eyes start to close, but I force them to stay open. "This is not what the curse intended."

"To the Nine Hells with the curse. We make our own destiny, Leonora. The teteoh are not gods any more than we are."

I can feel myself dying. I'm trembling and sucking in air as if through a tiny hole. I'm suffocating. Is this what Inés felt? A tear runs down my cheek. I will soon join her. We will follow the sun in its journey across the heavens. Will she be waiting? I will leave all the pain behind. I close my eyes. I am ready.

CHAPTER 29

El Calor

I awake in Martín's calli to a flickering hearth fire and the smell of herbs. Sweat drips from my forehead, running in little rivers down my neck. Blinking, I clear my vision and Tezca comes into focus, slumped in a corner, his face passive, baggy flesh underneath his eyes.

"Why?" I croak. "Why did you heal me? I did not give you permission to—"

"I did not ask your permission, and I will not ask your pardon. I'm a ticitl, a healer. My calling is to heal, and it takes precedence over your death wish. I've sat here all day and refrained from doing that which I must do," he says. "I did not heal you. She did."

I push myself up on my elbows, feeling a bandage of crushed plants on my stomach. I slowly pull it back and grimace as its leaves cling to dry blood. The wound has been sutured closed with some kind of hair, but it is red and tender, not entirely healed. Another scar.

"Don't excite yourself or you'll open your stitches." I turn to look at Zyanya, whose bald head resembles that of a priestess, except her mantle is green, while priestesses wear black. She's grinding plants with a mortar and pestle and speaks directly to the crushed herbs in the stone bowl. "Ometeotl, Mother and Father, supreme creator who resides in the Thirteenth Heaven, bring the cure for this sick flesh. It is I who speak, the ticitl." She places her hands on my stomach, just below the ribs. "The sap of the metl will help clean the wound," she says, rubbing it into the gash. My face twists in discomfort. Gods, it hurts something fierce. "Chicalotl is for the pain."

"You're alive," I say dazedly.

"After you broke our shield wall, I had to look after myself," she says. "Luckily, I'm really good at surviving."

"I'm sorry," I say. "They were going to kill my brother. I'm glad to see you, Zyanya."

"Here, drink this." She holds a dipper gourd to my lips.

I shake my head and shut my eyes, suppressing several different kinds of repulsion.

"Chalalatli. For your bewitched head," she says.

A crease forms between my brows. "My bewitched head?"

"I have held a jar of water under your chin and seen your shadowed reflection," she explains. "You are suffering from tetonalcahualiztli. Your tonalli is lost."

Ridiculous. My tonalli is not lost. I have not cut my hair, and my head is still attached to my neck.

Zyanya looks down at my stomach. I feel her small hands on my belly.

"You're an awfully sick woman, Pantera," she says, though I'm not wearing my mask. "Have you been attacked by a chaneque recently?"

"What?"

"They have a reputation for making you sick and stealing tonalli because they don't have tonalli of their own. Well, have you?"

"No."

"Are you sure?"

I shift uncomfortably on my mat, causing the reed to crinkle. "I think I'd know if I was attacked by a chaneque. I am not sick," I say crossly. "I am angry."

"Do you not think that anger is a sickness?"

With an annoyed shake of my head, I adjust my pillow and watch the smoke curling upward. In the center of the hut, the hearth fire crackles.

"Have you enjoyed a man or a woman's touch in the past few days?" she asks.

My first reaction is to glance at Tezca, and he's already looking at me, seemingly waiting for me to respond. My eyes skitter away from his. "What?"

"Pleasure, Pantera," Zyanya says as if it is obvious. "Sometimes, during sex, tonalli can leave the body. When was the last time you lay with someone?"

"I'm not going to answer that."

"Why not?"

"Because you're four years old."

"I'm ten, fool," she says.

"My point exactly. You haven't even bled yet."

"Did I say fool? I meant stupid. Stupid iztac colelehtli."

"Call me a white demon one more time."

"Iztac colelehtli."

"Are you two finished?" Tezca scolds us with a look.

I sit up on my mat, groaning with each movement. I settle into a slouch. "I'm sorry, tell me again why a child is the authority on healing?" I turn to Zyanya. "You're insulting and you're wrong, so I don't have to listen to you."

"She is not wrong," Tezca says. "You are barely alive, and it's thanks to Zyanya that you're alive at all."

"Death comes for everyone," Zyanya says. "No ticitl can prevent death."

"So, my tonalli is lost and I'm going to die? Is that your conclusion?"

"Yes. Unless you retrieve the tonalli from wherever it might be found or whomever might have taken it. I'm sorry I called you a stupid iztac colelehtli. I thought you already knew. Well, I feel better. I should apologize more often."

I don't argue. Can't. The combination of my supposedly absent tonalli, and being in agony, weakened, fatigued, blistered by the sun, parched with thirst, and too dispirited to bother, sinks me into a deep, dark pit of apathy.

"I can try to locate it," Zyanya tells me, "but I make no promises. Tonalli decides. Tonalli knows best."

I frown in confusion. "What does that even mean?"

"Tonalli is capricious and has a will of its own. It follows its desires, whatever they may be."

"Great," I snipe. "My tonalli hates me."

Zyanya places her hands on my temples and smears a smoky-smelling mud across my forehead. "Ometeotl, it is I who speak, the ticitl. I seek the tonalli of this bewitched head. Where is it? I seek the vital force, the tonalli, where has it gone? Where is it detained? I call the tonalli back. I call it back!"

A strange wind snakes through the hut with a spectral howl, and the hearth fire goes cold, extinguishing every candle in its wake. There is a moment of blackness as the light goes out, then the fire bursts back to life with an unearthly hue of violet flames.

Zyanya and Tezca trade glances.

My pulse quickens. "What was that?"

"Lord and Lady Ometeotl, the original source of tonalli, have spoken," Zyanya says.

"Can you be less vague?"

"How can I put this?" She scratches her bald head. "There is a way, but it is impossible. I suggest you pray and make the best of it."

"You mean until my inevitable death?"

"Tonalli is what makes you, well . . . you. You need tonalli to live. Without it, you will forget who you are, where you come from, your family, even your own name. One day, you will not be able to speak. It will be a living death."

"Wonderful. Thank you for the words of encouragement," I say.

"A powerful healer can retrieve the missing tonalli, but you must exchange something of equal value."

"Bargain for my tonalli? Something that valuable can only belong to the gods."

"Do you want your tonalli back or not? Decide quickly, while you're still . . . you." As she's about to leave the hut, she turns around to look at me, lips thinning, brows furrowing. "I'm sorry."

I wrestle with the mat, trying to find comfort on first one side, then the other, but I lose the fight. The ache in my muscles makes me feel more like a wooden doll than a woman of blood and bone. I roll over and stare at the wall. A haze of sleep sits somewhere at the back of my mind but is too far away to reach.

"Promise me you will never do that again," I say quietly.

"Never do what again?" Tezca says.

"Interfere."

"Xico was going to kill you."

"That's my worry," I say, "not yours."

"It's called helping, Leonora. You're welcome. That's what you do when someone is in trouble. You help them."

"And I am telling you not to. Ever."

"I'm confused," he says. "Is that not what you did for your brother on the field? Help him? Did you not interfere?"

I am quiet.

"What do you say we play a game?" he asks.

I turn on my side to face him. "What game?"

"The game where I pretend I don't know why you're really upset and you admit it yourself."

"What a stupid game."

"Just admit it, Leonora. It'll make you feel better. I promise."

"Admit *what*?" I say in a petulant voice.

"Are you going to say it, or should I?" He waits, but I remain quiet. "Very well. I'll say it. Inés is dead, and you blame yourself for it."

"Don't say her name." I reach for the Sword of Integrity and try to spring off the mat, but at the first movement, the wound in my side burns so intensely I fall back down, wincing.

"Do yourself a favor, Leonora. Decide what it is you want. Do you want to kill me? Or do you want to bed me?"

My nostrils flare as I look up at him. "I may have been weak last night, but it will not happen again."

If my words cut him, he doesn't show it. "Go ahead, then. Blame me for Inés's death and maybe you can move on with your life."

My tonalli-less, life.

"You could've saved her," I say finally. "You've done it before. You did it to me."

"I can't revive the dead, Leonora. What do *you* think happened when I healed you? Your tonalli was so poisoned I nearly collapsed. It gave me a headache for weeks. I've healed many wounds. New wounds, old wounds, wounds going back to childhoods. I took your injury into my body. I took your pain and your suffering. But this," he stretches his cloak to the side to show me his leg, and he has a scar right above the knee, "this you gave me. That's never happened before."

I bury my face in my hands.

"I'm sorry," Tezca says. He speaks softly, with a gentle, lilting quality to his voice that at the moment I find unexpectedly soothing. "I know she was important to you."

That night, some twenty warriors gather around a hearth with loud drums and shrill trumpets and dance to celebrate victory over the Spaniards. The men whirl and stamp with bells around their ankles, the song rising in intensity to honor Huitzilopochtli, the god of war. Every movement tells a story. People are on their feet, singing, drinking, and rejoicing in the night. Miguel is there, celebrating, and I think about his father. If I had saved him . . . There's nothing I can do now.

From outside Martín's hut, I can see the ahuehuetl blending into the teocalli walls, the forest all around. This remarkable tree has taken more than a thousand years to grow, and I wonder at the things it knows. The things it has seen. I think of my own life compared to that tree, and I realize how little I know. How little I've seen. To be that tall and strong and old. I feel a great emptiness and sadness inside.

Zyanya comes to me with a scowl. "Pantera, what are you doing? Why aren't you in bed? If you ignore the loss of your tonalli—"

"I will die. Yes, you've only mentioned it seven hundred times."

She frowns. "I don't understand. Don't you want to live?"

"What difference does it make if I die today or a week from now?"

"I'm sorry," she says quietly.

"Don't ever be sorry for me, kid. I won't be missed around here."

"You're not the only one who's done something wrong. Don't you want to make it right?"

"Zyanya, I've been fighting all kinds of wars since the day I left my mother's womb. I'm tired. I have very little fight left in me."

"And yet you're clearly not the sort of person who lies down when she ought to. It's all over now. The Spaniards retreated. We won. You don't have to fight anymore. You can rest."

"Just because there's no fighting, that doesn't mean there's peace. Even if the war were over, Spain is still in power. It will not be truly over until Spanish rule ends."

"Do you think that will ever happen?"

I seldom think far into the future. That's the thing about being doomed. "It will take a miracle," I say. "The viceroy believes he answers only to his god and his king, ordained by each to lead the people of the New World. I don't know about you, but if someone told me every day of my life that I was chosen by my gods to rule everyone around me, I would probably uphold my duty to my last breath too."

She watches me carefully. "What is a miracle?"

"Christians believe miracles are impossible happenings that cannot be explained."

Zyanya is quiet while she seems to give that some thought. She looks down, picking nervously at her dirty fingernails. "When Tezca brought you to me, I saw the wound in your belly and there was a lot of blood. There was no heartbeat. You were dead. Tezca and I thought you were dead."

"You brought me back to life?"

"No, I don't have that ability," she says. "A miracle did."

I smile briefly before feeling a spear pressed against my back. "Move, witch."

"Prince Xico, don't—!"

"It's all right, Zyanya," I say, then we turn toward the fire pit. I feel Xico's hand on my shoulder as he brings me down to my knees. I clutch my wound, wincing as pain sears through me.

"Tlahtoani!" Xico raises his voice above the music.

The drumming falters and the dancers halt. Everyone snaps their gazes to us, eyebrows raised. I see Tezca with his people, and he clasps a hand to his hilt. I shake my head at him.

Xico yanks my head back, forcing me to look to where Neza stands alongside Martín and Eréndira. Then, he says, "Iztac colelehtli."

I ignore the insult.

"How can a white demon defend our honor?"

I stay quiet, taking in Xico's anger. After a moment, I say, "I used to ask myself the same question. How can someone like me hold your pain while benefiting from an office that affirms the violence against you? I did not know the answer, so I withdrew, I became a shadow, I wore a mask. I was not strong enough to accept myself as I am. I speak Spanish like my father. And Nahuatl . . . Nahuatlahtolli like my mother. I am Spanish. I am Mexica. I walk the nepantla, the middle of two worlds, as do many living in Mexico. I embody this war from which all others are born. I am not the first Spaniard with Indigenous blood, nor will I be the last. I will not dishonor my father or my mother."

"Can we kill her now?" Xico sneers.

Neza comes forward. "There will be no killing of the daughter of Nican Nicah," he says, and I blink. *Who?*

Xico is wordless with rage, then Martín speaks. "She doesn't know."

"Don't know what?" I ask anxiously.

"Don Joaquín was no stranger to us," says Neza. "We knew him well. I am revealing to you the real identity of Nican Nicah. Your father was one of us."

If I wasn't already on my knees, my legs would go out from under me. "What?"

"Nican Nicah helped our people," Neza says. "He listened to what we had to say. He acknowledged the tyranny and corruption wrought by his own office and fought against it. He was La Justicia. We all are."

My mind whirls with scattered memories of my father. Jerónimo almost never talks about him, hardly even mentions his name. All I know is that he died too soon, and I miss him terribly.

"You and I are enemies from this day, tlahtoani," Xico says coldly. "My archers and I draw a clear line between you and us. I tell you this, if we cross paths again, be prepared to defend yourself."

CHAPTER 30

La Venganza

I lie awake, half dreaming, thinking of Zyanya's words. My tonalli has been stolen.

Martín sleeps on his mat in a corner of the calli, snoring softly.

In Tamoanchan, I would sit every night intending to write down fragments of what I had learned from the Nagual Headmaster Totoquilhuaztli. Instead, I would fall asleep. Fortunately, Master Toto had a habit of repeating himself, and this made it easy for me to follow him.

Although I tried, I was never the student Master wanted me to be. I was good with a sword, and I could shift into my nagual, which is more than most witches can accomplish, but I never understood his riddles and failed when it came to cultivating my tonalli, therefore my actions were meaningless.

"What good are you without your tonalli?" he asked.

Useless. He didn't say it, but he may as well have. My tonalli this. My tonalli that. It's all he talked about.

Martín wakes and goes outside to piss. He comes inside again and finds me sitting on my mat, leaning against the wall.

"Shouldn't you be asleep?" he asks.

"Shouldn't you be in the palace?"

241

A sad smile pulls at his lips. "They'd sooner skewer my head on the skull rack. He's the tlahtoani of Snake Mountain, Leonora. I will never be able to share Neza's bed or sit with him in the temple. Not like the Lady of Coatepec."

"He's a king. He can take another wife, however many."

He exhales. "The key word being *wife*." He sits next to me. "When he found out about Amalia, he was so angry. It wasn't my plan, but I couldn't help taking that bit of joy, to see him feel even the tiniest hint of what I feel when I see him with his lady. I don't know . . . I was a fool. And I regret lying with Amalia. But you knew that."

I hug my knees. "You love him."

"It can never be," he says faintly, his heart heavy with the knowledge. "Anyway. Enough about me. What's troubling you?"

"I can't shift." I don't even try to convince him that everything's fine.

"What do you mean?"

"I have no magic. Zyanya seems to think I was attacked by a chaneque," I say. "We heard them . . . on our way here. We didn't actually encounter one, did we?"

"I don't think so," Martín answers, "but I've heard you can't see a chaneque even if you try, unless it's their wish to show themselves. The creatures are guardians of the forest. And it's a big forest. I've never seen a chaneque myself."

This doesn't make me feel at ease. I'm tired, I haven't slept, I have aches and bruises and no tonalli. I'm not sure how I'm even breathing.

"For a long time," I say, "I thought I had to hide the Panther to fit into the human world."

"Why?"

"I don't know. To be normal, I suppose."

"Normal." He scoffs. "Whether you have magic or not, you're far from normal, Leonora," he says. "We all hide. I know what it's like myself. To hide my heart. To hide who I am."

The dim light of the torch on the wall touches his face. His pale blue eyes stare ahead. Although in most ways he looks like a Spaniard, with blond, almost gingery hair, he doesn't remind me of one. I never met Cortés or La Malinche, but I imagine Martín takes after his mother in many ways.

"I knew your father Nican Nicah," he says then. "And he knew me. He knew I was the bastard of Cortés. He said I had enemies in court and should anyone find out I was the rightful heir of Cortés, it would not be long before they had my head."

"What do you mean the rightful heir?"

"I was legitimized by the pope in secret."

He says this disinterestedly, as if it has no importance. My mind spins. Jerónimo sent Vicereine Carlota to live in Cortés's hacienda. To be rid of her as viceregent, yes, but to also have her keep a watchful eye on Don Martín, the Marquess of the Valley of Oaxaca. But he is not the rightful heir. The rightful heir of Cortés, El Mestizo, is a threat to my brother's viceroyal rule.

I get to my feet and prop my hands on my hips. "You tell me this *now*? Don Martín isn't old enough to challenge the viceroy, but *you* are. If Jerónimo knew, he would—"

"Get rid of the competition?" he says. "Yes, I know."

"Don Martín has your titles, estates, lands. What do *you* have?"

"My freedom. Some think I'm dead. Others believe I returned to Spain."

He catches my gaze and grins, patting the mat beside him for me to sit. I go to him and he puts his arm around me, then pulls me to his side.

"What now?" I ask, and he shrugs.

I rise before Tonatiuh appears and pray for three things.

First, I pray for strength to endure the loss of tonalli.

Second, I pray it will return to me.

Third, I ask to find peace.

A few houses over, in the Tlahuica settlement, Tezca is feeding the turkeys and collecting eggs, talking to them while they leap around his feet, gobbling. He lifts his gaze, and he knows, maybe from the sour look on my face, where I'm going.

I sling my sheath over my shoulder. "Don't try to stop me."

He tosses a handful of grain from a basin tucked under one arm. "Killing Nabarres won't end your rage."

"Yes, it will."

"Will you feel better when you have his blood on your hands?"

"Yes."

"Is this what Inés would want?"

"All Inés ever wanted was justice for her mother. This is *exactly* what she would want."

"It isn't justice. It's vengeance."

"It's a start," I sneer.

He comes to me. "Listen to me, Leonora," he says, serious, intense. "Are you listening?"

I squeeze my eyes shut and grit my teeth.

"I won't tell you what to do," he says, "but I hope you do the right thing, and this isn't it." A long pause. "You think you're all alone. You're not. My tonalli has been lost, stolen, and damaged far more times than I can count. Once, it left of its own free will. But it came back. Whatever mistakes you've made, it *can* come back. You lost someone you loved. You are allowed to grieve. You are allowed to be angry, hateful, full of rage. You are allowed to be whatever you are right now. Are you still listening?"

"Yes." My voice is weak. All the fight has left me.

"I know it feels as if nothing can ever be all right again. But I promise it will be. You will be. And you will recognize goodness in this world that once felt shattered. And you will hope again." He exhales, then says, "You don't have to die before you're dead."

I stare at him, hoping I don't look as miserable as I feel. "Did I . . . die? Zyanya. She said I died. Is it true? Was I really dead?"

"It's true," he says. "But you're alive now. There's a purpose."

"Purpose. Does everything have to have a purpose? Why did Inés die? For what purpose? Can you tell me that? You use that word as if the teteoh chose me to save the world and forgot to tell me along the way. What if I don't have a purpose? You know what I want? I want to end this belief that I am somehow naturally endowed with the power of a sorceress and skill for tonalli manipulation because I have the nagual of a god. This fantasy sickens me. I am no one's hero and no god's pawn. So leave me alone."

"Be careful," he says. "He's dangerous."

Good. It'll be a fair fight.

My journey from Snake Mountain to the capital is quiet, long, and painful. But the suffering caused by my wound is not nearly as bad as the confusion I feel from the loss of my tonalli, the miserable knowledge that Inés won't be waiting for me when I arrive, or the pure rage that consumes me when I think about Captain Nabarres.

Master often used to say that a Nagual's toughest battle is invisible because it lives between his own two ears. That is because tonalli is most concentrated in the crown of the head, protected by one's hair. You can master your nagual, practice Nagualist teachings, be the greatest of sorcerers, and have such strength that only the gods can tear you down, but without your tonalli, none of this is possible. He insisted that what makes a wizard a sorcerer is tonalli fully aligned to his nagual. Sorcery is learning to maintain the balance of your tonalli. Everything that goes against that threatens the Nagual Path.

I wait inside Nabarres's bedchambers, looking straight ahead at the door. That's the thing about waiting—it forces you to have a conversation with yourself, and when you quiet the mind, thoughts come to you. I don't like to wait, but for this man, I am a cat on the prowl. I am patient. I am still. I am quiet.

Finally, he walks through the door.

"Hola, Narcizo."

He looks at me, then shuts the door behind him and proceeds as if he's alone in the room, barely interested in raising his weapon.

"Would you like a drink, Pantera? Or would you like to kill me first?"

Once, I saw a jaguar feasting on a caiman carcass, when he spotted a group of birds. He went over to chase the birds and killed them as they tried to fly away, without eating a single one. He didn't need to kill them. He did so because he could. Some animals go on a killing spree for no real reason at all—not for food, not for territorial purposes—but more than that, they prolong the death just for enjoyment. I'm always in too much of a rush. I don't remember the last time I savored a moment.

I tilt my head to the side, looking at him. I note the healing scab on his cheek from when I scratched his face.

After pouring himself a drink, Nabarres drags a chair across the room and settles himself down in front of me. Then, he exhales sharply and gives me a weary glance, as if saying, *now what?*

"I should thank you, capitán."

"For what?"

"Giving me clarity," I say. "I've always been too eager to kill you. You do wicked, cruel things in the name of Spain. You said I couldn't beat you because I didn't know what I was doing. You were right. When you fail as often as I do, you learn. I traveled on foot from Snake Mountain without stopping, all because I wanted revenge for what you've done. I was wrong. You don't deserve death. You deserve to live. You deserve to suffer and die unremarkably."

He yawns. "Lady, it's late. If you're not going to kill me, why are you here?"

I take out a slip of parchment from inside my robe and read the letter.

To His Excellency Jerónimo de las Casas y Sepúlveda,
Viceroy of New Spain:

Your Excellency, as I write this, I am trapped in a prison of my
own making which can be escaped only through God's punishment.
Although His Majesty King Carlos has expressly forbidden any
mistreatment of Indigenous people, I have killed wantonly and
without provocation, merely because it pleased me to do so. I
have burned villages and dwellings to the ground without a
thought for children. I chose to instigate and support the war
against La Justicia. In so doing, I was the direct cause of the
death of innocents. I realize now that my actions were not those
of a God-fearing man, and I am deeply ashamed of what I have
done. I accuse myself by my own seal and hand and ask urgently
for God's justice.

Yours in repentance,
Narcizo Nabarres y Aragón
Capitán General de la Nueva España

Nabarres chuckles lightly. "What makes you think I will sign that?"

"You know as well as I that your signature alone gives no authority,
capitán."

He leans forward. Now, I have his attention. "And what are you
going to do? Steal my seal?" He chuckles and relaxes against his
cushioned seat.

Amazing, his pride. He thinks I've been sitting here all night
wasting candlelight. It strikes me that even now Nabarres still sees
me as a silly little girl, as if children aren't kings and queens, don't
wed and breed, and don't go to fight in war. How could someone as
insignificant as I, less substantial than a shadow, possibly acquire his
seal? The one he keeps locked in the lower drawer of his study table
and which carries the whole weight of his name and title. The one

that can't be stolen without the key which he keeps on his person at all times.

Had Nabarres bothered to look, he would have realized that drawer is open.

As if just coming awake, he tears his gaze away from me and looks at the desk. That's when he pushes to his feet, letting the chair fall behind him. I don't reach for my sword. He won't harm the viceroy's sister. At least not here. And not now. Instead, he seizes my wrist and yanks the letter from my hand.

"I thought you might want to keep a copy for your records," I say in a pleased manner. "Not to worry, capitán. I drafted an identical letter. It's already on its way to King Carlos."

Nabarres isn't just overcome. He's seething. "What do you want?"

He will live, and he shall know, for the rest of his days, that he was bested by a girl who knew what she was doing. "I have everything I want," I say. Before slipping out the door, I turn and say, "Adios, Narcizo."

My cloak swirls behind me, my hood pulled over my eyes. I dart from shadow to shadow and slip into the viceroy's chamber through the servants' passageway. Jerónimo is sleeping fitfully, tossing and turning in his bed. On the wall behind his desk is a portrait of a two-year-old Jerónimo when he was not the representative of the king but the viceroy's firstborn son. He's dressed in ridiculous adult clothes, already authoritative in a regal pose, and I'm holding his small hand. I can't help but smile. It seems like a lifetime ago.

I go to Jerónimo's side and softly push damp curls away from his face. I draw a relieved breath seeing he wasn't injured in battle. I needed to check for myself. He looks so much like Father it makes my chest ache. We are brother and sister. We are also opponents. He is a ruler first, a man second. His duty is to the viceroyalty.

"Move away from His Excellency," someone says, and I shoot up from the bed and turn around. Jerónimo's page has his sword leveled at me. My nostrils flare. I didn't know I had company. If I had my tonalli, I would've heard him.

The viceroy sits up quickly. "What is it?"

"An intruder, exclencia. Come with me. At once!" the page says. "Guards! Guards! An attempt on the viceroy's life!"

Three guards rush inside and assemble around me with their swords pointed at my neck, and I raise my hands in surrender. I think about wielding my blade, but this chaos is of my own creation, and I feel a strange sense of calm, as if I'm sleepwalking. I don't know whether it's a redefining of my relationship with myself or if I've simply come to accept my fate.

"¡Excelencia, venid conmigo cuanto antes!"

"I decide what to do, Estevan." Jerónimo looks at me, trying to catch a glimpse of my face beneath my hood. "Who are you?"

"Excelencia, it is not safe. The intruder is armed!"

Jerónimo orders his page to take my weapon, and I let him. "She . . . she is the Panther," he says in an awed whisper, recognizing my blade, and hands it to the viceroy, who scowls at the mention of that name.

"Mind your tongue, Estevan." He turns to me. "How and where did you get this sword? I demand you reveal yourself. Show me who you are."

And I do.

CHAPTER 31

La Viuda

I throw back my hood and pull down my mask. A weight lifts, as if shackles have fallen off my wrists. A new lightness fills me, and I wonder if it is this freedom Martín values, so much so that he would rather give up his power, position, and birthright than live without it.

On the viceroy's face is a haunting look of confusion and sadness, his eyes full of questions.

"Brother," I say.

"Why are you standing there fidgeting? Arrest the outlaw," he orders.

No man moves. "But she is the viceregent," Estevan babbles.

"And I am the viceroy." His temper flares. "If the witch is not on her way to prison in five seconds, you will be joining her, Estevan."

"Jerónimo, please, let me explain."

"Explain *what*?" he snaps. "What is there to explain? Betrayal? Treason? Heresy? Witchcraft? Don't bother. I don't want to hear it. Your deceit is hidden no more."

It is dangerous for me to feel so absolutely calm in such a nasty predicament. Perhaps, without tonalli, without the Panther, that part of my awareness is gone too.

"No," I reply. "Explain abuse. Explain oppression and neglect. Corruption. Scheming. Murder. I am Pantera, and I have not shut my eyes to the evil wrought by this viceroyalty."

"You will be silent," the viceroy says sharply.

"You did nothing," I accuse. "When Vicereine Carlota confessed to sinking *La Capitana* to fund the war against La Justicia. When she confessed to poisoning Doña Cayetana. You knew Captain Nabarres raided villages and torched houses and families. You ordered the attack on Snake Mountain that caused so many to die. You have allowed injustice and you have not judged it. Is this what your god commands, that you take by force everyone's property and lives?"

My brother is beside himself with rage. "Enough!" he thunders, and the men quake in their boots. "I have heard more of this nonsense than I need to. In my dreams, God speaks. Who speaks to you in yours?"

From somewhere inside the palace, someone screams, a woman, a piercing and dreadful sound that echoes through the corridors. The men look at each other wide-eyed, then toward the viceroy, who is distracted. I'm able to slip out and get away.

Without the Sword of Integrity.

Pulque is a strange kind of alcohol. Despite drinking for hours, my mind is completely clear, but my body feels fuzzy, like I have cotton stuffed inside. Wine will make me vomit and give me a headache, but not pulque. It's a different kind of intoxication.

The best pulque is made at the pulquería El Burro Blanco, the best pulquería found inside la traza where, at the moment, I sit with a milky bucket placed before me, along with a plate of corn-smut tacos, at no cost as long as I keep drinking. Inside, every wall and surface is adorned in red-and-purple murals, depicting all the major Nahua gods. There is Quetzalcoatl, god of life; Tezcatlipoca, god of sorcery; Huitzilopochtli, god of war; Xipe Totec, god of the seasons.

As the swinging door opens, I look up to see a hooded figure step inside. Lady Amalia enters the tavern and takes a seat in the chair opposite me.

"Is it true?" she asks, her eyes glistening. "The vicereine poisoned my mother?"

"You were the one who screamed."

"Is it true?"

I nod.

"I overheard what you said to the viceroy, so I followed you here." I take a drink of my pulque. "What do you want, Amalia?"

"I was worried about you. I needed to know you were all right. And now . . . I'm not so sure you are."

"Worried about me? Please. You hate me."

"I don't hate you," she says. "I may not always *like* you . . . but I don't hate you."

"This is no place for a lady with child."

"Leonora, it's the oldest trick in the book," she says, rubbing her flat belly. "I only made him think I was carrying his seed. But an imposter is of no importance to me. He's in prison now anyway. So, what are you doing here? Shouldn't Pantera be upholding justice . . . fighting evildoers?"

I want to cross my arms over my chest and sit there in proud defiance, but I can't. I have no pride left. "Just leave me alone."

"I know how you feel," she says. "The bitterness, the awful loneliness, the clawing anger. I've been there and back. On more than one occasion." She's pensive for a moment, then she goes on. "You know, I never thought Pantera to be real. In truth, to me, she sounded like a story parents tell their naughty children to get them to behave. 'You better be good, or the witch will come and take you away.' Witches." She chuckles as if the idea amuses her immensely.

My thoughts are at war, and I'm losing. "I wanted to right the wrongs I saw. Sometimes a cause can become an obsession. I put my duty before everything else. Was it worth it? What has Pantera accomplished?"

Her pale eyebrows lift in surprise. She's probably never heard me put myself down before.

"I endure the hurtful remarks . . . the lack of respect, respect that is only given when I don a black costume and wear a mask. Now that all is said and done, what do I have to look forward to? My friend is dead. I don't remember her voice. Isn't that sad? Before she died in the earthquake, she said to me, 'Don't be afraid, Pantera.' She didn't say Leonora. I despise her last words. They've haunted me ever since." My eyes brim with tears that refuse to fall. "I don't know why I'm telling you this." What difference does it make?

Her face is firm but sympathetic. "Maybe because I'm here—and I understand. My father is dead. My mother is dead. All three of my husbands are dead. I have nothing to inherit. I'm ridiculed for the marks on my skin. Being set apart means that sometimes you have to stand alone. When no one is around to talk in your ear, then you can hear the only voice that really matters. Your own."

Sometimes the right words come from the wrong person, and the wrong actions come from the right person.

Standing, I feel in my pockets and scatter some coins on the table.

"Where are you going?" Amalia asks.

"Snake Mountain."

She pushes to her feet. "Well, I'm coming with you."

"Why would you want to do that?"

"I've been a pawn since the moment I drew my first breath, Leonora. I am sick of it. When I first arrived at court," she says, "my mother had high hopes for me. We had no money, no prospects, and no favor. My mother was ambitious and taught me how to catch the eyes of men, rich men.

"When I was twelve, she married me off to a man of her choosing who still loved another, who bore him ten children, and after his death I was wed again, then again. I loved my mother, but when she died so did her plotting. I'm finished with it all."

I sigh tiredly. "You wouldn't last one morning outside la traza, Amalia."

"You're right," she says. "I can't handle a sword to save my life. I'm not good at violence, but I can be useful."

I rest my hands on my hips. "How?"

"I can think," she says proudly.

"That's it?"

"That's everything!" she says. "Hannibal in Cannae. Alexander the Great in Hydaspes. Odysseus at Troy. Some of the greatest battles in history have been won not by the hands of the greatest warriors, but by their minds."

"And I suppose you think you know about war because you read books?"

"Remember our previous game? War is one big chessboard," she says. "A good chess player knows his pieces. He knows their strengths and weaknesses. Likewise, a good military commander knows his troops. He knows how they work, how they react, how they think, how they perceive things, and most of all, how they feel."

I grumble in frustration. "This isn't chess, Amalia. This is life and death."

"Do not make the mistake of underestimating me, Leonora," she says. "I may not have been to war, but I assure you, I am a fighter. When I contracted the pox, I was in isolation for months. At first, I thought I had a cold. Then doctors thought it was a rash. Then the pustules started appearing. I was bedridden. I couldn't come into contact with anyone. Books saved my life. I learned to play chess. I grew to love the game. Each and every move you make is an opportunity to win. I challenge anyone who thinks me weak, and then we'll see who has the advantage."

I point a finger at her face. "You don't get in my way. I won't go out of mine to help you. Do you understand?"

She nods.

CHAPTER 32

La Bestia

We find accommodations for the night at the inn Los Tres Pablos, erected inside la traza, south of the palace. It's agreeable to Amalia's taste and habits. She's never set foot outside the Spanish part of the city.

At dawn, we enter the muggy, mosquito-filled woods. Amalia has overpacked with a heavy bag that she doesn't let me open. "You never know what you might need in the jungle," she says. Then, within the first ten minutes, her strap tears, and I see her bag is filled with several pouches of water, slips of parchment, a quill, ink, fruit, maize cakes, a pair of sandals, and some clothes. I give her a look.

"What?" she says innocently. "Someone has to journal our travels. I could die out here, you know."

"Are you sure you want to do this?"

"I should ask you the same question. You look tired. And hungover."

"I am not hungover," I say, irritated.

As the woods become denser, I expect war cries and chants at any moment, but all we hear are branches knocking together, leaves rustling, twigs snapping, trees rattling.

"Well, what is your great plan, Leonora?" Amalia says as we come to a path overhung by gnarled branches, barely wide enough for us to see where we're going.

255

"The plan is to not draw unwanted attention to yourself."

It doesn't take long before Tonatiuh begins to brighten to the east, and we stash our torches.

Hours pass. It'll take me longer to reach Snake Mountain with Amalia toiling behind me. And I don't know these woods quite as well as I thought. Has it begun? Am I starting to forget?

Our path twists and Amalia has to weave through a clump of hanging vines. I don't have my sword, so I can't hack our way through.

"Turn around. You're going the wrong way," I say.

She looks at me, brows knitted. "What do you mean I'm going the wrong way? I'm going the way you told me to go."

"No, we have to go right."

"But you said left."

"I said right."

"No, you didn't," she says, her voice taking an irritated edge. "You said to go left."

I stop walking to look around, then glance at Amalia again. And that's when I know. It's me, not her, who needs turning around.

"Leonora," Amalia says, looking at me with a peeved expression, "which way is left?"

"What?"

"Show me which way is left."

I falter. I'm quickly overcome by shame. Am I starting to forget the simplest things, like being able to tell left from right? My heart hammers.

"We're lost, aren't we?" Amalia asks.

"No."

She groans and buries her face in her hands. "Admit it. You don't know where we are!"

"Oh, where's your sense of adventure, countess?"

She violently swats the air. "I think it was sucked away by that exceptionally large mosquito."

"Perhaps you want to ask it for directions?"

Amalia continues sweeping it away with her hand, but it comes back more fiercely. "¡Maldito! You want a piece of me, you little sucker?"

"Maldita. Only females bite," I say, seeing the blanket of mosquitoes wrapping around her. "It's your perfume." I can practically hear them calling all their friends to the feast. "It attracts them." I scoop up mud and cover her face, arms, and hands. Amalia stands there, with an unamused scowl upon her face. "There. That should do it. When you're finished battling insects, do you think we can continue our march?"

She swats at a flying blue insect trying to land on her shoulder.

"Amalia, no!"

"What?"

I turn around, eyeing the damselflies futtering. "We follow the snake doctors."

"The what?"

"We're close."

The damselflies lead us to a wide stream, the water cascading down a series of mountainous outcrops, the kind of rocks hard enough to crack your skull on the way down. A waterfall hisses up ahead. *Horses never manage the trail*, I remember Martín saying.

Amalia looks behind her, spooked. "Do you hear that?"

"Hear what?"

"It sounds like a crying baby."

"I don't hear anything," I say. "Come on. We have to cross."

"I need rest."

"If we keep stopping, it'll take us a week to reach Snake Mountain." She scoffs. "If we even find it."

After we refresh ourselves, Amalia heads to the water and carefully walks across a fallen log above the stream, arms outstretched for balance. She makes it look simple, though I tell her to take it easy, and then her shoe slides off the log, splashing into the water and taking her along with it.

I hurry to her as she slips, then reaches for the log and hangs on to it for dear life. "I've got you," I say, pulling her, and she is nearly out of the water when a long sinuous tail wraps itself around her hips. She cries out as she's flung into the air, and I rush forward, grabbing her arm. A terrifying creature shoots up from the water, a doglike beast with a rubbery black hide and fur spikes. My eyes wide with fright, I flip out my knife and thrust it at the creature's head. With a violent shriek, it releases Amalia and disappears back into the water.

"What the hell was that thing?" Amalia pants.

"Nothing good."

When we reach Snake Mountain, night has fallen. The sky is starless. All the huts are dark. I halt at the entrance of Tezca's calli. Judging by his heavy breathing, he's asleep.

"Wait here," I say to Amalia.

Weary and burdened from our journey, Amalia dismisses me with a wave of her hand.

I throw aside the curtain draping the door and Tezca awakens.

"Pantera?"

My gaze slides to the girl lying next to him. My heart begins to race.

"Pantera, wait," Tezca says, pushing to his feet from the cot, naked as the day the gods made him. He lacks the decency to be embarrassed. But then again why should he be? There is nothing between us.

He holds my elbow and I face him.

"For a man who's particular about his bed partners, you sure have many."

He sighs. "You're angry."

"I'm not."

But something has changed. He can tell.

He rakes a hand through his long hair and looks around the hut as if seeking inspiration or help. "It's late," he says.

I have to swallow hard to push down the lump in my throat. "I just wanted you to know that I didn't kill him. You were right. I can't let my emotions get the better of me. The viceroy knows Pantera's identity. I am an outlaw and a fugitive from justice. If I return, I will surely be hanged. You will hear the news from the capital, so you may as well hear it from me. I'm sorry to have interrupted your sleep."

Never let it become personal. One of the four Nagual Truths. Although it pertains to the battlefield, this doesn't feel much different. Too late. It's personal. And it hurts. Nine Hells, it hurts.

As soon as I set foot outside the hut, I see Amalia on her knees, her hands tied behind her back, and Chipahua with his spear pressed against her throat.

I sigh, my irritation nearly visible. "I leave you for one moment. What did you do?"

"¡Nada!" Amalia says innocently. "I have done nothing!"

"Chipahua, what is this?" Tezca asks, emerging from the tent behind me. "Put down your weapon."

"Iztac colelehtli," Chipahua says.

"She is not a threat," Tezca assures him.

"I certainly am, or else he would not think me of any consequence," Amalia says cheekily. "I *will* say I do not usually have this effect on men."

"Now's not the time to be funny, Amalia," I say.

"I can't be funny if I'm dead," she says.

Lowering his spear, Chipahua lifts her with one arm and shoves her against a tree. He towers over her, and she is trapped in the little space between his arms and chest, but Amalia is hardly daunted.

We are led up the staircase of the pyramid, some hundred steps to reach the temple, with Chipahua and Tezca climbing behind us.

Our first sight at the top is Neza sitting in his high chair, with the snake wall behind him. Standing at his side are Eréndira and Martín.

"You . . ." Amalia says, looking at Martín. "What are *you* doing here . . . alteza?"

Martín levels a glare at her. "I could ask you the same question, countess."

"Is that her?" Neza asks Martín.

He nods. "That's her."

"My lord." I kiss the earth and motion for Amalia to do the same. Amalia awkwardly touches the ground, then her lips.

"If I may be permitted to introduce myself . . ." Amalia steps forward, clears her throat, and boldly says, "Greetings, I am Amalia Catalina de Íñiguez y Mendoza, Countess of Niebla."

She is met by silence, save for a chattering monkey swinging from branch to branch in the ahuehuetl overhead.

"I am Nezahualpilli," he says.

Amalia tries to pronounce his name but stumbles over it.

"Neza," he says.

"Ah, yes, *ahem* . . . King Neza, is it? Very well," Amalia says. "I've come to offer my services for any use you may care to make of them. I can read and write. My mother taught me to sew, spin flax into linen, card-weave fabric, play upon the harp, and sing. I've read a number of books. I don't know a whole lot, but I know a little about a lot of things. For room and board, I'd be happy to compose such a detailed account of La Justicia's glorious uprising that its fame through the ages shall rival the greatest rebellions in history."

"Tell me, countess," Neza says stonily, "what experience have you as a whore?"

Amalia's jaw tenses visibly. "What did you say?"

"Are you any good at whoring? I am told you entertain and pleasure a man then expect favors from him."

His meaning becomes clear. Martín.

"What is this? Jealousy?" She chuckles as if the idea gives her great enjoyment.

"Amalia," I mutter under my breath.

She sighs with exaggerated patience. "If it makes you feel any better," she says, "it didn't last long, and I'm not with child."

Neza rises, his face blanched with fury. "Get them out of my sight."

"Wait," I say. "My lord, it is the dead of night—"

He glares at me. "I have not forgotten the circumstances under which our shield wall was broken, Pantera."

"They were going to kill my brother," I say agitatedly. "I'm sorry I—"

"The clans are dividing," he says. "Prince Xico has turned against us after your slaughter of his men and cousin. Our alliance with the Tlaxcaltecah is no more. The Chichimecah refuse to band with us. There is distrust among the clans. The only reason you're alive is because you are the daughter of Nican Nicah. I offer you no threat, but don't presume too much upon that generosity."

There's a kind of tiredness that needs a good night's sleep and another that needs so much more. For me, one has become the other, starting out like a heavy cape and turning into heavy bones. I can't take on more, deal with more. I am breathing, but not really. I am alive, but not really. Everything seems to move in a blur. Losing your tonalli has this effect on you.

"Vámonos, Amalia," I say.

CHAPTER 33

El Demonio

As we turn on our heels to walk away, I slow my pace. A strange wind blows, a howl that rustles trees and causes them to murmur a terrible lullaby.

From the moaning breeze comes a rattling like shells.

A beast of bones swoops from the sky, wearing a necklace of human hearts and a skirt of shells. The gaunt skeletal creature flies into the temple. I stand rooted to the spot, my mind spinning, scarcely daring to breathe, for the stench of death is pungent. More creatures descend, swarming and permeating the temple with their hideous screeching. My pulse is erratic. I know what they are. I know what they want. And the terror swells in my chest. *Star demons.*

I crouch for cover, pressing my hands to my ears to block out the shrill screaming. I've never felt so useless in my life. The others are quick to raise their weapons.

Eyes darting around, one of the flying creatures comes for Neza. He pulls a bow from his back, sets an arrow, and draws the string back, but the creature closes her claws around the arrow before it can strike her chest. She lunges at Neza too fast for him to load a second arrow. He holds the creature at bay, taking swipes at her with his bow, and she takes several wounds but gets Neza in a clench. Chipahua comes to Neza's aid. Eréndira throws herself into a run, spreads her wings and swoops down on the creature, raking at the thing's flesh with her beak and talons, but the impact of the creature's outstretched claws sends her tumbling down, leaving a wake of white feathers.

Martín jumps to help a horrified Amalia batting away at the creatures. "¡Corre! Go!" Martín has long arms, but with his clumsy blows, his reach offers little advantage.

Tezca is engaged with his adversary, tearing at chunks of flesh and bones. When Tezca battles, I almost feel bad for his opponents. Now, I watch him deal with a winged creature, his blade curving through the air so fast it blurs. He wounds her, but he can't—won't—kill her. What in the Fifth Sun is he doing? Why is he holding back? *Shift, Tezca. Nine Hells, shift.* If I could myself, I would not hesitate to use that power. If I was worthy. If I had my sword. I call to my master, begging him to come to me.

My mind startles to life.

Star demons dwell in the darkness.

Light. We need light.

"Over here!" I call to the creature that Tezca is trying to fend off. I only need to goad her toward Huehueteotl's shrine, where a hearth is kept burning day and night for the god of fire. "What are you waiting for? Take me."

The creature's gnarled face turns, and she screams at me, tearing away from Tezca.

I don't move fast enough. I'm lifted at least two feet off the floor. The creature closes her clawed grip around my throat and seizes my face with her other hand, tilting it this way and that, studying me. I wheeze, forced to look at her skull. A prickly tremor climbs up my spine. She has two empty pits where her eyes should be, but even so, I feel her intense stare. I grab her bony wrist and tear what little flesh the creature has, feeling it squish in my fingers. The smell is hideously putrid, like a corpse that's been buried and dug up again.

"Obsidian . . ." I struggle to speak. "Obsidian Butterfly."

If her enormous knife-tipped wings are any indication, she is Itzpapalotl, the Obsidian Butterfly. She hisses. A forked tongue flicks out from between her bloodstained teeth. Her breath is worse than fly-infested carrion rotting in the heat. The appointed hour of my death arrives.

From the blurry edges of my vision, a bear charges toward us, hard and fast. I quickly shut my eyes and open them again. One moment I am looking at a big white grizzly, the next a large man, outfitted in armor. Swiftly, he draws a sword from his back and drives it into the ground. The blast of tonalli fills the temple with blinding light, as though I am looking directly at Tonatiuh at midday. The demons shriek their hideous cries, and the Obsidian Butterfly drops me as she flees. I can almost feel bones breaking as I land. I'm panting raggedly as I lift my head, my eyes watering from the glare.

"Where are they? Where did they go?" Martín cries frantically.

I raise my hand to my forehead to shield my eyes. The man slides his sword into his sheath and removes his helmet. "I don't know," he says, "but they're not here anymore."

With considerable effort, I try to pull myself up, fighting a wave of dizziness. "Ollin?"

He comes to me and helps me stand, holding me by the arms.

"Who in the Nine Hells are *you*?" Neza asks him.

I smile. "A friend."

CHAPTER 34

El Oso

A waterfall of questions cascades around us.

"Friend?" Tezca asks.

"How do you know each other?" Neza asks.

"Would anyone else care to know what those skeleton creatures were?" Eréndira asks.

"Or how she grew owl wings?" Amalia asks, looking at Eréndira.

"Am I the only one who saw a bear become a man?" Martín asks.

"Who is this giant?" Chipahua says.

"I am not tall enough to be Quinametzin," Ollin says.

For a moment I consider the possibility that my imagination is playing tricks on me. But my imagination isn't that good.

"Is it really you?" I ask.

When he brushes my cheek with the back of his fingers, I lean into his touch and close my eyes. It's really him. "It's good to see you, Tecuani."

My stomach flutters at the sound of my Nahua name. It's been a long time since I've heard it.

"I thought I'd never see you again." I smile and wrap my arms around him. "How did you find me?"

"Master Toto heard you," he says, and my smile fades.

His words only make me bitter. I've asked Master Toto to reveal himself countless times before, sometimes while in tears, but I've yet to witness it. If he didn't help me then, why would he help me now?

"I do hate to ruin your joyful reunion," Martín says, "but we have questions and no answers."

"I am Ollin," he says, commanding attention with his large frame and feather-trimmed shield. I notice his rank has increased. His armor is more elaborate, more colorful, and his wrists are covered in gold armbands. "The creatures that attacked you are known as the Tzitzimime. They are demon goddesses," he explains. His voice is calm, as is his manner, but his expression is worried.

"What do these demon goddesses want?" Amalia asks.

Martín snorts. "Are we supposed to understand the motivations of demons?"

"If we know what they want," Amalia says, "maybe we can use that against them."

"I'm going to assume they want to kill us," Martín says.

"The Tzitzimime were once celestial deities," Ollin says, "but after being banished from paradise, they became monsters of the night."

"Earthquakes will rattle the ground," Neza says, his tone a warning. "That will be the beginning."

"The beginning of what?" Martín asks.

"The end of the Fifth Sun," I say, hugging my arms to my chest to hide my twitching hands. "Star demons will come down from the sky to eat their fill of men and all will go dark forever. It is the prophecy."

"We defeated them today," Eréndira says. "Let them come. We will defeat them again."

"Brave words," Ollin says, "but foolish ones. The Tzitzimime represent the biggest threat to the Fifth Sun."

Eréndira lifts her chin as if to meet Ollin's challenge. "They may be demon goddesses, but they are not infallible. They are not unbeatable."

"Demons are stronger and faster than humans," Ollin says.

"We'll see about that," Eréndira declares.

"Are we supposed to give up without a fight?" Neza asks.

"Acceptance is a form of strength, tlahtoani," Ollin says. "The Tzitzimime have yearned for the moment they can devour humanity. With their queen the Obsidian Butterfly, and the Cihuateteo, their army of divine women, they will fulfill their purpose at last. They will return when the night is darkest. Come home, Tecuani. You will be safe there." He vanishes then, as though he was never here.

Home. How can I forget the paradise that raised me? I only have to close my eyes to see the peaceful lakes, the glistening buildings, the vast gardens. In Tamoanchan, I was not hunted, nor persecuted. I knew peace then. All I've wanted since I returned to the capital is to go back, see my master, see my friends.

I don't take comfort in knowing Master sent Ollin to help us. If I know Master Toto, this is only another ambiguous test, another riddle to add to my confusion. What does it mean? I press my mind for an answer, and I can almost hear him taunting me: *When you have found what you are looking for, you will no longer seek it.*

The last thing I want to do is solve another one of his riddles, but the end of the Fifth Sun is upon us, I am suffering from the loss of my tonalli, and I am without my sword. If anyone can help me, it's Master Toto.

CHAPTER 35

El Hermano

Directly under Neza are his noble advisors, the Council of Four, all powerful lords related to Neza, including Chipahua, who is his cousin.

If something is to happen to Neza, one of the Four will be the next ruler of Snake Mountain. The second-in-command goes by the title Snake Woman, his advisor, though the position is held not by a woman but a man, Neza's brother Ichcatzin.

As far as I can tell, Neza is also the leader of La Justicia, though he denies this and claims that La Justicia is one voice, and therefore he does not speak for all. La Justicia is made up of clans who would otherwise be fighting each other tooth and claw but share a common enemy. There is a Council of Chief Men—chieftains from each of the clans, including Neza, Lord of the Mexica; Tezca, Lord of the Tlahuica; Rahui, Lord of the Raramuri; Nucano, Lord of the Mixtec; and Eréndira, Princess of the Purépecha.

The Tlaxcalan prince, Xico, and his followers, the Chichimeca, have renounced their allegiance to La Justicia. I am to blame, and I know where I've gone wrong. Even though it was in defense of my life that I killed his men and cousin, he will not stop until I am dead. The other clans don't trust me. They barely trust each other. Never has a Mexica allied with a Tlaxcalan. The entire alliance is formed of clans that have loose and uneasy ties to each other. Over the years, Neza has been uniting the people under one banner. So far, the clans have fought together against the Spanish, but it was only a matter of time before they broke apart due to their own rivalries. Anything built on a shaky foundation is bound to crumble.

Council convenes immediately in Neza's presence, inside his House of Office. With sunken eyes and a grave voice, Neza warns of the great peril that exists as we face a declining Fifth Sun and an invasion from demons who are here to bring chaos, destruction, and ruin. "We must do whatever is necessary to protect our home from those who threaten to destroy it."

Ichcatzin, in his black-trimmed mantle and diadem of gold and crimson feathers, is a sight to behold, not only because he is magnificently dressed, but also because he is muscled with dense thighs and a thick neck.

"I am Keeper of the Hummingbird of the South," he says. He speaks like a warrior, not mincing words. "I maintain the balance with the Fifth Sun, the underworld Mictlan, and the Thirteen Heavens. The teteoh, for better or worse, bestow their favors when they are pleased, and withdraw them, or visit disasters upon us, when they are displeased. If they have chosen to unleash their fury, then they are quite plainly demanding more nourishment. We must placate and sate the gods."

I am so distraught that, unthinking and unmannerly, I blurt, "Why would the teteoh help us?" The other clans hated the Mexica because they demanded bleeding hearts and ate human flesh in homage to the gods. Neza abolished the practice, but it would seem that some, like Ichcatzin, aren't in agreement. "There have been four suns, and they've destroyed them all."

"Do the teteoh speak through you?" Ichcatzin hits me with a look that could halt a lightning bolt in mid-strike, and I mumble an apology.

"No, lord."

"Then the balance of the Fifth Sun shouldn't concern you," he says. I take notice of the family resemblance. He has the same stern mannerisms as Neza, and the same way of spitting out words as if they offend him.

"It concerns us *all*," I say. "We—each of us—face the same threat. And I don't see any gods willing to lay down their lives for the continuation of our sun, so it's up to us to save ourselves." Something he should know well as high priest. In the Fourth Sun, the gods convened in darkness to choose a new sun who would sacrifice himself to bring forth life. Tonatiuh. "The teteoh are not gods any more than we are. Tezca, tell them what you told me." My eyes shift to him. He has not said a word to me since Ollin came to us. It's unlike him, but I give no hint that this bothers me. His words have deserted him, and all he does is look away.

It seems Ichcatzin might argue for a moment, but he's too clever a politician for that. "Why is this murderer still breathing? She brings nothing but trouble, Neza. The alliance with Prince Xico and the Chichimecah is severed. It is *her* fault."

"They defected," Neza says. "If they can be deterred, then they have no place among La Justicia."

"Huitzilopochtli curse you, Neza! You would choose this witch over your own brother? Your own flesh and blood?"

Neza remains stoic. "I would choose that we not fight among ourselves while the Tzitzimime threaten our world."

Ichcatzin shifts his angry gaze to me.

I tug at the collar of my tattered shirt, making a show of the wound around my neck from the Obsidian Butterfly's clutch. "Take a good look, lord. This is the mark of demons that we can't defeat. Not by ourselves. You know they're going to come back. Do you really want to be under siege? I'd tell you to find somewhere secure to hide, but I know when I'm just wasting my time . . . lord."

Ichcatzin's lips tighten.

"We must put aside our petty squabbles," Neza says. "A tree that is inflexible is easily broken. We, too, must be flexible if we are to remain standing."

"I will seek my master's help in Tamoanchan," I say. "It's a one-day's journey. Two at most."

"The legendary paradise high in the mountains in the Namba jungle?" Neza asks.

I nod.

Ichcatzin scoffs. "Hundreds have gone on the fruitless trek into the jungle looking for it and none have returned. You are no less disturbed than they if you think you can do what they could not."

"In the Chebuye language," Neza says, "the word *namba* means labyrinth. There is no coming back from the Namba. Not alive, anyway. What makes you think you can find a place that is only mentioned in stories?"

"Because, as opposed to the treasure hunters, I've actually been there," I say.

Neza seems to consider my words. "Whether or not Tamoanchan can be found, you would be met with an endless barrier of hills, ravines, peaks, all covered in jungle and crisscrossed by rivers, including the scorching Bonnango, which kills anything that enters it."

"Malevolent spirits, man-eating tribes, and even deadlier creatures," I say. "I know." Under the Fifth Sun, men are weak enough. In a god's domain, I would be as helpless as a serpent hooked in an eagle's beak. But we must seek aid, and I must restore my tonalli. Master will know how to help.

Neza hesitates, then says, "Very well. Journey there if you must, but we will call upon La Justicia in your absence. Gather all the warriors we can and get them into position as quickly as possible."

"But," Eréndira says, "we are not enough. We'll need an army."

"I'll get you your army." Martín speaks up from the far side of the room.

"Whose?" Neza asks.

Martín glances at me. He nods and I nod back, because he is

271

Martín Cortés, El Mestizo, firstborn and heir of Hernán Cortés. A heavy burden, but he is ready to shoulder it.

"Mine," he says.

The following morning, I go inside the House of Darts. The armory is stocked with cartloads of weapons, spear-throwers, lances, clubs, and swords, even Toledan steel, as well as wooden shields, helmets, and various types of body armor. Tezca is sharpening his sword with a whetstone, pausing between strokes to gauge how the sunlight slides along the blade. A handful of knives lie on the table in front of him, waiting their turn. Eréndira is going through the variety of weapons lining the walls, assessing the assortment. As she sees me come in, she steps out of the armory, leaving me alone with Tezca.

I don't know what to say to him. I'm afraid to speak. If I open my mouth, there's no telling what might come flying out. In the few minutes I remain silent, I watch him and get lost in his expressions, analyzing his clenched jaw, his lips pulled thin. I can't stand his silence. *Talk to me. Tell me what's going through your head. Say something.*

"You're avoiding me," I say.

"So?"

"So tell me what I did."

"Not everything is about you, Leonora," he says, "difficult as that may be to believe. There are more important things that need my attention."

His words sting. But they're better than nothing. It's a start.

"You won't even look at me. I know you're angry, Tezca. So what is it? What have I done? If this is about Ollin—"

He stops what he's doing and looks up directly into my eyes. "Why would it be about him?" He stands, goes around the table, and moves toward me. When he stops, he's so close I can feel his breath on my face. He holds my gaze for a long moment, almost challenging me to answer, then nods, accepting what I can't put into words. As he walks away, my hand on his arm stops him. Slowly, he turns around.

My breath stalls in my chest. Finally, I find my voice. "What do you want me to say?"

"Well, that depends on who's asking. Leonora? Pantera? Or Tecuani?"

I sigh. "That's not fair. You know who I am, Tezca. The real me. No secrets. I don't have to hide behind a mask anymore."

He chuckles. "You're *still* hiding. You hide behind the mask of Leonora just as much as you hide behind the mask of Pantera."

"What do you want from—"

He looks at me, his dark brows knitted.

"—from," I repeat, "from . . ." I can't get past that.

"Leonora."

The loss of tonalli is a barrier of sorts. I have a sense of it. I am aware when I am forgetting, when there is something close but hidden, yet I cannot in that moment fathom what it could be. It's as if I'm following a trail and it suddenly ends. But I know there is a path, even if I don't know where it's gone, so that gives me some idea as to what is missing from my head.

"What do you want from me?" I say finally, my voice tight with frustration. "I told you, I'm cursed. My tonalli has abandoned me. I can't shift. I have no power. I'm not worthy of my own sword. I don't even have it in my possession. My brother hates me. I don't have a home. I'm terrified that this is how it will be for all that's left of my sorry life. I don't know what to do. I don't know what will happen to me. Is that what you wanted to hear, Tezca? Does that give you joy? Is that some sort of victory?" I say this in one breath, as if I couldn't wait to get it out of me.

A frigid silence hangs over us. Tezca seems to take in everything I said.

"I worry, you know," I say. "I worry for Jerónimo. I worry for the people. I worry for myself. I worried for Inés too. I worried for her safety. There were times when I treated her as if she couldn't handle herself, although I knew she could. I took her in and taught her how to fight."

Now, I can't stop talking. It wasn't until I began speaking that I realized how much I needed to say. It seems like there aren't enough words.

I draw a breath and continue. "You're the one person I don't have to worry about, Tezca. You are a sorcerer and the son of a god. Ours is a sun of blood and ruin and you give me peace. You *do* understand, don't you? What a relief this is?"

I don't expect Tezca's silence. I don't expect him to look so tired and so human, and I feel the urge to touch his shoulder and comfort him, but I resist. He's a lord. I don't think Tezca would punish me, as he's felt my touch before, but I am not sure he would welcome it now.

"I'm not the only one hiding am I, Tezca?" I say. "They don't know who you really are, do they?"

"I know my place," he says bitterly. His expression is full of outrage. I try very hard not to melt under its intensity.

"And what is your place? Pretending to be less than you truly are?"

"I am just a man."

"You know you're more than that."

"Don't presume to know what I am, Leonora," he says. "Whatever you think about me, I assure you, you don't know enough."

"Finally, we agree on something. Let's go with that. You're a sorcerer. Why didn't you shift last night?"

"It wouldn't have made a difference."

"Is that the best lie you could come up with?"

"I . . . can't."

"Why not? Why not, Tezca?"

"Leave it alone, Leonora."

"Tell me."

He looks at me and shouts, "You wouldn't understand!"

I stare at him, my forehead creased tightly. Tezca has never raised his voice before, but the fact that he thinks I wouldn't understand hurts as if he's just ripped my insides apart.

He lets his head fall, exhaling before he looks at me again. "I deceive others, it's true, but I have never hidden from you. My intentions, perhaps; the man, never. In all the ways that matter, I have always been honest about who I am."

"Are you honest with yourself?"

He frowns. "What?"

"Take a look at yourself, Tezca. Take a long hard look. The gods have given you so much and you squander it. I wish I had even a shred of your power. Sorcery that has taken me a decade to learn comes so easily to you, like it's nothing. Yet you behave like a mortal. It is an insult and a dishonor to yourself."

He gives me an incredulous glance. "Are you saying I should behave like a god?"

"I'm saying you could be more . . . if you wanted to."

"More." He chuckles at the word. "What if I don't want to be more?"

"Don't you want to find out who you really are?"

"No," he replies in a clipped tone. "No, I don't. I like who I am now." He pauses to take a breath. "Maybe I won't after I find out."

I frown. "What do you mean?"

"I *mean* . . . my father is the Black God, Leonora," he says, almost in a whisper, as if he's afraid of who might be listening. "Darkness is the source of my power."

I let out a ragged sigh of understanding. His eyes meet mine, and for the first time, I see the full force of fear he carries with him. I know Tezca has his own demons to contend with, but they've been quiet all this time. Now, they are much too close to the surface, coming out raw and hungry, and I wish they weren't. I know that's a selfish want; Tezca has a right to his fears, but in this moment, they are overpowering him.

"If there's one thing I learned from Inés," I say, "it's that you don't choose who you're born to, or where or when. But you can always choose who to be. Even if you find out the truth, if you ever decide to know, you can still choose, Tezca."

If my words meant anything at all to him, he hides it well. His attention is on the tip of his sword. He carefully flips the blade over and repeats the sharpening on the opposite edge.

"I should go," I say. "I have a long trip ahead."

"I've almost finished."

"What?"

"I'm coming with you."

"No," I say. "I must do this alone."

"I did not ask," he says. "You have no tonalli. No sword. Finding Tamoanchan is one thing, surviving the Namba is another. You cannot take risks as easily as you breathe, Leonora. I am coming with you."

CHAPTER 36

La Jungla

Tamoanchan, the paradisal realm where pulque was first made and Quetzalcoatl created humanity, cannot be found by chance. Mythical cities rich in gold, jeweled fish, and life-giving roses are seldom easy to find.

In the age of the First Sun, all the teteoh lived in Tamoanchan, ruled by the Heavenly Lord and his wife the Heavenly Lady. Some goddesses wanted to pluck the sacred roses, so they ripped the branches off the Flowering Tree to get them. When they did this, the tree bled. The guilty goddesses were expelled from Tamoanchan for their acts of sacrilege and desecration, and that is how they became the Tzitzimime. They consort with the Cihuateteo, divine women, malevolent spirits. Beware the night, parents tell their children, for the Cihuateteo may steal you. They haunt the crossroads, seeking victims—especially young ones.

The prophecy is in motion, the war with the Spaniards is not yet over, and we must all take huge risks, even at great cost and when we have everything to lose. Amalia will stay behind with Eréndira and prepare for battle, and Martín will go to his brother in Cuernavaca and provide us with the warriors we need.

The blisters on my heels have barely settled before Tezca and I march south into the wild unknown. We have no compass, no map, but to the east, we can see the great mountains of the Valley of Mexico, their snowcapped peaks jutting into the sky. I have with me parchment, ink, and a quill to journal my memories and reflections.

Tezca walks at a pace that I can barely match, but I don't argue.

"The faster we go, the sooner we get there," he says.

After a couple of hours taken at Tezca's brisk stride, just as dusk approaches, the terrain begins to change from rolling hills to rocky outcrops dripping with clear, clean fresh water and a wall of thick forest as far as the eye can see. Here we trek up the canyon and fill up our waterskins from the lake. The air blows as if from an oven, clammy and stuffy. I'm tempted to lift my trousers to cool off, but the gnats would have a feast.

"The moon will be up soon," Tezca says. "We should set up camp here."

As the stars can barely be seen through the thick canopy above, the wrath of Tlaloc comes suddenly. We are drenched in seconds, and within minutes the forest floor is flooded. I have to use a walking stick to get through the mud. In the towering trees above, birds ruffle their feathers in the raindrops, embracing the water. We settle in for the night on a flat, dry piece of land under an overhanging rock, and dine on honey ants. They are everywhere on the ground, their abdomens bulging with nectar.

Our dining choices consist of rodents and insects. As a general rule, if it's brightly colored, it'll likely kill us, so we can't eat anything that catches our eye. Restraint is part of our survival kit. With fresh water and insects we can survive, but no matter how many honey ants I eat, I am still hungry. I could eat a lizard. Or a beetle, if it's cooked right. But I know better. The insects of the Fifth Sun are often demons, experts at spinning magical deceptions.

Tezca builds a small fire to cook our voles and dry our feet and shoes. I am sweating from every pore, and wet feet will bring on jungle rot. The pustules are crippling, and you're next to dead in the

Namba if you can't walk. My vole is barely on the fire before I snatch it up and gobble it down.

There is rumbling. Then the ground shakes.

"It's Popo and Izta," Tezca says.

"We're getting closer," I say.

Popocatepetl and Iztaccihuatl were once lovers. Popo was a brave warrior and Izta the most beautiful of princesses. When Popo went to battle, Izta heard false news of his death from a rival and died of a broken heart. Upon his return, Popo learned of his beloved Izta's death and was inconsolable. The gods, touched by their plight, turned them into snowy mountains so that they could be together for eternity. Sometimes, Popo will spew ash, because the pain for his White Woman still burns deep within his heart. They are a symbol of love everlasting.

After we've finished eating, we try to make ourselves comfortable to rest, as comfortable as we can be with assassin bugs and a whole host of murderous creatures wandering out for the night. The vines have taken on the appearance of snakes and every shadow is a crouching wildcat.

The floor is coated with a carpet of vegetation and Tezca's sword comes in handy. As he's hacking away to clear the ground, a howler monkey comes at him, making a roaring sound that must be heard for some miles around. It stops when Tezca holds out his blade. The monkey spits at him but seems to have respect for his weapon.

At last I lean against a wide tree trunk covered with moss. I have to sit upright so I don't snore and mumble while I rest. Sleep overcomes me.

Tezca wakes me and informs me I'm snoring. I look around, befuddled. It takes me a moment to remember where I am.

"Are you all right?" Tezca asks.

I nod, but he knows I'm lying.

"You've barely said a word since we left. I've never known you to be so quiet."

"What do you care? 'Not everything is about me.' Isn't that what you said? There are more important things that need your attention."

"Good night, then." He adjusts his sleeping position and shuts his eyes.

"Tezca?"

"Just go to sleep."

"Tezca."

His eyes open. "What?"

"Tell me about Nican Nicah," I say. Perhaps I will learn new things, but mostly, I don't want to forget my father.

He takes a deep breath and leans forward, resting his arms on his knees. "He loved you," he says. "Nothing pleased him more than you returning to the palace after all those years he thought you were dead. He was so happy to have you back."

There is a silence long enough for his words to sink in.

He continues, lost in thought. "Don Joaquín advocated for our people. We gave him the name Nican Nicah because he would say 'I am here' every time he came to us. Then the plague began to spread. Nican Nicah did everything in his power to aid the sick."

And that was Father's downfall.

"There were sinister forces in play," Tezca says. "The Dark Mirror is intimately bound with its creator, and it worked evil into your father's best intentions. Tezcatlipoca is a trickster god. With the Dark Mirror, he can look into the hearts of mortals and tempt them into darkness. The outcome of that eventually brings . . ."

"Brings what?"

"Death."

I wipe away a tear with the back of my hand. "I don't understand. How did the Dark Mirror even come into my father's possession?"

"I have asked myself the very same question. The Dark Mirror isn't something you chance upon. It had not been seen since the Fall of the Toltecah."

"But," I press, "how did you know I had it?"

"I didn't. When Don Joaquín fell to the plague, I figured the medallion would be sent to Spain with the rest of our treasures. I couldn't let that happen. We will never know what your father saw in the mirror, but he was a good man, Leonora. My people grieved for him greatly. There are many who would fight in memory of Don Joaquín."

It doesn't take Tezca long to shut his eyes. I pull a piece of parchment from my bag, dip a quill into the inkwell, and begin scribbling. I write about my day. What I did. What I said. I write about Señor Alonso, Inés, my brother, my mother, Amalia, Tezca. The Dark Mirror. I pass my fingers over the slight indents in the material, feeling the curve of the letters, and a light smudge of ink transfers to my skin. I lift my hand and look at my blue fingertips, and I snort. I'm not a blue blood.

My hand starts hurting toward the end of the parchment. I'm waiting for the ink to dry, when I hear a slight rustle in the bushes. I positioned small sticks and branches crossed over each other close by to let me know if someone or something is headed our way.

I can feel I'm being watched from the brush, but whatever it is, I can't catch its smell, nor can I see it. I hold my breath, feeling the forest around me. In the Namba, you have to pay attention, or you'll end up dead.

I must have fallen asleep. When I wake up there is light and my first thought is, *don't move.* A large green boa, about three feet long, is curling up tight around my leg. She's not brightly colored, so she doesn't look venomous, but she can still constrict me to death.

I've learned benevolence toward all creatures, but I cannot say the same of demons. As the story goes, the Obsidian Butterfly fell from paradise along with the Tzitzimime and several creatures—scorpions, spiders, and other such deadly things. It's hard to tell a snake from a demon, but it's safe to assume both can kill you.

I hold my breath, feeling the boa's silky-smooth skin slither against my bare foot, and chant Inés's last words to me. *Don't be afraid, Pantera. Don't be afraid.* Death is about six inches from my face, when I hear a squirrel chattering in the tree behind me. The boa turns her head, her attention focused on the squirrel, not me. I start to breathe evenly again. As the boa is uncoiling herself from me, Tezca cuts her in half.

I look up at him angrily. "You didn't have to kill her. She was just looking for a meal."

"Tell that to the squirrel. Did you get sufficient sleep, or should I let you continue with your fourteenth hour of rest?"

I curse him under my breath and find my sandals.

The afternoon grows late, and Tezca is peeved.

"How do you sleep so much?" he asks. "Is that what you learned in Tamoanchan? To sleep?"

"What does that have to do with anything?"

"I thought witches were taught discipline."

I glare at him. "If you're going to insult me, do it right. I'm a sorceress, not a witch."

"You know, you scared away the bears," he says. "I'll pretend your horrific snoring never happened."

"That might be the most stupid thing you've ever said to me," I say. "There are no bears around here."

"How do you know?"

"The grizzlies live in the Sierra Madre, you fool."

"And where are we?"

"Not in the Sierra Madre—hold on. What's going on?" I say, the fog in my mind lifting enough to realize what he's doing, and I trot ahead of him. "Stop it."

"Stop what?"

"Your little memory game. Stop it."

"What memory game?"

"Save it, Tezca. I don't need your pity, and I can manage very well without you. I did for years before you ever came along."

"Would it be so terrible to maybe, just maybe, let me help, Leonora?"

It might.

We go on like this for hours, sniping at each other. I suppose it keeps me alive. I keep having episodes of forgetfulness and confusion about where I am, what I'm doing. Sometimes I lose a word, unsure if I said something already. Tezca can tell.

We come upon a river wide enough to allow the passage of a ship, beautiful in the light, innocuous. For all its peacefulness there is more danger in its depths than the trees behind us. Up ahead is a large waterfall. The river coils its way through the jungle like a serpent, a noticeable cloudiness blanketing the river, which could be mistaken for fog or mist from the fall but is actually steam rising from the bubbling water.

Bonnango, the boiling river of the Namba.

The mud on the bank is warm beneath my sandals. Tezca inserts a bamboo stick into the water. It comes out charred, to the point where it turns black and it falls apart.

"We're getting close," I say. "The river's heat comes from Popo."

"Are you sure this is the way?" Tezca says. "It doesn't look very promising."

"I didn't ask you to come," I snap. "I didn't ask anything of you at all."

He huffs. "We cannot cross to the other bank, and it'll take us days to find a ford. Or have you grown wings, Leonora?"

"Go back. If you don't trust me, go back."

"I trust you."

"But what? I'm not myself? Is that what you think? Say it. Be a man and say it, Tezca."

He throws up his hands and grumbles to himself, and I think about strangling him. I'm positive he's thinking the same thing. But neither of us gets the chance.

From the thicket, a spotted jaguar skulks on to our bank, fangs on display, and at least ten women rush out behind it with long spears. One of them comes over to us. Strings of beads hang down her neck, scarcely covering any skin, and a short skirt reveals the curve of her willowy figure. She walks with a sway of her hips, proud, smiling and expressive as she approaches, as if she knows she is making an entrance. She gives the jaguar a pat on the head.

Friend or foe?

She greets us in the common tongue. "We are Bungomanga, guardians of the sacred river." Grinning, she steps up to Tezca, trailing a finger up his chest and over his chin. "What brings you travelers to our territory?"

Tezca grabs her finger in his hand. She pulls it toward her, pressing it to her chest, and runs his knuckles across the swells of her breasts. Tezca looks like he wants to blink but can't remember how.

I stare at her incredulously. "I didn't catch your name."

She tilts her chin toward me. "It's Pantera."

Foe. "Pantera?"

"The one and the same."

For a second, I wonder if my head is playing tricks on me, but one quick glance at Tezca confirms we both heard the same thing.

"Tell me about you, Pantera." The name sounds odd on my lips.

"I am a witch, and I can take the form of a jaguar."

Sorceress. I feel a twinge of anger. "What else?"

"I am heroic and a symbol of hope."

"What else?"

"I am fearless and fight courageously to protect my people."

"If you are guardians of the river, you must know it well. How do we cross it?"

"There is only one way," Pantera says. "We have rafts in our village."

The walk to the Bungomanga settlement seems to be interminable. I'm struggling to breathe, I can barely move my arms, and the pain in my feet is all I can think about. My blisters have blisters. I have aches in places where I didn't know I had places.

I pull out my parchment and record the direction we are headed as far as I can tell, jotting down a careful description of the land we are traveling, my impressions of the women, and the one who calls herself Pantera.

We are led to a small community. The buildings are made of bamboo and other natural materials the jungle provides. More of the women receive us with pleasing smiles, making every show of friendship. As I watch children playfully chasing each other, I wonder where the men are.

Under the stars, we gather around a low table, sitting on woven mats laid on the ground, before a feast is piled high on banana leaves. There are dishes of fish, newts, tadpoles, and shrimp, simmering in different types of sauce, as well as tamales, snails, and agave worms. As guests we have to eat first, and I am starving, but I don't sample the food.

There's something wrong about this place. I can feel it.

Tezca is having his moment. He is being fed the pink flesh of a pitaya. With a chuckle, Pantera licks a rivulet of juice trickling down the corner of his mouth.

A vein in my forehead begins to throb. "Necesito hablar contigo," I say to him. "Alone."

Pantera doesn't understand Spanish but looks unhappy when Tezca stands and follows me under a tree.

I fold my arms over my chest. "What are you doing?"

"What do you mean?"

"I mean we should be on our way to Snake Mountain. You might recall why we're here."

"It's dark. We'll cross the river tomorrow."

I pinch the bridge of my nose, massaging it. "Gods, you are amazingly thick. What makes you think they'll let us leave? They're clearly hiding something. Don't you think it's odd that the tribe has women and children, but no men? And why would a distant tribe of the Namba speak Nahuatl, or any language we know of? Do they have dealings with other folk? They have plenty of food. Where do they fish? In the hot river? Not to mention, your girlfriend keeps a pet jaguar to do her bidding."

He sighs tiredly. "Have you finished?"

"No. While she was feeding you, did you notice the knife sheathed at the small of her back? I did. Why does she need a knife?"

"Maybe it's her fishing knife. Maybe she likes to cut her fruit to make it easier to eat. Maybe—"

My glare is enough for him to stop.

"You're looking for a problem where there isn't one, Leonora."

"Well, of course you would say that. The heroic Pantera was smitten the moment she laid eyes on you."

"So she calls herself Pantera. That doesn't mean she's hiding something."

"That's exactly what it means, you fool!"

"Leonora, don't start. I'm not going to do this right now."

"Why not? Because you know I'm right and you're too spineless to admit it?"

"I *don't* want to fight." His voice comes out like a thunderclap. He takes a deep breath, and in a softer voice says, "What is this really about?" He closes the gap between us, bending at the waist so his face is level with mine, and he looks right at me, as if he's trying to see into me. "Leonora," he says quietly. His eyes look hollow, weary. "I know it hasn't been easy for you."

"Don't talk to me like I'm broken." I push past him and slip away, trying to appear casual. If anyone asks, I will say I'm going to relieve myself, but nobody does.

The forest is black in every direction but very much alive. Its tune is the squabbling of parrots, the flapping of bats, the chattering of monkeys. It quickly reminds me that I'm inconsequential. I've been attacked, of course, by gnats and mosquitoes and midges. But the more dangerous wildlife has left me alone. I've been allowed to survive. So far.

I consult my parchment and head off down the path to the river. I'm starting to appreciate the benefits of journaling when the terrain gives way to a marsh of tall reeds. With a long branch, I test the dirt. The surface appears solid. Quicksand can form under certain conditions. I look around, making out murky shapes that could be slanted trees or lurking monsters. I take a deep breath. Any kind of strenuous leg activity is difficult, but there I am, hurrying to get across the wobbly patch of ground.

When I get to dry land, I drop to the ground and catch my breath. I look up and notice thinner trees and beyond them the riverbank. I'm not sure what I'm looking for, but I'll know it when I see it. Along the bank are bamboo cages, a row of them. They're all empty, except for one. Its occupant is a man, and he lies in a dazed stupor. I squat before him, holding my index finger to my lips when he startles, curling up in the back of his cage.

"I'm not going to hurt you," I say in Nahuatl, trying to pry the cage open.

"Help," he mumbles.

I give him quick acknowledging nods. "I'll get you out of here. Hold on."

The cage is so small he can't stand upright. He reaches through the bars and clasps my shoulder. "Behind you!"

I feel the sting of an insect on my neck. My hand reaches up. It's a dart. I extract it quickly and stand up, but I stumble. At the same time, arms wrap around me.

"Now, now, no need to fight unnecessarily. It's wasted energy."

I wake up in a bamboo cage of my own, my head throbbing. The sunlight hurts my eyes.

My stomach contracts violently, and I hunch over, my innards heaving, again and again. The grass is damp between my fingers. When it's over,

I feel bruised inside. I wipe my mouth with the back of my hand and lift my heavy eyelids, straining my gaze as I squint around for the prisoner from last night. His cage is empty. My bottom lip quivers.

Someone splashes me with cold water.

"A very good day to you, Leonora."

I shiver and brush away my hair from my cheeks, realizing how grimy it is. I lift my head to see an amused Pantera holding a bucket, accompanied by her pet jaguar.

"I apologize for the rough awakening," she says. "I trust you slept well. I certainly did; Tezcacoatzin has the energy of the jungle. He told me something of your story—I hope you don't mind that he did—and he said what a good friend you were."

Friend.

I'm caged. No weapon. No tonalli. No nagual. No power. But I still have my tongue. "Bed him. Kill him. Do what you will with him, for all I care."

With a smirk, she bends down before me and says, "You should see the look on your face."

"Since you're so interested, I'll tell you something about him few people know."

"And what's that?"

"On second thought, I'll let you figure it out for yourself. But if I were you, I'd be really careful. Who's to say that knife you're carrying around on your back won't be in my hand next."

Her jaw twitches, but then she laughs to show she isn't really angry. She turns around and as I follow her line of sight, I restrain a gasp. The prisoner I tried to help last night is being forced to the edge of the riverbank by two Bungomanga women, their spears held against him. I shout at him to run, and he lifts his head to look at me with drowsy eyes, then starts coughing as if he wants to say something but his throat doesn't give him the chance.

"The river gives us so much, but its power can be destructive," Pantera says. "We have our gods. They must be satisfied."

I've had about enough of this imposter. "The only one offering her blood today is you," I say.

Pantera grins. "You can try," she says, then saunters down to the bank. With her arms spread, she begins to chant. "Great goddess Tlanchala, Mother of Fish, turn not away. Bring to us your bounty. Let our people prosper. Accept our gift and return to us tomorrow." Her voice is echoed by the other two women as they push the prisoner closer to the water.

At first, I think he will be hurled into the river in some attempt to please whatever deity they worship, but then the water ripples, as if someone disturbed it from below, and out comes a creature, a predator with the torso and head of a woman and the black tail of a serpent. Flashes of sunlight reflect off her crown and the other jewels adorning her nakedness.

I curse and kick the front of my cage, my foot slamming into the bamboo. I am not going to die in this godsforsaken place, and neither is that man. As I'm shaking the bars of my cage, I feel myself jump at the growl of a beast. I turn my head to see Pantera's pet jaguar slinking toward her. Pantera slowly steps backward as the jaguar forces her to the edge of the river, fangs bared, swaying its tail slowly from side to side.

And then the jaguar turns its head to me. His brown eyes say it all. Tezca.

The golden, spotted fur on his neck and spine is erect, making him seem larger and more menacing. He growls his loudest, most fearsome growl. It's a weapon in itself, so ferocious that it rumbles across the jungle, reverberates through my body, and sends birds fluttering from their perches.

With a shrill cry, the water snake plunges back under the river, sending a burning shower over Pantera and the two women. They yell in agony at the scalding water, and at last the prisoner is able to slip from their clutches and flee into the trees. I kick my cage again, harder, and when it comes apart, I make my own escape.

CHAPTER 37

El Volcán

We run, our only thought to get away from the Bungomanga settlement. We don't stop until Tonatiuh's rays vanish behind the thick canopy of leaves, when our legs give out and we can go no farther. My feet are a battered mess. But it doesn't matter. After being caged, all I want is to move freely.

I bend over with my hands on my knees, gulping in breaths. "What took you so long?"

"You know me," Tezca pants, "I like to make an entrance."

"What was it you said to me not too long ago? Oh, yes. 'I don't go around bedding any woman who shows me the least bit of attention.'" Those were his words, all right.

"You're not going to make it easy, are you?"

No answer from me.

"You're angry with me," he says.

"I'm not."

"So why is the vein in your forehead about to burst?" he asks, making it clear my face doesn't lack expression.

"Oh, I don't know. Maybe because I was caged like a flea-infested dog."

We press forward.

"I'm sorry I didn't believe you," Tezca says. "I thought . . . maybe you were jealous."

I snort. "Of you? With her?"

"When I woke up in the morning, I felt . . . sick. I couldn't remember what happened," he says, frowning, "but I remember the snakes. They were everywhere, slithering, hissing, falling out of trees."

I didn't see any snakes. Did I? I would consult my journal, but I left it behind. "Wait," I say, gathering my thoughts. "Snakeweed." The herb called coatl xoxouhqui produces the seeds of the sacred morning glory ololiuhqui, which causes a rapturous, dreamlike state. Some are said to have visions of terrible things. Tezca must have been in a trance. "I saw the white flowers of the vine growing back at the settlement. You were deprived of your reason. You couldn't have known better."

When the sun sets, and we've lit our fires and eaten our rations of roast iguana, and strung up makeshift hammocks from the trees, Tezca asks to see my feet.

"My feet?"

"Yes, your feet. You're slowing us down."

I take off my sandals. Tezca sits in front of me. He pulls my feet toward him, inspecting my toes. They are bleeding with cuts and so swollen with blisters I can't move them.

Tezca's fingers drift, gentle. I wince at the stinging pain as he begins growing new skin over the open sores.

"I can't believe you've been walking like this," he mutters angrily. "You won't last a day once we begin our climb on Popocatepetl. If you lose your footing, you will certainly doom us. Is that what you want?"

I shudder as I listen. I hid this from him because I have no intention of letting him stop me from climbing. Not him. Not the loss of tonalli. Not blisters on my feet.

"Did you want me to be?" I say, my voice barely above a whisper. "Jealous?"

He keeps his head down, my foot cradled in his hand. "You told Pantera she could kill me for all you cared."

"I was in a cage. I said what I had to say. I won't apologize for it." But Tezca already knows that. "I don't want an apology."

"Well, then, what do you want?"

"What I've always wanted." He offers his hand to help me stand. When he pulls me up, our faces are inches apart. "I want you to live," he says. I look down. My feet are healed.

In the morning, we seek a path up the volcano. It takes us longer to go around the river, but at least we don't have to cross it and risk plunging to our scorching deaths. Halfway up, fog rolls in and it begins snowing. In seconds, we're enveloped in a bitterly cold, white blanket. Without a covering, I have to keep my head down to protect my eyes and blink constantly to keep them from freezing. I power up the trail, concentrating. I have a rhythm, one foot in front of the other. Darkness is approaching fast, and we have to keep moving.

The upper slopes are white. Trudging through fresh powder is a nightmare. It's almost like trying to get out of quicksand. The second half of the mountain becomes too steep to walk. We crawl, tunneling through snow that begins to bury us. We don't speak, just climb. I push along through a landscape of snow, ice, clouds and jagged peaks, slipping and sliding, grunting and gasping, miserable and full of pain and doubt.

A gust blasts down the volcano. Tezca guides us on a diagonal path, which is somewhat easier than heading straight into the snowstorm. But if we lose our footing here, there's nothing between us and the long falling slope of snow, dwarfed trees, brush, and rock. One slip and it's all over, but having Tezca with me makes the climb a little less rough, a little less terrifying.

"How far until we get to Tamoanchan?" Tezca asks.

"I don't know," I admit.

"What do you mean you don't know?"

"Either Tican lets you in, or he doesn't," I say.

"Tican?"

"Xochitlicacan," I say. "I couldn't say his name when I was little."

"Xochitlicacan?" He arches an eyebrow. "The Flowering Tree?"

"The very same, whose blooms are amulets of happiness. Tamoanchan has a strict code of entry. That's why treasure hunters have never found the city. You can only pass through the hidden door if its guardian allows you."

"We'll lose the light before we can find a campsite," he says. "There's a cleft through this ridge up ahead."

I'm laboring for breath, I can barely move my arms, and the pain in my legs is all I can think about. My hands are so numb I can't wiggle my fingers. They don't feel a thing. Cold, sweat, wind, snow, pain, pain, pain, and more pain. The climb seems interminable.

Finally, the incline ends and opens out into a flat expanse of snow. When I try to stand up straight, I nearly topple sideways, reeling from exhaustion.

"How are you doing?" Tezca asks.

"Just keep going." We'll freeze otherwise.

Thankfully, the snow is firmer here, my footing better. But then a sharp wind descends upon us, tossing about the snow and reducing my visibility.

I become angry. *Fine, Popo*, I think. *Do your worst.* Anger clears my head and brings back my focus. In spite of my agony, I won't rest until I find Tamoanchan.

Through a haze of swirling white, I lift my eyes, squinting, and just make out that Tezca has stopped some ten feet ahead of me. He turns around and says something, but his words are caught by the howling wind. I plop to my knees, scraping the snow around me. And that's when I know. There it is beneath me—a frozen lake caldera. Even ice-covered, the gurgling water is so incredibly clear that I can see rocks and boulders downstream. I'm close to the edge where it's shallow, so I test its strength and feel a quiver, like I'm standing on glass. Tezca is in the center of the ice sheet. He shouts something and makes a move toward me, shouting again, and then there's an earsplitting crack. He breaks through the ice.

"Tezca!" I scream. Only a croak emerges. My throat is too dry. I drag my feet through the snow toward the spot where the ice broke under him. I pull my gloves off and shove my hands into the lake, paddling to haul him out, but I can't find him or feel anything other than the unbearable sting of the bone-chilling water. I follow a current, stumbling and digging through the snow.

"No, no, no." I tap the ice, horrified to see the water pushing his body this way and that. "Tezca! I lied. I need you. Come back! Please, don't leave me."

I call to him again, but no answer comes. My body becomes too heavy to hold up, right before my legs give out, and I collapse on to the snow.

Lying there, blinded by the snowy wind, I see something—someone—walking toward me. "Tezca?" I croak. "Is that you?"

All I can distinguish before my eyes close is the blurred face of a woman.

When my eyes open again, a dog is staring back at me. I lie in a hut, my numb body slowly coming back to me as animal skins and a hearth provide warmth, a world of difference from the cold. A woman with curly, choppy hair slaps dough from one hand to the other, making tortillas. On the foot of my mat, a one-eyed hairless dog growls impatiently, his tongue lolling.

"I know, I know," says the woman, and she ladles beans into two bowls, one for me and one for the dog, and sticks a spoon and fresh tortillas into mine.

"Where am I?" My voice is hoarse.

"I'm sorry about Xolo," she says, giving me the bowl and a cup of hot sweetened chocolate. "We don't see many visitors. It's always been us two together."

Am I dead? The pain in my limbs tells me I'm not. It's nothing but a slight prickle compared to what I feel inside. It lets me know I'm alive. I'm still here.

And Tezca isn't.

It's your fault, says the voice somewhere in the back of my mind. *Why did you let him come? Tezca is dead because of you.* I cover my ears, as though it will block out the internal voice, but it carries on.

"I . . . I was with someone. Did you see anyone else out there?"

She shakes her head. "What brings you to Popocatepetl?"

"I'm trying to find Tamoanchan." I don't even try to lie. I have no pride left.

"Are you seeking jewels and riches or do you wish to pluck a rose from the tree of life?" she asks.

"I seek help," I say truthfully.

"You must look within for the reason you are climbing Popo," she says. "You don't find Tamoanchan. You find yourself."

I don't know what to say, so I drink.

"Climbing Popo means being born again," says the woman. "You have to learn to breathe, to walk. You have to eat. You can't cheat. Out there, you want to go faster to get to the top. But you have to take your time. You have to pace yourself. You have to stop. You have to sleep. Which reminds me, you should get some more rest."

My eyes narrow. "Who are you?"

"Me? It's not important."

I lie down on my mat. "Thank you for the food."

The sure knowledge that I must go on without Tezca undoes me completely. All pretense of quiet coping is lost and the tears come then, in choking sobs.

Tezca is now in Tlalocan. Those who drown are assured a place in the First Heaven, presided over by Tlaloc, but that doesn't comfort me. Tezca was a warrior. He deserved a warrior's death and a warrior's paradise. Nothing less. I cry myself back to sleep.

*

Xolo the one-eyed dog barks. I roll over and moan, but he barks again, louder this time, and then again.

"Shh. What do you want?" He bounces on the foot of my mat, tail wagging furiously. In the daylight, I can see his ugliness: long gangly limbs and a wrinkly head. The hut is deathly quiet. There's no sign of the woman from last night.

Xolo drags the animal skins off me with his teeth.

"All right," I say, slipping on my shoes. Xolo is already at the door pawing and whimpering. I open it and he dashes out. I think he might have a piss, but he races up the mountain instead. He's seen his chance for freedom and taken it.

"Dog, no!" I yell. "Get back here." My order is futile. He has already disappeared into the flurry of white.

"Bad dog! You'll freeze out here! You hear me?" I shout through cupped hands. I'm not certain if he'll be able to get back to the hut if he wants to, which he evidently doesn't. "You dumb, ugly dog— Nine Hells!"

I break into a run after him, fighting the snow and the pain in my head and in my limbs and in my body and in my heart. As much as I'm cursing him at the moment, I'm not about to leave the woman without her dog. I scramble up the mountain and pounce on him, but he isn't about to be captured. "Cut it out!" His freedom has already been established, and he veers from side to side. "Dog, stay!"

I follow his tracks to the top of the mountain and there I see him gazing into the vast valley, tongue hanging out to one side. I smile, or at least I think I smile. I can't really tell. I can't feel my face.

"Crazy dog," I mutter and drop next to him, panting. He gives me a look to let me know he's pleased with me and shakes a shower of snowflakes from his hairless body. The wind is intense, and I can't breathe, can't see, can't think of anything but Tezca and his final moments.

"What more do you want from me, Popo?" I shout. "You took Tezca! I'm tired! I have nothing left to give you!" It feels good to let my frustration out even though there's no answer from Popocatepetl, only the one-eyed dog, the frosty air, the wind whipping snow into my eyes, the freezing sweat on my back.

It's here I face my reality, the reality of living without Tezca, the reality of the end of the Fifth Sun, and somewhere in the midst of this comes a realization. Though I am prepared to die, I am simply not ready. I sneaked up on this sleeping volcano, hoping not to wake him, but he woke me. He sensed my need for an awakening and he shook me out of my slumber. Tezca and I only climbed because Popo allowed us. If the weather hinted at us to wait, we waited. And when Popo beckoned us to go, then we struggled and strained in the thin air with all that we had. One would think the most obvious way to get to the top of a volcano is to go up. But on more than one occasion, we headed down to get to another point before climbing again. My life has been like this. Sometimes, I have had to go backward to move forward. There are better things to achieve than death. Work toward living instead of dying.

It will be hard. I spent a decade practicing the Nagualist arts. It's taken me a long time to understand the great difference between having a nagual and being a Nagual. You don't master your nagual. You master yourself. We don't make war with another but with ourselves—our own imperfections, failures, addictions, and shortcomings. This is the wisdom of the great Nagual Masters. I've had to learn the hard way, the very hardest, and I am not blind to my faults. I am who I am. I fail and make mistakes, but at least I know I'm willing to try again. I know what I'm aiming for.

Xolo barks, and I open my eyes to see an arched door has appeared in the whiteness.

CHAPTER 38

El Paraiso

The wooden door towers high above our heads, a dusting of gold etched into its outline. There is no knob, no handle, nothing to grip.

Inés once said that my power lies in my ability to remember who I am. She did not know that I would come to lose my tonalli, nor did she know the "I am" wisdom of Nagualism—"I am who I am" or "I am as you see me." It means to have the awareness of who you are. When you have the awareness of who you are, you also have the awareness of who you were and who you will be.

Trailing through the Namba. Climbing Popocatepetl. Tezca's death. Those were big things. My realization is small, quiet, one that shakes me in its stillness, not in its destruction.

"I am Tecuani," I say and press my hand flat to the middle of the door. It begins to moan and crack, shifting its enormous weight and opening on unseen hinges.

I look down and see that Xolo has already leaped to the other side. "Good dog." The snow ceases, the sky clears, and the air warms as I step through the door into a lush garden of flowers with parrots and striking quetzals. The brightness here rivals the sun itself.

Before me stretch white temples and glittering palaces, shining all colors of the rainbow, ringed by water. Raised fields give way to forests as the land slopes up to the mountains.

I am home.

A gentle breeze blows my braid over my shoulder. I can breathe. My limbs are without pain. My grimy clothes are gone, carried away to a magical laundry or wherever dirty garments go, replaced by a jeweled tunic. Rings of green beads wrap around my fingers, and bangles adorn my wrists. On my feet, sandals of gold lace up to my knees with gilded straps.

A familiar voice calls me from behind. I turn around slowly.

There, in the light, is Tezca.

My body turns so rigid I wonder when I will snap in half. His red tilmahtli encircles his broad shoulders and cascades to the ground as he walks. He's never looked more intense, more handsome.

He smiles faintly. "What took you so long?"

"You know me. I like to make an entrance." I grin. "I thought you died. What happened to you?"

"I'm not sure," he says. "One moment I was drowning, the other I was coughing water." He waves a hand. "Here."

I bounce on my toes and fling my arms around his neck, burrowing my nose in his chest, and he pulls me in all the tighter, barely giving me space to breathe. I let myself sag against him and sink into the warmth of his hair and his familiar smell. His touch makes the air lighter somehow, the future a little less bleak. I don't remember the last time someone held me like this. I'm not able to sense his tonalli without my own, but I vividly remember the feel of it.

As we pull apart, Tezca looks down at me, searching my face for an expression he can read, as if silently asking a question.

"Tezcacoatzin," I whisper.

Saying his name is like a trigger. That's all it takes for him to cup his hands around my face and pull me close. I gasp when his mouth claims mine. He kisses me, hard, and I kiss him back harder, because this is it. This is what I've wanted. Since before I spoke to him, before

I even laid eyes on him. That first time I sensed his tonalli on *La Capitana*, I wanted him.

Deep down, I think I've always known, but I am made for war, and I resisted.

It's him. It's always been him.

Tezca's lips mold against mine, almost like they were made for me. I feel him—all of him—pressed against me. He is intoxicating. I forget about the world. I forget about everything. I don't want to stop, not ever.

We pull apart only as I'm lifted off the ground. One of the Flowering Tree's knobby roots wraps itself around my waist and holds me in the air.

"Oh, it's good to see you too, Tican." I laugh, struggling to break free from the gnarled branches. A flurry of butterflies descends on me, and I quiet. A woman walks to us under a pallium of gold and green quetzal feathers, her blouse and skirt dripping with precious jewels.

"The Flowering Tree has answered your call, Tecuani," she says, her voice graceful. "There, there, old friend." She pats the tree trunk.

Tican shakes his leaves excitedly, and I plummet to the ground.

Tezca offers his hand to help me up. "You've met Xochiquetzal."

"I have," he says.

The fairest of all the gods and goddesses in the Nahua pantheon, the Precious Flower, Xochiquetzal, guards the Flowering Tree. One touch of its roses ensures happiness, love, and good fortune. She is the goddess of love, sexuality, and flowers—lady of birds and butterflies.

"Tezca found his way into Tamoanchan too." As the Precious Flower gently bows her head and turns toward the city, a grassy path appears, surrounded by flowers and clumps of fruit-bearing prickly pear trees. Buildings are laid with a stone so white the city sparkles like a mirror.

It feels good to be back in the home that raised me. Life felt limitless here, like nothing could ever touch me. Even without my tonalli, I'm present in my memories, as if I never really left. But my thrill is short-lived. I'm visiting a past life, one that doesn't exist anymore.

We follow the path to the city, and in the main square, a crowd of curious onlookers gathers round us. A young man bursts forward. "Tecuani? Ca tehhuatl?"

I smile at him. Yes, it's me. "Quemah, ca nehhuatl. It is good to see you, Atzompa."

"Spread the word," Xochiquetzal tells him.

Paynani, or couriers, like Atzompa are trained to run as fast as the wind to deliver messages from one part of the city to another. I would often see Atzompa running up and down the temple, which is more than a hundred steps, to build stamina in his legs.

Atzompa pivots with a flair and announces to the murmuring crowd, "Tecuani has returned!"

At first, dead silence, then a cheer breaks out.

I beam, listening to my Nahua name on their lips. My smile doesn't last long, for my arrival is no celebration. The crowd suddenly parts, making a pathway for the approaching man.

Rumors say Master Toto was once very handsome. He's balding and what's left of his hair looks like dandelion fuzz on his scalp. The dirty soles of his feet tell me that he still insists on going barefoot because shoes bother his toes and make him walk funny, and he believes he loses something when his skin doesn't touch the ground. The goatee is new.

He walks slowly toward us in a sky-blue tilmahtli, his usual gourd hanging from his belt, leaning on his crutch as he goes. I've never known what his gourd holds. Maybe it's full of fish food, since he loves feeding the jeweled fish.

I bend to touch the earth with my palms and raise my hands to my lips. "Headmaster."

He nods. "Tecuani. You surrendered and saw all that you are. Now you have found what you were looking for."

"Master," I say, "I am suffering from the loss of my tonalli, and demons roam freely in the Fifth Sun. The Tzitzimime will have their taste of man-flesh. I have come to ask for help."

A chorus of disturbed gasps rises around us.

Master Toto lifts his hand. "Don't be hasty, Tecuani. You've just arrived, and the fish are hungry."

I frown. "Master, the Fifth Sun is—"

"In danger, I know. But rushing feet make mistakes."

"Will you help?"

"Yes. No."

Some things never change.

The fish come first, so I wait. My friends, my family, Mexico, and the entire Fifth Sun have to wait for Master Toto to command my presence. I'm patient at first, but when no message comes, I go about the city, hoping to cross paths with him. He's not in the temple, by the lake, in the training houses, nor anywhere in the adjacent grounds. Instead, I find the Precious Flower in the gardens, humming, on her knees like a peasant woman, tending to the soil, planting cempasúchiles.

"Why do you do that?" I ask as I come up behind her. "You're a goddess."

"I was not born a goddess."

"I know."

"But do you know how I became one?"

I shake my head.

A hummingbird lands on her hand, and I notice mottled spots and folds on her skin that weren't there before. The bird slides its long beak between each of her wizened fingers then flies away. She rises from her knees and faces me. Up close, a gathering of wrinkles creases around her eyes and mouth, and her long black hair shows streaks of white. The strange thing is, gods are ever youthful. The Precious Flower is the source of all beautiful things. No one can resist her beauty and look at her without love.

"I was born here," she says, "in Tamoanchan, the misty place in the sky where happiness-giving flowers bloom. I would spend my days knitting soft and exquisite fabrics for my huipiltin. Until I was stolen from my husband by the trickster god of the night to be his lover. He took me to his cold dark kingdom in the north. It was he who made me the goddess of love."

Trickster god of the night? The Black God. Understanding comes in a terrible flash. "He is your son," I say. "Tezca . . . he is a god."

"He is his father's son." Her voice is toneless. "He shares the same attributes as Tezcatlipoca. A strong warrior, and a skillful deceiver. His is a world of shadows, demons, and sorcery."

I shake my head, refusing to let her words get to me. I brought no offerings, no weavings, butterflies, or cuetlaxochime, her favorites. A plant as red as the blood of sacrifices. Wars were fought to gain her blessing. Why would she share information without proper worship? The Precious Flower, like all the gods, is capricious. She would not be telling me this if not for her own benefit. I'm not about to amuse her.

"You're wrong," I say. "Tezcacoatzin is not like his father. He sought the Dark Mirror to destroy it. He's helped people. He's helped . . . me."

If she was human, she would scowl. And even that would seem lovely on her. Instead, the garden turns bare and desolate, then the marigolds bloom and the fruit ripens again, as if she calmed herself. "Tezcatlipoca isn't always a destructive god," she says. "He can bring happiness and good fortune. He can be kind and very sweet. But he is impossible to predict, like my son."

Everyone has demons. Mine are never too far away. We all have things about ourselves that we hide and fight and ignore. Ometeotl is a god of duality. Male and female. Light and dark. Night and day. Order and chaos. Everyone has a dark side. Perhaps, for Tezca, it is not his favored side.

"Does he know he's a god?"

"Once," she replies. "A long time ago." There is an unexpected tremor in her voice, and because she's a goddess, the leaves on the trees quiver.

I stare at her, incredulous. "A long time ago?"

"My son has lived many lives, in many places; lives he cannot recall. He cannot truly die. But in the human world, he has had many deaths. In every lifetime, he begins showing abilities beyond any normal boy, so I come to him with the truth about his father. He is a great sorcerer, but he has forgotten who he is. It's best that he lives in the Fifth Sun, among humans, far from his father's wicked path. You understand, don't you, Tecuani?"

I feel my heartbeat in my throat. This is the immense weight I sensed in Tezca's tonalli before but couldn't understand—the burden of having lived multiple lives, each life an accumulation of different pains and sorrows. He does not remember, but his tonalli does. It remains the same, carrying the sum of all his past lives.

Tezca certainly is a great warrior, but his power is held back. If he remembered who he was, I can't help but wonder what kind of god he would choose to be.

Would he bring salvation?

Or destruction?

"The lake," I say. "You saved him."

"Yes. If my son had died, he would have returned to Teteocan,"— the Twelfth Heaven—"with his father, to be reborn. I'd have to feed his tonalli into another mortal body. But I don't have that kind of power anymore," she says. "Humans have the Christian God now. They have forgotten about me, and I . . . I have faded."

The teteoh need worshipers and offerings to be sustained like I need food and water. That gives them their power.

"I know how you feel about him, and the way he feels about you, but he must never find out," she says.

My knees feel weak and wobbly. I don't have the strength to carry this knowledge and keep it from Tezca. He isn't meant to live an ordinary life. This deceit will destroy him.

"You don't know how I feel," I say, my frustration rising.

"Tecuani, I am the goddess of love, among other things."

"Why are you telling me this?"

"I am telling you to stop," she replies. "You have been seeking answers from him, answers he doesn't have, and I have seen him struggling with himself in search of the truth. If my son ever remembered who he is, who he really is . . ."

"I don't fear him."

"You will."

I shudder at her words. They don't sound like a threat. They sound like a prophecy.

CHAPTER 39

La Escuela

Tezca's tonalli, his nagual, his ability to heal, his presence, his effect on women, his loose nature. There is a reason for it all. He is the son of the god of sorcery and the goddess of love.

The following day, when he touches my face and leans down to kiss my mouth, it lands on my ear.

"Is something wrong?" he asks.

My stomach knots. Everything's wrong.

"Leonora," he says, "you can talk to me."

I say nothing, avoiding his gaze. I can't look at him. Not in the same way. I have a foolish thought that I'm just another girl that Tezca will soon be finished with. I want to tell him the truth about his mother, the truth about himself, but I guard my tongue.

"What happened to no secrets? No lies?" he says. "What happened to trust?"

All good questions, ones that I don't have ready answers for.

It's been a day, and Master has not yet sent for me. I begin to despair, thinking that he has abandoned me once again.

Tezca and I wander into the House of Nahualtin, a great complex with chambers and courtyards filled with pines and fountains from which flow the purest water. Here sorcerers and sorceresses study the ancient wisdom of Nagualism. Witches and wizards in training are assigned to the House of Naguals, where they learn to master their animal forms.

Only those who do become sorcerers.

Ollin is there, and I greet him with a smile and a courteous nod, as his rank is higher than mine. As a Nagual Warrior, he's chosen to dedicate his life to teaching, responsible for the early education of hundreds of Nagual Apprentices, all at different stages of progression. Ollin was always a good student, always the one making the right decisions, disciplined, obedient, an ideal Nagual. I was not.

In the training hall, a full class of Nagual Apprentices is practicing tonalli manipulation with a few instructors, barely older than the students themselves, floating around correcting and explaining. On the other side of the hall, in a large open space, another group is taking part in mock battles against each other as teams.

"How can a killing tool be a means of attaining inner peace?" I asked Master Toto once, referring to the sword. The paradox of it all.

"When you find the answer, you will no longer have the question," he said.

When the Naguals see us, they stop their lessons. Ollin motions for the students to continue, and Tezca goes around the hall, taking in the lay of the room.

"Something is troubling you," Ollin tells me.

My eyes meet his, and I stiffen. "No. I'm happy to be home . . . to see everyone," I say, though there is no joy in my voice.

"I've known you since you were eight, Tecuani."

"Do you remember when we were children?" I ask, my focus on the students. "That was us not too long ago. What did we know about anything?"

I don't remember the details of my first class, what techniques I practiced, but I remember this great hall. I remember entering shyly, and kissing the earth with the other young Naguals. Here, I was simply a student of Nagualism and nothing else, moving from each of the seven levels to complete a rank.

On my first day, I asked how long it would take to become a Nagual Warrior, and that was my first error. Every other student knew not to ask this question. Later, I would learn that it could take anywhere between ten and twenty years, or I might never achieve it. There are only four ranks—Apprentice, Warrior, Master, and Headmaster, so we spend a lot of time on each, moving up their levels. And it doesn't always feel like you're making progress. Sometimes, it felt like I was getting worse rather than better. When my grading ceremony came, I had already completed seven levels as Nagual Apprentice and ten years of training. I knew the principles of Nagualism and the Nagual Truths, followed the Nagual Path, the techniques, the required forms, but Master Toto's answer wasn't the one I wanted to hear. Because I thought I deserved to receive the title of Nagual Warrior, he said, I was a very long way from attaining the rank.

"Don't you ever wonder what the point of all this is?" I ask Ollin. "Why we train so hard to become sorcerers, to progress to the next level and the next? How many times did we hear Master Toto say that rank isn't important?"

"It isn't," Ollin answers.

"Then what is?"

Ollin shakes his head as though disappointed by my question. "The Nagualist arts require dedication and hard work. All the great masters trained to have the perfection they show in their art. Our battles may not be on the battlefield, but still, we face them every day, in this hall, in our relationships, with ourselves."

One of the Nagual Apprentices drops his sword as he falters backward. Tezca goes to it, picks it up, and offers its hilt to the student, giving him an encouraging nod.

"I see the way you look at him," says Ollin.

I quickly change the subject. "The Tzitzimime," I ask. "How do we defeat them?"

"You go after the queen," he responds.

"But?"

"The Obsidian Butterfly is a goddess. She cannot be killed by mortal means, not even by the most powerful sorcery. Even then, I imagine killing a god has dire consequences that may upset the balance of nature. But a part of the queen can be killed in her physical form."

I think about this, watching two Nagual Apprentices pair up, raising their sword tips to touch. They move together under the guidance of an instructor. When their swords connect, one moves and the other intuits a response.

Ollin walks among the students. "To become a Nagual Warrior," he says to them, "you must find harmony with everything around you, and when that happens, you will understand how to see, how to feel, how to anticipate." He draws his sword and, with gestures, dares Tezca to attack him.

"Ollin, is this wise?" I ask. But wisdom, of course, has nothing to do with it.

Tezca takes up a sword from the array of practice weapons, and he deflects and reverses every one of Ollin's lunges. Tezca is the superior warrior, but Ollin wields a powerful sword, and it easily breaks Tezca's blade. Tezca exchanges his broken weapon for a tepoztopilli, a spear edged with jagged bits of obsidian, and manages to defend himself gracefully against Ollin's sword, Silverlight. However, Silverlight's power depends on its master, and it destroys every weapon that Tezca wields: a knife, a club, a pike, a baton, until finally, Tezca stands barehanded. Ollin swings Silverlight so hard the blade whistles in the air, but Tezca stops it by clapping a hand around its cutting edge. Students gasp, and even the instructors. Seeing blood gush from Tezca's palm, a wide-eyed Ollin loosens his grip on Silverlight's hilt. With a quick motion, Tezca snatches Silverlight and levels its tip at Ollin's throat.

I rush to Ollin and meet Tezca's gaze. "You're scaring them," I say. Tezca looks at me, looks at the students, looks at his bloody hand.

His eyebrows twitch, then he drops Silverlight as if it burns him. The wound will heal, but as Tezca turns and leaves the training hall, I hear the Precious Flower's voice in my head. *You will fear him.* I try to shake off the terrible thought, but I can't. It's already wedged there like a splinter.

Atzompa appears by my side. "The Headmaster will see you now."

CHAPTER 40

El Dios

Master Toto sits on a bamboo raft feeding the jeweled fish in the middle of the lake. I shield my gaze from the sun near a second raft at the water's edge.

I struggle to get on the raft and wrangle it toward him with my paddle. My legs wobble, and my stance, which is supposed to be upright, looks more like a crouch. The raft rocks beneath me, and I flop into the water. I emerge, sputtering, and turn to look at Master Toto, whose attention remains on the jeweled fish. Of course, this is another test, some kind of ambiguous lesson to find my balance. But apparently that too is lost and would rather not be found.

Nevertheless, I throw myself back on the raft and center my weight until the raft is mostly level.

Finally, I reach Master Toto and paddle so that my raft turns and I sit across from him.

"Master," I say, panting, "I need your guidance."

"You don't need anything from me, Tecuani," he says, his voice comforting. I relax into it, hungry for assurance.

"I can't figure things out."

"Then learn the lesson so you can stop repeating the class."

"But I don't know the lesson."

"Then meditate."

"I am suffering from the loss of tonalli," I say sadly. "I've lost my nagual."

"You cannot lose what you are, Tecuani. Do you think the trees become anxious when they lose their leaves?"

"Well, no, but—"

"Is a tree still a tree without leaves?"

"Yes."

"It knows what it is, what it is made of, what it can do. A tree does not rush itself. It remains true to its process. It knows it will flourish again, in its own time."

"But, Master," I say, "a tree can live without leaves, a tree can still be a tree if it loses some branches, but it cannot survive without roots."

At this, he looks up at me and, just for a moment, beams, quite delighted.

"Naguals must trust the Path, accepting they live fully," he says. "We must have the courage to accept the consequences of our actions, without guilt. Most witches never become sorceresses because they don't make it through their growth. They are resistant to moving through themselves, the pain, the wounds that need to be healed, and attempt to skip the process to go straight to their nagual. That doesn't work. The war of a wizard is not directed against other people, but against our own weaknesses. How can you be aware of your nagual when you have noise in your head? It is impossible to know your nagual when living in chaos."

"How do I get rid of the noise?"

"Slow down," he replies. "A warrior moves like a jaguar. Your nagual resides deeper than your wounds, Tecuani. To move into your nagual, you must move through your wounds."

I am quiet, immersed in the sight of the jeweled fish swimming around us, the sunlight glittering on their scales and tail fins of gold, turquoise, and jade. It's mesmerizing to watch them, almost meditative.

"Why help me?" I ask after a long while. "Why send Ollin? Why train me only to dismiss me to then help me again?"

"Dismiss you? Is that how you remember it?"

"You said I wasn't ready to become a Nagual Warrior. You . . . you said I still had much to learn."

"You had the same problem you have now. It wasn't that you weren't good enough. On the contrary, you were exceptionally good."

I frown. "I was?"

"Do you remember when you first came to class, and I had you watch the students? What did you see?"

"I don't know," I admit. "I didn't understand what they were doing."

"What about now? Watching a Nagual?"

"Well, now, I can see if they are doing it right . . . movement, footwork, sword style, concentrating tonalli in the right places . . ." I stop as I hear my own words.

"And how do you know if they are doing it right?"

"I suppose it's hard to explain."

Master Toto grins. "Yes. It's impossible to use words to explain a knowledge that has nothing to do with them." Supporting himself on his crutch, he stands up and steps over the edge of his raft, and I think he will plunge into the lake. Instead, he walks across the water toward the shore, never getting his feet wet.

I stare, marveling, and my own raft moves after him, an unseen paddle pushing it through the water.

When I get to land, Master Toto concentrates on taking gentle steps, his only concern putting one foot in front of the other. Following his lead blindly, I walk faster as his pace quickens. I don't notice the moment when he stops using his crutch.

"Master?"

An unusual wind swirls, as if alive, and wraps Master Toto's arms, legs, and body in an airy caress, then disappears. Instead of my master, a warrior stands before me covered with green feathers, face painted with white dots like the stars. The jewel of the wind sits on his chest, a necklace in the shape of a spiral conch.

He is the Plumed Serpent, the Precious Twin, Lord of Light, justice, and the wind, inventor of books, the arts, and the calendar, the giver of maize to mankind, a symbol of resurrection. The only god to refuse the blood of humans, asking only for small offerings of snakes and birds, butterflies and flowers.

"Quetzalcoatzin," I say his name reverently.

It's as if a screen has been lifted from my eyes, making me see the world quite differently, much more clearly, and much more distinctly. I realize now that he came to me as the woman on Popocatepetl. The crazy dog, Xolo, was Xolotl, his double, with whom he descended to Mictlan to gather the bones of the dead from the Fourth Sun. Those bones he restored to life with his own blood, and humankind existed again. Life returned and the Fifth Sun was born.

"In the beginning," he says, "Tezcatlipoca and I cooperated in creating life, but our destinies called on us to strive against each other for balance. Our first battle began when Tezcatlipoca became the First Sun. The Lord of Darkness was barely half a Sun. So, I struck him down, and he slaughtered all the people. I ruled over the Second Sun and created a new race of humans. Tezcatlipoca was vengeful and demonstrated his power as god of sorcery by turning them into monkeys. The other gods were angry with our doings, so they chose Tlaloc to be the Third Sun. Tlaloc raged after Tezcatlipoca stole his wife and made it rain with fire. The world burned away. Tezcatlipoca flooded the Fourth Sun and humans became fish."

The opposition between Quetzalcoatl and Tezcatlipoca that led to the creation and destruction of the Four Suns is recounted in the codices, but hearing the tale straight from Quetzalcoatl's mouth, in his own words, in his eerily calm voice, makes it feel overwhelmingly real.

He continues. "Then, the Fifth Sun began with Tonatiuh. I took the form of a human king in the city of Tollan. There was peace and wealth for all the Toltecah. The world was happy. Tezcatlipoca was not. He and his followers plotted my downfall. They descended upon Tollan and bent the city to their rule. I was overthrown and forced into exile. But I promised to return."

I know the Toltec tale. One day, Ce Acatl Topiltzin Quetzalcoatl will return and lead his people into a new age of glory.

"Why haven't you come back?" I ask.

"There is nothing I want more than to reclaim my kingdom and bring my people peace. But I cannot." A sadness in the wind passes over the lake. "After Tezcatlipoca burned Tollan to the ground, Ometeotl grew tired of watching us fight. They put rules in place for the gods of creation. Our first rule prohibits us from intervening in the lives of mortals. Only Ometeotl has that power." He pauses for a moment, then says, "But, then—"

"But then what?"

A gust of wind swirls up from the ground, then settles to stillness, as if he exhaled. "You're not quite mortal."

My mind tries to catch a thought. "What did you say?"

Quetzalcoatl shifts again, his clothes stretching a little, and a different man stands in his place, with curly brown hair and a pointed beard.

Nican Nicah.

I take a step back. "No."

"Yes," he says.

I wished so many times for my father not to be dead. For it all to be a cruel nightmare. The memory of him would fill me with such bitterness. When he passed, I kissed him on the forehead and whispered, "I've got an angel in heaven now." I didn't believe it, but it made me feel better.

Now, as I look at Quetzalcoatl in disguise, I struggle to say, "Papá?"

"Your mother . . . Tlazohtzin. She was a woman in love—and loved in return. I came to her one night in this form. Then her belly began to swell with the life I planted in her. You arrived early." He chuckles, as if remembering the very day. "You hungered for the world and demanded entry. Tlazohtzin wished she could delay your birth. She was only half-aware by the time you were delivered, with barely enough strength to muster her dismay at the news that you had been born during the first day of the Nemontemi.

"As she cut your cord, she whispered a blessing: 'My beloved daughter. Heed, hearken: thy home is not here . . . here is only the place of thy nest. Thou belongest out there for thou art a jaguar. War is thy destiny, war is thy mission. Thou shalt give drink, nourishment, food to the sun.'

"The Nahua blessing to girls expresses the hope that the little woman will wander nowhere. Her place is only within the house. It is not necessary for her to go anywhere else. Her duty is to supply drink and food, grind, spin, weave. For a boy, the highest honor is to shed blood in battle. For a girl, it is to offer herself to the work of domestic life. But thy home is not here, is it, Tecuani? Here is only the place of thy nest. For thou art a jaguar. Thou belongest out there."

I close my eyes, holding back tears.

"What am I? Your means to exact revenge against the Black God?"

"Revenge? No. No! Tecuani, I ended Tezcatlipoca's reign as the First Sun. I eliminated human sacrifice. He has been waiting for the Tzitzimime to destroy the Fifth Sun and rise himself as the Sixth Sun."

I fight back the tremors rippling under my skin.

Quetzalcoatl drops his guise and cups my cheeks in his hands. "Tecuani, you are my greatest love. It's true, you are the result of my planning, but I did not plan for you to lose your way in the woods. I did not plan for you to become Pantera. This was your doing. Not mine."

"You disobeyed Ometeotl's rules. You intervened . . ." I say to him, "with my mother."

"Yes, but I did not upset the balance. I restored it."

"Balance?" I shake my head in confusion. "What balance?"

"Order and chaos," he says. "You are my daughter, but you follow no direction but your chosen path, without any interference from me. Telling you the truth sooner would have meant my involvement. If one god breaks a rule, another is bound to notice and decide to do the same. When the teteoh fight, humans pay the price. My domain is here. In my realm, I can do anything. Create life. Grow lands. Change the direction of the wind. In the Fifth Sun, I can do nothing, like the other creator gods. Quite often, gods use vessels, but humans are fickle. They have wishes, desires of their own, and they're fragile. No human can contain a creator god's power. Not for long."

No human can, but a god . . . "Tezca," I say under my breath.

I stare at Quetzalcoatl, my mind spinning from putting everything together. Tezcatlipoca stole Xochiquetzal, Tlaloc's wife. That means Tezca was born in the Third Sun. His tonalli is thousands of years old.

Quetzalcoatl nods. "Yes."

"He is his father's vessel?"

"Tezcacoatzin is not a god of creation. He would not be bound by Ometeotl's rule. A lesser god with a creator god's power . . . well . . ."

I have to ask. "What did he do?"

"Tecuani."

"What did Tezca do?" I say louder. "Xochiquetzal told me he's lived many lives. She keeps him from his father. She keeps him from his power. She fears her son. He must've done something very bad. Tell me. I deserve to know."

"In Tollan," he says, "Tezcatlipoca was aided by great necromancers bent on the city's destruction. Two of them. Gods. They helped him lay enchantments. One of them was Huitzilopochtli. The other—"

"No . . ."

"He had another name back then. But it was him. Tezcacoatzin."

My breath leaves me.

317

Long before the Nahuas came to the valley, there were the Toltecs. No one is alive to know what happened to the great Toltec Empire. Some say plagues ravished the land. Others say droughts doomed Tollan. I desperately want to believe that. I don't want to believe Tezca helped destroy an entire civilization.

I stop the cry of outrage on my lips. "Did you know? Did you know our paths would cross? Did you know how I would come to feel about your nemesis's son?" This scares me more than anything. "What kind of twisted game is this?"

For a fleeting moment, I wonder about the familial connection, if Tezca and I are related. Yet, gods aren't humans. They don't share blood. They share tonalli. Besides, in this life, Tezca was born of mortal parents. As was I.

"Am I your vessel?" I angrily wipe a tear off my cheek. "It doesn't matter. The Tzitzimime will attack, Tonatiuh will no longer rise, and everything will end."

"My dear, containing the full extent of my powers would have incinerated every cell in your body," he says. "I forged a weapon. To the wielder of integrity, it is a sword of great strength. To the one who speaks high and clear, it is power."

"I did not come this far to bandy silly riddles with you!" I snap. "Demons wreak havoc in the Fifth Sun, and I don't know how to defeat them without my tonalli! It is beyond me or any of us!" He looks at me but offers nothing. "Why did I think you could help me? What a fool I was." I walk away.

"Tecuani," he says, and I turn around. "You will never win the wrong battle. When the time comes, choose wisely."

CHAPTER 41

El Traidor

I don't have long before my mind lets go completely. Tomorrow I might wake up and wonder what my name is, but I will not cower in the shadows waiting to fade away. I have lost too much, but I have not lost everything.

Tezca is with me as we go inside the Flowering Tree and pass through the doorway into the Fifth Sun, back to our world. I don't recognize this place. It seems to be a battlefield strewn with corpses. The reek of blood and rotting flesh assaults my nostrils. I shield my gaze from the light of day. Clouds of insects feed off mangled limbs and severed heads. With every step, we tread on the bodies of the dead. This isn't Snake Mountain. It can't be.

I step over a corpse and realize I'm not wearing gilded sandals anymore. Here, I wear my dirty clothes. Tezca's long hair is tied in its usual topknot and his sword is strapped to his back. Perhaps the doorway makes it impossible to take anything from one world to another.

Cries blare from a distance. One deafening wail after another fills me with horror.

We run toward the screaming as quickly as our legs can carry us, dodging and leaping over corpses. In a square before the temple-pyramid, crowds of people press shoulder to shoulder, over-flowing the area. A cold nausea drops into the pit of my stomach.

All eyes focus on the platform at the top of the pyramid, the teocalli of Snake Mountain. There, black-robed priests, like a flock of vultures, chant and blow their conches and pierce their earlobes with spines before cutting open the chest of a young man. Neza's brother Ichcatzin draws out the still-beating heart and holds it up triumphantly. The multitudes cheer. Ichcatzin smashes the heart into a stone bowl until nothing is left in his hand, and the corpse is kicked down the stone steps. Another man plods up the stairs.

I steal a quick glance at Tezca. The bulging vein just above his left temple tells me he is raging inside. *You will fear him.* No, I refuse to believe it. Whatever he did, whoever he was back then, it was someone else. It's not who he is now. I follow him as he elbows his way to the front, pushing past the mass of people.

The conches and drums fall silent. The crowd breaks apart, allowing Tezca to approach the pyramid and giving me an unobstructed view. At its foot, Tezca glares up.

"What is the meaning of this slaughter?"

Ichcatzin looks surprised but quickly hides it behind a smug grin. None who venture into the Namba ever return. I wager that was his hope.

"You have troubled yourself in coming, Tezcacoatzin," he says, loud enough to be heard by all.

"Where is Neza?"

Throwing his shoulders back, Ichcatzin lifts his chin and looks down, as if he is king and we should know it. "The teteoh give us health, nourishment, victory, whatever we need. My brother aban-doned the gods and now their wrath is upon us. Though he has forgotten the gods by whom he swore, I have not. Everything that is hard ripens and softens in time. And my dear brother has softened. Nezahualpilli is feeble as a reed."

Tezca turns around, facing the crowd. "You would let another come and take Neza's place? For what cause have you risen against your tlahtoani? Has he not been generous? Has he not fought for you? Has he not shed for you his lifeblood? Why have you forsaken him?"

"Look closely, Lord Tezca," says Ichcatzin, and he turns to face him again. "It is *he* who has forsaken the people."

"Where is he?"

"Nezahualpilli has lost their favor because he put his own desires before them, which he would know if he spent more time with his wife and less time romping with men."

Tezca draws his sword. "*Where?*"

"My brother is a coward," Ichcatzin exclaims. "We were once a mighty people. We must reclaim our power!"

At this, the crowd roars.

I fume. How dare he call Neza a coward? Neza has looked the lord of Mictlan in the eye, fighting to protect his people and bring them justice. He has shouted "enough"! Enough of oppression, of doing wrong, of idleness, of division, of slaughter! He is more of a man than Ichcatzin will ever be.

"It is almost dark," Ichcatzin shouts, pointing over the crowd to the row of dwellings behind them. "Go home, my people. The teteoh will protect us."

"Go home and do *what*?" Tezca says. "Tremble and wait while your priests shed more blood to appease the gods? All you are doing is offering yourselves to the demons."

The sacrifices will be for nothing. Quetzalcoatl said the gods of creation are powerless. We are on our own.

Someone tugs on my hand. A child, I think, then I turn around to see Amalia hidden amidst a tangle of legs.

I crouch. "Amalia? What are you—?"

"Shh." She puts a finger to her lips. "You must come quickly."

I nod and whisper-shout at Tezca, gesturing for him to follow me. He slides his sword back into his scabbard and we hurry away from the temple square.

As soon as we're alone, Amalia throws her arms around me. "I knew you were alive," she says. "I knew it." Embracing is a comfort I don't allow myself, and so I tense at first, the contact unexpected, almost unfamiliar. Spaniards are always greeting each other with kisses on the cheek, abrazos, and handshakes. I faintly tap her back, not quite sure what to do, then I find myself embracing her in return. It's the last thing I expected us to do. I never thought we could share something so intimate, but I hug her as if it can cure all my ailments.

"Come," she says as we leave the crowd behind. "We're losing light."

"Where are we going?" I ask.

"You'll know soon enough."

We leave the crowd behind for the backstreets, and Amalia leads us up a small, flat hill. Somehow, she moves ahead of me, climbing as if she's been doing it all her life, and I shake my head at the ridiculous sight. She's a Spanish noblewoman, trained from childhood in the art of singing, dancing, and playing musical instruments. I wonder how she climbs without complaint, but I utter no protest as I trail behind her. Tezca goes up two, three steps at a time, and waits for us at the top. He offers his hand, but I don't take it. I complete my ascent, bitter and annoyed to have to rest my legs.

At the top of the hill, the birds are chanting their evening song as we come into a campsite. Tents circle the remains of a fire, and stacks of weapons lean against trunks of trees with saddles and bridles and rabbit carcasses hanging from the branches above them. Chipahua is lying on the grass, picking his teeth with a knife. If he's pleased to see us, he doesn't show it.

An owl flies down from the sky and shifts into her human form as she lands.

"Princess," Tezca greets her.

"It is good to see you, Lord Tezca," Eréndira says, her head lowered. "And you, Pantera. I did not think we would meet again, my friends. Are you both well?"

Tezca and I nod.

Eréndira smiles, but it doesn't reach her eyes. "We will celebrate and have a great feast when this is all over," she says. "Ichcatzin has his own plans to defeat the Tzitzimime, which involve human sacrifice to win the gods' favor, a practice that Neza banned." A flicker of anger crosses her face, and she shakes her head, as if to clear it. "He is against the old ways of his ancestors, but Ichcatzin created a ruse to turn everyone against Neza and succeeded. The people injured him gravely, throwing stones when he tried to reason with them. He is recovering now."

My heart tightens. Neza. How could they do this to him?

"That is not all," Eréndira says grimly. "We have been scouting the forest. Our enemies are marching toward us. A force of Spaniards."

I shouldn't be surprised, but here I am, bringing a shaking hand to my mouth. Captain Nabarres must have been rebuilding his army while we were away. He's come to finish what he started.

"How many?" I ask.

"Thousands," Eréndira says. "Ten, twenty."

"How long before they get here?"

Tezca turns his head a little, straining his ears. "An hour or two. It could be sooner, but I doubt it. This terrain is difficult to navigate on horseback."

Amalia clutches the rosary beads around her neck. Chipahua says nothing, but he looks almost angry, as if it displeases him that he will not have his fight this very instant.

In the absence of Neza's leadership, Eréndira has gathered La Justicia, preparing and strategizing for battle, while Ichcatzin spills blood to appease the gods. The tribes are fiercely loyal to La Justicia, though after the Battle of Coatepec, their numbers have declined. Eréndira intends to concentrate her attack in one area, use the land to her advantage. We are in the forest and the forest is in us.

"Snake Mountain will not fall," Eréndira says. "The river can take thousands."

"That's your plan?" Amalia scoffs. "Drive them into the river? What if they surge up the hill? What do we do then?"

"Then they will come across Nucano and Rahui who are hiding in position with their troops," Eréndira says tersely. They are the Mixtec and Raramuri chieftains. "We have them cornered."

"Do we?" Amalia says. "It's hundreds of us against thousands of them. That isn't cornered."

"They will never make it this far," Eréndira says. "It's a long march and the Spaniards have been riding hard. They're going to be giving their exhausted horses a break. By the riverbank, if it is the will of the gods. They won't be expecting us there."

"Why don't we just wave a flag telling them where to go?" Amalia says.

Eréndira hears the sarcasm in her voice. "You will be quiet."

"I will not!" Amalia grumbles. "I cook, I clean your weapons, I warm your bed, I do as you say. I am not your slave. I am not your dog."

"Tell me more about your struggle," Eréndira says, her voice filled with derision.

Amalia, astonishingly, is quiet. After a long moment, she quietly says, "I'm sorry."

"What do you ask forgiveness for, countess? Did you give birth to Cortés? Or Alvarado? Or Pizarro? There's no reason for you to ask my forgiveness. You have not conquered me. I am still here, resisting."

Amalia exhales. "I can be of more use."

Eréndira tilts her head, curious. "To what use do you propose I put you?"

Amalia blinks, as if she wasn't expecting that question, then she straightens and lifts her chin. "I want to be in the fight."

Eréndira laughs. "Then your god has made you a fool."

"Many before you have thought the same," Amalia says. "But I am no fool. I have spent my time in the forest foraging for food and have befriended the creature in the water."

The creature in the water?

Eréndira recovers her wits before I do. "You befriended the ahuizotl?"

"I call him Rayo," Amalia says.

"Rayo?"

Amalia grins. "He's fast."

"None who see the ahuizotl live to tell the tale," Eréndira says. "Maybe you befriended a sickly dog."

Amalia pales with fury. "Tell her," she says to me. "We were attacked by this creature. We lived to tell the tale. Tell her, Leonora."

I say nothing, and Eréndira looks at me pointedly, urging me to answer.

"I think I would remember if we were attacked by the ahuizotl." I would've preferred to say that with more spirit, instead of an unsure, almost hesitant voice.

"You lie!" Amalia says. "You're a liar!"

I curse myself. I don't know if she's lying or if my memory is.

What I don't say is that it's getting worse. The sick part of my head is winning. It tries to kill me every single day, destroying my confidence and making me question every godsdamn thing I say. My recollection of my own life could be a fantasy. Were we really attacked by the ahuizotl? How did we survive? Is Amalia telling the truth?

I am shrinking away when Tezca comes to my side, stopping my retreat. "Save your breath," he says. "Every moment wasted is a moment the Spaniards gain ground on us." We share a brief glance, and one of his long fingers finds a strip of bare skin just under the hem of my shirt. He knows what ails me. My heart is thudding so hard, I'm sure he can hear it.

"The only path that gives passage to an army that size leads to the river," Tezca says. "I know it well. We can hold it and make our stand there."

"Getting them to surrender is our primary concern," Eréndira says. "If they refuse, you know what to do. Wait for my signal. We cannot let them reach the city."

"What's the signal?" I ask.

"You'll know it when you hear it," she says.

No matter what happens, whether our warriors advance or retreat, if the earth should open up and swallow our defense whole, we will wait for her signal.

Princess Eréndira is supported by her tribe, the Purépecha. Now that Lord Tezca has returned, the Tlahuica will follow him into battle. The Mixtec chieftain Nucano is in position with his people, and those who run fast, the Raramuri, will fight alongside their chieftain Rahui. If it wasn't for me, Prince Xico and the Chichimeca would stand with us.

"Neza's tribe is the largest," Eréndira says. "But without him, the Mexica are dispersed in and around Snake Mountain. Some will fight but not all. You will lead them, Nagual Warrior." I realize she's looking at me.

"Me?"

"You are Mexica."

"So is Chipahua."

"Chipahua is a Shorn One," Eréndira says. "His focus is on himself, not others."

I am not Neza. I am not a leader. I am not a general. Without my tonalli, my power, the Sword of Integrity, they won't listen to me, they won't follow me. I am no one.

But this is the first time someone has called me a Nagual Warrior.

Rank used to mean everything. A level one, a level five, a level seven Nagual Apprentice, I was always reaching for the next achievement. In the real world, my opponent doesn't care about my title. Training has nothing to do with rank. I didn't train for a title, and I still have much to learn. Master Toto told me I wasn't ready to become a Nagual Warrior because I thought I was ready to become a Nagual Warrior.

I understand now.

CHAPTER 42

El Triste

More dreadful climbing. Thirteen steps lead to the cuauhcalli, the House of Eagles, a truncated pyramid with a thatched roof of grass built into the slope of the hill and carved out of the rock itself. Once a temple for Tenochca warriors, the ruins still retain jaguar sculptures and a serpent-shaped entrance, with fangs, eyes, and a forked tongue, which is painted red with blood. The Tenochca abandoned the temple after the Fall so the Spaniards wouldn't find it. It remains hidden by the trees.

Neza lies inside on a pile of reed mats.

"I'm sorry, Leonora," Martín tells me. "I did everything I could, but they didn't believe my legitimacy." We are on our own. Though he is the true heir of Cortés, he was unable to secure an army.

The wound on Neza's head is a horrible gash of red. He grumbles as Tezca presses his hand against it.

"Stop bleating like a goat, Neza," Martín says. "Let Tezca heal you."

"The wounds of his heart I cannot heal," Tezca says.

I've never known Neza to be anything other than strong. It never occurred to me that he one day might not be. Seeing Neza shriveled and quailing presses a weight on my chest I haven't felt since seeing Inés's lifeless body. *Don't be afraid, Pantera.* I cling to her last words.

Martín paces the room in a huff. "We shouldn't be sitting here tending to this blubbering child when the enemy is soon to surround us."

"It's quiet now," says a young voice. Zyanya appears from nowhere, bearing a bundle of wood. She somehow looks older than I remember. "They say that's how it gets before the Tzitzimime come," she says, tossing a load into the hearth. "The tlahtoani's wounds are deep, but he will not die."

"No, no," Neza moans. A fit of coughing takes over his body. "This life no longer has anything for me. Let me die."

Martín's eyes glaze over with a sheen of moisture.

"They prey on the wounded first," Tezca says. "If they smell blood, they will come for the easy kill."

"If?" Martín says. "There's blood everywhere."

Ichcatzin and his priests made sure of that.

"My lord," I say, approaching him.

He groans. "What do you want? Can't you let me sleep?"

"The enemy is marching toward us and you wish to sleep? The Mexica are in desperate need of their true leader. I'm not you. They don't believe in me. I cannot give them purpose and lead them into battle. Only you can."

"Leave me alone."

Martín shakes his head. "Oh, noble Nezahualpilli. Where are you now when the people need you most?"

"I said leave me alone!" Neza thunders.

"Ichcatzin was right about you," I say angrily. "You are a coward."

Tezca finds me overlooking the forest. The valley spreads out green on all sides, though the view from the Eagle House is more strategic than scenic. The trees are straight and silent. Their leaves look painted on. My breath seems to die as soon as it leaves my mouth.

"What are you thinking?" he eventually says.

His warmth keeps the shivers at bay while I think of demons, destruction, and dying. "I was praying. There's no moon." The night is starless.

"I noticed."

When the darkness is total, the Tzitzimime will come down and devour us all. That's what the old people say. I turn. Tezca's face is still, his hair falling around his eyes. I've looked at him many times, but there's something different about him now. I see him as he is. Not a man. A god.

In the distance, a ribbon of light, faint at first, grows brighter. Torches: hundreds, thousands of torches. An army of immense size moves through the forest like a giant serpent of fire. My chest pounds with terror, my thoughts no longer centered on the Tzitzimime. Captain Nabarres has gathered all the men he can for his final battle.

"It is a good day to go to Tonatiuh," Tezca says. If he dies, he will be reborn. I guard my tongue. What if I die? What will happen to me?

"Do you think it's useless?" I ask.

"What?"

"Prayer," I say. The gods of creation and the lesser gods have limited power, but not Ometeotl, Mother and Father. Over the Thirteen Heavens they are king and queen. If Ometeotl wants to answer my prayers, they will, and if they don't want to, they won't, though I hope that my prayers are important to them.

"I know you don't put your faith in the teteoh," I say.

"Perhaps the gods are putting their faith in us."

We sit there, watching the Spaniards spread through the forest.

Any hope I had that they might surrender evaporates. A sickening feeling finds its way into my stomach, and I can almost imagine Captain Nabarres reassuring himself . . . *There's no way we can lose. We have catapults.*

Below us, a large river flows into the great lake. Eréndira leads some hundred warriors armed with spears and swords, ready to hold the pass and ambush Nabarres's army. They move with such stealth that not even the birds detect their presence.

Tezca desperately tries to hide his worry and concern. He wills his breaths to be smooth and steady. He smiles but even that looks forced.

"Leonora," he begins.

"I'm a warrior, Tezca," I say. "I will die a warrior if I must."

He nods, then he's gone.

CHAPTER 43

La Profecía

As I come down the steps of the Eagle House, Amalia is sitting alone by the hearth, clumsily gutting one of the dead rabbits. In the torch light I can make out her pouting pink face.

"You can go back, you know," I say when I reach the bottom. "You can go back to the capital if you find it unbearable here."

"No," she says.

"No?"

"Do you remember the first time we played chess?" she asks, and I shake my head. "You moved your pawn, then decided to move it back. I said you had already touched the piece, so you had to follow through. That is what I must do now."

I close my eyes and pinch the bridge of my nose. "This isn't a game of chess, Amalia. You are allowed to change your mind."

"This is my life now," she says without hesitation.

I sit on the dirt next to her with my arms around my knees, hugging them to my chest. "Look, I know you think I'm a liar—"

"I'm not angry at you."

"Then who?"

"Her."

"Eréndira?"

"She doesn't see my value."

"What do you care what she thinks?"

She shrugs. "I don't know."

"What happened to pawns becoming queens?"

"This isn't a game of chess," she mocks.

"Perhaps, but what holds true for the game, holds true for life," I say. "You can't win if you don't make a move. Wasn't it you who said that?"

Her expression turns bleak. "I'm not a warrior like you, Leonora. I'm just a girl."

She says Eréndira doesn't see her value, but she's the one who sees herself unclearly.

"You're not just a girl," I say. "You're Amalia Catalina de Íñiguez y Mendoza, Countess of Niebla. Look at everything you've overcome. The pox. Your mother's death. You were left a widow, three times, and still you managed to secure marital prospects. You play the game better than most courtiers, and you were ready to become Martín's mistress thinking he was Prince Felipe."

She grins, and I grin.

"Amalia, I've never seen you crumble in the face of adversity. You are the strongest of warriors." I reach out and nestle some loose strands of her dirty golden hair behind her ear, the indentations of the scars on her cheek visible. Inés didn't hide her scar. She was proud of her mark and wanted it to show she had survived a severe wound.

Chipahua appears from the bushes and says, "Never to flee, even if faced by twenty enemies, nor take one step backward." It's the oath of a Shorn One. Chipahua isn't a talker, nor is he patient with those of us who are. I've never known him to say more than a few words in one breath, but now, he tells us he has five children, one wife—a princess of Toltec descent—and several concubines who contribute to the wealth of his family, all of whom he has to return home to and protect against a great many enemies. He looks at me sharply. "What say you, Nagual Warrior?"

"How many are in your detail?" I ask.

"A handful."

"Assemble the men," I say. "Do you remember where you first saw me and Martín?"

He nods.

"That's where we will meet."

Chipahua hurries out to obey his new orders.

"What are you doing? The river lies west," Amalia informs me.

"We're not going to the river," I say. "We're going around it."

She snorts. "You plan to outflank an army of thousands with a handful of men? Leonora, they have catapults."

"We have Chipahua."

It's true, we don't have the numbers, but a considerable part of Nabarres's troops are inexperienced young men of humble birth under twenty-five years of age, many fresh from Europe, who volunteered for war in the hopes of making their fortunes. Ours are battle-hardened warriors, some veterans of the Fall, some belonging to fierce orders, like Chipahua, who loves battle. Eréndira says Nabarres has the Santa Hermandad in his power, Portugal's cold-blooded mercenaries, contracted to do the work of death. But if I know Captain Nabarres, he'll arrange them at the front and hope for victory. He won't send his brightest and best to the back, and he certainly won't be expecting us there.

"The forest becomes more impenetrable and treacherous on the journey to the Namba," I tell Amalia. "An army of Spaniards won't manage. A handful of men will. We look for a gap and attack their flanks."

"Why do you keep saying *we*? And what about Eréndira's signal?"

"Didn't you say you wanted to be in the fight?" I ask.

"To *learn*," she says with a huff, "not to actually fight!"

"Who says you can't do both? Look, either we stop them, or we die, Amalia. Those are our choices. I know you're scared. I am too."

Amalia sighs. "But I'm older than you."

"So?"

"So I'm supposed to protect *you*." She shakes her head, as if this greatly annoys her.

"Says who?"

"Everyone knows the older protect the younger." She stands and nods for me to follow her.

"I'm not climbing more stairs."

"Just trust me."

We go down the hill and move through a field of maize so high that we can stand up and not be seen. It's quiet. I can hear nothing except the rustling of stalks in the hot breeze and for a moment I wonder if Captain Nabarres has, against all odds, surrendered. I can't see anything except the path I'm on. My legs shake, threatening to buckle under my weight as I sway with the corn, like I'm part of the crop.

It's too quiet. An unsettling stillness surrounds us.

I walk behind Amalia, holding my breath, unsure whether there is danger here or not, whether my looted Spanish blade will ward off any attack or whether the best response would be to turn and run. A stalk snaps behind me, the sound sharp and brittle. I go rigid. I pay no attention to the scampering of a squirrel or the ribbit of a frog. Those sounds I'm used to, and I welcome them as good company. But heavier footfalls put me on edge. I grip my sword tighter.

With a wild unearthly shriek, a doglike beast shoots from the stalks in a flash of black and gray and white, yellow fangs gleaming.

The ahuizotl.

It skids to a halt, sharp claws scraping the ground. It's larger than a jaguar, and its long whiplike tail snaps the air. If I move, I'm dead. Its hideously ugly head has the appearance of a monkey with eyes that glow orange.

"Don't make any sudden movements," I whisper.

Amalia walks toward the creature. "This is Rayo," she says, and I blink. "He's stubborn, but we've come to a mutually beneficial arrangement."

I argue with myself, not recalling being attacked by this creature before, when Amalia pulls something small from her pocket and tosses it at the beast. The creature opens his gaping jaws in delight. It's too dark to see what the morsel is, but then I think about the eyeless rabbits hanging at the campsite, and Amalia cutting up the meat. She wasn't lying about befriending the ahuizotl.

I stumble back a step. "You've been feeding him?"

"You've been feeding him," parrots the ahuizotl. It impersonates me, shooting my words back in mockery.

"Fascinating, isn't he?" Amalia says. "He can mimic any sounds he hears, including voices."

I'm both riveted and petrified by this highly intelligent predator with rubber skin and five hands, including one at the end of his long tail. The creature crouches suddenly, tail whisking in anticipation, and Amalia deftly vaults onto his back. She's bonded with him. How I don't know, but before I can find out, a wave of wind and heat descends from above. Large flaming balls rain down. The Spaniards and their catapults are here. They mustn't have stopped at the riverbank like Eréndira said. This will be the end of Snake Mountain.

I'm not going to go down like this, squatting in a field of maize.

"What are you waiting for?" Amalia holds out her hand for me to mount. I don't refuse it.

Chipahua and no more than ten men, including Señor Alonso's son, Miguel, are waiting for us at our meeting point in the forest. They leap back and raise their weapons at our arrival. Rayo is agitated, jittering and making a pitiful cry. Amalia pats him comfortingly.

I dismount and go to them, nodding and gripping their forearms. "Tonight, we end this war," I say. "It ends here, be it life or death. You don't fight for me. I fight for you." I don't have a great battle speech nor strength in numbers, but I don't doubt myself, and the men don't doubt me, and that gives me a strength greater than any army.

"On me," I say.

I climb onto the ahuizotl's back, and we emerge slowly through the tangle of branches. The battle has commenced. The ground is covered with slumped bodies; swords separate limbs and heads; two Spanish catapults launch fireballs. These are fathers and mothers, sons and daughters, brothers and sisters. Each instant, their lives are stolen. But there, in the enemy's rear, is the favor I hoped for.

Weakness.

Amalia looks over her shoulder. "Do what you were born to do, Pantera."

I wear all black. No mask. A Spanish blade on my back. Hair braided tightly to my head. This is the ground I have chosen to hold. Should I fall, then I will die a warrior's death. The heaven where Tonatiuh lives awaits.

I close my eyes in silent prayer. *Ometeotl help us all.*

I give the signal to advance. Rayo charges forward, lusting for blood, and the men chant their war cries as they jump out of the bushes. The enemy scrambles to unsheathe their swords, shouting to each other, panicked, and their ranks open to let us through. Horsemen twist in their saddles, the foot soldiers in chaos as we strike, our weapons like snake tongues spreading poison. I have my right hand around the hilt of my blade and am feebly trying to yank it from a Spaniard's chest when Amalia yells my name.

A burly soldier, covered in mail from head to toe, is coming at us. I feel Rayo shudder beneath me, the way the ground does with an earthquake, and he mimics a howler monkey, but coming from him the sound is far more terrifying than the most furious clap of thunder. His tail lashes out at the Spaniard and rips the wretch's flesh. Echoes of his roar reverberate through the forest, announcing that he's awake and angry and warning fools to keep their distance. Even the might of the mountain seems inferior.

The hill is burning. Nucano, the Mixtec chieftain, is shouting orders to take down the catapults, but his warriors are either desperately trying to extinguish the flames, engaged in fighting, or dead. I glance around desperately, looking for the other chieftains, and the long, harsh scream of a lechuza cuts the air. Eréndira soars above our heads, her enormous white wings flapping soundlessly. The Owl Witch hunts under the cover of darkness. She dives and claws at the soldiers manning the catapults. They don't stand a chance.

Amalia is screaming at the soldiers to come and die. Rayo's long tail whips around as though searching for its next victim, and winds itself around a man's throat. The soldier is lifted off the ground, spluttering, kicking. Then he is no more.

A Spaniard tries to take my head. I show mercy by sliding my sword into his gullet. My hands are shaking with fatigue. Miguel is beside me, hacking at his cowering opponent. I nod at him, recognizing Señor Alonso's strength.

A line of men on horseback ride down the hill from the city. Furious, I wonder how the enemy made it past our defenses, where these Spaniards came from. One of them yells the name of Pantera; he is mounted with a lit torch in his hand. Martín. Neza is beside him. I feel a tired smile pull on my lips. They've come; Neza has called a small force into battle after all. They attack the Spaniards from both sides and set their wooden catapults on fire, rendering them defenseless.

My heart lurches when Martín falls off his horse. As he stands quickly, one soldier knocks him senseless, and Neza, who goes to help Martín, rams his sword straight through the Spaniard's stomach. Neza kneels beside Martín. Then Ichcatzin catches his brother's head from behind with a club.

Rayo takes off suddenly and I'm thrown.

I slam against the ground, rolling over a couple of times before my head strikes a rock. The last thing I see is Neza collapsing.

The earth is spinning. My eyes feel heavy as I open them. I try to push myself up and scream in agony. My left arm is broken at the elbow. A weight is crushing me, and I roll on to my side then give a cry of horror and desperately wrestle myself out from underneath a pile of tangled bodies. I'm surrounded by corpses and dying men. I rise unsteadily to my feet and dazedly bring a hand to my head. My fingers come away bloody.

Where am I? Who am I?

I don't know.

My mind is blank.

I look about in a panic, trying to remember. There is fire and smoke and men fighting. What am I doing here, in the middle of this bloodbath?

I'm brought down from behind and fall on my chest, the wind knocked out of me. My attacker grabs my hair and jerks my head up, forcing me to look at him. He stares at me with big brown eyes, a rage inside him.

"Your hour has come, witch," he snarls and swings his blade at my head.

I cry for help. He's about to deliver a two-handed strike, and I close my eyes, certain I'm doomed, but then I open them and see the point of his blade resting a scant inch from my neck. It's stopped short. The man topples forward and falls prostrate beside me.

I let out a horrified moan. At the same time, a boy in mail and a helmet appears and pulls his sword out of the dead man's back. The boy offers his hand and I stand up with effort. He gives me something—a sword, heavy and darkly stained, its guard shaped like two serpents. I feel the way it fits my hand, as if it's meant to be there, and I smile because I, Leonora de las Casas Tlazohtzin, am the wielder of the Light of the Feathered Serpent. The Sword of Integrity has returned to me.

"Jerónimo," I gasp.

His dark blond curls are bloody, as is his mail. "Are you hurt? Let me look at you." I go to him, but he moves back as if my touch is death itself. His eyes belong to someone else, cold and hard. He looks at me as though I'm a complete stranger. Tears blur my vision.

I think he'll say something. I hope he'll say he forgives my deceit, that it doesn't matter I'm Pantera, that he saved my life because I'm his sister and he loves me, but he says nothing.

I hear a choking sound, and I turn to see Xico on the ground.

I kneel beside him. I try to stem the flow of blood from his wound. There is so much of it. He gives one final splutter, and then is gone.

I close his eyes. "Rest now, warrior, and go to Tonatiuh."

I look up. My brother has vanished.

My arm is broken, my body feels as if it's been whipped with a thousand lashes, the dead and injured are all around me, and I have a passing thought that I could lie here and feign death, but such pretense would not help me stay alive. I see the first evidence that perhaps all is not lost when the sky thunders, rain comes pouring down on the forest, and the fires start to die.

"Kill me," someone rasps.

Nearby, a Spanish soldier is lying in a pool of his own blood.

"Por favor," he says. I'm about to show him mercy, but then Captain Nabarres shouts my name.

CHAPTER 44

La Destrucción

My enemy stands some twenty paces ahead of me, armored in a rich coat of mail that glints beneath his red cloak. He smiles as though I'm an old friend he's pleased to see.

I'm tired. Tired of this war with him. The last thing I want to do is fight him one-handed in the impossible rain, but there's still work to be done, for Captain Nabarres is free, far from defeated, and his army still outnumbers us.

This is my battle now.

I expect his usual baiting, with the two of us facing off and unmoving: how I have failed, how I'm just a girl, how I will never win.

To my surprise, there are no insults.

More thunder rolls in the distance. Perhaps it's a message from Lord and Lady Ometeotl to give me courage, because I have to use my sword hand to help lift my broken arm and twist the splintered bone into place. I grit my teeth and whimper, but still nothing compares to the torture of my body breaking and reshaping to take the form of the Panther. That pain is horrifying.

I go quiet, panting. Nabarres is neither weary nor wounded, no blood coats his graying beard or his sword. It's almost as if he's been waiting to face me. He takes his stance, sword at the ready, then he comes at me screaming, an ugly, animal sound. The rain pelts me, and I shout my best battle cry and whirl the Sword of Integrity in the air. Without tonalli, it's not easy to carry its weight. It's slippery too, and I swing it so weakly that Nabarres easily blocks my attack with his sword and lunges forward. I parry the first four or five blows, countering when I can, but his strength is overwhelming, and I begin to slow.

My breaths become harsh. My legs threaten to collapse in exhaustion. I don't know what keeps me standing, but I don't pause. I twist and thrust my sword out. Nabarres pulls back at the last moment, and I can see it now: he's tiring.

The tip of his sword drops when he changes grips. He has no clear dominant hand, although his left doesn't quite have the strength of his right. He's weaker with that arm.

Nabarres strikes once more. This time, he puts such momentum into a killing blow that, when I sidestep, he stumbles forward and his sword sinks into the mud. He rises from his crouch in fury.

When his sword rises above his head, I see my chance. I lift my own sword and bring it down on the hollow of his right elbow, just where his mail sleeve slides back, and I sever flesh.

Nabarres's arm falls away, blood jetting, blade still in hand. He stares wide-eyed at his ruined arm, but he doesn't scream. He's a brave man, and if he lives, he will do so with the knowledge that the finest swordsman in all Spanish America will never wield a sword again.

"Call to your men to stop fighting," I say.

Cradling his bloody stump, Nabarres looks at the carnage spread out around us, a scattering of fallen horses and men, some moving and groaning, some not.

"Kill them," he says. "Kill them all. Leave no heathen alive."

Nabarres gives the order to his page who has galloped up to aid him. The page rides away, barking orders at the soldiers around him.

I stagger for a moment in disbelief, so weak and tired that I almost drop to my knees, but then I hear unearthly screeches that can shatter glass. The fear returns then.

Tzitzimime.

I duck when a gaunt, slimy creature swoops in and sinks her talons into Nabarres's shoulders, before flying away with him into the stormy sky that churns with her kind. Nabarres screams in pure horror, thrashing in her hold. I almost pity him. She is a cihuateotl, a servant of the Obsidian Butterfly. The creature's wings aren't as large or heavily armored as her mistress's, but she rips Nabarres apart with the long, sharp claws on her feet.

The Tzitzimime and the Cihuateteo continue to descend like a veil of shadow. "Take cover!" I yell at anyone who will listen. However, the time for escape has passed, for the demons are hungry, and the battleground is wet with fresh blood.

"Get down!" I yank at a skinny soldier beside me. We stay low, racing to the trees. I whip my head around to see Zyanya behind me, frozen in place in the middle of the field, staring at the oncoming stampede of people and horses. She'll be crushed.

"Get out of the way, Zyanya!"

She's much too frightened to move.

"Zyanya, you have to run!"

Nine Hells. I push the young soldier forward and scramble toward her, stuffing her under my good arm as if she's a sack of beans, and rush to take shelter. We won't make it. Dropping to the ground, I shield her with my own body. Zyanya screams into my chest, and then I hear nothing more.

My ears ring with horrible silence.

"Can you hear me?" a childlike voice says. "Pantera?"

Everything hurts. My back is against a tree. I don't remember coming here. I put a shaking hand to my head. I'm looking up at a bald girl. "Who are you?"

"Come on," she says, helping me stand. "You risked your life to save mine, yet you don't know what I've done."

"What . . . what are you talking about? I don't know you."

"You will get out of this, Pantera. You'll live. You'll—"

We startle as a blaring screech cuts her words short. "What was *that?*" I cry, panic-stricken.

The bald girl quickly puts some distance between us and chants, "Ometeotl, lord and lady of duality, supreme creator who resides in the Thirteenth Heaven, it is I who speak, the ticitl. I return the tonalli of this bewitched head." She raises her right palm. "It has been detained, but now I call the tonalli back. I call it back!"

A gale of air is thrust into my body, sending me wobbling backward.

"Pantera?"

I'm on all fours, palms splayed on the forest floor, head down.

"Do you . . . do you remember?"

I raise myself up on one knee and lift my gaze. "Zyanya is forever," I say. A reference to the first time we met.

Her lips curve in a sad smile.

Her robe pools as she shrivels to the height of my hips. Her face becomes as gnarled as the bark on the woodland trees. White tendrils coil from her bald head like worms, squirming down her back. Finally, points emerge from the tips of her ears and thrust sharply downward.

I stare at the small creature, frowning in surprise and alarm as the truth sinks in. "Zyanya, you're a . . . chaneque?"

She draws a pained breath then speaks in a strange, creaky voice. "Without tonalli, adults die. Children become chaneques."

"Zyanya," I say, standing up, "you've been a chaneque all this time?"

Her floppy ears go up and down as she nods. "There is a medicinal plant which only grows in chaneque territory. It was dangerous and foolish to go in search of it. I was attacked by a chaneque and my own tonalli was stolen then. I tried to delay the change. My hair was turning white, so I shaved my head. Pantera, I didn't think . . . I don't know how . . ." she stumbles over her words. "You died on the day of the Battle of Coatepec. By the gods, you did. Neither Tezca nor I thought you would wake up again. And then I didn't know what to do when you did. You have to believe I never would've stolen your tonalli otherwise. I am so sorry."

I remember asking Zyanya why she was in the shield wall that day. I couldn't have known before, but I understand now. It wasn't because she was being punished for doing something wrong. She volunteered to die. She preferred to die rather than to become a chaneque herself. Now, it's too late for her.

"I thought of you as the enemy," she says miserably, wiping at a tear. "Can you ever forgive me?"

I go to her and kneel there, holding her hand. "There's nothing to forgive," I say with a smile.

She smiles back. I glance quickly over my shoulder. Terrified cries pierce the darkness once more, a shrill undertone to the thunder.

"Go," she says, handing me my sword.

"Zyanya."

She looks up into the canopy of trees. On every branch, there is a small, wrinkly creature with white hair. "I am not alone."

CHAPTER 45

La Hechicera

I'm not afraid.

My tonalli has returned to me. I'm a sorceress. I have power. There is chaos in the Fifth Sun. I won't wait for the enemy to come looking for me. I will seek her out.

The rain has stopped at last, and a muggy wind is blowing. As I approach from the tree line, a wingless demon is crouched feeding on the flesh of the dead. I whistle through my teeth. The creature twists her skeletal head toward me, a scrap of cheek hanging off her bloody jaw. Her slimy skin will surely feel the sting of my blade.

Screeching her monstrous cry, she lunges at me, blood-streaked claws extended. But before she can touch me, she shrieks, as much in pain as in horror, at the beam of green emanating from my sword. *I'm worthy.*

I throw myself forward. My blade hisses as it slices through the demon's neck. Her wretched cries are silenced as she crumbles to the ground.

Other demons lash out and catch prey with their savage claws. I swing the Sword of Integrity left and right, every strike hitting its mark. Chipahua is fighting a mob of creatures single-handedly, performing a dance of death for the flying Tzitzimime. I scream as my blade severs necks. My attacks are bolstered by simple spells. Not deadly ones. The night is dreary—not a good time to replenish tonalli. I can't conjure a storm or vanish at will. I'm certainly no great Nagual Master. But I'm a sorceress. One demon appears in front of me, and I dash forward with an uppercut, but the creature flies back. Raising my chin in challenge, I harness my tonalli and rise into the air to plunge my sword deep into her throat.

"Fight, you cowards!" Eréndira is shouting insults at the Spaniards. "Come back and fight like men!" They're completely out of control, running across the field, trampling on fallen comrades, disappearing into the forest, throwing themselves behind large oaks, knocking each other aside in their panic.

A cavalryman, hair disheveled, mail rent, with blood from a head wound running down his boyish features, leads a band of soldiers. I watch with satisfaction as my brother shouts so loudly the veins in his neck bulge, his sword whistling through the army of monstrous beings. But I know it won't be enough. We are not enough. There are too many creatures. It's only a matter of time before the massing Tzitzimime and Cihuateteo swarm up and overwhelm us.

I have to find her.

One demon drops from the black cloudscape, stretches her claws, and snatches a running soldier. Before I can see where she flies, another demon rushes at me from behind. I whirl and swing the Sword of Integrity, opening her stomach. She gapes downward, staring at her wound, and I drive my sword through her face.

I yank my blade free and lift my head to the sky, looking for massive obsidian-tipped wings. The tail of a snake. The claws of a jaguar. Fearsome goddess of the night, queen of the Tzitzimime, the most feared of the demon goddesses, a combination of insect and monster. The Obsidian Butterfly. Morning is close, and hers is the most important mouth to feed. A goddess doesn't simply stalk her prey. No, she'll have her demon servants bring her dinner. And she'll take it alive. Most animals don't eat carrion. Why should the gods?

It's blood they hunger for. It's blood they'll have.

Climbing up a pile of bodies, I slash my left palm and make a fist to let the blood drip. It's a small cut. It doesn't need to be a huge gash.

"Come on!" I hold my hand in the air.

As a demon hovers overhead, I sheathe my sword and leap to grab her foot. Screeching, she flaps her wings and takes off. I hold on tightly, legs dangling above the sea of bodies. The creature has foul, mush-like flesh, and my grip keeps slipping. But I have claws of my own. My nails sharpen into dagger points, and I dig them into the demon's ankle. The tips pierce bone. The demon plummets to the hillside with a shriek, and before I let go of her foot, I draw my sword and bury it in her hip.

I push my tonalli downward, slowing my fall before my feet gently touch the brush at the bottom of the hill. Here, a horde of demons are massed into a protective circle around the Obsidian Butterfly, all of them smeared with human blood. The Demon Queen's mouth is smeared too, and from it a forked tongue flickers between red teeth.

There are holes where her eyes and nose should be, but I know she's looking at me. Still. Intent. Calm. Menacing.

Tonatiuh, my ally, is a long way off, so I point my blade at her, knuckles white upon the hilt. "O fearsome goddess. O clawed warrior. O queen of the night," I say. "I am a servant of the Nahualli Order, wielder of the Light of the Feathered Serpent. In the name of the Lord of the Dawn, go back to your abyss, Obsidian Butterfly. I command you, creature of darkness, go back to your abyss and torment us no longer. I said be gone!"

Dazzling green light burns before my eyes, as though Quetzalcoatl himself has come down from Tamoanchan. Almost at once, rocks begin to dance around my sandals. The ground rumbles with the pounding of heavy feet.

Something is coming.

Something big.

The sky tears with lightning, brightening the battleground in streaks of white. A great charge of jaguars, cougars, bears, and wolves, hundreds of them, one after another, knocks down trees and tramples the forest floor. Hawks, bats, vultures, and eagles claw and bite viciously, each seeking the next demon to destroy.

Naguals.

An army of sorcerers.

With a roar of triumph, I gaze upon a fellow Nagual, a white grizzly crushing demons, his fur splattered with red. Ollin. I laugh at his rage.

The Owl Witch shoots down from above us and makes a strike. The Demon Queen flies backward with a wrathful shriek, her great wings beating, hurling Eréndira to the ground. Wounded, the queen flutters unevenly into a grove of trees.

A shape flashes from the dark, and I spin around. A spotted jaguar shifts and hacks at a demon, then another and another, in a whirlwind of blades, a jaguar one moment, a man the next. How Tezca does that, I don't know. But it seems like the most natural thing in the world, shifting one form into another. For a moment, I waver. All I want is to call on the Panther and rip the demons limb from limb with my own fangs, but Quetzalcoatl's words come to me. *You will never win the wrong battle, Tecuani. Choose wisely.*

Tezca stops, looks at me, and smiles. He smiles because he can sense my tonalli. And I can sense his. At once, he comes to me and draws me to him. He kisses me, and I put my arms around his neck, and his body presses against mine, and I taste him as he holds me, as his tonalli enters me. I feel the difference in heat, a pounding power, a dozen pleasures all at once, and I realize he is my sun.

"Send my regards to the Obsidian Butterfly," he says. His grin is like a secret against my lips.

He moves back, then charges into a run, a jaguar again.

Something buzzes behind me. I look over my shoulder to see a darksome cloud: not a raincloud but a cloud of insects, a plague swarming over the field. Lesser demons. Vile things. I remember the words of my master, my father, that tonalli is always flowing like water. It's not something we can control, but we can create the ideal situation within ourselves for tonalli to work. It feels as though every last nerve in my body is being set on fire, and when I can no longer contain it, I scream and send the full power of my tonalli blasting through the air, in a tremendous wave that rattles the earth and bathes the night sky in turquoise-green light. The demons screech and wail, flying off in a fright. Then the winds halt, the debris settles. The spell is already weakening and the light is dimming by the second. There's no time to waste, so I make a run for the trees. For the Obsidian Butterfly.

Deep in the forest, the bushes stir. It could be the wind, but I know better. The warning gives me a moment to react.

"I know you're here," I say.

The flash of an arm or a leg—or a tail—is gone before I can see more.

"Stop the games. Show yourself."

Using my blade to light my surroundings, I gaze up at an ashen-gray skull with a mane of black hair, a shell skirt, and a bone cape. The Demon Queen. One of her wings is broken, leaving her incapable of flight. Wreathed in darkness, she looks like a wraith. She *is* the darkness.

I fall into her gaze, those empty sockets more piercing than eyes. A coldness shoves into my mind. The Demon Queen forces her way inside, sifting through my memories, pausing long enough for me to see Señor Alonso's head tumbling into a basket, Father fading on his deathbed, Inés's body as she lay in my arms.

When she slides out of my mind, my breaths come in labored pants and my heart aches with every gulp of air. "So bitter. So full of regret." Her voice is the rumbling of thunder, the deep cracking of the earth. "In truth, I care little for your petty sorrows. Humans beg for divine intervention at the slightest inconvenience, then forsake divinity when the affliction is removed. Miserable, wretched creatures."

"What is it you want?"

"What all the teteoh want. Blood."

"Will you settle for a goat?"

"I demand true sacrifice!" She flaps her good wing, sending a line of obsidian shards at me, but I quickly throw up my forearm, and my shield of tonalli takes them, each one dropping to the ground. "Tell me, daughter of Tlazohtzin . . . would you like to see your mother again?"

I swallow in a futile effort to ease the grip tightening on my throat.

"My mother is dead," I say quickly.

She gives me a cruel, bloodstained smile.

I slap my hands to my ears to stop a wail of pain in my head, the image of my mother writhing in agony as she gives birth to me.

Get out of my head! I want to shout, but my heart plummets as I understand.

The Cihuateteo, her army of divine women. Childbirth is a battle; a babe is sent down to the earth by the gods, and the mother has to fight and struggle in order to bring it into the world. Tlazohtzin died a warrior's death. By her labors she became a cihuateotl, a fierce wielder of chaos and shadow.

A demon goddess.

My mind swarms with terrible thoughts. I've killed many demons tonight.

Leonora . . . My mother's voice comes through to me as though from far away. More than anything, I wish she were alive.

Clenching my jaw, I shake my head, willing myself to focus. This is what the Demon Queen wants. She will not have this triumph.

"Go back to your abyss, Obsidian Butterfly," I say. "Take your demons with you."

Enraged, the Demon Queen shifts into her nagual, a monstrous deer, and my lips curl, because all night I have been waiting to shift into mine. The shift doesn't hurt any less, but there's no resistance within me, and the transition is smooth, quick. It's a vicious and bloody fight to the death, two beasts pouncing, locking jaws, each pulling down the other. I leap atop her. Before my fangs dig into her neck, she shifts back into her goddess form. I go from horizontal to vertical, from four legs to two, and it takes me a moment to realize that I'm dressed, not naked.

I'm grinning like a fool until the Demon Queen rips the Sword of Integrity from my hand with her long snake-like tail, casting it away. Before I can make a move toward the sword, she wraps her tail around my waist. I try to squeeze out of her slithering embrace, but the more I struggle, the tighter she grips and for a moment I think my bones will be crushed.

"I'm . . . sorry . . ." I gasp.

"Oh, what was that? You're sorry?"

"I'm sorry . . . but this is not how I die!"

I force my nagual soul out of my body. A wisp of my tonalli tears through the demon and coalesces into the shape of the Panther, radiant, blinding. Startled, the Demon Queen releases me from her grasp and her skull whips in the Panther's direction. I assert my will over the Panther, and she roars and claws at the ground. As shining and mighty as the Panther is, she serves only as a distraction. I stand up on shaky legs and scramble toward my sword, but the Obsidian Butterfly's long, scrawny fingers claw at my braid.

Raising my palm, I blast the Demon Queen against a tree and hold her there as I scoop up my sword.

She chuckles. "You foolish wretch. You can't kill me. I'm a goddess."

"Funny story," I say, approaching her. "So am I." I hold my sword up, arm arching. "I am Tecuani, daughter of the Plumed Serpent. In the name of all that is good, your chaos ends now, Obsidian Butterfly."

I stab her through the face and twist my sword, making sure I get the job done. And with that, the Demon Queen is consumed and disappears, leaving behind nothing but black smoke.

CHAPTER 46

El Amanecer

The battlefield falls silent. With the Obsidian Butterfly defeated, her army has no leader and they retreat.

We've won, but no trumpets sound, no banners wave. It seems like a hollow victory as I look around at the slaughter spread out before me. Captain Nabarres is gone, and the Spaniards lost, although, to the dead, losing or winning makes no difference. All Captain Nabarres left behind is a field of fallen men and women, some who fought for him, others against him, but all now united in death.

In the pale glow of dawn, I see Miguel lying on his back with another body flopped over him. I hurry over. His eyes are closed, and he seems to have stopped breathing. I'm checking for a heartbeat when he opens his eyes.

"Did we win?" His voice is a raspy whisper.

"We did."

He coughs.

"This isn't what your father wanted for you," I say. Señor Alonso made it clear. Before his death, he feared what Miguel would become. "He knew you'd make a choice. And he knew he wouldn't like it. But he'd be proud. You should know his last thoughts were of you."

"Why are you telling me this?" Miguel croaks.

"I promised him." I put a hand on his chest. "You fought bravely, warrior." I help him stand.

Viceroy Jerónimo approaches, combing through the dead, searching for surviving comrades.

"Leonora." He wipes his eyes, the blood from his forehead and fist merging into a scarlet mess across his face. "Are you unharmed?"

"I am."

"Good."

"You could've fled . . ." I say. "Gracias."

He bows his head toward the heap of bodies. "God bless their souls." He makes the sign of the Cross. "I've never seen such carnage. It's going to take weeks to remove the wounded and give our slain warriors a Christian burial. It's my promise to every man who fights under the flag of Spain."

A clicking cry steals our attention. The ahuizotl Rayo crawls to a halt beside us, bearing Amalia and Eréndira. The clawed hand at the end of his long, sinuous tail grasps the air.

Jerónimo takes a step back, hand closing over his sword hilt. "What in God's name?"

Amalia keeps hold of Rayo's sleek mane, while Eréndira slides off the creature's leathery hide and comes forward.

From the battlefield, Chipahua, Martín, and Tezca, as well as the other chieftains, Nucano and Rahui, and what's left of La Justicia, gather around, bloody and battered. Warriors who fought and gained victory.

Jerónimo eyes the faces staring back at him, some new, a few familiar. "Which one of you is Sin Rostro?"

Neza . . . An awful hollowness fills me. Ichcatzin is a murderer. He killed Neza, his own brother.

Coward. That was the last thing I said to Neza. I despise my words. I curse myself for speaking wrongly.

No one says anything. The understanding that the king of Snake Mountain, the fearless leader of La Justicia, has gone to Tonatiuh, pushes away any words.

Eréndira breaks the grim silence, lifting her chin. "We are *all* Sin Rostro," she says. "We are one face. One voice."

I look at the warriors, each giving the other an acknowledging nod. And I know, whatever the day is to bring, we will meet it together, for as many tomorrows as it takes, till death if need be.

"Very well," Jerónimo says. "Be it known to all present that I, Jerónimo de las Casas y Sepúlveda, virrey de la Nueva España, as of this day declare the Long War over. With God as my witness, I free these lands so that no man carrying a Cross may have authority here and whosoever breaks this peace should prepare to face punishment, for such an act shall be considered treason against New Spain.

"Abuses have been widespread. The New Laws designed to protect native people have been ignored, and I will be directing them to be enforced. No more obedezco pero no cumplo. We will obey and we *will* comply. If anybody does not agree, let them speak so we may know our enemies."

All stand in silence.

"People of Snake Mountain," Jerónimo continues, "I know I have made mistakes and I have much to learn. I am more sorry than I can say for the atrocities perpetrated against you. I will strive to do better. There is much work to accomplish, and it is my hope that ways can be found so that we may advance together to a future of justice and reconciliation."

He holds out his hand. Eréndira stares, making no move to grasp it. The Purépecha princess has resisted the Spanish since she was a young girl, for longer than I have lived, and I think she will immediately refuse, but Neza is gone now, and she is responsible for her people. So maybe she's thinking about them now. She wants them to prosper. She wants a way forward. And the way forward for La Justicia is to work with the Spaniards.

Jerónimo keeps his hand held out for a long moment, until at last, Eréndira shakes it.

My brother's expression is grim as he briefly glances my way.

Lowering his head, he exhales, as if struggling with himself. He may have come to my rescue in battle, but that doesn't mean he's forgotten my deception. I don't know that he will ever trust me again, let alone wish to see me.

Jerónimo leaves without a word, and I go to Martín. I wrap my arms around his neck and feel him hesitate before embracing me. He weeps into my hair, but I don't know whether it's heartache or rage that consumes him. When his breathing slows down and his heartbeat steadies, I pull away slightly to look at those blue eyes. "He died a warrior."

"It's my fault," Martín says miserably. "I begged him to get up and fight."

"Ichcatzin will pay," Chipahua says. He should go home to his wife, concubines, and children, joy from the glory of battle flowing through him. Instead, a savage bloodlust fills him. "The traitorous bastard will pay."

"We are warriors," Eréndira says. "We raise our swords. We raise an army. We raise the dead if we must."

I turn around and start across the field.

"Pantera," Eréndira says to my back, and I turn to face her.

"Princess."

"What will you do?" she asks.

I shrug.

We regard one another for a moment, before Eréndira says, "Thank you . . . for everything. You are a true ally."

I stare at my feet, then raise my eyes to where Amalia is climbing down from Rayo. Eréndira follows my gaze. "She can be annoying," I say, "and stubborn, but she never acts without thinking. She is also brave and strong, and she cares deeply about those closest to her."

Eréndira breathes, nods, and walks toward Amalia.

*

Darkness surrenders. Dawn comes. I blink toward Tonatiuh, for he brings a day I was never promised, yet am glad to see. A new beginning is possible, and possibilities bring hope.

Tezca finds me sitting on the brow of the hill overlooking a field of maize, surrounded by the forest. He lies down on his back beside me, his hands laced behind his head. A gentle breeze tousles his hair, and he closes his eyes. He looks peaceful, as if we spent the night frolicking, playing a game. It's been a while since I thought that, amid all the fighting.

I'm still taking him in when he opens his eyes and looks at me. There's a glimmer in them, and his mouth twitches in a small smile.

"What?" I ask.

"Nothing."

"Why are you looking at me like that?"

"I'm looking at you the way I've always looked at you," he says, the timbre of his voice low and sultry. "I'm not making you nervous, am I, señorita?"

I snort. "You're a funny pirate, aren't you?"

His laugh is hearty, quite infectious.

"So . . ." he says, smiling from ear to ear, "you've become a hero after all."

I slap his chest, unable to stop myself smiling too. He catches my hand and pulls me down to stretch out beside him. Resting my head on his shoulder, I squint up at the clouds.

"It's odd," I say quietly, feeling the thin grass between my fingers. "When I lost my tonalli, I stopped dreaming. I could tell I was asleep, but I didn't dream."

"And now?" I feel his breath on my forehead.

"I can dream awake." I sit up and hug my knees. The maize field stretches out below us, and the patterns of the blowing stalks make pictures in my mind. "You know how when the corn is young and just beginning to grow, the leaves stand up straight, but when the husks become burdened with seeds, they stoop? That's how my head was. Heavy. I think I needed to lose myself."

Tezca leans in, his arm propped behind my back. "Leonora."

I glance up, and our noses almost touch. "Hmm?"

"Who taught you the Elegant Speech?"

"The what?"

"Tecpillatolli," he says, "the lordly speech spoken by the Nahua ruling class. The style is difficult. It's been forgotten since the Fall. No one speaks High Nahuatl anymore, at least not like in the days of Moteuczoma. I heard you speak it last night to the Obsidian Butterfly."

I chuckle lightly. "You heard wrong. I can't have done that."

"Why not?"

"Because I'm not nobility, Tezca. I don't speak High Nahuatl," I say, but then I remember Quetzalcoatl's words. *To the wielder of integrity, it is a sword of great strength. To the one who speaks high and clear, it is power.*

High and clear. Nahuatl is a clear language. Quetzalcoatl was referring to High Nahuatl.

"It was a riddle . . ." I say, coming to the realization.

"Yes," says Tezca. "The Elegant Speech can seem that way."

My brows furrow. "What?"

"Contradictory. Puzzling. Saying one thing and meaning another. Like a riddle."

"I . . . I must have learned it in Tamoanchan," I say in a daze, thinking about Master Toto's riddles. I thought he was merely testing my mind, but I understand now. All along, Master Toto—Quetzalcoatl—was teaching me the speech he must have spoken to the Toltecs as their king. I summoned a Nagual army with the Sword of Integrity. That kind of power shouldn't be casually let loose, so Quetzalcoatl built a safeguard. As Tezca said, no one speaks High Nahuatl anymore.

It dawns on me. Ichcatzin, like Neza, is nobility . . .

I must never let the Sword of Integrity fall into the wrong hands.

I don't tell Tezca about Quetzalcoatl, my father. I don't tell him about Xochiquetzal, his mother.

"I don't know," I say after a moment. "I don't have all the answers. I just want to sit here and see Tonatiuh rise. It's beautiful, isn't it?"

"Quite so," Tezca says. I turn my head and realize he's looking at me.

"You were right, you know?" I hold his gaze briefly before finding the horizon. "You said one day I would hope again. Do you see that, Tezca?"

"See what?"

"A new day." My lips curve, feeling the first of Tonatiuh's rays touch my skin. Silence wedges itself between us for a moment, then I say, "On second thought, my legs are feeling restless."

"So what are you waiting for?" He growls, and I catch a glimpse of his golden spotted fur as he leaps down the hill. A magnificent beast of power and strength.

I drop into position. There's no pain. The shift feels perfectly natural.

And we run.

Epilogue

He slowly ascends to the top of the pyramid, the man in the feathered headdress. He wears such an array of adornments it is a wonder he can even move. Gold upper armbands, turquoise on the lower arms, shell necklaces, golden bells up and down his sides and legs, and a cape of skulls and bones. He is dressed in the teotl-form, the manner of the divine.

The man-god presents himself in the temple, carrying an obsidian mirror. He sits on the chair with the high back in front of the stone wall carved with snakes.

He gazes into the mirror's glassy surface. He sees not his reflection but something else.

"O master," he says. "O our lord. O lord of the near and far. You who does as he pleases, whose abode is everywhere, whose servants we are, by whom all live. I come to appear before you, to reach you. I call out, I cry out to you: come, bring yourself here. Your wrath, your anger—enjoy, take pleasure, delight in castigation. I fall before you; I throw myself before you. O master. O precious nobleman. O our lord. I humbly beg of you, perform your office, do your work, make haste."

He beams with satisfaction at the young face looking back at him, a black stripe painted below the eyes.

Glossary

NAHUATL

Ahmo – no

Ahuehuetl – cypress tree

Ahuizotl – a doglike aquatic creature with a hand at the end of its tail

Calli – a house or household

Chalalatli – a medicinal herb

Chicalotl – a medicinal herb

Chichyotl – sorcery of witches who can shift into owls

Chaneque (pl. Chaneques) – a small, sprite-like creature, guardians of nature

Chichtli Mocuepa – owl shape-shifter

Coatl Xoxouhqui – snake weed

Cocoliztli – pestilence, plague

Cuetlaxochitl (pl. Cuetlaxochime) – poinsettia

Ihiyotl – animating force located in the liver

Iztac Colelehtli – white demon

Metl – maguey plant

Nagual – a shape-shifter

Nemontemi – the Dead Days, last five days of the solar calendar

Nepantla – in between, place in the middle

Octli – alcoholic beverage made from fermented sap of the maguey plant

Ololiuhqui – morning glory seeds

Quemah – yes

Tecpatl – sacrificial knife

Tecpillatolli – elegant speech spoken by Nahua nobility

Teocalli – temple

Teotl – a god, god tonalli, divine energy

Tepoztopilli – a type of spear

Teteoh – the gods

Tetonalcahualiztli – sickness, tonalli loss

Teyolia – animating force located in the heart

Ticitl – a healer

Tilmahtli – a cloak/cape worn by Nahua men, designed for various classes in society

Tlahtoani – one who speaks on behalf of a group, a king

Tonalli – life force made from teotl

Tonalpohualli – sacred calendar

Totomonaliztli – pustules, smallpox

Tzin – an honorific suffix attached to the end of a name, sometimes conveying affection

Tzitzimitl (pl. Tzizimime) a star demon, a destructive goddess

Xiuhpohualli – solar calendar

SPANISH

Ahuehuete – see ahuehuetl

Audiencia – highest governing council in New Spain

Corrida – a bullfight

Criollo – a person born in the New World of Spanish descent

Doña/Don – titles of respect attached to a first name

Encomendero – the holder of an encomienda

Encomienda – a grant by the Spanish Crown to a colonist conferring the right to demand tribute and forced labor from the Indigenous inhabitants of an area

Gachupín (pl. Gachupines) – a Spain-born Spaniard, a peninsular

Lechuza – a screech owl

Mestizo – person of mixed Spanish and Indigenous descent

Pulque – see octli

Virey/Virreina – the representative of the Spanish monarch in a region of New Spain

Acknowledgments

Heather Cashman, look what you did. Despite a global pandemic, you believed in this project and me from the beginning, even when I wanted to pull the plug. I will never forget when I read your email of interest in representing me. It was one of the brightest moments of my life. It hasn't been an easy journey, but you've kept me sane. You're the best agent in all the land. If I could insert a hugging cat meme here, you know I would. A special thank you to Vicki Selvaggio and everyone at Storm Literary: you're the best.

This book would not be what it is without the brilliant and hard-working minds at Harper Voyager. Thank you to my US and UK publishing teams and HarperCollins worldwide. David Pomerico, thank you for giving my book a home and helping it take flight. Mireya Chiriboga, my GIF queen, thank you for loving my characters and for indulging me when I very seriously asked, "Can we get Henry Cavill?" Elizabeth Vaziri, I'm overwhelmed with gratitude for your eagle eyes and for taking such good care of this story. It's been a dream working with you all. My extended gratitude to Natasha Bardon, Laura Bowles, Kat Howard, and all who had a hand in this manuscript. Sadly, I won't be able to name everyone at the time I'm writing this.

Acknowledgments

Micaela Alcaino, I tell you all the time and I will tell you again—your design wizardry is out of this world. Thank you for creating such a majestic cover and illustrations. I will be billing you for the sight I've lost staring at your beautiful art. My eternal gratitude to David Bowles for his invaluable insight and expertise in the Nahuatl language.

Mom and Dad, hola! Even though you thought that my writing was just a hobby, you never dissuaded me from pursuing my passions. Thank you for instilling in me perseverance and encouraging me every step of the way. I love you.

I would not have survived the querying, submission, and publication process were it not for my family and friends. Mynra Berna, you deserve un coctel de elote for listening to my endless audios on WhatsApp. Andrea Encinas, you are the Virgo-est Virgo to ever Virgo. Gabriela Romero Lacruz, I'm happy to have connected with you and excited to share a debut year (among other things!). Mariella de La Maza, thank you for downloading Goodreads just to rate the book, you sneaky momma. Joanna Nava, mi comadreja, I love my beautiful SOBAR jacket! Lorraine Storms, thank you for your friendship in cyberspace and blessing my feed with chickens. It's so great to have coworkers and friends like Peggy Parolin and Gloria Magallanes who have been nothing but supportive throughout my publishing journey. Peluchemon, thank you for just sitting next to me while I wrote this book, but don't tell Fer. Mi gabs, thank you for always being my champion. Ferny, Nancy, Paty, Larissa, Ale, Liz, Adriz, Nanas, Ana Paty, Rose, Gilda—thank you for understanding when I disappear into my writing cave. A special thank you to my dog, Gaston, for keeping me company while I write and never complaining when I read aloud, except when I'm late to take him on walks or feed him. I'd also like to thank my grandmother, best friend, and uncle, to whom this book is dedicated, for your never-ending encouragement. Tio Go, you would have been the first to purchase a copy. Tita, you always believed in my writing. Priscy, I'm still waiting but I know it'll be worth it. I miss you all greatly.

Acknowledgments

Last but never least, dear reader, muchas gracias. Thank you for picking up this book from the millions available. I didn't study at Harvard. I didn't major in creative writing. I don't have a PhD. I'm a border kid who dared to dream. I failed a hundred times. I doubted myself a thousand times. If you're reading this and are an aspiring author with big book dreams, I'm rooting for you.

About the Author

MARIELY LARES is a Mexican American novelist. Born in the only hospital of a small town in Southern California—which, fun fact, is also Cher's birthplace—she grew up straddling two worlds, crossing the border from her hometown to Mexico almost every day. The daughter of Mexican immigrants, she holds a degree in computer science engineering and lives in San Diego, where she can be found doing all the outdoorsy things, rescuing dogs, and writing her next book.

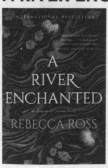